Murder in Monaco
Death's Lovely Mask

By John Flagg

Introduction by Nicholas Litchfield

Stark House Press • Eureka California

MURDER IN MONACO / DEATH'S LOVELY MASK

MURDER IN MONACO

"It began as one of those casual dates…I'd met her the night before in Monte Carlo." So begins agent Hart Muldoon's latest mystery. Nancy Trippe works for *National Alert*, a tell-all magazine, and offers him four thousand dollars for a job finding some stolen letters that "might involve murder." When Muldoon visits the publisher's mistress, Amy Grant, he finds that murder is indeed involved—Charles Pless has just been poisoned. Someone substituted cyanide for his adrenalin heart pill. Now it's up to Muldoon to track down the letters while trying to discover who killed the promiscuous publisher. Was it Alva Creighton, author of the compromising letters? Harold Jones, her body-building boyfriend, trying to protect her? Ballentine Black, the blackmailing ex-agent? Or Trippe herself, working her way up the ladder of success?

DEATH'S LOVELY MASK

Hart Muldoon is in Venice on a case for the U.S. government, only this time he is asked to betray a lover: "It was getting to be deep down in somebody else's dream now…Too many villains and too few cops. A Prince in love, an Arab drowned in the Grand Canal, a whore spouting romantic nonsense beneath pornographic pictures in a beach cabana, hatchet men in unlikely guise moving toward a Masked Ball and a payoff, a jerk husband trying to hire me to track myself down to his wife's bed, a salty old New England character whose motives were apparently far from what I had first suspected, and above all a girl named Linda whose cool and level gaze had sent me skittering toward the cliffs of guilt. Linda whom I saw as damned and yet who had crawled under my skin as no other woman had been able to do…"

John Flagg Bibliography
(1911-1993)

The Persian Cat (1950)
Death and the Naked Lady (1951)
The Lady and the Cheetah (1951)

Hart Muldoon series
Woman of Cairo (1953)
Dear, Deadly Beloved (1954)
Murder in Monaco (1957)
Death's Lovely Mask (1958)
The Paradise Gun (1961)

As John Gearon

The Velvet Well (1946; reprinted in Australia as
    The Deadly Web, 1956; and in France as
    Le Puits de velours, 1949)
"Faces Turned Against Him" (1951, *Suspense*)

Plays

Without Guile (1934; with Edward Crandall)
De Luxe (1935; with Louis Bromfield)
A Bright Young Thing (1936; with Edward Crandall)
Two Hearts in Candid Camera Time: A Revue (1937;
    with Wilson McCarty and Edward Crandall)

The Further Adventures of Fearless Agent Hart Muldoon

by Nicholas Litchfield

American writer John Rex Gearon (1911-1993) might be considered something of a man of mystery. There's a plethora of news clippings featuring his name, and yet bibliographical information on him is sparse and sketchy. Ostensibly, his identity in the sphere of literature is composed of two illustrious works that brought him distinction, a *nom de plume* that he attached to a string of thrillers, and one epic, eye-catching failure.

His diverse career began in the 1930s and tailed off in the early 1960s; during those years, he tried his hand at numerous forms of writing. Early on, he was a radio scriptwriter for the Office of the Coordinator for Inter-American Affairs (OCIAA), which sought to boost political and economic relations between the US and Latin American nations. He then found fame as a playwright, often collaborating with actor Edward Crandall. They sold, in quick succession, *The Doctor's Confession* to well-known theatrical producer and director Jed Harris (Mantle, 1934), *With the Wind* to Broadway producer Albert Bannister (Dickstein, 1934b; Cohen, 1934), and *Without Guile* to Elsie Ferguson and Ethel Levy, who toyed with producing it for the Shubert Theatre in Boston (Daily News, 1934b; Mantle, 1935). Notable Broadway performer Katherine Warren, who later became a significant film and television actress, led the cast for tryouts at the Cliff Theater in Sea Cliff (Burnett, 1934; Dickstein, 1934a).

His biggest play, *De Luxe*, proved his biggest disappointment. Jed Harris purchased that one, too (Dixon, 1934). It was a play in two acts and five scenes about wealthy American expatriates living in Paris at the end of the Coolidge era (Daily News, 1934a), and 20th Century Pictures acquired film rights as part of a policy to "employ the legitimate theater as a laboratory for possible screen presentations in the future" (The Tampa Times, 1934). It was a collaboration between Gearon and Pulitzer Prize-winning author Louis Bromfield that looked like it would score big. Pre-New York performances began at Boston's Shubert Theatre (Times Union, 1935b), and "an unusually large number of theatrical and motion picture magnates" made reservations to attend (Times Union, 1935a). The Broadway production was just as grand. Marlene Dietrich hosted a party of friends at the Booth Theatre to witness the performance (Field, 1935c). Noel Coward even sent a telegram to international society figure Elsa Maxwell, the lead actress, on the opening night (Shapiro, 1935). The much-talked-about play attracted a distinguished cast that included Melvyn Douglas (before he won his two Oscars). It was pretty much the theatrical event of the year—but for the wrong reasons.

First-night reviews were forgiving. *The Boston Globe*, though accepting that the plotting was unfocused, believed the narrative was "grippingly dramatic, with graphic episodes and vivid characterizations" (The Boston Globe, 1935). Elsewhere, all too speedily, the critics drew their knives, and the bloodletting began. The *Times Union* called it "a rather pointless saga of the slimy side of cosmopolitan society and it is divided up into a series of detached incidents in the lives of compete rotters of both sexes" (Field, 1935b). *Hartford Courant* said it was peopled with "an assorted lot of variously dissolute social derelicts on Paris' Left Bank, mostly both unpleasant and uninteresting" (Carey, 1935). *The Brooklyn Daily Eagle* called it "a de luxe bore," insisting that neither of the writers "know how to write plays, being still of the opinion that drama is something in which people talk a long evening away and find at the end that they have said nothing" (Pollock, 1935). The *New York Times* remarked that the authors had "let themselves down badly into the juicier quagmires of buncombe" (Atkinson, 1935). There were many more negative reviews, but perhaps *The Brooklyn Citizen* wins the prize for most savage. Having previously described it as "a long, incoherent, talky bore" (The Brooklyn Citizen, 1935b), they later offer this witty summation: "The trouble with 'De Luxe' was that too many of the characters were either dead or dying on their feet from boredom and moral decay, with the result that a funeral aroma was communicated to the play itself." (March, 1935).

The New York premiere was at the Booth Theatre on March 5, 1935 (The Brooklyn Citizen, 1935a), and despite the glitzy showbiz crowd, the beating it took from critics ensured it didn't linger in the theater for long. The curtain fell for the final time a mere eleven nights later (Cohen, 1935).

At some point during that decade, Gearon switched from being a playwright to working as a newspaper columnist. He wrote as John R. Gearon for the Book Reviews section of *The Cincinnati Enquirer* in 1941, reviewing both fiction and nonfiction. His articles also turn up in The Book Rack section of *Detroit Free Press* in 1942, his byline without the middle initial. In August 1942, he was at a military camp in Texas, having enlisted in the Army (Bower, 1942).

By 1946, Gearon had moved away from journalism and was focused on writing fiction (Bowers, 1946). His sophomore effort, *The Velvet Well,* published by Duell, Sloan & Pearce in 1946, garnered strong reviews. It was a "well written" (Bronte, 1950) novel "packed with action, excitement and suspense" but "touched off with just the right amount of humor and craftiness" (Browning, 1946). Famed crime writer Dorothy Hughes and eminent magazines like *The New Yorker* also praised the story and the author's flair for suspenseful prose (Litchfield, 2020). Penguin Books and Collins (now HarperCollins) reprinted the novel some years later, and producer Anthony Z. Landi acquired the rights with a plan to release it as a movie (Scheuer, 1952). It eventually surfaced in movie theaters, but as a French picture, *Un Papillon Sur L'Epaule,* filmed in Spain in 1978.

At the start of the Fifties, the author seemed to have acquired a pen name: John Flagg. Why, and why that name, is a bit of a puzzler. Eight postwar espionage thrillers followed, each issued by Gold Medal Books, starting with *The Persian Cat.* It was a mystery tale of "barbaric excitement," set in Paris and Tehran, featuring "boudoir politics, murder, spying, oriental puzzles and strange perfumes used by stranger characters" (Bardon, 1950). The narrative style and the rakish protagonist, special agent Gil Denby, are blueprints for his later novels starring former OSS agent Hart Muldoon. My thoughts on the first two, *Woman of Cairo* and *Dear, Deadly Beloved*, can be found in the previous Stark House collection, published in 2020. The succeeding two novels are equally enjoyable adventures that take Muldoon to the most luxurious pockets of Europe.

Murder in Monaco, from January 1957, is an elaborately plotted murder mystery with old-school intrigue and a chic setting. Here, man-about-town Muldoon is frittering away his money on the French Riviera and the Principality of Monaco, enjoying a hedonistic lifestyle, rubbing shoulders with models and Hollywood starlets, an Italian princess, and a famous Spanish painter. Though content to remain in the fictional seacoast town of Verens, Muldoon is behind on his rent. The lure of a pretty stranger, Nancy Trippe, in a plush club in Monte Carlo breaks up his idyllic routine. Nancy is an ambitious features editor for the *National Alert*, a small-circulation magazine founded by her boss, Charles Pless, specializing in biographies of international celebrities. Broadly speaking, it's a sleaze publication focused on digging up embarrassing revelations. Pricey and harmful, its exposés on public figures commonly tarnish careers.

Charles Pless, his mousy wife, Myra, and Nancy Trippe are making the most of their business trip to Antibes, hoping to unearth juicy gossip on newsworthy holidaymakers. Past feature stories have humiliated ex-Governor Thorne, who's currently in Verens, but the latest target is Alva Creighton, an enormously successful American novelist. She knows Charles well and knows that disgraced former FBI agent Ballentine Black is on the payroll, selling dirty secrets to the magazine, so she's in a stir about the *National Alert*'s upcoming story.

As a former government spy, Muldoon has the expertise to be useful to Nancy Trippe, but the four-thousand-dollar job she offers him is steeped in mystery. Precisely how he can serve her is unclear, and her trustworthiness is highly suspect. However, he doesn't have time to scratch his head. Events unfold at a breakneck pace, the key players appearing left and right and menace emerging at every turn. In the space of hours, theft, rape, and multiple homicides send Muldoon rocketing across the Riviera on a thankless mission to unpick a heavily knotty plot that concerns blackmail letters, sordid affairs, inheritance money, and bloodthirsty revenge. All good fodder for a grisly mystery.

Gearon has explored similar themes before, but with *Murder in Monaco*, he adds some neat surprises, binding his characters together through bruising past associations and questionable self-serving objectives. Good dialogue and biting humor add to the fun, and delightful, larger-than-life female characters, like the formidable bully Alva Creighton and the wily Miss Trippe, add solid backbone to the story. The final act is right in Gearon's wheelhouse—a bombastic ballet at the Opera House in Monte Carlos, with Death cavorting about the stage, followed by the grandeurs of a gala ball at the nearby Sporting Club. The action-packed dénouement is suitably frenetic, although the big drama would have been better served in a theater or gala setting.

Readers will no doubt be stymied by the lack of police presence. At no point does anyone wish to report a crime. Why allow the shady local authorities to interrupt the action and foil people's plans? Besides, freelancer Muldoon is around, with his Luger and his government influences, to play detective and resident law enforcer. The chief quandary is the small matter of exactly who is paying his fees.

The subsequent mystery, *Death's Lovely Mask*, published in July 1958, is the jewel of the series. While soaking up the delights of Naples, Muldoon is bribed by old associate Hirem, a topmost government official, to go to Venice and investigate Linda Pawling. She's a promiscuous beauty. Amorous and seductive one day, and then cold and aloof the next. Muldoon is currently having an affair with Linda and is rapidly falling in love with her. To complicate matters, she has a husband, George, who suspects she's cheating on him and wants to get rid of her lover. George is a troubleshooter for the powerful German-American Oil company, which controls the oil reserves in the Donrd-Arabia desert. Hirem wants Muldoon to press Linda for information regarding a possible conspiracy and a potential governmental uprising.

Prince Sir-el-Donrd "Ali" of Donrd-Arabia, a graduating Yale senior who's the favorite son of ailing King Donrd, is next in line for his father's throne. Though the State Department is keen for "Ali" to rule, the Arab chieftains fear that he's too westernized to govern the region. His romantic associations with Judith Garnter, the daughter of an Israeli senator, threaten to destabilize power in the country and hinder American oil interests. The prince intends to travel to Venice to see Judith, who's staying with her elderly mentor, the puritanical Mrs. Winthrop, an aristocratic acquaintance of King Donrd. There's talk of elopement, and Hirem has concerns that there may be a plot to harm "Ali" or Judith and permanently end the affair.

The intricate plot allows for lots of majestic settings, speculative guesswork, and character study, with a large assembly of suspicious characters circling around the royal target. Gearon is a writer who excels at magnificent guidebook descriptions of dreamy, aristocratic hideaways, quirky, colorful people in the public eye, and grandiose architecture. Extravagant, filthy-rich magnates and glamorous playboys often populate his pages. As with other books in the series, this tale of political intrigue involving a reigning monarch and his heir lets Gearon draw attention to the chocolate-box scenery and the exotic revelries of the well-to-do. This time, the memorable backdrops include an exquisite castle situated in eastern Spain, along the Iberian Peninsula, and a wild masquerade ball in the Palace of Countess Feretti, beyond Venice's Rialto Bridge, with resplendent costumes and an atmosphere of boisterous, depraved recklessness.

The Knoxville Journal fittingly called the story "wild and sexy" (Smith, 1957), and it's that and more. It's gripping and chaotic, told at speed, and bristling with tension and murky drama. Death and duplicity surround the intrepid Muldoon, who is continually one step behind a killer, never sure who to trust and how to connect the pieces of the puzzle. As the story takes the form of an exhilarating race across Europe, full of murder, mayhem, and misplaced allegiances, Muldoon gets caught up in the chase, relying on luck and witness statements to stay within reach of the prince.

Famed book critic Anthony Boucher considered *Death's Lovely Mask* "much the best of the international adventures of Hart Muldoon" (Boucher, 1958). He valued the "opulently visualized scenes" and the almost operatic, "larger-than-life intrigue." His complaint had to do with the "tastelessly exaggerated sex." Titillating scenes between Muldoon and the busty young tigress Nina Apperatti, a victimized Italian actress whose pornographic movie scenes are graphically described, perhaps prompted the criticism.

Truth be told, Muldoon's frequently witty, reliably suave narrative is strewn with somewhat crude, chauvinist comments and sexual innuendos. Steamy romance can become riskily gratuitous, and Gearon makes a habit of pushing the envelope. Nudity and promiscuousness are especially rife in *Death's Lovely Mask*. The out-of-control masquerade ball at the palace, heaving with bawdy, indecently clothed revelers, has the feel of a bordello. The lewdness of some of the characters, notably Pietro Apperatti, Nina's pervert cousin, whose costumes range from "postage-stamp bathing trunks" to transparent, sheer satin loin cloth, beggars belief. His lack of propriety and overly erotic, debauched behavior are deliberately unpleasant. And yet, the brazen Pietro and other flamboyant oddballs who jostle for attention are a requisite ingredient in the John Flagg novels, whose books are concertos of villainy and mischief—filth and sin within worlds of wondrous beauty.

Everyone has blood on their hands in *Death's Lovely Mask*, and Muldoon is scarcely better than those around him. He has casual affairs with minors and married women, lies and deceives whenever it suits him and kills without compunction. From one adventure to the next, you question his ethics and shake your head at his antics.

Somehow, Gearon makes him presentable, wrapping him in courage and worldly intelligence and sending him out on worthy foreign missions.

All of the Muldoon tales are worth exploring. Gearon's adroit humor and skill with language raise his stories from puerile pulp to something more creditable, and the varied, sumptuous localities brought to life in these two gratifying adventures provide much to savor.

—January 2024
Rochester, NY

Nicholas Litchfield is the founder of the literary magazine *Lowestoft Chronicle* and editor of eleven literary anthologies. His stories, essays, and book reviews appear in many magazines and newspapers, including *BULL*, *Colorado Review*, *Daily Press*, *Mobius Blvd*, *Pennsylvania Literary Journal*, *Shotgun Honey*, *The Adroit Journal*, *The MacGuffin*, and *The Virginian-Pilot*. He has also contributed introductions to numerous books, including eighteen Stark House Press reprints of long-forgotten noir and mystery novels. Formerly a book critic for the *Lancashire Post*, syndicated to twenty-five newspapers across the U.K., he now writes for *Publishers Weekly*. You can find him online at nicholaslitchfield.com.

Works cited:

Atkinson, Brooks (Mar 6, 1935). "THE PLAY: End of an Epoch the Theme of 'De Luxe,' by Louis Bromfield and John Gearon." *New York Times*, p.22.

Bardon, Minna (May 27, 1950). "New Line." *The Cincinnati Enquirer*, p.7.

Boucher, Anthony (Aug 10, 1958). "Criminals at Large." *New York Times*, p.BR16.

Bower, Helen (Aug 30, 1942). "The Book Rack." *Detroit Free Press*, p.53.

Bower, Helen (Jun 23, 1946). "Book Shelf: Novel Casts Light on Balkan Politics." *Detroit Free Press*, p.16.

Bronte, Miss (Apr 22, 1950). "Seven Lively Penguins." *The Daily Telegraph*, p.23.

Browning, John (Jul 13, 1946). "Weekly Book Reviews." *Henderson Daily Dispatch*, p.3.

Burnett, Henry N. (Jul 26, 1934). "Heat Fails to Halt Summer Theater Activity in Nassau." *Brooklyn Daily Eagle*, p.8.

Carey, Ralph W. (Mar 17, 1935). "Among New York Theaters." *Hartford Courant*, p.23.

Cohen, Harold W. (Jun 27, 1934). "Stage and Screen: Addenda." *Pittsburgh Post-Gazette*, p.8.

Cohen, Harold W. (Mar 19, 1935). "Stage and Screen." *Pittsburgh Post-Gazette*, p.6.

Daily News (Feb 17, 1934a). "Jed Harris Has Play By Louis Bromfield." *Daily News*, p.275.

Daily News (Jul 19, 1934b). "Schwab Schedules 2 Farces, 1 Thriller." *Daily News*, p.41.

Dickstein, Martin (Jul 20, 1934a). "Theater News." *Brooklyn Daily Eagle*, p.9.

Dickstein, Martin (Nov 17, 1934b). "News of the Stage." *Brooklyn Daily Eagle*, p.15.

Dixon, George, (Jun 19, 1934). "Actors Fund." *Daily News*, p.37.

Field, Rowland (Feb 19, 1935a). "'De Luxe' Opens Tonight At Shubert, Boston." *Brooklyn Times Union*, p.14.

Field, Rowland (Mar 10, 1935c). "Both Sides of the Curtain." *Brooklyn Times Union*, p.10.

Field, Rowland. (Mar 6, 1935b). "The New Play," *Brooklyn Times Union*, p.15.

Litchfield, Nicholas, and John Flagg. "Intrepid Agent Hart Muldoon's Treacherous Paradise." Introduction. In *Woman of Cairo and Dear, Deadly Beloved*, Stark House Press, 2020, pp.7–11.

Mantle, Burns (Mar 18, 1934). "Lunts and Noel Coward Join As Producing Firm." *Daily News*, p.136.

Mantle, Burns (Mar 24, 1935). "Boston's 1 Play; Shubert May Do 'Without Guile.'" *Daily News*, p.76.

March, Michael (Mar 6, 1935). "The Premier." *The Brooklyn Citizen*, p.14.

Marks, Tim (Feb 16, 1935). "This Man's Town: 'De Luxe' Will Open At Boston, Tuesday." *Brooklyn Times Union*, p.12.

Pollock, Arthur (Mar 6, 1935). "The Theatre." *The Brooklyn Daily Eagle*, p.21.

Scheuer, Philip K. (Nov 5, 1952). "Milland To Present Self as Bavaria's Mad King; 'Larceny' Binds Couple." *The Los Angeles Times*, p.67.

Shapiro, L.S.B. (Mar 7, 1935). "Lights and Shadows of Manhattan: Miss Maxwell Debuts." *Montreal Gazette*, p.3.

Smith, Harrison (Jan 13, 1957). "Crime Corner." The Knoxville Journal, p.42.

The Boston Globe (Feb 20, 1935). "The Stage: Shubert Theatre 'De Luxe'." *The Boston Globe*, p.21.

The Brooklyn Citizen (Feb 23, 1935a). "Booth Theatre to Get 'De Luxe' on March 5." *The Brooklyn Citizen*, p.8.

The Brooklyn Citizen (Mar 23, 1935b). "Three New Productions Set For Next Week: This Side of the Footlights." *The Brooklyn Citizen*, p.8.

The Tampa Times (Oct 27, 1934). "20th Century Buys Rights to 'De Luxe'." *The Tampa Times*, p.12.

Murder in Monaco
By John Flagg

ONE

It began as one of those casual dates, with only a dim "maybe" in my mind and nothing else to do at three o'clock on a hot July afternoon. I'd met her the night before at a brawl at the Sporting Club in Monte Carlo given for some sullen, big-breasted Italian movie star. We'd exchanged a few polite words in the shadow of a potted palm, rubbed up against each other in a languid rumba, discovered—before she rejoined her own party—that we were both staying in the little seacoast resort of Verens, and arranged to meet at the peculiar hour of three the next afternoon at the Café Armand where, she informed me not without grandeur, she might be found sipping an aperitif. It seemed, according to her, we might have mutual interests to discuss. Her name was Nancy Trippe. There was nothing to indicate on first meeting that actually she was a case even Kraft-Ebbing forgot to list.

She was sitting in the sun just beyond the shadow of the café awning, reading a copy of *The Christian Science Monitor*. Innocence—sweet and apparently untouched by the world-below-the-waist—shown from bright, well-scrubbed features almost devoid of make-up. Naturally blonde hair was swept back into a prim schoolmarm bun. She seemed oblivious of a body built for business and if, while sipping a chaste pink liqueur, the simple sports dress occasionally slipped low enough to afford an unobstructed view of the twin peaks of Shangri-la, it appeared to be an accident. She looked like the senior class queen of some Midwestern university in search of European "culture" on an American Express quickie.

Behind her, the ancient houses of Verens climbed the twisting streets toward the middle corniche and the villas of the millionaires. Immediately below the little square where the café was situated were the red-tiled roofs which kept the rain and sun from the canvases and manuscripts of the art colony, and farther down the hill was the harbor edged by a white crescent of beach, a palm-lined boulevard, smart shops and the imposing bulk of the Bellevue Hotel. Out in the bay white yachts seemed glued to glass and beyond them was an improbable view of the Riviera coastline stretching all the way to Cannes.

But Miss Trippe was impervious to the seductive panorama. When my shadow fell across the editorial she looked up with the brave smile of the captain of the losing hockey team, leaving me to wonder what, if anything, I had won. Certainly hockey wasn't the game I had in mind. Not since Pless's note had arrived at noon. Her eyes were cool, placid and as remote as the illusions of my childhood.

"Oh, Mr. Muldoon. How nice of you to come. Please sit down."

"The name is Hart. After all, we've rumbaed together."

I sat, told a waiter to bring me a double Courvoisier, and pointed to the newspaper. "Don't let me interrupt you."

"Oh, that. I make it a point to study the opposition carefully."

"Opposition?" I said as though I didn't know. "You represent the *Mohammedan Monitor?*"

She smiled kindly. "Didn't you know? I'm on the editorial staff of the *National Alert.*"

"Never heard of it," I said glibly. "But it sounds depressing."

"We have a small circulation but tremendous influence. We specialize in frank, capsule biographies of celebrities on the international scene. Really quite valuable."

She made it sound as respectable as the *Encyclopedia Britannica.* Since noon I had made some discreet inquiries about the sheet, and what I'd heard made my hair stand on end. But it was hard to associate this corn-fed beauty with the scuttlebutt I'd managed to pick up.

"As a matter of fact, we're in Europe to get some material for the November issue."

"We?"

"I'm staying with Mr. Pless and his wife in their villa at Antibes. Mr. Pless owns the *National Alert.* His wife was a friend of mine in college." And then with a smile that was almost shy, she added, "That of course is how I managed to land a job on the magazine."

"Oh," I said, feeling tired already. The slipping neckline revived me somewhat and I called up the memory of that brief rumba to give me hope. I still didn't con any connection between this meeting and the note in my pocket, but for some reason—probably professional habit— didn't mention it.

"Verens is a funny place for your kind of research," I said as I attacked the cognac. "The material you'll get here is better stuff for the gossip columnists. Who got into whose bikini at high noon in what cabaña and why the bed in the royal suite of the Bellevue broke down at two A.M."

She appeared not to have heard. "At the moment there happen to be some interesting people in Verens."

"Then why waste your time with a bum like me?"

"Now, Hart ..." she said with maddening tolerance. "No masochism, please. You see, I just happen to know a little about you. "

"That's a depressing thought."

"Not at all. The sort of work you do fascinates me."

I gave an inside groan and said, "How did you know?"

"Files," she said calmly.

"Once again, please?"

"Files. For the magazine. We keep them on many, many people. The theory is, you never can tell. You understand?"

"Why me?"

She fingered the aperitif glass. "At the moment that's irrelevant. What matters is that I know a great deal about you already."

"For example?"

She smiled and spoke like a travesty on the weather report. "Boy hero in the OSS during the Second World War. Gone bitter with the sight of the business-as-usual boys. Stayed in Europe as a freelance. Handled some dangerous assignments for various individuals and governments—some of them odd jobs for odd individuals and odd governments."

"The money wasn't odd."

"That we can discuss."

I put down my drink and sat up straight. "You're not trying to offer me a job?"

"I certainly am."

"On the magazine?"

"Not precisely."

I laughed. "Forget it, sweetie. You can't afford me."

Her smile was honey. "Maybe the manager of your hotel would think differently."

"What does that mean?"

"You're two weeks behind in your bill, and no prospects except me. I hate to be so vulgar, but I believe in facts, don't you?"

I restrained myself from telling her about the cryptic note from Pless and said instead, "I'm doing okay."

"Don't get angry. Such a waste of adrenalin. I'm not offering you peanuts. I'm offering four thousand for a week's work. A thousand in advance."

I stayed in shock for about half a minute. She was enjoying herself now. I began to wonder whether she was a case for a head doctor.

"*You're* offering?"

She smiled serenely, leaned forward, almost brought one breast completely up over the neckline. "Well?"

Playing with it, I said, "Will we work together ... I mean closely?"

She followed the direction of my gaze and modestly pulled up the dress. "Please don't joke. This is very serious."

"How serious?"

"It might involve murder."

I put one hand in my pocket and fingered the note from Pless. It was an odd coincidence, Pless's urgent request to meet him at a villa up on the middle corniche at six o'clock, and now this offer from Pless's secretary, or whatever she was to him. Yesterday this time I'd never heard of either of them. For half a second I was tempted to tell Nancy Trippe about the note, but a kind of instinctive professional wariness took over and I resisted the temptation. Might as well hear his story and his offer first.

"Whose murder?"

"I don't want to worry Charles—Mr. Pless. But as it happens there are several people here who would be only too glad and ... something I found out today."

"Don't you have your own investigators?"

"One of our investigators is here in town, but we've just had to fire him. I never did trust him. And ..." suddenly she put her hand over mine on the table top and I felt the tension in her fingers. "Look. This is no schoolgirl fantasy. And I can produce the money. You've got to help me."

"Who is this other investigator of yours?"

She looked away. "A man by the name of Black. Ballentine Black."

"That creep!"

"Ah! You know him?"

"By reputation. I understand he was canned three years ago from the FBI under a cloud."

"Rumors are always highly exaggerated. Unless, of course they appear in the *National Alert*. He's done some good work for us, but recently ..." She shrugged.

Watching her, I made a quick decision at least to pretend to play along. I was damn curious, and besides it might come in handy in the later interview with Charles Pless. "My olfactory senses have been dulled by time and poverty. I suspect a bad stink but what's the angle?"

"Do you happen to be going to the gala performance at the Opera House in Monte tonight?"

"I hadn't planned to."

"Change your plans. Everyone on the Riviera will be there. And when I say everyone I'm including a lot of doubtful characters. Mr. Pless has taken a box. I'll be in it."

"So?"

"So we can meet as though by accident in the main foyer between the acts."

"Why by accident?"

"I'll explain that then. During the second part of the performance I might meet you at the Café de Paris and ... well, we can have a discussion in detail."

"Why can't we talk right now?"

"I always like my facts straight. There are a couple of points I must clear up first. I'll have a thousand for you."

Quickly I figured out time and mileage. I decided to risk it. "I'll be there."

"Good. I think we can work together."

"It has possibilities."

She looked me in the eye with that queen-of-the-campus candor. "I think so, too."

Then her eyes wavered and went beyond me and I noticed a flicker of wariness. I turned. Coming down the cobblestone street was a large, angry-looking woman who strode through the town, slack-clad, shopping basket over one arm, a washed-out blonde in tow. I knew her to be May Bracken, a self-proclaimed Lesbian who lived in Verens on a small income doled out by a remote and apparently stunned English father. She professed to be a painter, and in this place of doubtful, dilletante talents, no one contradicted her too loudly. The blonde in tow had been, until recently, a chorus girl at the Lido nightclub in Paris after basic training in second-rate London theaters. As they drew abreast, May Bracken bestowed a fierce glare on me and an open, boyish smile on Nancy.

"Nancy, darling. You won't disappoint us for tea this afternoon. Betty and I would be devastated if you forgot."

"How could I forget?" Nancy said, her voice oozing a secret warmth.

Betty looked neither pleased nor annoyed. Her pink little face was an absolute blank. Miss Bracken led her like a sleepwalker down into the town. I raised a questioning eyebrow at Miss Trippe.

She said, "They're sweet. I like to know all kinds of people."

"You might get out of your depth."

For the first time there was something beyond sweet innocence in her smile. "Nonsense." And then at my continued silence she said almost, half compulsively, "Miss Bracken reminds me of an English teacher I had at South Dakota. I always managed to get 'A' in English."

There was an odd note, derisive and steely, in her voice.

"You always get 'A'?"

"Yes," she said in a matter-of-fact voice. "Yes. So far."

"I'm tough on my pupils. I need more than a shiny big apple."

"I'm prepared for that."

"You begin to interest me."

"I began to interest you last night, Mr. Muldoon. Otherwise you wouldn't have shown up today. I believe we can work together— without friction."

"I hope not entirely without it!"

"We can discuss it tonight." She took out some francs from a businesslike bag and put them on the table. "These are on the expense account." But before she rose she turned suddenly and said, "Has Charles Pless talked to you?"

"About what?"

She held my gaze for a long moment, and I began to feel uncomfortable. Then she laughed and brought the handbag down to her lap. At first when her hand moved to my leg I thought it was accidental.

"I want a boss who goes on living," she said. "Otherwise I'm out of a job. I like my work."

"Listen …"

"We'll talk about that later, at the Café de Paris. It's been very nice." Primly she stood and primly she walked down the narrow street swinging the bulky bag, leaving me to wonder whether I had dreamed her up out of a hazy hangover and whether I had dreamed the neat little automatic I'd seen nestling among the cosmetics and franc notes in the bag.

TWO

I flipped hot and cold and tried to resolve the conflict in the bar of the Bellevue. I was allergic to neither sex nor money, God knows, but Nancy Trippe's cool nympho approach, combined with the coincidence of the note from Charles Pless and the reference to murder, set up storm clouds over riches and pleasures to come. An enterprise that included a jerk like Ballentine Black didn't have a cozy sound. What kind of a job did she have in mind that she felt it necessary—as the wandering hand had certainly suggested—to seal the contract in some bedroom?

The Bellevue bar was small and quaint, a leftover from the days when the hotel had been winter headquarters for English ladies and their Edwardian gentlemen long before Verens had been invaded by the blatant exhibitionists of the hep set. Nothing much had changed except the clientele. Wicker chairs, a big electric fan in the ceiling, potted palms, an oil painting of Windsor Castle, and an aged British bartender with the memory of hoary Colonials and gin and bitters in his red eyes. I stood up at the small bar and tried without success to pump the bartender.

"Black, sir? It's possible that he comes here. Everyone …" He paused significantly and repeated, "Everyone seems to come here these days."

I looked around for more loquacious sources of information. It was only four-thirty, a comparatively off-hour for this room, but I recognized some of the faces that had bobbed up during my two weeks in the resort; faces that had floated around me at parties, on the Bellevue beach or at the casinos or nightclubs. Some of them I had known in Paris or Rome. At a corner table an Italian princess was being overdemocratic with an Australian heavyweight while her husband—boredom cut from stone—half listened to a Hollywood starlet whose eyes reflected last night's tactical mistake.

Nearby a sleek New York model who had recently attached herself through marriage to some millions of the Detroit motor industry appeared to be advising a world-famous Spanish surrealist painter how to create his next masterpiece. She looked up long enough to give me an aristocratic and tolerant smile—one must be kind to the lower classes—and then went back into an inaudible stream of atrocious French. Further down the room two blond boys in faded denim and sandals sulked dreamily over some mild wine. But in the far corner, in the shadow of a potted palm, my eyes struck possible gold in the person of Alva Creighton. It was difficult to avoid meeting Alva if you moved, for one reason or another, in and among the set of rich bums and their lassies who float from one smart European resort to another with the seasons.

Alva was an enormously successful American novelist whose epics of Midwest farm life were monotonously serialized in the women's magazines. She was edging past middle age, square-built, given to hopelessly inaccurate pronouncements and possessed with the burning conviction that she was chic and a leader of the international set. Her snobbery would have shocked most of her readers right out of their gingham aprons but this snobbery was not extended to well-built and attractive young men. At the moment she was cooing into the handsome, suntanned face of a youth who recently had been discarded by a well-known film star after she had picked him off the bench at Malibu, where he had been a lifeguard. I figured Alva's latest book must have hit the bestseller list. The young man's services came high.

I took a deep breath, a deep gulp, and glass in hand, wandered from the bar toward Miss Creighton. Knowing her relentless storehouse of ill-assorted facts and her addiction to gossip, I hoped for a glimmer or two about Trippe and Co.

She wasn't too pleased to be interrupted, but apparently decided to be chic at all costs. "Dear Mr. Muldoon," she said in an incredibly phony British accent. "You know Harold Jones, of course."

"Only from a distance."

"Hi." Harold gripped my hand and gave me an all-American smile. "I think I met you at that marvelous party Princess Cerotti gave last week."

"It's possible. May I sit down?"

When no one said yes, I smiled and sat. Alva cleared her throat and was off to the races. "The Cerotti is a dear … I don't care what anyone says. Winston speaks well of her, you know … used to know her when Maxine was still alive. But I do wish she would stay clear of the wrong dukes, if you know what I mean."

Not having the slightest idea what she meant and not caring to guess the identity of Winston, I nodded sagely.

Harold said, "Alva has been telling me everything about her trip to Tangiers."

"Everything?"

Harold didn't smile. Humor was a liability in his trade.

Alva cackled. "How naughty of you! But you're quite wrong, Mr. Muldoon. I stayed with Barbara and I also stayed chaste. The Arab is an acquired taste, I'm afraid." And then, with barely a break, "This place is being ruined already. The beach is alive with tourists. Really, must they look as they do? I wouldn't be here if …" She broke off, then continued quickly, "Bea was up for Elsa's party and she tells me Capri has been completely destroyed by Americans. This is almost as bad. I'm trying to persuade Harold to hop over to Porto Fino in a few days …"

"Did she succeed?" I asked Harold.

Instead of answering, Harold looked away. Was it merely the practiced gesture of the wary businessman? Watching Alva's narrowed eyes, I wondered. There was some kind of slow-gathering tension here.

"He's so naive!" Alva gushed. "So fantastically American, like one of the characters in my books. A sweet smile, fluttering eyelashes, the odor of Ivory Soap, and as lost as any callow farm boy. I'm attempting to indoctrinate him into what—for loss of a better phrase—we might call the ways of the world!"

"Alva …"

"Now, dear boy, no more of that idiotic nonsense. You're playing with fire. You're coming to the opera gala with me, and no arguments."

Harold frowned, but he refrained from comment.

"As a writer," Alva said with malice, "I find it somewhat tiring to go on creating my material after I leave the typewriter."

Whatever the implication, I let it slide for other fields. "Speaking of your books—you're from Wisconsin, Alva, aren't you?"

"I was," she said shortly.

"Do you ever go back?"

"God, no! Let's not be depressing. I got the types and the plot when I was young. I don't need anything more than an occasional reminder, such as this charming boy." She laid a motherly hand, encrusted with diamonds, on the charming boy's knee. I thought he looked a little green around the gills. I was beginning to edge up to a lead-in to Trippe and Co. when she suddenly put down her drink and stared beyond me. "No!" she said.

I turned to see a tall, Lincolnesque man of about sixty approaching the bar. He wore a neatly pressed white suit much too formal for daytime wear in Verens, and a black shoestring tie, and he seemed to emanate an aura of curious dignity and benevolence. He was made to order for a mint julep, but I saw the bartender pour something light on the rocks.

"This is fantastic!" Alva said in a voice suddenly tense. "What in the world is he doing here?"

"Not knowing him, I can't say."

"But my dear … that's Governor Thorne. *Ex*-Governor Thorne to be exact." She named a state in the Deep South. "Before the last election, the world suddenly fell on his head!"

Only mildly interested, I asked, "How?"

"That filthy sheet killed his sister!"

"Filthy sheet?"

"The *National Alert*!"

I straightened to attention. "I gather you don't like the magazine."

She jabbed a cigarette into the end of a jade holder and leaned toward Harold for a light. "I can't tell you … I simply can't put into words …" She paused, puffed angrily, got control of herself and said, "Look at that poor, tragic man! A year ago his position seemed unassailable. He and his sister made the state mansion one of the most charming and hospitable houses in America. Everyone stayed with them at one time or another. And then this abominable magazine printed that filth …"

"What filth?"

"It purported to have proof that many years ago, in her youth, the governor's sister Virginia had spent some years in a New Orleans bawdy house."

"Was it true?"

She shrugged. "You know those impoverished Southern families. Anyway, it's irrelevant. Virginia never married. She sacrificed herself to her brother's political career. She was a charming and very cultured woman. After the story appeared she went to her room and blew her brains out!"

"Ah?" I turned it over in my mind. The ex-governor stood in lonely grandeur at the bar, looking as out of place as a Man of Distinction in a children's playground. Was this one of the threats to Charles Pless's life that Nancy Trippe had hinted at? Was there, after all, murder in the balmy air of Verens?

I watched Alva with growing curiosity. There was more than mere love of unsavory gossip in the way she had told the story. The hand holding the jade cigarette holder was trembling. I took a deep swig and said casually: "What goes with this *National Alert?*"

"It makes me ill to think of it. And what's worse, I am, in a way, responsible for it."

"You?"

"Yes, God help me. If I hadn't been so kind, so helpful ..." She smashed out the cigarette and reached for her drink. "It was four years ago, just after the publication of my *Love and the Earth*, you know. The publishers went all out on exploitation and publicity. One of the stunts was a well-photographed account of my return to the scene of the novel, the horrid little town in which I was born, North Fork, Wisconsin ... But I'm boring you."

"Not at all."

"Well they had one of those ghastly Old Home Week affairs with all the impossible provincial characters from my childhood—people who had once laughed at my attempts to write—fawning all over me, and speeches about North Fork's genius and similar sickening events. Well, there was a young man—not unlike Harold here—very handsome and very modest, a farm boy who had gone through the state college on a scholarship and was interested in journalism. I ... that is ... well, I took an interest in him. Purely professional, you understand."

"Of course."

"I encouraged him. Gave him letters of introduction to people in New York who might help him. My agent, two or three magazine publishers, people like that. It was a gesture ... one of those things. I never expected to hear of him again. How wrong I was! Within two years he was managing editor of *Inside* ... the very successful Picture Magazine. Then he married Myra Brock, who came equipped with cash. Out came *The National Alert* and my little farm boy turned into one of our contemporary monsters."

"Success story, eh?"

"Disgusting. Just half an hour ago we were treated to the spectacle of Mr. Charles Pless lording it over the cabañas on the beach." And then she added, in sudden unexpected fury, "His memory may be refreshed in a manner he doesn't expect."

In the silence her hand inched across the table to the discarded cigarette holder. It looked like a bejeweled crab.

"What's this magazine really like?"

"It's terrifying! Slick and expensive ... on the face of it it's very respectable. It poses as a crusader. Actually it deals in filth and slander."

"Your dislike of the magazine seems almost personal."

Her chin came up, her eyes narrowed, and for a moment the muscles of her flabby face jerked in fear. Then she laughed harshly. "Nonsense!"

"Did you come here to Verens to see Charles Pless?"

"Really! What an idea!" The muscles jerked again. "Now I know … Someone told me about you, Mr. Muldoon. You're some sort of professional sleuth, aren't you? How stupid of me not to have remembered."

"What difference does it make?"

"None, of course. None at all." And then she said, "Oh, my God, the governor has spotted me. What will I do?"

"Ask him over, of course."

"But one can't …" She sighed. "What bad luck, with that Cerotti woman in the room. It will be all over town in an hour. But I can't escape. He's coming over."

Quickly, before the governor arrived at our table, I whispered, "What about the girl named Nancy Trippe?"

She turned away. "She's Pless's secretary. Any other information you'll have to get from various hotel detectives." She turned on a too-bright smile for the governor, who bent over her hand. "Governor! What a lovely surprise! What ever brings you to Verens?"

"The climate," Thorne said with a gentle smile.

Alva introduced Harold and myself and hurriedly began to gather her bag, her cigarette holder and her artillery together. "But how delightful! You're staying in the hotel?"

"Yes." He sat in the fourth chair as Alva snapped shut her bag.

"How nice," Alva said. "We must see one another. So much to talk about. Unfortunately—and I am devastated—Harold and I promised Willie to run over for a cocktail before dinner."

The governor kept smiling, but I detected the shadow of irony at the corners of his mouth. "Your popularity is my loss, my dear Alva." He stood with her. "But perhaps soon …"

"But darling, of course! I'll call you as soon as I'm free. We have so much to discuss."

"Perhaps more than you imagine."

Alva's hand froze in the act of adjusting a silk scarf. "Oh?"

The governor looked down into his glass. "It seems, my dear Alva, that a certain magazine has decided the feature story of its November issue will be Alva Creighton."

Slowly the hand fell from the scarf. "Who told you?"

"So you know already."

"The bastards!"

"I quite agree," the governor said.

"Well, by God …" She caught herself up and looked furtively at Harold. She leaned back toward Thorne and said, "My dear, I'm not in the least worried about that absurd little sheet. Not in the least.

But I'm interested in knowing how you … Can you meet me here in half an hour?"

"What about Willie?"

"The hell with Willie."

"I'll be here, Alva. I intended to wait here anyway."

"Wait? For what?"

He smiled dreamily. He shrugged. For some reason I felt a chill on my spine. Alva took Harold's arm and they left the bar. The governor and I sat down again. The dreamy smile had left his face, and he suddenly seemed old and tired. He drained his glass, leaned back and closed his eyes. I thought he'd forgotten my presence.

But after a moment he said, "Young man, try never to fall into the depths of an obsession. There's nothing that will age you more quickly." He opened his eyes and looked around the room. "Sometimes I think I'm dreaming." He rose to his feet. "I'm sorry, but Alva only mumbled your name."

"Muldoon. Hart Muldoon."

"Ah, yes. Perhaps we will meet again. I think I will take a stroll on the promenade before returning to join Alva. The swim and a drink seem to have made me sleepy."

"Sir …"

"Yes?"

"About obsessions …"

He raised an eyebrow and for the first time really looked at me. "Yes?"

I hesitated, cleared my throat and said, "It's not worth it."

Surprise gave way to chilliness. He straightened up and nodded formally. "It's been pleasant. Perhaps next time we meet you will explain your enigmatic words. Good day, sir."

He walked away from me, out through the bar, erect and proud, oblivious to heads turned suddenly away. I had a picture of his walking this way down between the columns of the governor's mansion, in happier days.

I finished the drink and went out into the lobby. The clerk at the desk was cold and uncooperative, but I did manage to drag some information out of him. As I had suspected, Black was not registered at the Bellevue. Yes, Charles Pless was known to the hotel; he maintained a cabaña on the hotel's beach. A thousand-franc note helped to elicit the information that Pless had rented the Chateau de la Mer out on the road to Cap Ferrat.

I went to the public booth and called the chateau. A servant informed me Mr. Pless was out and would not be back before dinner. Miss Trippe? She was not in, either. And Mrs. Pless had gone into Cannes to do some shopping. I hung up and stepped back into the lobby. I was beginning to feel like an old hound dog let loose once more in the morning wood. But there was something wrong with the scent.

I decided to shower and change before going to my meeting with Pless. As the ancient gilt elevator lifted me up to the fourth floor I took out Pless's note and read it over again. "Mutual London friends have suggested your name. I believe we can work out a deal that will be advantageous to us both. The matter is urgent and perhaps even dangerous. If you are interested you will meet me at six at a villa named Petit Chanson, which is rented by a friend of mine who can be trusted completely. It is situated on the middle corniche towards Monte from Verens, just beyond the Chateau Noir. In the meantime, whether or not you decide to come, I would appreciate it if you keep this matter completely confidential—even to the point of destroying this note." It was signed Charles Pless.

I folded the note carefully and put it back into my wallet. I had no intention of destroying it. If nothing else, it might come in handy as a bargaining point with Nancy Trippe....

I stepped out of the elevator into the long, deserted hall. Daylight had given way to pink splotches from the silk-shaded lamps along the white and gilt paneling. I had the key to my room out when I noticed that the door was open half an inch. My muscles went tense. I hesitated a moment, then shoved the door inward with my foot.

The silence was oppressive. I stepped over the threshold. The wall lights were on, revealing most of my belongings strewn about the room or hanging from the open drawers of the bureau. Someone had done a damned messy job. I stood in the doorway, every nerve tense with listening, a Pavlov dog reacting to the old familiar stimulus. The open bathroom door, the half-open closet door, the space beneath the bed, all moved quickly through my line of vision like shots in a film. I began to figure that whoever had made this mess had left my room, probably some time ago.

Suddenly the phone beside the bed began to ring.

I stood in the doorway resisting the pull of that ringing phone. But after a moment it got the better of me. Keeping one eye on the closet door I edged to the phone and grabbed it up from its cradle.

"Yes?"

"Mr. Hart Muldoon?" A woman's voice, strained and muffled.

"Yes."

"Thank God. He was expecting you at six but you must come right away."

"Who is this?"

"My name doesn't matter. But please ... don't ask any more questions. Just come out here, if you ... Please!"

"Come out where?"

"The villa where you expected to meet Charles Pless."

Her words seemed to belong to a world of fantasy. The world of reality was much closer in the unmistakable sound of a wire coat hanger moving on the iron rod in the closet.

Automatically I said into the phone, "I'll be there," and hung up.

I was too late for any constructive action. The character who stood in the closet doorway was holding an automatic in a thoroughly professional manner. One part of my mind thought, You've made life interesting again, Miss Trippe—but this was just a bit too interesting for comfort.

"Now," the character said in the sweet accents of Brooklyn, "you and me … we'll have a talk."

"Come out of the closet, sweetie. I can be had."

"I'm counting on that."

He looked as though he meant it.

THREE

He moved as if he'd never trusted anyone in his life. And he was business. Faded blue eyes, lost in a pink sea of yesterday's excess, were called back in the necessity of the moment to taut awareness; the arm with the gun was stiff, but not stiff enough to freeze. He padded around me to the door like a sly old tomcat and then, facing me, reached behind and turned the key in the lock.

I had a moment to case him and what I cased I didn't like. He was in his middle forties and obviously regretted it. His hair was thin and dry, a tattered veil over a gray scalp; the face was beginning to fall away around a nose probably made pug in some forgotten battle of his blustering youth. The bulldog head appeared to be set on the shoulders without benefit of neck, and a belly protruded mournfully into a too-tight blatant sports shirt that seemed to symbolize some dream of gaiety he'd never attained. Perversely, the threatening pink-blue eyes contained the dying glimmer of some choir-boy supplication. He was full of fear, and therefore dangerous.

"You practicing up for TV, Black?"

It was a long shot that paid off. The tightened mouth told me.

I went on easily, casually, hiding what I felt. "You guys go in for real corn when you get canned out of the bureau."

"Buy yourself a couch, you punk. I didn't come here for a head session."

"Not much else to come for."

"Come on, pretty boy. I'm late for a date."

The voice, now deprived of official authority, was a harbinger of violence to come. In a way, I knew what to expect. Those creeps have to have it that way. The gun in one hand reassures the other fist, makes it feel safer. Maybe I was lucky it didn't carry a hunk of iron pipe. The blow came on the side of the face and sent me sprawling across the bed. I went with it, knowing a show of fight on my part would raise the ante, perhaps even to a trigger-happy finger.

He stood over the bed until I rolled around on my back.

"I'm the mailman, Muldoon. I want the letter."

"You're higher than a kite."

That cued him into another clout on the head. Then, like an old department hand, he frisked me completely. He came up with my wallet, my passport, an entrance stub to the casino, the names of some gals up and down the coast, and the note from Charles Pless. He fingered open the wallet with his free hand and after a quick examination dropped it to the bed. Then he flipped open the note from Pless and read it. He stuffed it into his pocket and stared down at me and for the first time there was a flicker of uncertainty in his eyes.

"Maybe you're smarter than I figured, after all, Muldoon. Maybe you didn't jump at that Trippe bitch's bait after all. Maybe you're playing it cozy."

He backed away and jerked the gun in a pantomime order to get up. I managed to get up without groaning and buttoned and zipped myself back into place. There was still a sting in my brain. I fished a cigarette out of a pack on the bedside table and, not looking at him, lit up. When I turned he'd backed off and the trigger finger was slack.

"All right," I said. "Now that you've had your kicks for today, how about telling me what the hell this is all about?"

I could see he knew I wasn't conning him. But habit persisted. "Come straight, Muldoon. I don't have time for the curves. Three o'clock finds you playing footsie with that Trippe bitch at the Armand's café. Three-thirty or a little later someone frisks my room at the Hermitage. Something Trippe wants bad is gone from my room. What do I figure?"

"You're slipping, Black. You could have checked. I came right back here from the Café Armand and have been down in the hotel bar ever since. A few questions would have saved your energy. You're getting a little old for this kind of roughhouse."

The gun was sinking out of business range. I began to feel less like a bull's-eye. I pressed my point. "If you had your doubts, why didn't you trail me from the Café Armand?"

Black's hand went into the pocket in which he'd put the rumpled note. "What's with Pless?"

"You tell me. I never met the guy."

Black said, "Pless! Poor benighted son of a bitch." And then quite suddenly all the threat went out of him and he whined, "You got a bottle in that top drawer. I could use a drink."

I didn't move. "Get it."

He hesitated, shrugged, went to the drawer, fished out the bottle and took a deep swig, tilting it up to his mouth like a nursing baby. Then he held it out to me.

"No thanks. I'm particular."

He shrugged again. "You going to keep that appointment with Pless?"

"Any reason I shouldn't?"

He looked away. There was something in the way he did it that made me uneasy. "Not if you don't mind getting up to your neck in sticky tar. You'll never get out, sweetheart. Not with that bunch." Still holding the bottle, he sank into a chair and with great ostentation placed the gun on the coffee table in front of him. "Let's you and me talk business."

"I've never been one to disregard good, honest, free enterprise."

He smiled uneasily and took another stiff one from the bottle. "Listen. It's this way. If you haven't got the letters Nancy Trippe has. The way things are, I haven't got a chance of getting near enough to her to lay my hands on them. But if she's beginning to snuggle up to you ..."

"You think if I get these letters—whatever they may be—you and I are in business."

"That's about it. Alone, they wouldn't do you much good. But with me ... Me, I got the angles."

The poor creep was serious. It never occurred to him that I wouldn't jump at some deal that I knew stank, even around the outer edges. Conking me on the head was only a friendly gesture in his lopsided world, and I could see that he had got to the point where he depended largely on the bottle for his values. But in a way he and Nancy Trippe had a lot in common: supreme faith in the power of the fast buck. For my own information I decided to play along.

"What's in these letters? What makes them so hot?"

Instead of answering he said, "I'm serious, Muldoon. There's enough in this for both of us. At worst, enough for a roll in the hay for a couple of years. At best, old-age insurance."

I didn't remind him that he looked as though he could use less of the former and more of the latter. "You still haven't answered my question."

"Get them back for me first ... then we'll talk."

"Suppose it wasn't Miss Trippe who lifted them from your room.

Suppose it was someone else. Pless, for instance."

"Pless?" He looked up at the ceiling. "Don't worry about Pless. I'm telling you it's Trippe we got to deal with." He clenched the bottle and suddenly looked away. "She's the only one who knew I had them here in Verens. That's why I thought she had contacted you—to pay you to get them. I should have known better. That bitch! I've seen them all, but this one—"

"Are these letters the reason why you're no longer working for Pless?"

Again his eyes went out of focus. Something seemed to amuse him, but whatever it was he kept it to himself. "Pless? Without me he'd still be nowhere, even with his wife's money. I mean nowhere he wanted to be. Pless has to be somebody people point to, somebody the columnists write about. The *National Alert* did that for him, and half the stuff in the *National Alert* came out of my special files." He tilted the bottle up and let the whisky trickle into his mouth. "Nothing was too good for me in the beginning. I was the white-headed boy; I was good old Biff, until Trippe decided to knife me in the back. That milk-fed bastard ..." He caught himself up and laughed dryly. "What he didn't know, and what Trippe didn't know, was that I had their feature story for the November issue tucked away in hiding."

"November issue." I remembered where I had last heard the November issue mentioned.

"Without those letters they got a million-dollar suit for slander on their hands."

"But now it seems they have the letters again ... and you've got no old-age insurance, eh? Not while they're in Pless's hands."

"Pless? You got it wrong, sweetie. Pless doesn't even know what's set up for his November issue. Not yet. That's Trippe's little bombshell."

"How much did the lady offer you for the letters?"

"The lady?"

"Alva Creighton."

Slowly he put down the bottle. "So Trippe told you."

"No. Alva Creighton mentioned the November issue down in the bar. Or rather someone mentioned it to her."

"Who?"

"Governor Thorne."

He leaned forward. "Thorne. Here in Verens? How did he know about the November issue?"

"Why don't you ask him?"

He sagged back into the chair, grinned foolishly, and looked away. "The streets won't be safe for a hardworking magazine writer ... or editor, for that matter. What the hell ... Thorne isn't gunning for me.

It's Pless he blames."

"Isn't he right?"

Black shrugged and looked amused again. "I like it that way." And then with a ridiculous show of what he imagined to be candor he said, "All right. The letters were written by Alva Creighton. They say things she regrets. She wants to forget them by burning them. I've got her to about the twenty-thousand touch, and I'm going higher. You get the letters back from Trippe and I'll do the rest."

"Why cut me in at all?"

I thought for a moment he hadn't heard. Then he looked down at the bottle in his hands. "I haven't been so good lately. I need somebody to work with."

I made a show of pacing thoughtfully. And, in fact, I did do a little thinking. It was obvious that Black needed me. It was obvious that he needed anybody. He was shaking himself up to the finish line fast, with only a desperate dream to hang to. His days as a smart solo operator were drowned in the bottle he held so desperately in his hand. Maybe that's why Pless had fired him. I'd have to edge up to Pless on that one. I needed Black around for future reference, but in the meantime he must be kept in deep freeze. Or in alcohol.

"Well," I said after a moment, "I've got a big hotel bill. I need something quick and easy."

"What did Trippe offer you?"

"What do you think? I'm seeing her later tonight."

"That means she hasn't sprung you yet. She will. I'd like to know what the hell she has in mind."

"Leave it to me. Now, how much are you cutting me in for?"

"A third."

"That's fair enough."

He looked at me for a long moment and then, poor slob, seemed satisfied. I figured that even in his best day, Black had been nothing more than an office worker in the bureau; J. Edgar wouldn't have let Black loose in the field on anything more important than an inquiry at the information booth of Grand Central. At the moment booze was helping him dream up a rosy world with me propping him up along the way.

"Be my guest," I said. "Order dinner from room service and anything liquid if you run out. I'm going to change and start digging."

"You going to keep that date with Pless?"

"Why not?"

He hesitated, seemed about to say something, changed his mind, and shrugged. Then he said, "You get a knife fitted for my back, sweetheart, and this will be the last job of your career. Cross me, and so help me, I'll get you, Muldoon."

He meant it.

And then almost compulsively, he added, "I learned this. Doing the dirty jobs to keep the big wheels respectable doesn't pay off. Not in the end. I got a hate as big as Texas for the human race. And maybe I was soft-talked out of a slum, but I got no tears for the Alva Creightons of this world, and I got no tears for that bastard Pless. I got no tears for you."

He was sailing away to dreamland with that bottle. It took a little more talking, but not much. Ten minutes later I left him sprawled on the bed like a five-year-old, nursing the bottle.

I left the room, locking the door behind me, and went down to the main entrance. The doorman gave me and my battered MG the fish eye. The little car coughed its way up a steep, narrow street to the middle Corniche. A fat red moon was just rising from the sea, and there was the odor of orange blossoms in the night. I pointed the hood toward Monte Carlo and stepped her up. The ancient Roman road twisted around the hills and gorges, past the wedding cake villas and flowering mountainsides. After a bit I came to the walls surrounding the Chateau Noir and slowed down. The wall gave way to a lower wall of pink stone crawling with bougainvillea, and beyond the wall I saw the tiled roof of a small villa.

I turned in at the gate and found myself in a tiny circular courtyard. A sleek Mercedes sports car was parked near the door. The car looked familiar. I cut the motor and stepped out on the flagstones. It was very still here, full of the fragrance of the flowers that clung to the pink walls of the villa. A slit of light was visible between the drawn curtains of a window to the right of the main entrance, but otherwise the house was in darkness. I took time to light a cigarette. The sound of a powerful motor came roaring down the corniche and then died away in the distance. Before I reached the blue door, it opened and a woman's figure was silhouetted against a dim light from inside.

"Yes?" Soft, staccato tension.

"Hart Muldoon."

The shoulders slackened. "Oh, I … Thank God. I'd just about given you up. Come, in please."

She stepped aside and I walked past her into a small hall with dark, wide floorboards, a provincial table and chair. Light came from a wrought-iron lantern wired for electricity which created a shadow of grotesque pattern on the white walls. The door clicked behind me and I turned. The woman resolved into a girl, no more that eighteen or nineteen, wearing a simple blue linen sports dress.

Even in the filtered light, I could see she was not the type who would ever have to write the Lonely Hearts Club. Her dark hair was cut short in the boyish Italian fashion, but there any resemblance to the opposite sex ended. There was a sweetness in the face that robbed it, perhaps, of sensational beauty, but she was not a rubber-stamp Hollywood type, dewy-eyed with thoughts of the cash register. Fantastic dark eyes leveled at me, taking me in all at one glance. Then she moved swiftly past me over the threshold into a room to the right of the hall.

I followed without waiting for a whistle. The room was small but chic; a few very good pieces of old country furniture against white walls, bare except for a couple of striking abstracts, a corner fireplace, a chaste modern couch, a large window with a view of the moon-drencher Mediterranean far below.

"Nice," I said.

"As you can imagine, I didn't bring you here to discuss interior decoration."

Behind the matter-of-fact accents there was something just about to go out of control. She was fighting desperately to keep emotion at a distance, and it occurred to me that perhaps, with her, it was not an entirely new fight.

"It seems a pity to be so businesslike on such a night," I remarked.

She frowned. "There's a man here."

"I'm not that kind of detective."

"You don't understand. He's dead."

A little chill crept through the room. "How inconvenient."

"Yes," she said in the same unearthly, forced calm. "It's very inconvenient."

"Murder?"

She nodded. The knuckles of her hands, clasped together, were white now.

"Did you do it?"

"I don't know," she said. And then quickly, "No. No."

With an effort, she detached one hand from the other and lifted her arm to indicate a door by the fireplace.

"Don't you trust the French police?"

The hand fell back to the comfort of the other.

"He mustn't be found here. He must be taken away somewhere."

I nodded as though it were the most logical suggestion of my day. I wanted, for at least a few more minutes, to keep hysteria at arm's length. I started for the door. She made no move to follow. She simply stood there as though carved from stone. I remember thinking, She's too young for this. I throttled any more questions, went to the door, and pushed it inward. I stepped into the room and reached along the wall for the light switch. Before I pressed it, I looked back into the gay little sitting room. The girl was still standing where I had left her.

There was something oddly touching in the stern loneliness of her posture. She's too young, I thought again and snapped on the light.

The man on the bed was a big athletic blond of about thirty-five, wearing Italian silk slacks and a pink sports shirt. He was on his back, eyes closed and, at first glance, merely seemed to be peacefully sleeping. There was no sign of a wound or marks of violence. On the table beside the bed there was a half-empty glass of water and a wristwatch. The sports shirt was badly buttoned. On the floor beside the bed were sports shoes and argyle socks that obviously belonged to the stiff, naked feet.

If this hadn't been enough to spoil the illusion of peaceful sleep, small details, some of them distinctly unpleasant began to creep in. The man's arms were straight down along his sides and the fists were clenched tight. Through partly open lips I saw that the tongue had been bitten almost in two and that part of it was turned grotesquely in his mouth.

I went back to the sitting room. She was standing exactly where I had left her.

"It's Pless," I said.

The fingers loosened their grip on one another as though life were draining from them. Just before she slipped to the floor she whispered, "Pop—I didn't—"

FOUR

The cognac trickled between her lips. It finally brought her back to consciousness. She looked up at me from the couch, uncomprehending for a moment. Then memory flooded back and she pushed herself up on one elbow.

I took out a pencil and a little black book which I'd retrieved from the shambles Black had made of my room. I thought a professional presence would reassure her.

"We'll begin with names."

She hesitated. "First I've got to know whether you'll help me."

"What kind of help do you want?"

"He mustn't be found here. It would make too many people unhappy."

"What people?"

"His wife, my father, others ..."

"You care more about that than finding out who did this?"

"In a way—yes." The curious, unnatural calm was returning. She sat up and groped for a cigarette. When I lit it she looked me in the eyes for a moment, then away.

"You and Pless ..." I said.

"Yes?"

"You were on … ah … friendly terms."

"Yes."

"Why did you call me?"

"Charles mentioned your name. He said you might be able to help him. He was terribly upset about something. After—after it happened I couldn't think of a soul to call for help. Then I remembered your name and the fact that you were staying at the Bellevue."

"What was he upset about?"

"I don't really know. He wouldn't tell me. I guess he didn't want me to worry. But he had been upset for the past two days … and apparently something happened this afternoon."

"This afternoon?"

"He came here directly from the Bellevue beach. He always swims there in the afternoon. Apparently something that was said there … someone he saw … I honestly don't know."

"Tell me what happened."

She puffed at the cigarette, closed her eyes for a moment, tilted her head back and blew smoke toward the ceiling. Her hand was almost steady now. "It would kill my father," she said. "He hates messy things and messy people." Almost dutifully she added, "And so do I."

"Would I know your father?"

"It's unlikely. He owns a drugstore in Vinesville, Ohio."

This bit surprised me. I would have sworn she had a social register background.

"He's important in Vinesville. On the board of aldermen, director of the Community Chest—things like that. There has never been even the hint of scandal in his life."

"And Mamma?"

"She died when I was five. I'm an only child."

"And how did you land in this mess?"

Carefully she deposited the ash from her cigarette in a tray. "It's like a dream …" She sighed. "I graduated from college last spring, and I came to Paris to be … to get away from …" She caught herself. "I came to Paris to study painting. I met Charles Pless at a party in Paris about six months ago. He—" She stopped again, stubbed out the cigarette, brought her hands together and then said in a matter-of-fact voice, "I suppose you have to know these things. Otherwise it wouldn't make sense. Charles and I—we had an affair. It—it became serious. I mean serious on his part. And serious on my part, but—but for different reasons."

"Once over again please."

"I can't explain. Don't ask me to explain now. Anyway, what matters is that it happened. When he came south to Verens for the summer he took this place for me."

"He was keeping you."

Her chin went up and color spread across her face. But she controlled herself and finally said, "I suppose you could call it that. Yes."

"Somehow, you're not the type."

And then to my surprise she leaned forward and said angrily, "Why not?"

I retreated. "All right, you are the type."

She leaned back again, contrite. "That was silly of me. Childish. You happened to hit a sore spot ... Oh, this is so neurotic and unpleasant, talking about myself with—with Charles in there." She looked at her watch. "We're wasting time. Someone might come."

"Take it easy."

"Poor Charles."

The statement was genuine enough, but it didn't have the emotional force of a woman in love. The girl was beginning to puzzle and intrigue me. She didn't quit fit into any of my convenient pigeonholes.

"You might as well know my name. It's Amy Grant. It was Amelia in the beginning, after my mother."

"All right, Amy. Now tell me exactly what happened. But first, why are you so certain it is murder?"

"He told me," she said. "Just before he died."

Now I needed time to light up. After a second I said, "Begin from the time he arrived, and tell me in your own words."

"Charles usually came here in the afternoon or late at night. I seldom went out. I just stayed here and worked at painting or puttered around in the garden and waited for him. Today he didn't arrive until almost four. As I've told you he was very upset about something that had happened on the beach at the Bellevue this afternoon."

"Did he give you any idea at all?"

"No. He said he wanted to talk with you about it first. I've never seen him so—"

"Yes?"

"It's hard to explain. So angry, so determined, yet at the same time afraid."

"What happened?"

"I fixed him a drink and we talked a little. Then ..." She stopped.

Casually, I said, "Then you went to the bedroom."

She looked away and nodded her head. I could see that the effort to be calm and detached was almost heroic.

"Now I have to explain ... I must explain. Charles had a heart condition. At times he would have to take adrenalin ..."

"You mean—" I said brutally— "after sexual intercourse."

She closed her eyes and nodded miserably. "He carried a pill in his pocket—in case. It's terrible, but somehow the story was all over Paris. How it started I don't know. It was a kind of dirty joke, and it was humiliating to him."

"Let me get this straight. You mean many people knew Charles Pless carried a life preserver?"

"Yes. I always suspected it was a form of hypochondria. I don't think he really needed it at all, but he believed he did."

"He was afraid of death?"

"Maybe … Yes, I guess so. Anyway, after—I mean—there in the bedroom, he asked me to get the pill from the small side pocket of his jacket. He seemed to be having a little trouble with his breathing, but nothing unusual."

"You'd seen him that way before?"

"Yes."

"What was the pill like?"

"It was a capsule, really; a little yellow capsule."

"Go on."

"He was joking about it from the bed. I got a glass of water for him and handed him the pill. He put it in his mouth and swallowed and I was about to turn away when suddenly—" Now, for the first time, her voice rose, and emotion—horror—cracked through. "And … oh, dear God, he suddenly cried out and went into convulsions. It was only an instant really … it seemed impossible. His tongue … he screamed, but I couldn't understand what he was saying. I was almost blank with terror. He was trying to tell me something I couldn't make out the words—except one—Murder."

"Go on."

"Even in my terror I thought of a doctor. I didn't know who to call, but I started for the phone. I backed from him toward the phone; I couldn't take my eyes from his face. He doubled up there on the bed, then he straightened out, completely rigid, his hands down at his sides and his fists clenched, as you saw him. And the veins of his forehead were standing out as though they would burst. He wasn't seeing me anymore. And then, then quite suddenly … he was dead."

The silence was broken by the cry of some night bird out in the garden. I cleared my throat and said, "What did you do?"

"I don't remember. I must have tried to dress him—but that was later. Yes, of course, I did. I kept thinking Pop might walk in at any moment—Pop, who is thousands of miles away in Ohio. I remember dressing myself and standing in the bathroom before the mirror and I remember washing my hands—washing. I remember later pouring a drink of brandy and sitting here in this room unable even to think. And then out of the white blankness came your name and I went to the phone to call you."

"Maybe you're lucky," I said.

I got up and went to the window overlooking the garden. I was aware of her sitting on the couch behind me, hands tightly clasped, tense with waiting. There was a contradiction here. If I knew anything about people I knew she wasn't the sort of girl who could have slipped into an easy and sloppy relationship with a guy like Pless. There were holes a mile wide in her story and there were at least ten dozen questions in my mind. But there was something else … something that surprised me; I was almost certain she had not killed Charles Pless and I was equally certain I was going to help her. I'd done plenty of pratfalls in my time as Sir Galahad; and although I suspected this might result in the biggest pratfall of all, I knew I was going to play on her team.

"Someone will be missing him," I said.

"Not yet. His wife thinks he has a business engagement in Nice for dinner. There's to be some sort of a party at their villa later … but not until ten or eleven, and he wasn't expected back until then."

"That gives us a little time. We'd better get him away from here."

"Then you will help?"

I turned. She was leaning forward, and the expression of relief in her eyes was almost worth the worry it gave me.

"Look, Miss Grant. I don't know why you got yourself into this mess, but it's hardly your own business anymore. You'll have to come clean with me sooner or later. We'll leave it till later right now. All this is very inconvenient for me—someone has done me out of an employer right at a time when I needed one bad."

"I have a little money. Not much, but …"

"We'll discuss that later, too. In the meantime, for the next half-hour you'll have to keep your head and all the guts you can summon."

"What do you want me to do?"

"Pless is a heavy man. You'll have to help me carry him out to his car."

She stood up. "I'll manage all right."

I started for the bedroom, then stopped and turned. "You didn't love him?"

She brought her chin up and looked me in the eyes.

"No. But I'm grateful to him. I'd never been with a man before Charles. I was afraid; he taught me not to be."

She was standing between me and the drawn curtains of the window, facing the courtyard. As she spoke the sound of a motor came closer. Headlights grew stronger on the draperies. The motor died. And then suddenly the headlights were turned off. Neither of us moved or said a word. We stood as though mesmerized, listening to the footsteps coming across the paved courtyard.

FIVE

The staccato sound of the knocker filled the room with urgency, Now that possible disaster was rapping at the door, Amy was calm. She said, "What now?"

I stretched my lips into a hypocritical grin of assurance, hopped over to the windows overlooking the courtyard and tugged a crack in the draperies. Out there something belligerently feminine was standing at the front door, something cloaked, bejeweled, big and middle-aged. A hand, flashing diamonds, clawed up at the knocker again in jerky impatience. She looked like death in drag.

A Renault with a prissy little bonnet had come to rest between Pless's Mercedes and my MG. It didn't tell me much. It was the kind of car let loose by the hundreds from the rental services of Cannes and Nice.

The figure at the door wheeled about me majestically and peered, unseeing, in my direction. The light was on the woman's face now and I recognized it. I let the draperies fall back into place and turned to face Amy. She was standing in the middle of the room, hands clasped tight in front of her, like a Quaker gone tense at a prayer meeting.

"You've got a lady novelist at the front door. Maybe she needs a new plot."

"Lady novelist?"

"Alva Creighton. Do you know her?"

"No."

"Why are you so startled, then?"

"Why?" She looked away. "Charles has spoken of her. It's just something that Charles said."

The locked hands had become a lie detector machine. A visitor at this moment would be enough to lock anyone's hands, but there was something else here. Something that didn't fall right. What the hell did she know about Alva to send the blood scurrying to her feet?

"You're not going to answer the door?" she said.

"She must know Pless's Mercedes. Everyone does. Let her in and see what brought her here. It might be revealing. Try to act casual."

"But you ..."

"I'll be doing the French farce bit from behind the bedroom door."

"I'm afraid of her."

"I've got something reassuring here," I said. "Something persuasive."

I took out the Luger. She looked at it with blank eyes for a moment, and then shuddered. The knock came again, desperately insistent now. Middle age knocking frantically at the doors of lost youth? I signaled Amy to get moving, and beat a retreat to the bedroom. Through the partly open door I got a clear view of the entire living room.

Amy was out of my line of vision when she went into the hall, but she reappeared a moment later leading a gaudy Alva Creighton decked out like a peacock for some Riviera night gala.

"I'm sorry to be so crassly insistent," Alva said with a steely smile. She looked around the room questioningly, then her fiction-seeking eyes found the bedroom door and the smile became more knowing. With obvious "chic" she looked away from the bedroom but raised her voice for the benefit of whoever she imagined was in there.

"The blue hour," she said with relish. "Such an inconvenient time for callers."

But she sailed down into the room, diamonds flashing, egrets waving, and in one deft movement, divested herself of the gold evening wrap, revealing something Balenciaga must have dreamed up for a woman half her age. Amy had stopped uncertainly inside the archway to the hall, as though trying to draw her unwelcome guest back into the hall by means of magnetic will. She was scared, and barely able to conceal the fact.

Alva calmly settled on the sofa, fished out her holder and cigarettes from a gold evening bag and lit up. She was seething about something, but apparently enjoying her own anger and the drama she was playing.

"Thank you so much. I will sit down," she said ironically. And she rattled on, "I'm due in half an hour for dinner at Ciro's, in Monte. I shall probably be a little late. I hope not too late, Miss Grant. I have a governor—an ex-governor, true—dining with me, a last-minute substitution. Oh, no, my dear," she continued with heavy-handed sarcasm, "don't bother about a drink. By the way, in case you're puzzled my name is Alva Creighton. Does that ring any unpleasant bells?"

"I don't understand," Amy said weakly. "We've never met. Why do you assume ..."

Alva gave a peacock laugh to go with her finery. "My dear child, if I didn't know you were too young, I would swear you had been coached by one of the Gish sisters. Do you intend to honor me with one verse of 'Ave Maria'? You have that look about you." And then she added swiftly, in the same tone of voice, "It's quite obvious that Charles Pless is in this house. If I had no other reason to think so, I would certainly have recognized his Mercedes. Do come out of that bedroom, Charles. It's so—inhospitable."

Amy snapped out of her fear.

"You're mistaken, Mrs. Creighton. Mr. Pless is not here."

"Are you going to try to deny that isn't his car out there?"

"No. The Mercedes belongs to Mr. Pless. He was here for tea. When he was about to go he found the battery dead. He called his villa and had the chauffeur come for him in the limousine."

Inwardly I groaned; now we were in deeper than ever. But I couldn't help but admire Amy's cool conviction. She almost had me believing it. I watched Alva to see whether it fitted. The novelist looked uncertainly from Amy to the bedroom door, then back at Amy again. After a moment she said, "I suppose that's just brazen enough to be true. Did he call his wife to request the chauffeur to come?"

Alva was accepting the story. And suddenly, watching her, it came over me that she wanted to accept the story—that in some way it suited her unknown purpose.

Amy said, "I'm sorry, but I'm about to dress to go out. If you have anything you wish to say …"

"And the other car in the courtyard."

"Oh. Why—that's mine, of course."

"I see. Then we are alone?"

"Yes."

"Good! It makes it easier. I don't have to undress in public."

"Undress?"

"Strip down to my weaknesses. With just you to hear it isn't too bad. You see I know all about you and Charles Pless and I do hope you won't waste our time by denying it."

Amy didn't. Instead she said, "What do you want?"

"My property."

"I see."

There was a sudden complete silence. The two women seemed to know what they were talking about, even if I was in the dark. Alva blew smoke up into the room, waiting. I had the feeling that, in the stress of the moment, Amy had forgotten about my presence behind the bedroom door and, in fact, the silent presence on her bed. She walked slowly down into the room.

"You can't be serious. You can't refer to another human being as your property."

"Why not? When there was a for-sale sign up."

"That's a terrible thing to say about a man."

"Oh come now, my dear. Do you think I was born yesterday?"

"No one could possibly think that," Amy said with unexpected malice. Hatred was beginning to crackle and sputter in the quiet room.

Alva smiled with frightening sweetness. "It's lucky we women never took the Marquis of Queensbury and his silly rules seriously. They were intended after all for men who are more hypocritical about these matters."

"May I ask how you found out I was living here—and the other details you have just revealed?"

Alva's smile held. Very carefully she said, "Shall we say a mutual friend?"

It was immediately obvious that she had scored heavily. Amy's clasped hands fell apart. In a tired voice she said, "Oh."

Having won her point, the older woman permitted a note of humanity to creep back into her phony British intonations. "My dear, when you have lived and known as much as I, you will come to realize that there isn't a male alive who won't—when pressed—kiss and tell."

"I can't believe it." The misery on Amy's face astounded me. Whoever had kissed and told must have mattered a great deal.

"Now, my dear," Alva went on in the same clipped caricature of mother-to-daughter talk. "Harold Jones is who he is. It's naive to have expected loyalty to the old school tie. The boy is ill-suited to the roles of either Romeo or Sir Galahad. His other attributes are—shall we say, more amusing."

Harold, the muscle man! Live and learn, I thought. I glanced over at the dead man on the bed. I amended that first thought. Had it been learn and die?

"Please say what you've come to say," Amy was saying in a tired voice.

"The boy is corrupt, but foolish. The combination has its advantages for a woman like me. Unfortunately you have instilled in him juvenile and uncharacteristic delusions. He's beginning to see himself as The Man in The Gray Flannel Suit. He's beginning to use foreign words, like decency. It's your doing, of course, and I want you to undo it immediately."

"How?"

"Oh, come now. You can't go on playing with fire, or, to really mix the metaphors—have your cake and eat it too."

"But—"

"But nothing! You're not that naive. You've managed to convince Harold that this business between you and Charles Pless is merely some sort of neurotic slip on your part, that actually, at heart, you're a simple little child with love and babies and heaven at ten cents a week on your mind. It's not at all fair. It's like despoiling a work of art—especially when you have no intention of giving up Charles."

"What makes you so certain?"

Alva's head came up like a walrus's for a tossed fish. Her small eyes glittered dangerously.

"Now, please! I want you to leave Harold alone!"

"What right have you to—"

"The right of any heavy investor!"

"Suppose I refuse?"

"I don't believe you're that foolish!"

The novelist's voice was as cold as the Greenland ice cap and even less comforting.

Too late, Amy retreated from boldness to discretion. "I think you're imagining things."

"Nonsense!" Alva's artillery sought her out relentlessly. "I know Harold is coming here tonight to take you to the gala at the Opera House in Monte Carlo."

"He told you?"

"That's irrelevant. I know a lot of things. I know you've been seeing one another; I know, as a matter of fact, exactly how you met on that island two weeks ago and what happened on the beach that Thursday and incidentally, how many times!"

The color that rose to Amy's face might have been anger or shame or maybe both. "Please go," she said.

Alva didn't budge.

"Not before you have agreed to tell Harold that you're through with him!"

"Get out!"

"Oh dear, you sound just like one of my Hollywood scenarios! Well, my girl, I have news for you. Life isn't like my scenarios. It's a hell of a lot more sordid and urgent and … and desperate! I don't begrudge either of you a little fun in the bushes, but I'm damned if I'll sit back and see you make it a life's habit!"

"Your mind is a garbage pail!"

"Possibly, but it's still quite alert. And I'm curious—as one garbage pail to another—just why you insist on leading poor immoral Harold down the garden path of middle-class dreams. Just how have you managed all this with Charles? How are you going to explain flaunting Harold tonight at the gala in Monte? Really, as a professional writer I am interested."

"I should think that was my business, and Charles', and above all, Harold's. Harold is old enough—"

"Oh, my God. Platitudes! Harold or no other man is old enough, until of course it's too late for them to be concerned about matters of this sort."

"Mrs. Creighton!" Amy said angrily. "I really don't understand you. You seem to think that Harold is someone you can buy and sell. I don't happen to think so. As for Charles, he was—" she caught herself up—"he understands."

"Charles Pless is giving you his blessing? I don't believe it for a moment. I know how he feels about you. He told me himself."

"Told you? When?"

"In his cabaña this afternoon, at the Bellevue beach."

There was a moment's silence. I pricked up my ears. Alva seemed to be regretting this revelation.

Quickly she hurried on. "I think you're lying about Charles's knowing; you've been seeing Harold on the sly. I suppose Charles is fool enough to think he's just a convenient escort to take you to the gala." She leaned forward. "Now listen, my sweet. Unless you send Harold packing when he calls for you tonight, I will have a heart-to-heart talk with Charles and tell him some of the things I was gracious enough to leave out this afternoon. I'll …"

"You'll what?"

"I'll talk not only to Charles, but to his wife and friends and anyone else who cares to listen from here to Marseille. I'll talk up the sweetest little pornographic storm that even this coastline has seen. I'll …" Alva was getting out of control.

Amy brought her up, at least for a moment. "Is this some sort of blackmail? Surely you wouldn't—"

"Blackmail! I love that word coming from anything belonging to Charles Pless. My dear, he crawled into my bed at the Commercial Hotel in North Fork, Wisconsin, when he was a callow youth, and he's been blackmailing everyone in sight since then. At least his organization has. And not only that … if he doesn't return those letters …"

"Letters?"

"Never mind. That's between him and me, or rather his organization and me. But blackmail! Really! His own medicine. And speaking of medicine, he might get the wrong kind—something he hadn't bargained for, one of these days …"

"What does that mean?"

"There's an absurd little man over in Cannes. He's been telling the world he has a pill ready for Charles."

"A pill? What kind of a pill?"

"Nothing more serious than cyanide."

SIX

Amy didn't move. She stood with one hand on a small wooden chair, leaning on it for support. She stared down at Alva Creighton, eyes wide and unbelieving.

The silence stretched into a meaning of its own. It penetrated even

Alva. Her anger and frustration faded into a small feather of fear. After a moment she said, "What's wrong?"

She looked from Amy about the room, as though afraid of what she might find. Her gaze came to rest on the half-open bedroom door which concealed me. She shivered and reached for her cloak.

"Cyanide tablet?" Amy finally managed to whisper.

Alva stood up, drawing her cloak about her shoulders. She tried to make her voice light, but it trembled beneath the weight of some urgent emotion.

"Everyone knows about it, my dear. It's just a joke, of course."

"You didn't say it as though you thought it was a joke."

"Well it is, I assure you. This creature—someone Nancy Trippe produced at a party in Cannes—he got drunk and began telling the world he had a cyanide tablet for Charles Pless. Now you see how absurd that is. I suppose even Charles heard the story. The creature is obviously some crackpot ..." She stopped and the simulated lightness shattered in the light of a sudden thought. "Why, I guess even you had heard the story. Certainly Harold—" She broke off.

"If Charles had known ... Charles was the sort of person ..." Amy too choked off her words at the sudden alertness in Alva's face.

"Did you say was?"

"I meant ... when I spoke to him last."

"Why, I don't believe you meant anything of the kind. May I freshen up in your bathroom?" She began moving toward the bedroom door and me. I got the Luger out.

Amy said sharply, "Don't go in there!"

Alva stopped dead. She had her back to Amy, but she was facing me and I got a clear view of her expression through the crack in the door. It was a curious mixture of fear and satisfaction. There was a moment's utter silence. Then slowly Alva turned back to face Amy. "There's something very wrong here," she said. When Amy said nothing she went on: "Why of course! What a fool I've been—all the time I was talking to you about Harold, you knew something was wrong. You knew, because ..."

"Mrs. Creighton."

"No." Alva made a circle around Amy toward the hall door. There in the archway she wheeled about.

"So Charles didn't like your liaison with Harold! You had a quarrel ... His car—he never left this house. You paid that funny little man to—Oh, my God! I can see it on your face!"

Behind the door I thought fast. I could step out now and give Amy another and quite logical reason for the agitation she had shown when Alva had approached the bedroom. I might even try to reason with her. Or I might lock her up in one of the rooms in the villa for a few hours, until I had a chance to track down whoever had finished Charles Pless off. But that would leave Alva out of circulation as a possible decoy—or, even more to the point, a possible murderess. I needed more than vague suspicion.

I paid a long hunch. It began to pay off almost immediately.

"Listen to me," Alva said dramatically. "I don't know what's happened here. I don't know anything. I haven't even been here. If—if, I say— you send Harold back to me intact and keep our names out of this mess."

"Mrs. Creighton …"

"If you don't comply, you'll regret it."

With her own mouth Alva had implicated herself as a strong suspect. How convenient to frame her young rival. How convenient to have the publisher of the magazine she feared and hated out of the way. Had she somehow managed to slip the poison tablet into Charles Pless's jacket at the Bellevue beach? Was the story of the person from Cannes true; had she paid a price for that cyanide tablet? All of it was barely possible, and yet it was hard to believe that even Alva with her flare for the dramatic, would have dared to come to the villa to discover whether the tablet had taken effect.

"I shall expect Harold to join me after the gala, at the Sporting Club. You can give him that message, if the police haven't intervened in the meantime."

"Mrs. Creighton, you must listen to me."

"I've heard quite enough, thank you. I suppose I can even wish you luck. But keep Harold and me out of this filthy mess."

She turned and hurried into the hall, kicking a table over in her undignified flight. There was the sound of the outer door slamming, high heels on the pavement of the courtyard, the motor of the Renault sputtering to life and choking furiously as it fled from the scene.

I came out of the bedroom, tucking the Luger into my coat pocket.

"Why did you let her go!" Amy cried. "She'll broadcast it to the world."

"I don't believe so," I said as calmly as possible. "Anyway, we'll play it three to one she won't talk—at least not yet. It will give us time and, aside from money, time is what I need most."

"Money…" she said in a tired voice.

"Yes, sweetie. Money."

"I … Right now … Maybe later …"

"You're broke?"

"At the moment. But if you can wait …"

"I'm impatient."

I started for the hall door.

"Wait!"

I turned. She was hanging on the back of the chair in desperation. "You didn't mention the money before she came in. You ..."

"Didn't I?" I said coolly.

"Oh," she said. "I see. You mean what you heard ..."

"So you had a date with dear Harold. Why didn't you mention it?"

"There was hardly time. It's so complicated."

"Did you quarrel with Pless about Harold?"

"No. He'd found out about Harold. I told him the truth. He was very decent."

"The truth?"

She averted her face, but not quickly enough to conceal the utter misery in her eyes. "I have no one."

"Look," I said letting the burn show through. "I'm not particularly interested in your extra-curricular activities with an ex-lifeguard named Harold Jones. At least not in the moral values involved. That's your own business!"

She sank into the chair in weary despair. I thought I must be losing my marbles. But I took a step into the room and, of course, was lost.

"What do you know about this story of the cyanide tablet?"

"I don't know," she said listlessly, and then looked up, aware of the significance of my step back. Hope came back into her face.

"Do you think Alva made up that story? Did Charles ever mention such a person?"

"No. It came as a complete shock to me. Do you believe it?"

"Come on. We've got to get moving."

"Where?"

"We have a dirty job to do. Then I've got to track down some people and this story of Alva's."

"Yes. Yes, all right." But she still sat there. I guessed that her mind, womanlike, was not on the dangerous present but on the emotional implications of her scene with Alva Creighton.

"Snap out of it, Amy! Someone may come at any moment—Harold, for example. We've got to get what's left of Charles Pless out of this house."

That brought her back. "Where?"

"We'll get him into his Mercedes and I'll ditch it somewhere along the Corniche. When they find him, they may think at first that it was simply a heart attack. It will give us that valuable time I was talking about." I looked at my watch. It was seven-ten.

"What time was Harold supposed to call for you?"

"About eight-thirty. We were going direct to the Opera House. The gala begins about nine."

"Good. I want you to follow along in my car and pick me up. Now take a swig of brandy because the next few minutes won't be too pleasant."

She looked at me with an expression of sudden disconcerting sweetness. "You're a very kind person."

"The hell I am! Come on!"

It took a good ten minutes of lugging, pushing and heaving to get Pless's heavy body out of the bedroom and into the front seat of the Mercedes. He leaned there against the door, leering glassily at the moon. Amy, full of little surprises, stepped back from the car and dusted off her hands as though she had just completed a good morning's cleaning. Her transitions from childish fear and helplessness to cool detachment were beginning to puzzle me. She went back into the house without having to be told, came out a moment later and locked the front door. She took the keys of my car without a word, regarded the dead man for a moment with a sort of distant and thoughtful pity, then turned and climbed into my car.

When I got in behind the wheel of the Mercedes she called out. "I'm ready whenever you are. Which direction are you taking?"

"Toward Nice."

"Okay."

The moonlight was full on her face now and revealed what the apparently calm voice had not revealed; she was green around the gills.

I swung the Mercedes around until the long bonnet faced the entrance gates. For a moment I lay in wait until a car coming from the direction of Verens sped past, then carefully nosed out into the road and swung toward Antibes and Nice. In the overhead mirror I saw the light of the MG as it swung out into the highway. They began to bob along behind me like a couple of worried chicks. I stepped the big powerful car up to about fifty. The road was too twisting and narrow to try any fancy tests of horsepower. Amy kept coming along at the same pace, too trusting, I thought, too dependent. Could I really get her out of this mess?

Suddenly, behind the lights of the MG, another pair of headlights appeared. Two determined bright shafts of light bore down on the MG. I could see Amy's figure outlined against the rocking glare. I slowed down, took one hand from the wheel and reached for the Luger. I brought the hand on the wheel in arc to make a sharp turn. Pless's body jerked stiffly against me and then away again to its former position against the door.

Worried now, I watched the overhead mirror. In a moment the lights of the MG came into sight around the curve; the chick in pursuit of the mother hen. I kept waiting for those other headlights to appear, but they never came into sight. Whoever it had been must have turned in at some driveway along the Corniche. I relaxed a little and got the Luger back into my pocket. The Mercedes, heading south now, made me think of a leopard in the night. The road twisted around the face of a mountain and then off to the right, far below, were the lights of the Hotel du Cap and the surrounding villas out in Cap d'Antibes, and up ahead was the glow in the sky above Nice. Out at sea a great liner was creeping through the night toward Italy.

The scene was utterly improbable. I had the eerie feeling that Pless, tilted stiffly to the east, was contemplating a panorama that had become so familiar to him as he had raced back and forth along the Riviera; contemplating it perhaps in preparation for one last game of chemin de fer at the casino.

The overhead mirror showed me the lights, signifying Amy Grant, bouncing along behind me. The girl had me wondering. Was it simple naiveté that had led her into a liaison with a phony like Harold Jones, the ex-lifeguard?

A lot of other questions ticked off in my mind. For instance, had Alva Creighton known when she walked into the villa that Charles Pless lay dead in the bedroom? That visit was suspiciously like a scene in one of her popular novels and might, in the end, be a daring cover-up.

The road swung and dipped down the mountainside toward the glowing night sky of Nice. Two miles from the city I came to a spot where, a few nights before, a happier and lustier event had taken place involving me and a redhead from Turin. It was a small observation area, secluded from the main road by extravagant foliage, overhanging a wide, sweeping panorama of the coastline. Luck was playing along. The parking area was deserted as I swung the Mercedes off the Corniche and came to rest under a giant Cypress tree.

Amy drew up beside the entrance to the parking area. In a moment I was beside her at the wheel of my own car. We had one last fleeting look of Pless staring emptily at the moon. Then I swung the little car around and headed back toward Pless's villa. The road was oddly deserted for this time of the evening. A warm breeze was blowing in from the sea. Out beyond the moon, on the horizon, massed cloud banks were beginning to form.

I hoped my silence would start some compulsive conversation. It finally worked. In a flat voice she said, "I suppose this makes us some kind of criminals. After the fact, or whatever."

"Would you rather take your chances with the police?"

"I think I trust you," she said.

"I'd rather have the cash."

"I told you—"

"Forget it, for the moment. Maybe I can get someone else to foot the bill. Tell me—did Charles Pless know that you were going to the

Opera House in Monte with Harold Jones this evening?"

"Yes."

"And he didn't object?"

She hesitated. "No. Not really. It's difficult to explain. I suppose the whole business made him unhappy, but—"

"The whole business?"

"I told him how Harold and I felt about one another."

"Which is?"

She stirred restlessly beside me. I thrust a pack of cigarettes at her. She lit one for each of us, bending down to escape the breeze in the open car. Still bent over, she said in a muffled voice: "We had it out—Charles and I—this afternoon, when he came from the Bellevue beach. He knew I had met Harold ... that I had seen him several times ... that we had fallen in love."

I stifled a groan, took the lighted cigarette from her, took time off from the road to case her profile. It was as clear as a statue in the moonlight, and it told me just as much.

"When did you meet Harold?"

"A week ago Thursday. Charles had gone up to Paris on business. I hired one of those little boats at Juan le Pins in the morning and crossed to one of the tiny islands—you know the pine islands where people go for picnics and bathing. There was no one else there except this young man. We got talking. It was very strange; I felt no constraint with him, nor he with me. It's as though we had taken up from some point in our past. We ..." She stopped.

"Yeah," I said, "Alva Creighton was quite graphic about what happened next."

She was silent.

"Do you deny it?"

After a moment she said quietly, "It's a matter of interpretation. The Alva Creightons of this world dirty up every word, every emotion we know. And this place—this beautiful coastline—everything turns to filth here."

"Look, sweetie, do you really know anything about Harold?"

"Yes!" she said vehemently. "Everything!"

Oh my God, I thought. "How do you think Alva Creighton got hold of the details of what went on between you and Harold on the beach? Mental telepathy?"

"He didn't tell her," she said desperately.

"But who did?"

"Someone must have seen us." And then in sudden weariness, she said, "I don't know. I must have time to think."

But I didn't give it to her. "Now look, Amy. I'm way out on a limb for you now. Once you begin moving dead bodies around, it entails more than a traffic ticket. I expect you to come clean."

"But I have!"

"Do you seriously expect me to believe that you discussed your undying love for Harold with Charles Pless this afternoon and then went into the bedroom with him— It doesn't make sense."

"Perhaps it doesn't, but it's true."

I flipped the cigarette out and stepped on the gas. The car rattled angrily along, reflecting my own mood. A sleek Rolls went purring past in the direction of Antibes. The breeze was beginning to increase in strength.

Amy put her hand on my arm. I glanced at her. She was looking at me, a worried child now, afraid of losing Papa.

"I know it sounds silly," she said earnestly, "and it's difficult to explain. Charles was very fond of me. But there was something odd in his feeling—a sense of guilt. In some ways he was like a father to me. He was unhappy about losing me; I can say that without ego. And yet in some ways I think my confession about Harold relieved him of his sense of guilt. Anyway, he asked me so sweetly, I ... I couldn't have refused."

"It's so illogical that I suppose it represents the ultimate in feminine logic!"

"You don't believe me?"

I looked at her and, despite myself, smiled. "You're the damnedest little—" I stopped. The moon reflected tears on her face. The softie in me jumped to my mouth.

"Take it easy, Amy. I'll buy the story. I think you're a romantic little idiot, but I'll buy it!"

She said, "I'm not crying. It's the wind."

"Sure, it's the wind."

We were less than a quarter of a mile from the villa now. I was beginning to feel strangely warm and comfortable. I wished to hell there were nothing ahead in this evening except Amy and a few idle hours. I figured it wouldn't take much to demolish the legend of Harold.

"What are we going to do?" she asked.

"I have some work ahead. Small stabs in a big dark. Alva's story of the guy in Cannes to track down, and heart-to-heart chats with some people who would be only too glad to see Pless out of the way. And an expedition to the Bellevue beach."

"The Bellevue beach? Why?"

"Somewhere today, someone planted that poison pill in Pless's pocket. What more logical place than the beach, while he was in swimming?"

"Oh. Why, of course! He came right to me from the beach. Oh, Mr.

Muldoon, do you think—"

"Hart."

"Hart. What am I to do now?"

"I want you to dress and wait for Harold. Keep your mouth shut about what's happened and go with him to the gala in Monte and seethe with gaiety. I have a feeling the person we're looking for will be in that Opera House. It will worry them, maybe enough to be indiscreet."

"I'm not a very good actress, but I'll try my best. When will I see you?"

"I'll be at the Opera House later. I have a date there with Nancy Trippe."

The effect was surprising. "That woman!"

"Why do you say that?"

"Charles hated her!"

My ears pricked up. I turned. She was staring straight ahead.

"Why?" I asked.

"He wouldn't tell me. All I know is that it was one of the reasons he wanted to see you. Some investigation having to do with Nancy Trippe."

"Do you know her?"

"I met her at a party in Paris, the night I met Charles. She tried to—"

"To what?"

"Nothing. She was just—just unpleasant."

The gates of the villa came sliding into view. I swung the car into the courtyard and switched off the motor. In the sudden silence there was no sound except the breeze in the foliage. It made a curiously sinister, whispering sound. Amy made no move to leave the car. We sat there silently. The urgency of time ticking away slid off into some other life. I didn't want to leave her. I wanted to sit there and let the rest of the world go hang. And giving in to the impulse, I tried to take her in my arms.

She pushed me away, meaning it. Her whole attitude changed in an instant.

"You too!" she said bitterly.

"Why not?"

"Would you like to use the bed he was murdered in?" Her voice was low and full of fury and self-loathing.

"Now, sweetie."

"This is bargain night. A penny off because of risk!"

I decided to shock her with calm. "Maybe I'll take you up on that later. I can wait." I said quietly. "In the meantime stop playing the femme fatale. Go in and get dressed and hide whatever you may feel from Harold."

The mention of Harold's name did it. The tears that suddenly came couldn't be excused on the breeze. "We're alike, Harold and I. People always expect … expect that!"

She got out of the car, slammed the door and stood there glowering at me. I shrugged and turned on the motor.

In a kind of panic she cried, "You're not walking out on me?"

"No."

"Oh, Hart. I don't know what got into me. I didn't mean—"

"Forget it. I'm wasting time. I'll see you in about two hours at the Opera House, if they don't pick Pless's body up first and come here to question you. Remember, if they do, tell them Pless came for tea and then left. You know nothing more."

She moved toward the door of the villa. A sudden uneasiness overcame me.

"Keep that door locked until Harold shows."

"I'm not afraid," she said in the little-girl voice of the prize Cub Scout.

"Maybe that's the trouble."

I waited until she was inside and then backed out into the corniche. Mountains of black clouds were marching in across the sea.

SEVEN

I got back to Verens into the slow-gathering evening glitter of the nightly Riviera masquerade. The occupants of the luxury hotels and private villas up and down the coast had changed, or were changing, from bikinis and sports clothes into dinner jackets and evening gowns for parties, galas, the casinos or theatrical performances in Nice or Monte Carlo. Limousines were lined up in front of the Bellevue and there was, in the air, that soft, aphrodisiac, early-night feeling peculiar to summer on the Riviera. The hunting horns were sounding to a varicolored prey. The course my fox would ride was strewn with diamonds and Paris gowns, but it might be no less deadly than the darkest trail in the forest. And, for the hunt I had in mind, my uniform would be not a pink riding coat, but the inevitable dinner jacket.

I squeezed the car into a space on the boulevard and started for the hotel entrance. Across the promenade, a few rugged individualists were still lolling in dimly lit cabañas on the Bellevue beach, and now and again the lights of the boulevard reflected a white arm or face splashing in the waters near the diving float. I decided to put off my visit to the beach for a few minutes and went quickly through the hotel lobby to the house phones. A few calls established a few barren facts: Governor Thorne's room didn't answer, Harold Jones's room didn't answer, and Alva Creighton's room didn't answer. I called my own room with the same results. I figured Ballentine Black was out in a boozy dream or too cagey to pick up my phone. I wanted a stronger foundation before I spoke to him again, and decided to wait until after I'd made my visit to the beach.

I went to the desk. I didn't like to part with the thousand-franc note—my wallet was getting pretty damned thin—but it helped open up the clerk on duty. Yes, monsieur, the Governor had left about thirty minutes before in a car supplied by the hotel management. Monsieur Harold Jones? The clerk remembered seeing him go through the lobby from the elevators less than ten minutes ago; he had seemed to be in a great hurry. Oh yes, he had picked up two tickets at the concierge's desk for the gala over in Monte tonight.

"But wait, monsieur. There is a note for you."

I opened the note, which was from Alva Creighton. It read: "Urgent mutual concern to discuss. Ciro's Monte Carlo, between eight and nine; the Opera gala between nine and midnight; the Sporting Club at Monte from midnight to about one."

I tucked the note into my pocket, left the hotel lobby and crossed to the entrance to the Bellevue beach. The attendant at the entrance smiled in recognition. "You desire a cabaña for a swim, Monsieur Muldoon?"

"Not at the moment. Is Marius here?"

He grinned discreetly and gestured down the steps. "If he is not otherwise occupied ..."

"Good."

I went down the wooden steps to a wide platform overlooking the beach, which during the day was a casual outdoor café. At the moment it was deserted. I sat at one of the iron tables. I knew I wouldn't have to look for Marius. I lit a cigarette and waited. In a moment he came out from one of the rows of cabañas; stocky, burned almost black by the sun, dressed, as always, in soiled linen slacks, sandals, a gaily striped cotton shirt open on his hefty chest, and a battered white canvas hat.

"*Bon soir*, Monsieur Muldoon. I can be of service?"

"Sit down a moment, Marius."

He regarded me for a moment with his habitual expression: partly insolent, partly tolerant, the rest appraising. Then he sat and lazily took one of my offered cigarettes.

Marius was technically the manager of the Bellevue beach and usually could be found there from eleven in the morning until closing time at ten P.M. Apparently a firm believer in free enterprise, his activities were multitudinous and, to say the least, all-inclusive. He was a legend here, famous or infamous according to one's needs or moral principles. The celebrated or the notorious or the merely timid availed themselves of his varied services, whether it was the procurement of blonde or brunette, male or female, or half an hour's diversion with a bevy of *poule de luxe*. It was said that he had prospered to the point of owning an apartment house in Nice, a bawdy house in Marseille and a wine shop in Verens. It was said also that he combined a deceptive peasant-like directness with a general philosophy that resembled a wedding between the minds of Jean Paul Sartre and the Marquis de Sade. It was rumored that if he remained on the underside of the law it was with a certain sense of security; a brother was a power in the local *gendarmerie* and an uncle sat in the Chamber of Deputies. He was pictured as being the final and shrewd appointment of a luxury hotel that provided all the comforts away from home, the key to all the dreams of well-heeled tourists and unaggressive playboys.

All of this contained some element of truth. But I remembered another Marius, a fearless leader in the Maquis who had worked closely with my OSS unit around Lyons in the last days before D-Day.

"So, *mon cher*, you are alone."

"Only for the moment."

"I am reassured." He looked thoughtfully toward the entrance ramp. "Loneliness is, of course, a permanent condition. However, we can attain the illusion of non-loneliness. For example I have just returned from saying the same words to a young lady in Cabaña Twenty-one. A ravishing Hungarian, certainly no more than eighteen years of age, whose accomplishments astounded even me. Yet she too suffers from the melancholia of loneliness—a condition that might, under certain circumstances, be alleviated by therapy."

"Not now, Marius."

He shrugged. "For you, she would be generous."

"I've come for another reason."

"Ah?" I knew that a list of his various enterprises was being reviewed waiting to check me off at the proper line.

"I'm on a job, Marius. A delicate job."

He sighed. "The most fatiguing work is so often delicate."

"At the moment I'm working for an American publisher by the name of Pless. Charles Pless."

If he knew I was lying there wasn't a flicker of change in his expression. "Ah, Pless. A very interesting person. I have promised myself to study him during his stay in Verens." He brought his gaze dreamily to me. "You have still some connection with the forces of the government of the United States—or the police?"

I laughed. "Come now, Marius. You know better. I'm like you are. I'm making others pay for my own disillusionment. We're a dangerous lot, we ex-war heroes!"

He didn't smile. Instead he sighed. "You, too," he said.

"I work for people who pay the price!"

The unwavering intensity of his gaze made me uncomfortable. I began to boil.

"I remember you well," he said softly. And then a film of cynicism fell over his voice. "Ah, very clever and wise, my good friend. Governments in these days are, at best, able to offer only short-term employment. What is patriotism today is apt to be rank treason tomorrow, no? The needs of the individual are limited and do not include abstractions. The need is met, one says farewell, and ..." He shrugged with an odd sort of anger. "*C'est rien!*"

The conversation was taking me where I didn't want to go; where, in fact, I never wanted to go again. I fled from words to action. I took out my wallet and extracted a five-thousand-franc note and placed it on the table. It was almost the bottom of the barrel for me. Marius regarded it for a moment, then gently pushed it back toward me.

"We will discuss that later. Even the devil himself can deviate from his pattern on the strength of memories. What do you want to know?"

The money lay between us like a barrier. I picked it up. "Someone has been threatening the life of Charles Pless. Have you known of this?"

He shrugged. "I know what everyone else seems to know—and that one cannot take seriously."

"What's that?"

"A tourist. He stays in some modest *pension* over in Cannes. He, who obviously is not used to drinking, takes to drinking too much. He boasts that he means to poison Mr. Pless!"

"Then it's true."

"But one can only laugh. It is a big joke. Everyone talks of it. This man is mild, and small. He is what you Americans call a milquetoast. On the other hand there are so many others who are not at all mild, who might wish your employer dead!"

"Do you know the name of this man in Cannes?"

"I believe he calls himself Cooladge, like the name of one of your Presidents. Roger Cooladge. But I assure you."

"An American?"

"But what else?" he said with an expressive wave of the hand.

"Do you know of the *pension* in which he stays?"

"Yes. It is quite undistinguished, and run by an English woman. It is known as the Pension Brett."

"How is it that you have all this information, Marius?"

He hesitated. "I was paid to find it out last week, by a compatriot of yours."

"Who?"

He smiled. "Ah, no. Even the memory of old adventures—you ask too much."

"Marius, it is of great importance to me."

His eyes hardened. "I am sorry, *mon cher*."

I was about to remonstrate, when an unexpected sight brought me up short. Harold Jones had just come down the steps from the boulevard. He was dressed in a dinner jacket and there was something curiously furtive in his movements. He didn't look in our direction, but turned quickly into the line of cabañas on the left. By the time Marius, caught by the expression on my face, turned to look, he had disappeared. I pushed my chair back and got up.

"What is the number of Pless's cabaña?"

"Fifty-three. Over there." He pointed to where Harold had vanished. "The last one in the row."

"I'll see you in a few minutes, Marius."

Just before I started down the wide wooden promenade in front of the dimly lit cabañas, I turned. Marius was looking after me. He had the expression of a man who has lost a beloved dog.

I hurried down the promenade, past the cabañas which for the most part were dark and deserted. When I came abreast of Cabaña 21 I couldn't resist casing the Hungarian goulash Marius had offered for supper. From what I could see, the dish looked tasty enough to make me regret more pressing commitments. The lantern on the outer deck of the cabaña threw a discreet and revealing light on a ravishing blonde who lay back on the chaise longue dreaming into the moonlight. She wore a very brief bikini and bra and seemed about to slip out of the first and burst out in the other. She gave me a tentative smile, and it was hard to keep my mind on the business at hand.

I filed her away for future reference and heroically continued on toward the last cabaña in the line. There was no sound down here but the soft lapping of the Mediterranean on the beach and the murmur of traffic from the boulevard above. The main lights of Cabaña 53 were out, leaving the lounges and canvas chairs blue in the moonlight of the outer deck. But a light was burning in the inner room which opened into the showers and lavatory. And someone was moving in there.

Softly, careful not to bump up against the furniture, I went to the door of the inner room, getting the Luger into working position as I went. I got to the threshold and stopped in surprise. I don't know just whom or what I had expected to find there, but certainly not the picture now revealed. Harold Jones was down on all fours, frantically examining the floor space beneath the discreetly placed day bed.

I tucked the Luger into hiding and said quietly, "Can I help?"

The young man wheeled around in consternation. All the effected cynicism that had been on his face when he was having cocktails with Alva Creighton in the Bellevue had evaporated. He looked like a kid caught red-handed in the cookie jar.

"Hello, Harold."

"Oh! Mister …"

"Muldoon."

He scrambled to his feet.

"A friend of mine lost something here this afternoon. I thought—"

"A lady friend?"

He looked away. "Yes. Some trinket—an earring. Nothing very valuable, but …"

"That's thoughtful of you. Any success? No? Maybe I could help you."

I made a move into the room.

"Oh, no. It isn't worth it. I thought she might be amused, if …" Nervously he looked at his watch. "Gosh, it's getting late. I've got to get on."

He started for the entrance. Then he saw the Luger in my hand and stopped short.

"What does this mean?"

"Harold," I said softly. "Papa wants to speak with you."

EIGHT

The sound of the Mediterranean eroding the coastline was like the nibble of mice on cheese.

"What the hell are you doing in this business!" Harold finally managed to say.

"This business?"

He tried to recover from his slip. "I mean—I know you're some kind of private eye. Alva Creighton told me. Who are you working for? Why did you follow me here?"

"I'm working for Pless," I said blandly.

"Pless! When did you see Pless?"

"Today."

"Oh." He looked relieved. "You mean Pless has hired you to tail me?"

"Partly. He doesn't like you fooling around with Amy."

"Fooling around!" he said angrily: "That's no way to talk about Amy. And Pless had better—"

"Better what?"

He retreated quickly. "Nothing."

"And Pless has another idea," I said quietly. "Perhaps he's oversensitive, but he's got this idea. He thinks someone wants to kill him!"

That took the wind out of Harold's indignation. "I don't know anything about that," he said.

I took a nose dive. "Then why did you and Pless have an argument here in his cabaña this afternoon?"

"Argument!" Panic crept in around the edges of his voice. "Now listen, Muldoon. I never came near this cabaña this afternoon."

"You deny being on the beach?"

"No. I was swimming. But I never came near this cabaña. I saw him here, talking to someone, but—"

"Talking to whom?"

"I don't know. I think it was Alva Creighton. Yes, it was Alva." He said the last as though remembering it for the first time, and remembering it was a sense of shock.

"Did Alva send you here to find something?"

"No. Oh no," he said quickly. Too quickly. I could see he was plenty worried now. I decided to follow through while I still had the advantage.

"Look, Harold, I'm willing to give you a break."

"A break?" he said uneasily. "Why should I need a break?"

"Let's put it this way. Suppose that something should happen to Pless. It would leave you way out on a limb, Harold. Who but you would have a better reason for—"

"No." He began to look ill. Then he said, "I've nothing to conceal. Mr. Pless knew—" He caught himself up quickly. "Knows that ... I mean how Amy and I feel about each other. In fact ..."

He stopped as though suddenly the flow of his own words would betray him. Or someone else.

"If you have nothing to conceal, why did you come here?"

"I told you the truth," he said belligerently. "A lady lost something here. An earring. I won't tell you her name. I don't want her involved."

It was pretty damned thin and the expression in his face admitted it but I knew he wasn't—at least for the moment—going to change his course.

"What do you know about this guy Cooladge?" I asked bluntly.

"Cooladge? Oh, that crackpot? Why?"

"Just answer."

"Not much. I met him at a cocktail party yesterday afternoon over in Antibes. He's a funny little bird. Completely out of place. Someone brought him."

"Who?"

"Miss Trippe. Nancy Trippe."

Somewhere behind us, probably out at the float, a woman began to laugh. The laughter was strident and breathy, as though she were being tickled. Then it was choked off and there was nothing but the lapping of the waves and the distant echo of traffic up on the boulevard.

"Miss Trippe brought Cooladge to the party?"

"Yes. She was apparently amused by him. I think it was said she had picked him up in a bar over in Cannes."

"Was Pless at the party?"

"No. His wife was there, though. She left early."

"Did she talk to this man Cooladge?"

"I don't know. She could have. A lot of people did. Everyone thought it was a joke." His eyes lit up. "Say, maybe it wasn't such a joke after all. He was telling everyone how he had this capsule or something— a pill, maybe—and that it was cyanide and that he intended to give it to Pless. Is that what you mean by someone threatening to kill Pless?" He seemed suddenly vastly relieved. "You mean that little pipsqueak? We all thought it was a big laugh!"

"Is Cooladge an American?"

"Oh, sure."

"What's he like?"

"Like a caricature; something you see on a small-town platform on the Fourth of July."

He reached into his pocket and drew out a pack of cigarettes and lit up. I noticed his hand was shaking in excitement. "Say, maybe this guy Cooladge is your bird after all, Muldoon. Maybe he really meant it. Maybe he wasn't just a quaint little drunk."

"Maybe not. He's damned convenient, isn't he?"

"Convenient?"

"I mean if anyone really has it in for Pless, there's always this character Cooladge to take the rap."

Harold puffed at his cigarette, then looked away. "Yeah," he said, deflated. "I suppose there's always that—if anything happens to Pless."

"Where have you been for the last half hour, Harold?" I shot it out at him to take him off balance. But he was ready this time.

"I took a walk. I wanted to think."

"And you finally thought yourself down here to Pless's cabaña."

"Yes," he said.

"And now you intend to pick up Amy."

"So you know that too. Well, why not? Pless knows. Amy told him. I'm picking her up and taking her to the gala over in Monte and we don't give a good goddamn whether the whole world knows after tonight."

"Impetuous," I said. "But indiscreet."

"Maybe it is. That's the way it's going to be, though."

"And what about Alva?"

"Never mind about Alva. That's between Alva and me."

I smiled. Angrily he crunched out his cigarette. And for just a moment he let his gaze rest on the bed. Then his chin came up with a comic sort of nobility.

"Now get this, Muldoon. If Pless hired you to tail me, it's too late."

"Too late?"

"I mean … well, I mean I'm working differently from now on and that's the God's honest truth!"

"Come on, Harold," I said quietly. I tucked the Luger back into my pocket. "Come on, let's sit out on the deck, look at the sea, have another cigarette, and talk reasonably."

"I'm late now."

"It might be wise to be a little late tonight. It might be better if I understood you a little better. I mean better for you."

After a moment he shrugged. I noticed his gaze go back once more to the bed, then he followed me out to the moon-drenched deck. I had a premonition I was in for one of those sessions for which a psychiatrist gets twenty an hour. It might be valuable time wasted, but I had a hunch. I sprawled on the lounging chair and he sat rather stiffly on a canvas-backed chair facing me, conscious only when it was too late that the moon fell directly on his face. We both lit up. For a moment I watched two swimmers racing for the float a hundred yards off shore. Far out at sea the lights of a yacht were moving in toward Cannes. The woman on the float laughed again.

I let the silence bear down on what I suspected was his compulsive need to talk. It worked.

"I think maybe you're a pretty decent Joe, Muldoon."

"It's a dangerous thought."

"No, I mean it. You sense those things. Pless has probably filled you up with a lot of crap about me and Amy. Maybe the truth isn't much better, but at least it's the truth, and you can give him a full report. Amy knows …"

I leaned back and blew smoke up at the sky. "Where did you meet Amy?"

The change in his voice was remarkable. An unexpected softness crept it. It made me think of treacle pudding on a hot August day.

"It was the damnedest thing, like a dream. You see, sometimes when I want to get away … get away … well, from …"

"Alva Creighton?"

"Things like that. Well sometimes I hire one of those tiny little sailing boats down at Juan and go over to one of the islands. If you're lucky you have the island to yourself: a lonely beach, a box lunch, a bottle of wine, and plenty of time to think and no one to say yes to or fend off. I was luckier that day. The island wasn't deserted. It was populated by Amy. Just Amy and me. We got talking. We shared the box lunch. The sun was hot, and we got back under the pines. The afternoon passed. We talked and talked."

"And talked," I added dryly.

The look of suspicion evaporated beneath the sticky glow of memory. "By the time we headed back to Juan in our separate boats it was almost sunset. It was as though we were parting from a lifetime shared. And it was as though I had discovered myself—I mean who I really am—for the first time."

"Where was Pless during this fascinating exploration?"

"He'd flown to Paris on business for the day. That's why Amy was free."

"And Alva?"

"She was furious. I missed a cocktail date with her. I …" He leaned forward. "Look, I want to explain something. I mean about Alva and me."

"Can you keep it decent?"

"Maybe not. Amy understands. And I suppose that's all that matters. Amy had—has—Pless in her life. I've had Alva and a few before her; a series of one-way tickets out of the kind of a world I grew up in."

"What kind of a world was that?" I said in my best couch voice.

I knew it wouldn't matter much who his listener was at this point, as long as the tone of the questioning was sympathetic. In his newfound discovery of himself he had to talk about that past. He did so now with a vengeance. "Technically, I'm a farm boy."

"So was Pless. Heaven protect us from the farm boys!"

"Only technically, though. My parents died when I was only five; they were killed in a train wreck outside Sioux City, Iowa. They'd been to the State Fair, only fifteen miles from home. Home! A broken-down, unsuccessful farm. I was the only kid. I was sent out to live with my mother's cousin in Long Beach, California. They had a hot dog stand on the boardwalk. Uncle Bart and Aunt Maud! Jesus, if ever a penny-pinching bastard and a slimy bitch existed, it was those two! Aunt Maud was nothing more than a fat, sloppy whore. Saturday night she used to do it for beer money under the boardwalk with old drunks who couldn't get it any other way. Before I was fourteen Maud had me bedded down with a nympho widow who lived in the same rooming house. Maud got a new hat out of it."

"Charming."

"That's the way things were. Charming, like you say. In high school I got on the swimming team, but it didn't bring me any close friends. I didn't want friends; I was afraid they'd find out. And anyway Bart and Maud kept them away, and I thought if they didn't know too much … I was a muscle hero in the daytime and they wouldn't have suspected the other. You see?"

"Somewhat."

"Well, I had this body and I looked older than my age and in Maud's way I was older than my age. I got a job as a lifeguard at Long Beach and I began to see that maybe I could get out of it. I knew I'd never get out of it in the Horatio Alger tradition … my marks at school stayed near the bottom of the class and there wasn't even a wisp of a daydream of a scholarship to college. In high school I was left back three times."

I hadn't bargained for the works. I'd hoped for a digest version. I could almost hear the ticking of my watch. But I didn't stop him because I hadn't decided yet whether he was leveling or whether he was a highly sophisticated con man.

"The things I wanted were corny—I didn't know any better. Decent clothes, a snappy convertible, the expensive Hollywood restaurants I'd read about. I thought if you got these, people respected you. On the beach, I met people. I found out what they wanted, and it wasn't hard to give. Sex in our household was something for pennies a throw, but I was holding out for the buck. I'd learned that enough bucks meant out."

"You're beginning to sound like one of the exposés in Pless's magazine."

"Maybe.

"Anyway, you got out!"

"Yeah. Through Brenda Willis."

"The movie star."

"She was no star when I met her, believe me. She had a small contract with World Pictures but she was really being kept—in a small way—by an assistant director on the lot. In a motel out on Vine. She found me on the beach and we went riding in her secondhand Buick and soon I was going to the motel when the assistant director was at work.

I began to dress better. She was very intelligent about things like that. Good shirts and even a cheap dinner jacket and sometimes we'd head for night spots down in Monica or out on the Strip where the assistant director couldn't spot us. Well, all in one year things suddenly broke for Brenda and up she went like a sky rocket with her cleavage showing in every magazine from Beverly Hills to Broadway. She dumped the assistant director and took me along for the ride. I even had a screen test, but that came to nothing. But I went up with her in my own way. I watched and learned. Better clothes from an English tailor, a new car, a Hollywood-type apartment near her big house out on the Palisades. I had the keys. You understand."

"It's not difficult."

"Maud and Bart went out of my life—for a price. When Brenda came to Europe last spring to make a film, I came along. Well, you know what happened. She met this Viennese director. He was good for her career and good in bed—a convenient combination for a girl with ambition. They got married. Brenda went back to New York to study, and that was that. I drifted down to the Riviera, and it wasn't much different from Long Beach. Ask Marius. Anyway, I met Alva Creighton. We got along. We made each other's lives a little easier. It didn't matter too much—until I met Amy."

"And now?"

"The whole world has changed." He laughed. "Can you believe this? I've got myself a job at the American Express Company in Nice beginning the first of the month. Only about sixty a week, but over here Amy and I can live on it. Amy is telling Pless today; she thinks he'll understand, but what the hell! We'll get along. We're going for one last fling tonight at the gala in Monte, and tomorrow I'm checking out of the Bellevue and out of the lives of the whole stinking crowd!"

"And Alva understands all this?"

He looked away. "Alva's all right. She'll be a good sport. I think I can even keep her as a friend!"

"You didn't learn as much as you should have under the boardwalk in Long Beach!"

"What does that mean?"

"Did you tell Alva what happened between you and Amy on the island that day?"

He looked startled. "It's funny you should mention that. I didn't exactly, but somehow she guessed most of it. I wanted to be honest. I filled in the rest, I suppose. After all, I owed her that."

I flipped my cigarette out onto the beach. I could see someone standing down near the water line, just a black shadow against the moon. Even as I looked it glided off into the shadows of the cabañas. I straightened up, bringing my legs over the edge of the chaise longue. "Why did you tell me all this, Harold?"

His voice was keyed to mild reproach. "I wanted to be honest with you. I want you to make Pless understand that I'll take care of Amy and how we feel about each other; that I haven't kidded her about my past."

"Maybe. What were you really looking for in there, Harold?"

He got to his feet, went to the edge of the platform and stared out over the sea. Over his shoulder he said, "I told you. It was an earring."

"Belonging to Amy or to Alva Creighton?"

He turned. "I don't know why you're making a federal case out of this. I didn't have to tell you what I did. I wanted you to realize that I'm leveling with you. I …"

I interrupted. "Did you drop something there yourself, Harold?"

"Damn it, I told you. What the hell is all this about?"

"Trouble," I said quietly. "Bad trouble."

Fear flitted over his handsome face, and then it was gone. He held up his watch and squinted at the illuminated dial.

"You can make your report to Pless. I've got nothing more to say. I'm late now. Amy is expecting me. You can add that to your report, if Amy hasn't already told him."

Harold strode off into the darkness as though his biography paralleled Abraham Lincoln's. Love can make anyone self-righteous.

I waited until the footsteps died away on the wooden promenade, and then I went back into the small inner room of the cabaña. I got down on my hands and knees and took over where Harold had left off. A detailed search of the floor revealed nothing more startling than a box of matches and a hairpin. Automatically, feeling like a burlesque version of Sherlock Holmes, I stuffed them into my coat pocket. Finally I gave up trying to be a human vacuum cleaner and started to rise to my feet. It was then that I noticed the tiny object caught in the folds of the flowered material that covered the bed. Quickly I bent over and snatched it up. The blood began to boil a little faster. Between my fingers I held a tiny yellow capsule!

Out in the harbor the klaxon of a yacht moving in to its mooring made a harsh sound in the silence. I stood there wondering at the curiously hollow feeling growing in my stomach. I was pretty well convinced that the yellow capsule would turn out to be a genuine adrenalin tablet, the one Pless *should* have taken. I'd have to check to make certain, but if my suspicion proved correct, the implications were obvious. Someone had removed the capsule from Pless's coat in this cabaña, probably while Pless had been swimming, substituted the cyanide tablet and then, probably panicking at the sound of someone approaching, had let the real adrenalin capsule slip through his, or her, fingers in the effort to make a quick getaway.

A slight sound out on the promenade made me stiffen. I stuffed the tablet into the inner pocket of my side pocket. I stood very still, listening, my hand on the Luger. The sound was not repeated. After a moment I thought I had imagined it, and relaxed. I took one last look around the cabaña and went out onto the deck. The promenade was deserted. I lit a cigarette and started back toward the main entrance.

The blonde Hungarian was standing far back under the canopy of her cabaña, smoking a cigarette. At first I thought she had changed into a two-piece Bikini, white bra and trunks. Then, with a warm shock, I realized that the whiteness was the part of her body which the sun had not been permitted to reach.

The Hungarian smiled. The urgency of the immediate future faded off into other people's business; the immediate present became a matter demanding action. Amy Grant and Pless and Nancy Trippe and Harold were obliterated. The girl stood under the lantern, where shattered light fell upon firm breasts. Marius had made it clear that my credit was good for this one. He had offered her to me like a dream in the midst of battle. I thought, This is on the house!

I got off the main route quick. This Hungarian detour—like so many other detours in my life—was making life possible again. She opened vistas that were familiar enough and yet, as always, breathlessly new. And there were a few unexpected variations. "I luff Americans!" she whispered ardently. "I am luffing everything with the American label!"

The chaise longue was wide and utilitarian—it wasn't difficult to give her an example of American goodwill. International relations were cemented in a highly satisfactory manner.

When the conference was over she lay back, eyes closed, and, to my astonishment said, "You know Little Budapest?"

"What?"

"A restaurant. A cabaret. In the street which is named Eighty-third Street in New York City."

"Who doesn't know it?" I said and wondered who did.

"Ah—it is famous, of course. In this place people will come to see me and I will sing to all the Americans in the United States of America, because I cannot give enough. I wish to. It is arranged. Marius has sponsored a marriage with a gentleman who owns this famous restaurant, and a contract is signed. You will tell all your American friends? I go in two three weeks' time, on a ship."

"You will be the sensation of Yorkville," I said, as I finished arranging myself for public inspection again.

"You do it very good," she said politely.

"Thanks. I can say the same for you."

"I will be at the Hotel Bristol in Room Twenty-three, after midnight. I will cancel all other engagements for tonight."

"I'll be there."

"It's funny," she said. "Very funny. I mean how few men can do it good. After all, this is more fun than anything else. Do you not agree?"

"Fervently."

The future began its annoying nibble. I heard the sound of a footstep out on the wooden promenade. Pless and the others began to take shape again.

I moved out of the comfortable orbit of the cabaña lantern. It was a mistake.

The footsteps I had heard suddenly resolved into a scurrying sound on the wooden planks, coming down behind me. I didn't have time to turn. I heard the beginning of a Hungarian scream. The blow on the back of my head sent Hungary and the stars splintering across the heavens.

NINE

I came up and out of a black cloud with a close-up of Marius shutting off the background.

He said in French, "It is nothing ..."

His face moved aside for a more enticing vista. The Hungarian had thrown a terry robe around her shoulders, but with Magyar generosity had neglected to fasten it. She was a nervous Hungarian now.

"It is a scandal! Terrible."

I shoved the wet towel from my forehead with a groan and pushed myself up on the lounging chair. There was no one in the cabaña but the Hungarian, Marius and myself. Out there on the float that damned woman was still cackling.

Without much originality I said, "What happened?"

"Mitzi came running for help. Tell him what you saw."

"It was horrible," she said dramatically. "I was lighting a cigarette, and I was admiring the stars and then I see you go out on the promenade and for some reason you stop there in front of the cabaña ... and then out of the shadows comes this long stick, and ..."

"Stick?"

Marius held up a beach rake. It had a long handle, ending in vicious-looking iron claws.

"You were lucky," he said. "He missed you with the claws. Only the handle hit you."

I shook my head, which was beginning to clear. I looked up at the girl. "Did you see who it was?"

"Oh no. I see only the long pole come down out of the shadows ... I scream and I hear someone running off. Then I myself run to get Marius."

"A hit-and-run, eh?" I rubbed the back of my head. It felt as though there should be a bump there, but so far it had not risen. Then I remembered and dug my hand into my pocket. The yellow capsule was still there. I brought it out and thrust it at Marius.

"What is this?" he asked.

"Do me a favor for old times' sake."

"*Mais oui.*"

"Can you contact a chemist?"

"Yes."

"Good. Would you get this to him and have it analyzed?"

"I am not understanding," the Hungarian said.

"Call me here at the beach in an hour," Marius said. "There is an all-night chemist on the Rue Foch. I have had dealings with him."

I swung my feet over the edge of the chaise longue. Everything tilted up for a minute, then righted itself. Reluctantly the blonde drew the robe tight.

"You all right?" Marius asked.

"I will be. Have you a cigarette?"

The blonde fished one out of the robe and Marius lighted it for me. My head was clearing fast; there was only a dull throb now. I thought of the iron claws of the rake and shuddered. Whoever had used it must be damned desperate.

"Marius," I said. "You know a young American who swims here. Harold Jones?"

He grinned. "*Oui.* A companion of Mrs. Creighton."

"That's the one. Did you see him leave about five minutes ago?"

He frowned. "No. But I had a telephone call in the office. I would not have seen anyone come or go."

"I'll ask the attendant on duty at the entrance."

He frowned. "You think it was Jones who ..."

"I'm not sure."

I started to get to my feet. Solicitously the blonde bent over to help me. "Room Twenty-three," she whispered. I squeezed her hand and turned to go.

"I'll call you in an hour, Marius."

He called after me, "Be sure you get paid in advance!"

The advice was grimly amusing; the guy who could sign the checks was dead. All I had so far was a blue-eyed Indiana heifer, corn-fed and broke.

My legs wobbled a little, then began to do their bidding. By the time I got to the steps leading up to the boulevard I felt almost as good as new. The attendant there was no help at all; he had been across to the hotel twice on errands in the past fifteen minutes. No, he did not remember anyone answering to the description of Harold Jones.

His cocky indifference was exasperating. As I climbed the steps I suddenly had the sense of a slow moving mass of evil circulating around a bright and glittering center, and inexorably closing in—on whom?

I crossed the boulevard and went into the lobby of the Bellevue. The gilt clock over the desk stood at seven forty-five. Time was being chopped off fast, bits of ice ticking off with the minute hand to melt in the steaming pool of the past. I had a sudden picture in my mind of Nancy Trippe grinning up ahead at the ten o'clock time, too aware of minutes missed, time lost. It seemed impossible that only an hour and a half before I had left the hotel in answer to Amy Grant's phone call …

I stepped out of the elevator on my floor into a crescendo of muffled sound. The door of the suite at the end of the hall was open on a noisy cocktail party, and out of it came a babel of voices punctuated by shrill laughter. Just inside the door of the suite an aged woman with dyed red hair stood like a battered statue, curiously rigid and still, holding an empty champagne glass. She looked down the hall as though her expected guest—long overdue—was death.

I fit the key into my lock. Bent over, pain caught up with me unexpectedly for a moment. The knob advanced and receded, dissolving into an object on a Dali landscape. Then suddenly it was back in place, firm and commonplace. I looked up. The redheaded woman was staring fixedly beyond me at some distant point in her memory. I turned the key and stepped into my room.

The lights were all on, blazing across the rumpled bed, the empty bottle on the commode, the note propped up on the bureau top. Ballentine Black was gone.

The manner of his getaway was obvious enough. Curtains fluttering at the French windows which opened on a balcony attested to his boozy exit from the locked room. The balcony adjoined the balcony of the next room, and it would have been comparatively simple to pick a moment when the next room was empty, to escape.

I stood there inside the door and heard myself groan aloud. I'd counted too much on that bottle and too little on Black's psychopathic drive. The note he had left on the bureau top only confirmed this last thought.

> "You didn't con me, Muldoon! I'm unconned. I got a job. It may pay off. Maybe not. If I slip I'm finished but God damn it I'll see to it I don't go down alone! And you, you bastard, and the whole double-crossing lousy crowd of … You get past a stopping point, and no one puts the stop on me. Get out of my way sweetheart or you get hurt real bad."

There was some more, most of it almost unintelligible except for some obscene references to Nancy Trippe.

I had a picture of Black lying there on the bed nursing the bottle and his hatred for the world, and rationalizing himself into a big-shot operator and maybe even worse—because in his present state of mind Black was a killer. The note had been written from the depths of despair and fury. The world owed him a death for having permitted him to be born.

A kind of frustrating panic washed over me. The sounds of the cocktail party in the suite at the end of the hall became the sound of hysterical mice scratching on the lid of a sealed box. The events which had taken place since my meeting with Nancy Trippe in the café were becoming unreal and disjointed—motive, deed, relationship and words jumbled together in a madman's tapestry.

I looked at my watch. It was almost eight, two hours away from my rendezvous with Nancy Trippe. The urgency of time brought me back. I sat on the edge of the bed and picked up the phone. After a moment Amy's voice answered on the other end. It sounded strained and tight with apprehension.

"Are you alone?"

"No."

"Has Harold arrived?"

"Yes. We're about to go to dinner."

"Where?"

"Just a moment." Off the phone I heard her speaking to Harold. Clearly I heard the taut nervousness in her voice as she said: "No. No, darling. Just a friend ..." And then she said, after a moment, "A little restaurant at the top of the town called Petite Marmite. Then we go on to the gala."

"Has anyone called?"

"No."

"Look," I said in a cool, paternal voice, "get out of there immediately, before any unexpected callers arrive. I'll see you at the theater."

"Is there any news?"

"Plenty," I said, keeping the irony out of my voice. "Things are moving along."

I hung up and lit a cigarette. Then I got the operator again and after a little trouble got the number of Pless's villa. A butler answered. Yes, Mrs. Pless was in but she was dressing for dinner. Yes, he would give her my message but madame might not be in in half an hour. Yes, he would tell her it was important. No, Miss Trippe had not as yet come in, nor had Mr. Pless.

After I rung off I got the operator to find me the number of the Pension Brett over in Cannes. She took an interminable time but finally a dry, feminine, very British voice, desperate to conceal a faint trace of cockney, spoke.

"Pension Brett. Margaret Brett speaking."

"I'd like to speak to Mr. Cooladge."

"Mr. Cooladge seems suddenly very popular," she said dryly. "But he isn't here anymore."

"He checked out?"

"Yes. At about noon today."

"Have you any idea where I can reach him? This is important."

"That's exactly what the lady who called an hour ago said. I couldn't be very helpful."

"Lady? What lady?"

"Oh, come now. Who is this?"

"I'm Mr. Cooladge's nephew," I said glibly. "I've been trying to track him down."

"Well!" she said in a stern voice. "It's nice to know that little man has *some* relatives who care about him. He most certainly needs relatives!"

"How do you mean?"

"The man isn't well," she said sharply. "He isn't well at all."

"In what way?"

"I believe he needs the attention of a psychiatrist."

"Oh." And then for form's sake I added, "We were afraid of that happening. That's why I'm so anxious to find him."

"Well, I'm sure it's none of my business. I have no idea where he moved to. He seemed highly nervous and unwell."

"Did he leave alone?"

"Yes … Oh, wait …"

"Yes?"

"There is something that might help you. This morning he suddenly expressed a desire to go to the gala over in Monte tonight. I thought it was odd. He isn't at all the sort who would enjoy that kind of thing, but then Mr. Cooladge was odd, anyway. Seats are very difficult to get, but I managed to get him a balcony seat through the concierge at the Carlton."

The gala seemed to be a magnet drawing all the people involved in Pless's life to it.

"Thank you," I murmured into the phone.

"Quite all right, I'm sure. I do think it about time someone took care of the man …"

"Miss Brett."

"Yes?"

"Did my uncle … I heard a disturbing rumor that he had been taken with some obsession … about a man called Pless."

There was silence for a moment; then she said in a clipped monotone, "I know nothing of it. He is an odd man. Drinks far too much, but I never inquire into the personal lives of my guests. Now if you don't mind ..."

And that was all for Miss Brett. I hung up. Too late I realized I had bungled things by bringing Pless's name in too soon. I should have stuck on the trail of possible visitors to the *pension* or the woman who had called.

But I began to move faster now, feeling less like a fly stuck in molasses. The Opera House in Monte was a focus for my activities. Nancy Trippe had made an appointment to meet me there; Harold was taking Amy there; Alva Creighton and the governor were going there; and now the shadowy Mr. Cooladge, who had boasted of his plan to murder Pless, was headed there.

I showered and changed into dinner clothes in ten minutes flat. It was eight-fifteen when I approached the concierge in the lobby. He wasn't much help.

"Sorry, monsieur. It is impossible to get even a single seat for the gala. They were completely sold out at five this afternoon."

I left the lobby and hopped into the car. It went roaring up out of Verens as though it had a life of its own. Ten minutes later it slowed down as it approached the imposing gateposts of the villa Charles Pless had rented at Cap d'Antibes.

TEN

The Chateau Noir stood on a rocky promontory in fashionable section, not far from the famous Hotel du Cap. It was a big rococo building set back on vast property—more like a casino in appearance than like a private home. Built during the nineteenth century by a wealthy Russian fur merchant with a penchant for royal surroundings, it contained much black marble, some real, some ersatz; Greek columns, incongruous cupolas, wide terraces and intricate gardens. From what I had heard of Pless, it didn't surprise me that he had chosen it as his legal headquarters for a season in the sun. A long, curving drive led up to a shiny black façade where bronze doors were hung between two fat white columns. An English butler conducted me across marble floors, through a vast reception room dominated by a double curving staircase, to a comparatively small sitting room where everything was pastel and gilt and fragile. He told me Mrs. Pless would be down directly, brought me a drink and left me to the vacuous stare of some fat angels who hung heavily in a too-blue ceiling.

The house was so still I could hear a clock ticking out in the hall. It made me conscious again of the urgency of time and I looked at my watch. It was almost eight thirty-five. In another twenty minutes the gala would be starting. I gulped at the drink impatiently. I paced the carpet for a moment, then lowered myself into something uncomfortably Louis Quinze and lit a cigarette.

The place had the chilly stillness of a museum at night, permeated by a pompous weight designed to crush laughter—a pleasure dome, without pleasure. Even the smoke from my cigarette seemed to hang in the midst of damp, motionless air. The gay restaurants, the tinkling orchestras, the crowded casinos of the coast seemed far away and dreamlike. I had a momentary, macabre vision of marble men and women locked in stony copulation in vast corridors, commemorating some mirage of love and passion.

Somewhere out in the night the sound of a car starting up dispelled the tomblike fantasy. The draperies fluttered heavily at the window. I had the uneasy feeling that someone was watching me. I twisted around.

A woman was standing in the doorway to the hall. She had made no sound on the marble. She was slim and mousy, wearing an unbecoming beige lace dinner gown. She wore little or no makeup, which was a mistake, because her blonde eyebrows and lashes appeared to be almost nonexistent. There was an expression of perpetual apology in her pale eyes.

"I'm Mrs. Pless. Myra Pless."

"Yes, of course."

She stood there uncertainly, as though waiting for an invitation to come further down into her own drawing room.

"I'm sorry to have kept you waiting. I was dressing. As it is, we'll be late for the gala."

"We?"

"Nancy. Miss Trippe and I. Charles said to go ahead without him if he wasn't back by a quarter to eight. He had some sort of business appointment."

"Business appointment?"

"Yes. He called from the Bellevue beach late this afternoon. As a matter of fact, I thought he was to be with you, Mr. Muldoon."

"He told you that?"

She looked nervously over her shoulder. "Well, I knew he was going to try to contact you. Have you seen him?"

"No."

"Oh. Then I suppose you're here to see him. I really don't know ...."

"No. I came to see you."

She looked startled and uneasy. "Me? Whatever for?" And then she said, as though fighting panic, "Oh, no. Your business is with Charles."

"Didn't he tell you why he wanted to contact me?"

"Not exactly, but I guessed. He didn't deny it when I asked this morning. He didn't admit it, but neither did he deny it."

Once again she looked nervously over her shoulder and seemed reassured to find no one there.

"Deny what?"

"About that strange little man over in Cannes. The one called Cooladge. And other things."

"Ah, then you know about Cooladge."

"I don't understand this at all. Why have you come to see me? Has—has something happened?"

"Not yet," I lied. "That's why I'm here—to prevent it."

"Oh, I see."

She came down to the sofa and sat primly, looking washed-out and almost too tired to continue the interview. Listlessly she took the cigarette I offered.

"What is it you want to know?"

"First, about this man Cooladge ..."

"It's so odd," she said. "Like a dream. Yesterday I went to a cocktail party over in Antibes. I hardly ever go to such things, but Nancy felt I should. I'd only met the host once—in New York at some party for the magazine people, I believe. Anyway, it was awful, this party. A strange mixture of riffraff. Some of them were described to me as fashionable. I wouldn't know; I'm not interested in fashionable people. In fact I'm not interested in parties. I have a fear of crowds, you see. I ..."

"And you met Cooladge there?" I interrupted impatiently.

"Yes. Nancy came in with him. She was amused by him. She'd picked him up in some bar in Cannes, I believe. Nancy is always doing things like that. I used to think it was part of her charm ..."

"Used to?"

"I mean ... I do. Yes, I do think it's part of her charm. She's an original, of course. Anyway, this party was in a little *boîte* in Antibes owned by some well-known jazz musician. The host—don't ask me to remember his name—had taken it over, you see. It was terribly crowded, and the music gave me a dreadful headache. I have these dreadful migraine headaches, and ..."

"And Miss Trippe brought this man Cooladge in?"

"Yes. It was sort of a joke. At least she seemed to think so, and apparently so did everyone else. It was something exotic, something different ... You know how those people are. Anything for a new thrill. Dreadful, really ..."

I kept my temper.

"Tell me about this man Cooladge."

"Well, it's difficult to describe him. He was short and thin, middle-aged, a gray little man. He followed Nancy around like a dog. He seemed mad about her."

"Oh?"

"That sort of thing would amuse Nancy. She's perverse."

"Yes?"

"Yes, quite. Well, Mrs. Creighton took him in tow for a while …"

"Alva Creighton?"

"You know her then. I've met her before, of course. She frightens me. So intelligent and talented. Women like that always make me want to crawl back into my shell."

She looked pretty well back in it already. Watching her as she talked with little ZaSu Pitts flutters of the hand, I figured she must have a good deal of money to have hooked Charles Pless. She was almost the most colorless woman I had ever met: a pale, tired, beige-colored woman.

"Alva Creighton talked with Cooladge, too?"

"Oh yes. I tried to avoid him but he attached himself to me. He said I looked sympathetic and like a real American, whatever that may be. He didn't realize who I was. He went into a long rigmarole about what a fine girl Nancy was … a splendid example of the independent American working girl, he said." She paused to give a little laugh; it was unexpected and curiously venomous. "Then … then he began to talk drunkenly about Charles. He called him a monster. He said he had come to kill him. He said—" She shuddered—"he said he had a cyanide tablet for him!"

"Cyanide?"

"Oh, I know it's ridiculous. Nancy came up and winked. She thought it was a tremendous joke. But it upset me terribly. I left the party …"

"Alone?"

"Yes. Nancy was annoyed with me for making a scene. Anyway, I'm not so sure that it's merely a drunken fantasy … There was something so—well, fanatical … unbalanced about this man Cooladge. Last night I told Charles. He laughed it off at first, but when I told him I was really worried he said he knew of a private investigator staying at the Bellevue and would contact him. That, of course, is you."

"I see."

"I was afraid he was just saying it to calm me down. But it's good to see you on the job. Now you will certainly get in touch with this man Cooladge and find out whether or not he is … a mental case." And then she added, quite inexplicably, "I'm very sympathetic with persons who have mental or emotional problems."

She went on explaining her interest in psychiatry, but I stopped listening to the words. I was trying to figure something that didn't fall right. Why had Nancy Trippe approached me for the same job that her employer Pless intended to approach me for? What was behind this Trippe mouse anyway? Why the crazy appointment at the Opera House, of all places?

I interrupted her flow of words. "Have you any idea where your husband is at the moment, Mrs. Pless?"

"I never have much of an idea," she said with surprising candor. "But unfortunately I can make a very good guess ..."

"Oh?"

"There is a young girl," she said. "There always has been. I suppose there always will be. They say he's keeping her in a villa up on the corniche. I believe her name is Grant."

She said it very calmly, but suddenly the calmness evaporated. She leaned forward and whispered tensely: "For God's sake, help me! Things are closing in on me!" Before I had a chance to stop her she went on in an excited voice, "I'll pay you as much as Charles is paying you. More. You'll need money. I understand that. How much?" Hysteria was taking over now. Obviously afraid of my "no," she said, "Would three thousand be enough? I can give it to you in cash. Really I can. Now. Right now. I'll give you more, if necessary. Only you must—"

"What?"

"Find out about this girl. Not only that. Stop them from talking, humiliating me. They will smother me ... I can't seem to get out from under ... smother me!"

I didn't exactly groan aloud, but I felt the groan down where it hurt. The three thousand was suddenly dissolving into a litter of loose marbles. What this baby needed was not a private eye but a head doctor. But even as I was thinking that, a change came over her.

The hysteria disappeared and she straightened up in the chair and said with remarkable calm, "I can see what you're thinking, but it's not true. I'm in a nervous state, but nothing more. Who wouldn't be, with what I have to contend with? I'll give this money to you in cash if you'll help me."

"You have that much cash in the house?"

"You don't believe me ..." She stood up. "Come with me. Hurry. Charles may come back at any moment, or Nancy may come down!"

Uneasy but curious, I followed her out into the vast reception hall. Her heels made little clicking sounds on the marble as we climbed the stairs. It was warm and humid outside, but in here a cold draught seemed to be sweeping down from the upper halls. On the second floor she led me down a wide hall strewn with statuary to a double door at the end. She pushed open the doors and we stepped into a large, ornately furnished sitting room. On either side of the sitting room, doors opened into bedrooms, dimly lit now and deserted. With a jerk of the arm she indicated the bedroom on the right. I could see an enormous Louis Quinze bed complete with silk draperies already turned down for the night.

"That's my room," she said bitterly. "The other room belongs to Charles—when he's here."

Through the open door of the other room I saw dinner clothes laid out on the bed; dinner clothes that Pless would never wear unless they buried him in them.

She went directly to a French impressionist painting that hung on the wall next to Pless's bedroom door.

"Charles believes in cash, too," she said. "I keep it around for him as other wives keep children!"

She put her hand on the picture frame and drew it outward revealing a small wall safe. But almost immediately she drew back and gasped. The safe's door was already open half an inch. She flung the door wide. A light flashed on inside the safe. There was nothing there but cold steel walls.

She wheeled about wildly. "Everything is gone!"

"What was there?"

"About four thousand in cash and—and some private papers of Charles!"

"What sort of papers?"

"I don't know ... something to do with the magazine. But how could this have happened? I was here only ..."

"Who else knew the combination?"

"Charles, of course, and ..." She stopped.

"Well?"

"Nancy knew it ..."

Suddenly she stiffened. "Nancy! Where is she? I kept expecting her to come down as we talked. She never takes more than a few minutes to dress."

She turned and darted for her bedroom, with me a few feet behind. She went past her bed to what appeared to be a discreet closet door, different from the pink paneling of the wall only by a knob and lock. Frantically she turned the knob and pushed, but the door refused to give.

"It's locked ... the key is gone. Please help."

I pushed her aside and threw my weight against the door. Fortunately, it was fragile, and at the first pressure I could feel the wood giving. On my third try the panel burst inward on darkness. I checked my forward movement over the threshold and shoved Mrs. Pless back into her own bedroom.

"Stay there."

Across the darkness I could make out draperies fluttering against a moonlit window and the delicate iron work of a balcony outlined against the pale night. I felt along the wall for the light switch, crouching and tensed for any sign of movement, my free hand clutching the Luger. Finally I found the switch. The room was suddenly bathed in a sick pink light. The scene it revealed was so unexpected that I stood frozen for a moment. Behind me Mrs. Pless let out a muffled scream.

The room was in wild disorder: chairs overturned, drawers flung onto the floor, part of the window draperies hanging in shreds. But I was hardly aware of it.

For on the bed lay Nancy Trippe, as naked as a girl in the final number at the Bal Tabarin. Her arms were stretched above her head, bound by the wrists to the headboard with torn sheets. Her legs were similarly secured to the footboard, and a pillow case had been wadded into her mouth. She was writhing about, desperately trying to free herself. And her eyes were the eyes of a half-crazed animal—or so I thought.

I managed to make it to the bed before Mrs. Pless and tore loose the gag. The voice that was freed upon this unlikely scene was unexpectantly strong and full of rage.

She looked from Mrs. Pless to me in white fury.

She shouted: "The son of a bitch raped me!"

ELEVEN

Nancy didn't look up at me. She sat on the edge of the bed clutching a robe about her with one hand and the glass of brandy I had fetched in the other.

"But we must call the police!" Mrs. Pless said for the third or fourth time. Somehow, though, I felt the words were a concession to form rather than an expression of outrage.

Nancy said, "No. It will only make matters worse."

She looked up at me, then away. I admired her spunk. There was more to this girl than merely a smooth operator on the make. Maybe I'd done her an injustice in my thinking so far. "Who was it?" I asked her.

She took another pull on the brandy.

"I haven't the faintest idea," she said in the tone of a person who has made a decision. "I had just showered. I came out of the bathroom and I was just over the threshold when I realized my bedroom lights were off. I stopped, but it was too late. Someone grabbed me. I tried to scream, but he tore away the towel I was carrying and wrapped it around my head. He was strong … I thought he was going to kill me. When he pushed me down on the bed my head hit the headboard. I must have gone out for a moment. When I came to, my hands and feet were already bound and—the bastard!"

Mrs. Pless said, "It's disgusting!"

I turned in some surprise. It was almost as though she were disgusted with Nancy. She caught herself up quickly and said, "Poor dear … I'd better call a doctor."

Nancy said coolly, "Don't be a fool, Myra! I'm all right!"

And, oddly enough, I knew that she was all right. You'd think she'd just been engaged in a boring and rather awkward rumba.

"But, darling …"

"I said I'm all right, Myra!"

Mrs. Pless said, "The safe has been robbed!"

An odd conspiratorial look of understanding and even despair passed between them. It was a quick look, but as hard and as sharp and as final as the blade of a Damascus sword.

"Yes," Nancy said finally.

"You knew?"

"Of course I knew. I gave him the combination!"

"You what!" Myra's voice rose shrilly.

"When someone has his fingers at your throat and the rest of your anatomy otherwise occupied, it's no time for heroics."

"But then you must have heard his voice," I said.

She looked me straight in the eye. "There was nothing about him that was familiar to me—his voice or anything else." She said it with such conviction that I knew she was lying. She finished off the rest of the brandy, gave Myra Pless a penetrating look and said, "Take Mr. Muldoon downstairs, Myra. We must dress. We're late for the gala now."

"You're not planning to go to the Opera House—not after what's happened!"

"Why not?"

"But you can't!" Myra spluttered. "Not in—in your condition."

"My dear Myra, rape is merely a state of mind, unpleasant but by no means crippling." She looked away. "It's not the worst thing that's happened to me in my life." She stood up and took a deep breath and the note of bravado came back into her voice. "Give me fifteen minutes and I'll be as good as new."

"Nancy, I really don't think …"

"Well I do!" The high note of exasperation was back. "It's lucky for us Charles hasn't come back yet. He'll think something is wrong if we don't show up at the Opera House." She stopped and looked at me again. "Just what are you doing in this house, Mr. Muldoon? Our appointment wasn't until …" She choked off the last words too late.

"Appointment?" Myra said sharply.

"Date," Nancy amended. "How is it that you turned up here?"

"Ask her." I pointed to Myra.

"Myra?"

"It's a long story," Myra said quickly. "Later, we'll talk about it." She started moving toward the door. "Come on, Mr. Muldoon."

"You go ahead, Mrs. Pless. I'll be down in a moment."

Myra Pless hesitated, then shrugged and left the room, going through the shattered doorway into her own bedroom.

Nancy moved impatiently toward the bath.

"Look," she said over her shoulder, "I don't have time for chitchat."

"Why are you so anxious not to call the police in?"

On the brink of the bathroom she turned. "None of your damned business."

"But it is my business. It's my job!"

"What does that mean?"

"Should I try to dig Black up?"

"Black? What do you know about Black?"

"I didn't mean to upset you."

"Listen," she said angrily. "For two cents I'd chuck the whole damned show. I'm fed up to here. If Black has told you anything … if he's told you any screwball stories …"

"What kind of stories did he tell you on the bed?"

For a moment she said nothing. Then the bravado seemed to leave her. A kind of weariness crept into her voice. "Leave me alone. I feel as though I'll never be able to scrub everything away. So many things."

We stood looking at one another. I felt the old fatal symptoms of sympathy beginning to stir. Christ, I thought, not this one too! I fought the feeling down. I waited.

"What has Myra told you?" she finally asked in a tired voice.

"She's afraid of something."

She looked at me again with a curiously inscrutable expression. "Myra … Myra is not very well, you know. She's sometimes given to fantasies about even her closest friends."

"Are there many?"

"Friend then."

"Who could be closer … a door into her bedroom."

"Don't, please. What did she say?"

"She's too scared to say much of anything."

She seemed relieved.

"I see. Does she want you to work for her? Oh, for God's sake get that smug expression off your face. As Sherlock Holmes you don't impress me! I'm just warning you. Myra … Sometimes I don't know what I am around here. Pless's whipping boy or Myra's trained nurse—and I'm fed up!"

"You're getting out?"

She looked at me again as though the thought had just struck her. "Yes," she said. "I believe I am getting out. And now leave me alone or I'll …"

The vehemence was back. I remembered the automatic I had seen in her handbag.

She started to turn.

"I won't keep you," I said. "I have to hunt up a guy called Cooladge."

That got her. She wheeled back. The tired mask slipped and there was fear in her eyes. "Something's happened!"

"Why should you think that? Everyone tells me you thought Cooladge was a joker."

I turned and started for the door. The cliff-hanging technique worked. Behind me she said, "Oh, my God!"

I got almost to the threshold of the ruined door to Myra Pless's bedroom when she called, "Come back!"

I did, but slowly. She was leaning against the door frame of the bathroom for support now. "That's why Charles didn't come back. Something has happened."

"Maybe."

"Charles is dead."

"Do you care?"

Without hesitation she said, "His death would not be convenient— now. But how do you … Where is he? That girl on the corniche. Do the police know?"

"A lot of questions there. The answer to the last one is 'no.'"

"But why? What are you up to?"

"I'm going to get whoever did it," I said calmly.

Mechanically she came back into the room and sat on the edge of the bed. She looked tired and haggard. I thrust a cigarette at her and she took it automatically and permitted me to light it for her.

"How?" she finally asked.

"A doped-up adrenalin pill."

She nodded. "Yes, of course."

"You knew it would be that way?"

"Let's say I was afraid it might be that way."

"Cooladge?"

She hesitated a moment, then looked up at me and said, "Who else?"

"You tell me."

"A lot of people knew the story Cooladge was telling …"

"But a lot of people couldn't have got hold of his cyanide tablet, if he really had one. And you just don't go into a chemist's and buy a cyanide tablet and have them make it up to look like the particular adrenalin tablets that Pless took."

"No." The quality was back. "I suppose it all comes back to Cooladge in the end."

"How did you meet him?"

"Marius at the Bellevue beach first told me about him. He said there was this character drinking in the bars of Cannes who had threatened to get Charles. He thought I should know. I dug Cooladge up. Poor, stupid idiot. I think he had flipped. He had this mad plan for getting rid of Pless. It was so insane it was funny. He was so far gone he apparently thought it was almost natural to discuss his plan with the world, as though everyone else would agree with him. But try as I might, I couldn't dig up a motive. I don't believe his name is really Cooladge ... I ended up, though, thinking he was harmless. I guess I was wrong ..."

"Why did you bring him to the party in Antibes?"

"Why?" she shrugged. "It was a gag, really. But I guess I hoped he would talk. He did. But I never found out who he really was. Did it happen in the villa, the one Charles took for that girl?"

"Yes."

"Oh, my God!" She laughed shortly. "Little Miss Muffet in her dirndl and flat shoes."

"So you knew about her all the time."

"Who doesn't! She's been damned inconvenient. She's just ..."

"You wouldn't mind seeing her put out of the way."

"I didn't say that!"

"You didn't have to. And Mrs. Pless?"

"Oh, it doesn't matter to Myra ... I mean ..." She added hastily and without much conviction, "She was used to those things. She is—tolerant about Charles."

She looked me in the eyes again and I felt a little shiver on my spine. There was something here I didn't understand, something cold and repellent. Then her gaze wavered and she got shakily to her feet.

"I suppose Black must know something. I have a feeling he'll turn up again in Monte. He's got something to sell again."

"Then it was Black who did the rape act."

"Yes. He's been sniffing around me for months, without getting to first base."

"That's not the way he told it to me."

"Naturally not! He'd like the world to think there isn't a woman on the coast he hasn't laid, the rotten little bastard ..."

"And what has he got to sell? What did he get from that safe aside from the four thousand in cash?"

Again she hesitated. Then, with apparent candor, she said, "All right. You might as well know. There was a manila envelope containing some letters written years ago by Alva Creighton to Charles. They'd make even *your* hair stand on end!"

"What were they doing there?"

"Myra came across them by accident just before we sailed for Europe. She was upset, naturally, and brought them to me. She wanted to know what to do with them. I ... I decided to keep them."

"Why?"

"Let's call it insurance. Charles and I had had some difference of opinion over the policy of the magazine. I thought they might be valuable to me if he ever decided to fire me. I wanted to keep this job—then."

"Blackmail?"

She shrugged. "In a mild way. Unfortunately Myra mentioned the letters one day while Black was in the room. He got hold of them in Paris. He went to Alva Creighton and told her we were planning to use the letters as a basis for a filthy story on her in the magazine, and that he might be able to get them for her—at a price."

"And?"

"She hadn't come up to his price as of yesterday afternoon. Of course Charles knew nothing of it, and the story never would have been published in the magazine, but Alva didn't realize that. Black was being difficult and nasty ... he was in a position to do us a great deal of harm. I decided to get the letters back. It was simple enough. I went to his room yesterday afternoon while the woman who runs his *pension* was entertaining her lover. I got them back."

"You haven't told Alva the truth—that the magazine would never have published the story, that Black was just scaring cash out of her?"

"Not yet. I was planning to tell her tonight, if I saw her at the Opera House. Now, with the letters in Black's hands again—well, Myra and I may have to buy them back at a good price."

I crushed out my cigarette. "Sweetie," I said easily, "it's a good story and maybe half true. Now tell me what Black has that you and Myra are *really* anxious to buy back."

She looked startled. After a moment she decided to level. "All right. There is something else. I won't tell you at the moment; it's not fair to Myra. I must first find out ... Look, I'm just as anxious to dig up whoever finished Charles off as you—maybe for different reasons—before the police begin unearthing a lot of filth. Maybe we can work together."

"Maybe." The skepticism in my voice was all too clear.

"All right. You might as well play it that way as any. I've got to find Black. Give me an hour or so; I think I can come up with something."

"What's your idea?"

"You go on to the Opera House with Myra. She can get the ticket at the box office left in Charles's name. He took a box, but there are three separate tickets. Myra and I each have one, and the other is left in Charles's name."

I hesitated for only a moment. There wasn't much to lose. She wasn't apt to make a break for South America or the Aleutians. I wanted to come up with Black again myself.

"You think you can produce him by ten?"

"I guarantee it!"

"What time did you get back here tonight?"

I saw the defenses rushing into place. "An hour ago, more or less."

"Where were you?"

"I had tea with friends in Verens."

"Anyone I can check with?"

"Miss Bracken. May Bracken."

"And Myra? Was she out?"

"Myra? I believe she had a fitting at a dress shop in Nice this afternoon. Then she went to the hairdresser. Ask her."

"I will." I started for the door.

"By the way," she said behind me, "who's paying your bills?"

"Mrs. Pless has made me an offer."

I looked over my shoulder. The glance was rewarding. She looked as though she'd just picked up a fistful of lightning.

TWELVE

When Myra Pless and I entered the box Charles Pless had engaged, the gala ballet performance at the Opera House was in full bloom. The rococo auditorium with its semicircular rows of boxes and balconies was almost as glittering as the stage. The Pless box was on the grand tier, the second box from the stage on the left. We entered it through a little private sitting room where one could retire when boredom with the stage performance set in, an arrangement left over from the days when visiting grand dukes and British earls entertained the ballet girls in private between the acts. It was like Pless to have engaged this box—which normally would have held eight people— for just Nancy, Myra and himself.

Across the way, were row upon row of white shirt fronts, ribbons and medals, Paris gowns and summer furs and diamonds flashing in the reflection of the stage lights.

I conned the audience for my own personal celebrity list. Their faces began to appear to me. Alva Creighton and the governor were sitting in the third-row center, apparently enthralled by what was taking place onstage. I could make out Prince Rainier and his lovely bride. After a while I found Amy and Harold sitting in the eighth row on the side. They seemed to be looking through the performers and the scenery into some dream of their own. Occasionally each would turn slightly to look in the direction of our box. I searched the rear of the orchestra and the balconies for some sign of Ballentine Black, without any success. Was Nancy talking to him at this very moment, and, if so, what the hell about?

And somewhere in those rows might be the face I wouldn't have known—the face of the man they called Cooladge.

Ultra-modern atonal music seethed from the orchestra pit accompanying a currently fashionable ballet company from Paris. What was happening on the stage would not have been condoned at the Folies Bergère, but the cloak of art made the graphic depiction of various primitive urges and civilized vices respectable. The program notes referred solemnly to Freud, and the dancers were lost—according to the program—in "an endless, spaceless Sodom and Gomorrah." A surrealist setting suggested faintly some Dali-like version of the Riviera, but the props in the foreground consisted of a gigantic bed and three kitchen chairs, on and around which three nearly naked men and a girl spent more time entangled in disturbing—and sometimes unlikely—contact than on their classic points. It seemed to me a character called Death was having himself a ball.

Beside me, Myra whispered, "I'm worried. We should have insisted that Nancy come along with us."

We sat far back in the shadow of the velvet draperies, away from the glare of the stage lights.

"She can take care of herself. You should know that." She glanced at me and then away. She stirred restlessly, letting her program slip to the floor.

"What in the world is keeping Charles?"

Nothing in *this* world, I thought grimly, but I muttered something reassuring. Onstage, Death had locked his legs around the girl.

I felt welded to the gilt chair while action might be gathering into a whirlwind out in the streets. But there is a time for action and a time for waiting and some part of my training had forced me into this waiting time, just as some part of my intuitive equipment told me that in some manner the Opera House, where a performance that was a nightmarish reflection of the life on this plush golden coast was a focus point, a center of the whirlpool for the forces surrounding the death of Charles Pless.

I held up my watch at an angle to the glow from the stage. It was ten-five. I wondered whether anyone had as yet stumbled on the body of Pless. After a moment I said, "It's almost time for the intermission. Let's beat the crowd out. We can go up to the Café de Paris for a drink."

"But if Nancy comes, and Charles ..."

"They can get along without us for a few minutes."

"Well ..." She seemed uneasy. "Just one drink."

We left the box through the tiny little sitting room, and went out into the long curving hallway behind the boxes. It was deserted, as were the grand staircase and the ornate foyer. We went out into the night. I noticed that the moon had gone and warm gusts of wind were sweeping in from the harbor. Limousines were lined up all the way from the Opera House to the square which opens out in front of the casino. We walked up past the limousines and the chauffeurs who stood in little clusters smoking and talking. The wide terrace of the Café de Paris which faces the casino was only thinly populated. We found a table in the rear and ordered drinks. I wasn't surprised when Myra Pless said primly that she wanted a Dubonnet.

I dove right in. "Tell me something, Mrs. Pless. You wanted to pay me three thousand for some kind of a job. What is the job?"

She drew her hand away from the table and clasped the big awkward beaded evening bag, something that looked as though it might have been inherited from great-aunt Harriet.

"I've been overwrought in the past few months, and perhaps my suspicions are unfounded—but ..."

"Suspicions?"

"It's as though—as though all the poison were coming to a head suddenly. You see, meeting this man Cooladge was sort of a climax to my fear, because there have been others I feared—for Charles, I mean."

"Others?"

"Ballentine Black. I know he hates Charles."

"And?"

"This is very difficult for me to say. But I must, Mr. Muldoon. It's Nancy I'm afraid of now."

"Nancy! I thought she was your best friend."

"She was. And is, I suppose, in a way. No, that isn't true. It's so involved, so difficult to explain."

"Try to. Where did you meet Nancy?"

"At the state university Nancy was a sophomore when I arrived for my first term. She was on her way to being a big wheel on campus.

Charles was already a big wheel—president of the senior class and the editor of the campus paper. Nancy was working on the paper, among other things, and she and Charles were friends. I was nobody. Worse than that, I was a scared nobody. You can imagine how flattered I was when Nancy took me up."

"Where did you come from?"

"Upstate. Upstate in every sense of the word! My father had done very well in the dairy business. My mother died when I was a baby, and my father was a strict church man. I was never permitted any freedom. I always felt he resented me because my mother's fatal illness began at my birth. Anyway, it was only through the insistence of my English teacher that he finally permitted me to go to state college. I didn't have any friends. I was very lonely. And then, in the middle of my first year, my father died and I came into some money."

"And Nancy Trippe took you up."

She regarded me blankly for a moment. "Yes. We became inseparable. I never made a move without her advice."

"And that advice was …"

"Well, an odd thing happened. Charles was already talking about some job on a New York magazine where he could get experience. He had met Alva Creighton, and she had given him some letters of introduction to important people in the literary world. He and Nancy were already talking of an idea for a magazine of their own. Sometimes the three of us would go out together and talk half the night. They seemed to include me in their plans. I guess I was flattered."

"I can imagine."

"They needed money. Nancy's parents were poor, and so were Charles's."

"I see."

"The money my father left was held in trust until I as twenty-one. It came to about sixty thousand dollars."

"Is that all?"

"I know. Gossip has me a millionaire. But you must remember that sixty thousand was a great deal to Charles. And Nancy convinced me that it would be a good investment. Theoretically, she was right."

"Theoretically?"

She puffed nervously at the cigarette and looked away. "It all sounds so cold-blooded in retrospect. Charles needed my money. I wanted to be with Nancy. I needed her absolute loyalty and understanding. She made everything sound so plausible. I would marry Charles, and she would come to live with us. We would have the sense of security that marriage would give. Charles would make us rich. Nancy would work behind the scenes on the paper. Charles would be free to live his own life."

"And you gave him the sixty thousand."

"Yes. In return he made a will—I was to get two-thirds of the estate; Nancy, one-third. As you can imagine, with the success of the magazine my sixty thousand investment is worth at least twenty times that amount today. I mean if—" She stopped.

"You mean if Charles should die."

"Well, yes."

"And has everything turned out as you planned, Mrs. Pless? Have you found the happiness you were promised?"

"Happiness?" She smiled, her eyes derisive. "How can a prisoner be happy?"

"And the loyalty you expected from Nancy?"

"I was a fool—I knew nothing. Instead of finding security I found myself a target of derision. Charles has flaunted his girls and his affairs. Nancy has—"

"Yes?"

"She has betrayed me," she said quietly.

"In what way?"

She shook her head impatiently. "I want to go away. I want to leave them. I never want to see them again. I … I hate them!"

I said nothing.

After a moment she calmed down. Quietly she said, "It's like being caught in a cobweb of evil. Nancy is cold and calculating; I know that now. She used me just as Charles used me. They must pay. And in a way they are paying—they are destroying each other."

"Destroying each other?"

"Charles has changed. He claims he didn't realize how sinister the magazine's policies really are. He claims Nancy ran things in a highhanded way. He has some new girl. He wants to get rid of Nancy and me. But …"

"But what?"

"Oh, it's so horrible. So unbelievably horrible. Nancy keeps talking about the money, how it might be with us if anything happened to Charles. She paints a wonderful picture of the life we would have together. And all the time I know … Oh, it's hideous!" She shuddered delicately and sipped the Dubonnet.

So we had a motive for Nancy Trippe, at last; it wasn't the case of killing the goose that laid the golden egg.

"If you've felt this way about your husband, if you have been afraid of Nancy, why didn't you break off with her long ago?"

She looked me in the eyes. Her expression was curiously sad and lost.

"It's not easy to break off a thing like that, Mr. Muldoon. I can't explain."

"What do you want me to do?"

"I thought if you could persuade this girl that Charles is going to go away … that if you helped me to stand up to Nancy … that … Well, Charles and I might have a chance!"

"Is that all you had in mind?" I asked skeptically.

Instead of answering, she suddenly put down her glass and looked beyond me in slow gathering fear. I turned. Out beyond the last row of tables on the edge of the square, a man was standing. He was curiously battered and unreal. He carried a large manila envelope held tightly to his side. He seemed to be leaning against the night, staring at us with bleary-eyed fixity. It was Ballentine Black.

I started to rise, but Myra Pless clutched my sleeve.

"Don't go near him," she whispered. "He hates Charles and me. There isn't anything he might not do."

But to my surprise Black seemed to come out of a deep sleep and began to move towards us. Myra clasped her bag and started to rise.

"We must get out of here," she whispered frantically.

I took her hand reassuringly, sat down myself and held her there. "You're safe with me, Myra, remember that. We're together in this."

"But …"

"Let's see what the poor fool's up to. Apparently the three thousand in your safe wasn't enough—and he must have Alva's letters in that envelope."

She was trembling, but managed to stay put as Black lurched between the tables towards us. I saw the headwaiter turn and give me a questioning look. I smiled reassuringly. I was curious.

"Ah, good evening," Black said with the leering bow of a stock-company villain. "A bit of luck. Customers everywhere I look …"

Drunk as he was, he managed to keep the manila envelope and himself well out of my reach.

"Lovely evening," he said mockingly. "A lovely evening for negotiations. Any takers?"

"What the hell are you talking about, Black?"

"Ask the lady. Ask sweet Lorraine here, or her girlfriend …"

Myra started to rise. "I must get back …"

But Black intercepted her quickly, grabbing her wrist and forcing her down again into the chair.

Myra said, "How dare you!"

"It's easy, I assure you! It's time you two …" He leaned down and whispered something in her ear. The effect on Myra was astounding. Her face settled into a mask of immobility. He straightened up and looked down at her with a triumphant leer. Their gazes were locked for a moment in some intense understanding. Then she nodded.

Before I could say anything, the headwaiter arrived. "Is anything wrong, madame?"

"Wrong? Certainly not."

Black looked at me and laughed. When the headwaiter drifted off he said to me, "Crawl out of this, you square. You'll only get boxed in."

"I want to talk to you, Black."

I made a move to rise, but he jumped away like a ballet dancer.

"Listen, Muldoon. I've held deuces most of my life. I got aces now, and I'm playing them. Cut out of this game, sweetie—it's too god-damned steep for you!" He wheeled around and lurched off between the tables. Myra grasped my sleeve.

I turned on her. "What was that all about?"

"Let him go. I'll explain later. It's something to do with Nancy."

"Are you protecting her, or him? After what he did earlier …"

With surprising calm she said, "What can we do about it? Bring a charge of impairing the morals of a minor?" Beneath the calm was a new note, hard and derisive.

She rose primly. "Come along. We must get back."

I paid the check and we left the café. Black was nowhere in sight out in the square. Myra Pless seemed in a hurry now, or maybe her apparent rush was an excuse to avoid further discussion. There was a new, enigmatic urgency in her hitherto negative manner.

THIRTEEN

Intermission was on at the Opera House. The smartly dressed audience was spilling out through the lobbies into the streets under a cloud of cigarette smoke and conversation. We pushed our way into the main foyer.

"I don't see her anywhere," Myra said nervously. I noticed that there was no concern for the missing Charles. "What in the world is keeping her?"

I would have given something to know that myself.

"I must powder my nose," she said. "Why don't I meet you over there on the grand staircase?"

"I'll be there."

She went up the stairs to the upper foyer, and I took a position halfway up where I could get a good view of the entire main lobby. I was still uneasy about the scene with Myra Pless and Black. What sort of a threat had Black whispered to clam her up so tight? And what had that crack been about customers? Did he have something more than those letters of Alva Creighton's, something that would put more buyers on the market than merely Alva?

Beautifully gowned women and their escorts were arranged in gay chattering groups down the marble steps like extras in the grand finale of some expensively staged revue. Down below, on the floor of the main lobby, there was a mob around the champagne bar at one end. But among the sleek pack I could make out none of my foxes—or wolves.

The five-minute warning bell signifying the end of intermission sounded faintly over the babble. The warning was lost in laughter. No one paid any attention. No one but me; for some reason I felt a sudden chill of apprehension start up my spine.

Behind me a voice said, "Please give me a cigarette. I've got the shakes."

I turned and saw Nancy Trippe, who had descended from above. She looked cool and trim and completely unraped. In fact, it occurred to me that she looked ready for it again. However, beneath the careful cool veneer, she was worried.

"Where have you been?" I asked.

"To the can," she said elegantly.

"Then you must have seen your pal, Myra."

"Myra?" She looked somewhat taken aback. Then quickly she said, "No. There's a crowd up there. Incidentally, it was a waste of time. I couldn't find Black."

"Did you try?"

"What does that mean?"

"I think he's in a mood to be found. Myra and I saw him just ten minutes ago, at the Café de Paris."

"What! And you let him go?"

"You've got me mixed up with Superman—or the police. I couldn't hold him."

"But—but—did he speak to Myra alone?"

I looked at her closely. Apparently she regretted the question almost immediately. She turned away and said with studied carelessness, "I—I wouldn't want him to upset Myra. She's very easily upset, you know. Is he here in the theater?"

"I don't know. He went off into the darkness like the villain in a bad melodrama."

"That son of a bitch! He ..." She stopped, arrested by the sight of someone coming down the stairs. I followed the direction of her gaze. Amy and Harold were descending toward the chattering mob in the lobby. They looked like a couple of sleepwalkers. I felt a chill of apprehension. Amy was as pale as chalk. She gave me a blind, unseeing look. Harold seemed almost to be supporting her entire weight with the grip he had on her elbow. And I noticed something unexpected in the glamor boy; his usual immaculate appearance was somewhat marred by a long tear in the right sleeve of his dinner jacket.

"My God!" Nancy said. "What cheek! What colossal cheek! Flaunting her second-hand gigolo here, with Charles dead in her house."

"Excuse me ..."

I left her side and started for Amy and Harold. Dimly I was aware of two faces turned toward us from the mob around the champagne bar. They belonged to Alva Creighton and Governor Thorne. And even at this distance I felt the malevolence in Alva's eyes as she spotted Amy.

I reach Amy and Harold in the middle of the lobby, just as the last warning bell sounded. The people around us began to drift slowly toward the auditorium.

"Where are you two going?"

Amy turned a gaze on me that was filled with fear. Harold kept moving her toward the street doors.

"I'm taking Amy home," he mumbled. "She shouldn't have come. If I had known ..."

"She told you?"

"Just a few moments ago. You must be crazy, Muldoon, getting poor Amy in this lousy mess."

"Maybe, I'm getting her out of it. What's wrong? Who's been tearing your clothes?"

Harold tried to jerk his free arm out of sight.

"I caught it on the rail."

"Are you planning to call the police?"

He tugged at Amy's arm. "How can I, now, after what you did with Pless's body? You goddamn well better get Amy out of this or I'll break every bone in your body."

"Listen ..." I stopped, struck by the weary despair on Amy's face. "Amy, what's happened?"

She looked up at me as though recognizing me for the first time. "I don't care about the money ... really I don't. I'm tired. I must go home. Harold, darling—please." There was a note of rising hysteria in her voice.

It was obvious that whatever had happened I wasn't going to get any answers from these two. I made a quick decision, knowing as I made it that I might regret it. "All right. Take her back to the villa. Stay with her until I get there. And don't let anyone in—not a soul."

"It's too late," Amy said in a voice full if inexplicable sadness. "Too terrible—too late ..."

I watched them go out into the street. A little feather of knowledge was tickling my brain, faint and maddeningly elusive.

I turned. The lobby was almost empty again. Inside the auditorium the orchestra had struck up the opening chords of music. Myra had joined Nancy on the stairway. They were both staring at me with a sort of tense questioning in their eyes. Over by the bar, Alva Creighton and Governor Thorne were also watching me. It was an odd, eerie tableau—these four people, each of whom had been involved for different reasons with Charles Pless, standing there, very still, very wary, waiting, as the fashionable audience drifted back into the theater like weary peacocks, leaving the great marble hall full of a silent threat.

I stood in the center of the lobby. They began to converge on me. Alva and the governor reached me first. "I must speak with you," Alva said in a low voice. "It's terribly important. And the governor wants to speak with you, too. Can you be at the Sporting Club in twenty minutes? We're leaving now." She turned a false, ravishing smile on Myra and Nancy as the two women approached.

"Such an attractive pair," she said maliciously.

"I could say the same for you darling." Nancy met fire with fire.

Myra closed her eyes uncomfortably. The governor cleared his throat uneasily in this battle of bitches. "Well Alva, my dear …"

"Yes, right away, Governor." She started for the door with a prima donna sweep of her cloak. "Like everything else in this world, the ballet no longer amuses me."

"Yes," Nancy said with the weapons of her kind. "Even lifeguards wear thin in the end."

Blandly Alva said, "Quite right. However, I'm still old-fashioned enough to prefer them in trunks, and without brassieres." And then with one last shot to Myra Pless, "Do remember me to dear Charles, if and when you see him again." She swept out into the night, dragging the embarrassed governor behind her.

"What did that bitch want?" Nancy demanded.

"I don't know yet. Is something wrong, Mrs. Pless?"

She passed her hand over her eyes. "Wrong? Everything is wrong. It's so ugly. Why doesn't Charles come?"

"Poor dear, she's tired," Nancy said. The note of tenderness was as unexpected as it was incongruous. But when she put her hand out toward Myra the other woman drew away.

"Come on," I said.

"Where?" Myra asked.

"We're going back to that box."

"Why?"

"Don't ask so many questions. Maybe we'll have a visitor. We won't stay much longer."

"I simply can't understand why Charles hasn't appeared," Myra said again.

Nancy hesitated. "I'll give you ten minutes more. Then I'm cutting out. I've had about all I can take. Incidentally, where did sweet-eyed little Amy and the lifeguard go?"

"Back to her villa."

I led them up the deserted staircase into the circular hall behind the boxes. From far away the ballet music was marching toward its dissonant climax. Here in the thickly carpeted hall the music was a distant calliope; everything was soft and dreamlike, perfumed and closed in, cream and gilt paneling and crystal chandeliers curving out of sight. Ahead of us a party was entering Box 3. It consisted of two aging women and two dark young men. One of the women I had seen earlier in the evening at the end of the hall on my floor at the Bellevue—the woman who had stood in the open door with a champagne glass in one hand, who had seemed to be waiting for Death. They were sucked into the open doorway of their box as though by a vacuum.

The door of Box 2 was slightly ajar. I pushed it open into the little sitting room. Then I held fast, as though my feet were caught in ice.

"What is it?" Nancy said sharply.

She pushed in beside me and gasped. I heard Myra Pless make a little sighing sound behind me.

For a moment there was only the sound of that little sigh against the relentless beat of the music rising up against the velvet draperies. Then Nancy whispered, "The poor creep!"

The man lay half on his side by the fragile sofa of the sitting room. He was facing us, and at first it appeared that he was merely lying there, too weak to rise, after suffering some blow that had bloodied his nose. But he was very stiff and very still, and from between his shoulder blades protruded the curved ivory handle of a stiletto. It was quite obvious that Ballentine Black had made his last deal.

FOURTEEN

The two women were waiting for me out in the hall. They were tense and angry, rather than frightened, as though they had been quarreling.

"Well, what now, Sherlock Holmes?" Nancy said bitingly.

"He got into a fight. He was stabbed."

"How clever of you!"

"The manila envelope with Alva's letters is gone."

They didn't seem surprised. They said nothing. They seemed to be waiting for something else.

"What else was in that envelope?" I asked quietly, and immediately saw, at least on Nancy's part, that this was the question they feared.

"Why don't you ask Alva Creighton? She probably knows. She probably has her letters back. I wonder how much she paid what thug to do this pretty job!"

"I think I'd like to talk to Harold Jones about that—after I talk to Alva."

"Harold Jones?"

"The coat of his dinner jacket was torn when he left the Opera House a few minutes ago. He had obviously been in a fight."

"Where did he go?"

"He's taking Amy Grant back to her villa."

The two women exchanged a quick glance, knowing, rather than sympathetic. I could see that Mrs. Pless was thoroughly frightened.

"What else can you come up with?" Nancy asked contemptuously.

"Whoever stabbed him was not a professional."

"How do you know that?"

"The knife. It's a Damascus knife, the sort one might buy in a curio shop, too unique for these parts. It should be simple to trace."

"Curio shop?" Nancy's voice was suddenly guarded.

"Why? Does that mean something to you?"

Instead of answering, Nancy said sharply, "Are you going to call the police?"

"Hardly. We haven't got one-third of an escape hatch between us. I've got to manufacture one, and quick."

"How?"

"I want you two to go over to the lobby of the Hotel de Paris and wait for me. I'll be only a few minutes."

Myra stepped forward. "Mr. Muldoon, something terrible has happened. I mean even beyond this poor man Black. What is it? Where is Charles?"

"Take her to the hotel," I said to Nancy. "Tell her what happened—over something soothing."

She looked me in the eye. Her mind was off on something else, clicking along swiftly.

"Yes," she said. "I suppose you're going to talk to Alva. Maybe you're just wasting time, but it's worth a try. Come on, Myra."

She put out her hand, but Mrs. Pless drew herself up and walked past the outstretched hand down the curving hall toward the marble staircase. Nancy and I followed.

"I'll handle her," Nancy said in a low voice.

"Tell me," I said casually. "Where were you before you came back to the Pless house to dress for dinner? I mean, where were you before Black showed up in your bedroom?"

Her hesitation was hardly noticeable. Then she spoke with apparent candor. "All right, you might as well know. After I saw you at the café, I went to Cannes to try to hunt up Cooladge. He'd already checked out of his *pension*. Then I went back to Verens and had tea with the two women you saw at the café—May Bracken and her friend."

"I suppose you can check on that."

"It was later than I thought when I left May's studio. I went to the hairdresser next to the Bellevue to pick up Myra, but she had already left; there was a message saying she had taken a taxi back to the villa. Myra was dressing when I got back. I went into my own bedroom to bathe and dress, and you know the rest."

"Did you run across Harold Jones in Verens?"

"No."

We had reached the main entrance to the Opera House. Myra turned on the pavement, waiting for us.

Nancy hesitated for a moment as though about to say more, changed her mind, and went to Myra's side.

"I'll see you two in a few minutes," I told them.

They went slowly up the hill toward the Hotel de Paris, and I turned down toward the Sporting Club. People were already leaving the Opera House, bored with the ballet and anxious to get on to the promised splendors of the gala ball at the club. As I passed groups on the way down the hill, bits of conversation, disjointed and out of context, reached me—a babel of French, German and English murmuring into the night air, the English rising shrill and aggressive above the rest. "… too absurd to be born with a mustache and a croupier's blessing … Gave a better performance, my dear, in *The Swan* … The German officers are no longer with him … Absolutely exquisite in the *pas de deux* … Got the job from De Quaivis by dressing as a boy … Five hundred thousand francs last night on number thirteen … And she calmly passed my two spade bid … Spoiled! The place is lousy with Americans! … No, darling, he's keeping the one in pink. Papa bought her for him last Christmas … Can't blame Pless, with that dreadful, washed-out wife … Saw him with Bertie last night, and my dear, Bobbie doesn't even suspect! … Odd creatures you couldn't possibly know from some outlandish place in Michigan!" And "I'll never find … never find … never find …" rising and falling in the soft night air like a counterpoint to my own bleak thoughts—the tired music of this over-plush coast, music for the funerals of Pless and Black.

The luxurious main room of the Sporting Club had been redecorated for the gala to represent a vast undersea effect. Nylon seaweed dripped from the ceilings; balloons shaped as octopi, shark and twisting eels, hung in mid-air; mobiles vaguely resembling mermaids floated and turned on unseen wires, and an orchestra, playing now to a nearly empty room, was decked out in some obscure marine garb. I found Alva and Governor Thorne alone at a large table set for about sixteen beneath a disturbing canopy of fish net.

"Thank goodness you came before the rest of the party!" Alva said. "Can I order you a drink?"

"No. I have only a few minutes. What did you want to see me about?"

Alva leaned back, sucking at her long cigarette holder. "I've been talking to the governor. I told him what I am now going to tell you. I stopped earlier this evening at the villa where Pless is keeping that American girl. I strongly suspect that Charles Pless is dead!"

She seemed disappointed that her bombshell fell so flat. But I wondered whether it was only an act.

"That's too bad," I said calmly. "Did you see the body?"

"No. I didn't have to; I'm a writer. I could tell by that girl's behavior. Pless's car was there. She seemed very nervous and frightened. I strongly suspect she and that man Cooladge poisoned Charles."

"What motive would she have had?"

"She's been after Harold Jones!" she said angrily. "That's sufficient reason. Ask her."

"Why do you tell me this? Why don't you go to the police?"

"Don't be a fool. The governor and I have been overheard publicly to express our opinions of Pless. It might be uncomfortable. That's why I asked you to stop here. We want to employ your services—for two purposes."

I turned to the governor. "Do you agree?"

He cleared his throat uncomfortably. "Well, Alva has told me what she fears. I believe she might be right. During the intermission she saw this man Cooladge."

"Where?"

"He was in the upper hall of the Opera House," Alva said quickly. "He was talking to that girl, Amy Grant. She seemed terribly upset and angry."

"And?"

"Something about the way they were talking confirmed my suspicions. And—" she smiled—"I'm afraid I have been rather foolish and indiscreet ..."

"In what way?"

"Well, after I left the villa, after seeing Amy Grant, I got to thinking. After all, if Charles Pless had taken some sort of a poison pill, thinking that it was adrenalin, someone might remember I had been in his cabaña at the Bellevue beach this afternoon."

"You saw Pless at the beach?"

"Yes. I wanted to talk to him about some letters of mine he had."

"Did you?"

"Yes. We spoke for a minute or so …" She leaned forward. "I might as well be frank with you. When I got to his cabaña no one was there. I had some crazy idea—I can't tell you why—that maybe the letters might be hidden inside the cabaña. I went in and started to search. Charles came in and found me. He was not amused!"

"Did you tell him why you were there?"

"Yes. He didn't seem to believe me. He belittled the value of the letters. He told me he had never intended to use them for the magazine, and that whoever had told me so was lying. I simply didn't believe him."

"He might have been telling the truth."

"That Ballentine Black had promised to get the letters for me. He never kept his promise, and I didn't trust him."

"What else did Pless have to say?"

"He seemed very preoccupied and discouraged about something. He hardly listened to me. Then he saw the governor down the beach and he got up abruptly and left!"

"Was that before or after his swim?"

"His swim?" She looked blank. "He never went swimming at all. He never changed his clothes."

I was aware of the orchestra and the metal mermaids floating idiotically above our heads. And I thought, Pless never went swimming at all. Something turned over slowly in my stomach.

"But as I say," Alva went on quickly, "after I left Amy Grant's villa I got to worrying. If Pless were dead, someone might trace me to his cabaña this afternoon. I lost an earring while I was searching there for the letters … When I got to Monte I called Harold and asked him if he would not please go to Pless's cabaña and find the earring."

"Did he?" I watched her closely. "Why are you telling me all this?"

She sighed. "I've been a fool. I know that you are a first-rate investigator. I want you to try to find out who killed Pless—if he is actually dead—and I want you to get my letters for me before they fall into the hands of the police!" She dug in her bag and plucked out a check. "Here. Here is a check for one thousand. If you can do as I ask, there will be three thousand more!"

I took the check from her and put it into the pocket of my dinner jacket. I thought, at last, an employer. But I wasn't too happy about it. There was something too candid about Alva's manner.

I turned to the governor. "You haven't said a word, Governor. What do you think?"

"I don't know what to think," he said slowly. "Alva is very clever about these things. I know that if Pless is already dead I'm in hot water. I didn't disguise the fact that I came to Verens to have it out with him."

"Are you sure you didn't have it out with him, Governor?"

"No," he said quietly. "I didn't." Then he added with dignity, "By having it out with Pless I had no intention of killing him, if that's what you think."

"Is there anything else either of you cares to add?"

Alva looked at the governor. He cleared his throat and after a moment said, "Well, it's a small thing. It may not mean a thing, but ..."

"Go on."

"That man, Cooladge. Funny how he always seems to keep popping up. As I was leaving the hotel in Verens to come to Monte for dinner, I happened to look down the boulevard, and there he was."

"Alone?"

"No. He was standing in front of that fancy gift shop next to the hairdresser's. He seemed quite upset. He seemed to be having a violent argument with one of the ladies you were with a few minutes ago in the lobby of the Opera House."

"The one in red or the one in beige?"

"The pretty one in red."

I stood up. For the first time that night I sensed a genuine trail. Yet the first moment of elation quickly evaporated. I'd been a fool to let those women out of my sight or to permit Harold to take Amy back to the villa. I looked down at Alva. I had a hunch I would be seeing her sooner than she expected.

"I've got to get going. You'll hear from me."

"But, Mr. Muldoon ..."

Alva's words were lost to me as I crossed the dance floor toward the entrance. I looked at my watch. It was almost midnight. A gala would soon be over at the Opera House and in a matter of a short time, Black's body would be discovered. Not much time left now.

I was certain now that unless I could prevent it, another murder would take place before the hour was up.

I reached the street and began to run.

FIFTEEN

Myra Pless was sipping coffee in the lounge of the Hotel de Paris. Nancy was nowhere in sight.

"I had about given you up," she said. "Nancy has gone back to our villa."

The hell she has, I thought, but I kept panic out of my face. "Why didn't you go back with her?"

"I've decided to stay here at the Paris for the night." She looked at me with a curious sort of calm. "Nancy told me about Charles."

"I'm sorry."

She seemed barely to have heard me. "I might as well warn you. Apparently you are working on the case. You have only an hour more. After that I intend to call the police."

"Mrs. Pless ..."

"Nancy and I have quarreled. I never want to see her again. I feel absolutely nothing about anything. I'm sitting here drinking coffee just as calmly as though I were expecting friends to join me. No one will join me, but it doesn't matter. Nothing matters anymore."

"I don't believe Nancy went back to your villa. Do you?"

"No," she said flatly, "I don't. I suspect she has gone to Cannes to try to find that man Cooladge."

"Yes," I lied, "I think so too. In fact, that's where I'm headed."

"Good luck. But I'm warning you. An hour—no more."

I left her sitting there like a waxen image who had never known life, and went down from the lounge to a pay booth near the main entrance. There I called the number Marius had given me.

Luck was really beginning to come my way. He had more information that I had bargained for. Yes, the tablet had been analyzed. It was, as I had suspected, merely an adrenalin tablet. But Marius had gone further. He had actually traced the tablet to the place of its purchase: a chemist in Cannes. The chemist was fairly certain it was the same sort of tablet he had made up only the previous week in a batch of fifty for Charles Pless.

I thanked Marius and hung up. It was obvious now that whoever had murdered Pless had had access to that bottle of tablets. This particular tablet had been planted in the cabaña. Unfortunately for the murderer, Pless had not gone swimming, had in fact not changed his clothes, so that the tablet could not have been taken from his jacket and the poison tablet substituted. Now, instead of throwing suspicion away from the real culprit, the little tablet had narrowed the field down to the few people who might have been able to get hold of one of Pless's tablets.

I hurried from the hotel across the square to where I had left my car. What a fool I had been to let Harold take Amy back to the villa! It wasn't only some crazy psycho named Cooladge I feared; there were a few others, including Harold himself. I knew Amy was in danger.

I went charging up out of Monte like something they experiment with out at Los Alamos. The moon had gone and black clouds were piling in from the sea. The wind was warm but surprisingly strong, sweeping up across the hillsides and the villas, through the gorges and the lush orchards with a curious, hot presentiment. Before I got past Cap Ferrat it began to rain, slanting in, big-dropped, warm and unpleasant. The car had no top, and things began to get difficult. The narrow twisting road was dangerous even on a clear night, but I took chances now out of sheer desperation. Several times I swept past cars coming up out of Monte, running parallel to them for an instant in the vain hope of spotting whoever was at the wheel. I had no idea what make of car Nancy would be driving, let alone the stranger named Cooladge.

I was lucky enough to get through Nice without the gendarmes stopping me. On the other side of Nice I roared up to the middle corniche and in a few minutes was approaching the spot where Amy and I had dumped the body of Pless in his shiny Mercedes. The trees and the rain formed a veil over the little picnic area; it was impossible to tell whether things were as we had left them. The rain let up for an instant, then came down with sudden unbelievable fury. I was forced finally to slow down.

About half a mile beyond the picnic area I saw a car ahead, drawn up to the side of the road. It was leaning far over to the right on a flat tire, and a woman was silhouetted against the lights, waving frantically for help. I was almost past when I suddenly jammed on the brakes. A woman in a rain-soaked evening gown stumbled to the door on my right and tore it open.

"Monsieur," she began in bad French. "My car, it is disabled, and …"

"Hop in!" I said in a muffled voice.

"Oh, thank God, an American!" She put one foot up into the car and then suddenly began to draw back, but I leaned over and jammed the Luger into her stomach. "Get in here, you bitch. I haven't got time for games."

"You!" she said in despair. "What lousy luck!"

She got in, clutching her bag. Still keeping the Luger in her side, I reached over with my free hand and snatched the bag from her reluctant fingers. Inside I felt the outline of the neat little automatic I had seen at the café that afternoon.

"You're out of your way for the Pless villa."

"I was going to Cannes."

"The hell you were."

"You can take that gun out of my ribs now."

I did so, stuffing it down into the pocket next to my door, away from her reach.

"You come along with me, sweetie. Your friend Myra …"

"What about Myra?" Her voice was sharp with anxiety. "The worm has turned. She told me she was finished with you. I left her back at the Hotel de Paris."

"You're lying! Myra is the soul of loyalty."

I laughed on that one and stepped on the gas.

Above the roar of the motor she shouted, "If you've frightened Myra, by God, I'll …"

But she let that one die, realizing how empty the threat would have been at this moment. After that she didn't try to make conversation. She might have drowned if she had opened her mouth. Sheets of water were dropping from a thundering sky.

Headlights, wetly descending on us, outlined for an instant the gates of Amy's villa. I drew the car off the road and turned off the motor.

"We'll walk from here." I got the Luger back into action and prodded her out of the car. In a flash of lightning I could see that the thin dress was molded to her body like wet gauze, and her hair was plastered to her head.

"Walk up ahead of me!"

She obeyed without protest. Once she stopped quickly, uncertain of what was ahead, and I came up against her, feeling the firm curves of her body pressed against my own wetness. It was only for an instant but it sent a disturbing shock through me. The lights of the villa finally gave a dim outline to the gateposts, and we went into the little courtyard. I breathed a sigh of relief when I saw that. So far, there was only one car here, a little Renault that must be Harold's.

Nancy was playing it too docilely, too compliantly. It set the hair on my neck bristling. But I shoved the Luger into my pocket again, grabbed her arm, and pushed her along toward the side of the villa.

We reached the end of the house and, groping in the darkness of the slashing rain, I led her down around to the seaward side of the villa. Here there was a terrace which normally gave out on a wide panoramic view of the Mediterranean far below. Now there was nothing but seething darkness down there. Jutting out from the house was a covered colonnade wide enough to offer shelter from the rain. Under the colonnade the French windows opening into the living room, protected from the storm, were open on the heat. I warned Nancy with a squeeze of the elbow and pushed her in under the colonnade. It was comparatively dry here, with only an occasional gust of warm rain at our backs.

And suddenly it was as though we had come in out of the storm into the shelter of a theater. The stage was the living room of the villa, and on that stage were two characters, Amy and Harold. They were handsome enough for any production on Broadway, but only time would tell whether their methods would have pleased a

Broadway audience. Words spoken even softly came to us with surprising clarity; the acoustics were excellent. And I knew, standing outside the patch of light from the open French window, that there was little chance of our being observed. Nancy seemed suddenly as absorbed with the play taking place on that stage as I; I felt her arm going tense.

Amy had changed from her evening gown into a simple bathrobe. She was sitting huddled up in the corner of the sofa, legs beneath her, staring disconsolately into a half-finished glass of milk. Harold had removed the torn coat of his dinner clothes—perhaps to reveal his famous body—and was pacing back and forth nervously. Every once in a while he would pause and look at his watch.

In my ear Nancy whispered vehemently, "Sweet domesticity!"

After a moment or so Harold stopped his pacing and said: "Keep hold of yourself, darling."

"I'm trying to. But what's keeping him? Oh Harold, you don't think ..."

"There's no good speculating. I'm giving him another twenty minutes."

"It's like a nightmare from which I'll never wake up. What a fool I was! If only I had never called in Muldoon. If I had called you instead. We could have gotten Charles out of the house, just as Muldoon did. I know it sounds heartless—but if I had only known!"

"It came as a shock to me too, baby. And to think I never suspected!"

"Oh, darling, what can we do!"

Harold, summoned by the note of needing, came lover-like out of some movie production to soothe the heroine. He sat beside her on the sofa while she pressed up against him, not weeping, apparently beyond the tears she had so obviously shed.

Harold, reared near the source of Hollywood dialogue, rose to the occasion. "I'm sticking by you, darling, to the end."

This ominous statement seemed to calm, rather than to frighten, the heroine. Huddled together like two handsome puppies, their hands met, intertwined, parted for careless exploration.

Nancy whispered, "They charge several thousand francs for this kind of an exhibition in Nice."

"You would know," I whispered back.

"Thunder always frightened me," Amy said.

"I'm here, baby," Harold said nobly. And to make his point, his hand as proof positive against thunder, lightning and the elements in general, moved with practiced carelessness beneath the little-girl bathrobe.

"Oh darling. We mustn't—not now. It's wicked."

Harold didn't seem to think so. His intentions were becoming manfully obvious. Amy began to resist with feminine insincerity. I hadn't bargained for this. Nancy smothered a giggle and said: "When in Rome ..."

"Cut it out!"

And then, as though on cue from some hidden censor, headlights swung across the window on the other side of the sitting room, the side facing the courtyard, and faintly, above the sounds of the storm, came the complaining whine of a car. The whine ceased abruptly. The two young people untangled themselves. Harold sprang to his feet. The Frank Merriwell personality was replaced for the moment by the practiced Don Juan, ready for the emergency and quick adjustments. Amy drew the robe about herself guiltily. Love and sexual play were hurled into some convenient cubbyhole for future reference, and the fear it had momentarily extinguished, returned. Unconsciously, as though for comfort, her hand moved toward the glass of milk. Harold started moving to the hall even before the chimes of the front door began to ring through the house. I felt Nancy tense and got a firmer grip on her arm.

As a member of the audience I had the sensation of waiting now for the climax of the second-act curtain.

There was a pause, short actually, but in my mind intolerably stretched out. Then Harold appeared again in the archway to the hall. He stepped aside. A man stepped timidly across the threshold. He was middle-aged, short and thin, and altogether undistinguished. He wore an ill-fitting, old-fashioned dinner jacket that would have been more at home at some Kiwanis dinner west of Chicago. His small face was drawn and pale. He stood there, his lips trembling, unable to utter a word.

"My God!" Nancy whispered. "Cooladge!"

Even as she spoke I knew her apparent surprise was phony. She had known this man was coming here. But I was only dimly aware of Nancy at the moment; I was concentrating with a kind of cold fascination on the unlikely scene taking place in the living room of the house Charles Pless had rented for Amy Grant.

No one spoke or moved. I imagined I could hear the ticking of a clock above the storm. The man simply stood there, hopeless, destroyed, looking at the girl on the sofa. Finally she said something I couldn't hear. It brought the man into stumbling life. Somehow he got across the room, fell on his knees beside Amy and threw himself against her, his head in her lap, his arms clutching her to him in a kind of frenzied appeal for strength.

Amy, lost in some dreadful dream, began to stroke his head as though a child had come to her for help. After a moment she spoke in a voice which was completely drained of emotion.

"Pop! Oh, Pop! Why did you do it?"

SIXTEEN

It wasn't a complete shock. Some dim little stirring in my subconscious had suspected it. But seeing it, hearing it, like this, left me stunned. Nancy's arm beneath my hand hadn't even flinched. It told me that, of course, she had known. She took a step forward, but I dug my fingers into the flesh above her elbow and she came back to my side.

"I couldn't believe it, Pop," Amy was saying. "When I saw you at the end of the corridor in the Opera House I thought I was dreaming. I thought my mind was slipping. I thought, it can't be—he's thousands of miles away in Vinesville. He can't be here. He's probably having dinner tonight with Mr. and Mrs. Cross at the Iroquois Hotel. He'll be sitting there in the dining room over the three-dollar *table d'hôte* telling about the last letter from his daughter and how she loved studying art in Paris and— Oh, those lying letters! It couldn't be you, Pop, I thought."

Harold cleared his throat uncomfortably. "He needs a shot of something strong."

"Over there." Amy pointed to the commode in the corner. As Harold went to pour a shot of cognac, Amy's father managed to straighten up. He got slowly to his feet and looked dazedly around the room. Then his gaze settled blankly on Harold's athletic back.

As though guessing his thoughts, Amy said, "I love him, Pop. We would have been married. Now ..." Her hands fell into her lap. "Sit down here."

Harold, turning with the drink in his hand, said, "We'll be married all right. Nothing can stop that."

Mr. Grant managed to say in a trembling voice: "I don't understand anything anymore."

Harold handed him the brandy and Grant drank it down in one gulp. It seemed to help. Harold said with misplaced gallantry, "I'm in this with you to the end, Mr. Grant!"

I thought, he must have seen the same movie twice; but on second hearing there was something curiously touching about Harold in his new role.

"He's not well," Amy said hopefully. "Look, Harold, anyone could see that. He's not responsible ..."

"I'm tired," Grant said. "So terribly tired ..."

He put his hand to his head and closed his eyes. Harold went back to the commode to replenish the cognac. Grant downed the second drink and shuddered. Then he seemed to be shaking himself out of a trance. "Oh, Amy, I've been half crazy. It's as though right and wrong got all jumbled up. I went half out of my mind when I got the letter."

"Letter?"

"Oh, how I curse that day. At first I thought it was from you, with the Paris postmark on the envelope. Then of course I realized it wasn't your handwriting. I had just come back from a committee meeting at the lodge, and Beulah was fixing my lunch. I remember sitting there at the table with the letter in my hand, and I was thinking the magnolia had gone to seed so early. Then I opened the letter, and my world just busted apart, honey ..."

He stood up now and began to pace back and forth. "I couldn't believe it at first. It was some woman I'd never heard of. Nancy Trippe, she signed herself."

I looked at Nancy. She was staring into the room with a kind of hopeless anger. But she didn't move.

"Miss Trippe?" Amy said in a puzzled voice. "That's the woman who worked for Charles. I don't understand. What did it say?"

"It seemed to be a kind letter—from someone who was concerned about you."

"Concerned about me!"

"Yes. It said that it regretted to tell me that you had fallen into an unsavory relationship with Charles Pless, and advised my coming immediately to Paris. It also suggested that it would be wisest not to let you know I was coming and that if I got in touch with her—Miss Trippe—at an address she gave, she would be only too glad to help me straighten things out."

"But I don't understand," Amy said.

"Neither did I. But I was almost out of my mind. My little Amy—so innocent and unworldly ..."

Amy brought her hands together and closed her eyes in distaste. "All right, Pop. What happened?"

"I took a plane to Paris as soon as I could get a passport. Miss Trippe had left a message for me to meet her in the lobby of the Georges Cinq Hotel on the tenth, at three in the afternoon. That was a week ago. She was very sweet ..."

"Sweet!"

Besides me Nancy shrugged impatiently.

"I thought so, anyway. She seemed so clean-cut, and—well, so concerned about you. She told me she was up in Paris on business for the day, and explained that you were living here outside of Verens in a villa Pless had taken for you. I couldn't believe it! I couldn't believe that my little girl ..."

"Go on, Pop!"

"I was all for coming here right away and facing Pless, but Miss

Trippe convinced me that that was unwise, that Pless was a very persuasive man and had a hold over you. She advised me to come to Cannes without letting you know. She said she had some sort of a plan; she explained that it was not only you she was thinking of, but Mrs. Pless—her friend. She said that Mrs. Pless didn't suspect the truth, and that it would kill her."

I looked at Nancy. I didn't expect a blush, of course … even had I been able to detect one. But her face was an absolute blank now. My hold on her elbow was very firm indeed.

"At her advice I came to Cannes. I hated it—all those brazen women in their bikinis and smooth-talking foreigners. I stayed in that *pension*, waiting, and my hatred for Pless and what he had done to my little girl became the only thing I could think about. Sometimes Miss Trippe would visit me and she was most sympathetic and understanding. She didn't blame me at all for feeling as I did, but she said it would be bad to let you know I was here just yet. I did nothing but sit in that room and go to movies and think, until my mind seemed to hurt. Really, Amy girl, it hurt! Then I began to think of killing Pless. Oh, don't look at me like that. You don't know what I've been through …"

"Oh, Pop, if you'd only got in touch with me, I could have explained."

"Explained!" Grant said in sudden anger. "Explained! This filth? Never!"

"You were always so sure you were right!" Amy said with unexpected spirit.

The father and daughter were caught for a moment as their gazes locked in some secret understanding. Then Grant calmed down and went on in a dry monotone.

"I lay awake all night, night after night, thinking of ways to kill Pless. And then one afternoon when Miss Trippe was there—I don't know how it came up—she mentioned the fact that Pless took adrenalin tablets. Well, I'm a pharmacist. I began to have dreams of how I would substitute a cyanide tablet for one of those adrenalins. It would be fairly simple if I could get hold of the cyanide and one of those tablets Pless took. Maybe no one would ever know. Maybe they'd think he had died of a heart attack. It got so I couldn't think of anything else."

"I see." Amy's voice was listless, devoid of hope.

"I got to drinking. I couldn't stand the thinking and the dreams. I started drinking and you know, Amy, I never drank much; one drink was always too much for me. I started hanging out in the bars. I would talk to people about how I planned to kill Pless. It wasn't real; it was like telling a movie plot about someone else. I would tell complete strangers. People seemed to think it was funny … and then this strange thing happened …"

"What?"

"I'd been out drinking. I came back to the room, and there on the bedside table was a bottle with two adrenalin pills. Beside it a small package. It contained cyanide."

"My God!" Harold said.

Nancy moved back against me, then recoiled as though the contact had given her a shock.

Grant said: "I don't know who … I was drunk, not in my right mind. I had some funny idea that it was an act of fate, almost supernatural. There they were, the ingredients of my dreams, waiting and ready. I—I prepared the cyanide tablet. When it was finished I went out to an all-night bar and drank some more. Then I went back to the room and hid the poison tablet in my suitcase. I took the remnants of the cyanide down to the harbor and threw it into the water. I was drunk, but calm. I felt the way you feel when you've left church. I felt as though all I had done was right and good."

"When was this?"

"It was dawn, the day before yesterday. I went back to the *pension* and fell into a deep sleep. I was awakened about noon by a knocking at the door. Miss Trippe was there to see me."

"She came right to your room?"

"Oh yes. The woman who runs the *pension*—an English woman— is out most afternoons."

"What did Miss Trippe want?" Amy asked.

"She sat and talked for some time. She seemed nervous and upset. She said that perhaps she had made a mistake, but then in the next breath she would say to forget what she said, that she must have time to think. Then she asked me to go with her to a cocktail party at Antibes. … I felt sorry for her … She made me think of you. So— well, American, and innocent."

Harold managed a laugh. Amy gave him a warning look. Besides me, Nancy sighed deeply.

"What happened at the party?"

"Once I got drunk the cyanide pill came back into my mind. It was funny … when I was talking to Miss Trippe—sober, and with a raging headache—the pill had gone completely out of my mind. But drunk again, I couldn't stop the words. It was horrible. I'd say to myself: Be careful, shut up. But the words kept spilling out. I told people about the cyanide tablet. I boasted about it."

"Who did you tell?" Harold asked him.

"Lots of people. I don't remember them all. You were there. Maybe I told you."

Harold avoided Amy's eyes. "Who else?"

"Some middle-aged woman who wrote novels."

"Alva!"

"I think her first name was Alva; I couldn't be certain. Then I talked to some woman—very quiet and timid, and quite sympathetic. Brown hair, pale green eyes. Her hands kept fluttering like ZaSu Pitts's."

"Mrs. Pless!" Harold said.

Mr. Grant's mouth fell open. "Mrs. Pless? His wife?"

"Yes, Pop," Amy said quietly.

"My God, what she must have thought. She never let on. I told her I had a pill and that I intended to kill her husband. I was drunk, and out of my mind again."

"Did you tell Miss Trippe the pill was in your room at the *pension?*"

"Yes, but I don't think she believed me. No one seems to believe me. And maybe they were right, in a way. Once I had made up the pill, once I had the means to kill Pless, once I could talk about it … It's funny, but to me it's almost as though I had already done it. I didn't need to do it now … I can't explain."

"Go on." There was a rising note of excitement in Amy's voice that matched my own feelings.

"After I left the party I took a bus into Cannes. I went to a bar. I was alone now and I couldn't think straight. I had a funny feeling of something gone wrong, of something I should straighten out—a feeling of apprehension and fear. I thought of taking a taxi out here and confronting you, Amy, but then I lost my nerve. I thought of going straight to Pless, but I didn't. I was like a person in a dream whose feet are stuck in mud. I tried to read that English language paper, the one about what people are doing along the Riviera. I read about the performance at the Opera House, and I saw Pless's name on the list of patrons. I had some crazy idea that if I could get a ticket, if I could approach Pless without his knowing who I was, if I could humiliate him in public … Anyway I finally went back to my *pension*. The landlady was out, and so were the rest of the guests. I went to my room. I thought, I've got to get rid of that tablet of poison before it destroys me. I've got to wake up from this nightmare. I went to the closet and dragged out my suitcase—and the pill was gone!"

In the silence a gust of wind whipped around our legs. Nancy's arm was limp in my hand. I could almost feel bravado seeping out of her body.

Amy leaned forward. "Pop—are you telling the truth?"

"The truth? Why wouldn't I? I'm willing to tell Pless when he comes in—if he comes here tonight!"

"What!" Amy jumped to her feet. Hope had flooded back into her face. "You don't know about Charles?"

"Know what?"

"Pop, listen to me. Have you any idea who took that tablet?"

"None. I woke up about noon worried about it; I realized I might get into trouble. I decided to check out of the *pension* and go to Monte. I just checked my bag at the railroad station there. My landlady had got me a ticket to the Opera House, and I thought I might see Pless there. Then I was planning to come to you."

"Did you stay in Monte?"

"No. I got there at four, so I had five hours to waste. I took the bus back to Verens."

"Why?"

"I thought I might be able to find Miss Trippe, and that she would tell me what to do. I couldn't find her anywhere. I hung around the entrance of the Bellevue Hotel. I knew she often went there in the afternoons. I saw the woman called Alva, but she didn't see me. And I saw that woman you now tell me is Mrs. Pless."

"Where?"

"She came out of the hairdresser's about six-thirty—the hairdresser next to the Bellevue. She looked up and down the street as though looking for someone, and then she went into the gift shop next to the hairdresser's. She came out in a few minutes. Whoever she was expecting didn't show up; she seemed impatient and nervous. After a while she went across the street to the public beach, and I didn't see her again."

"And Miss Trippe?"

"She finally came along. She stopped in front of the hairdresser's and went in; then she came out and looked up and down. Then she started back toward her car. I went up to her; she seemed upset to see me. She told me to go back to the *pension* and wait—that she might call me later. I told her about the missing pill. She got terribly upset. She told me to keep quiet about it, and when she heard I had a ticket to the Opera House she said she would talk to me about it there, that at the moment she was in a terrible hurry. She drove off."

"Then what did you do?"

"I went back to Monte. I sat on a bench on the promenade and slept for a while. When I woke it was late, and the performance had already begun at the Opera. I went there, and then … You know the rest. I saw you in the upper hall—or rather I first saw this young man here having a violent argument with another man."

"That was Black," Harold said calmly, "before I took him down the hall and knocked him down. Before I got hold of the envelope with Alva's letters. The little bastard was trying to blackmail me about something. Then I came back down the hall and there you were talking to Amy."

Grant turned to his daughter. "I've been crazy, baby. I've caused a lot of trouble, but thank God I've told the truth before it was too late. Maybe someone really intends to use that pill on Pless. You can't talk ..."

Amy looked away. "It's possible," she said faintly.

"Amy. Amy, my little girl. What's happened to us? Why can't it be as it used to be when we were always so happy?"

"I was never happy, Pop," Amy said with weary cruelty.

"Mr. Grant—" Harold broke off. Now all the characters on the stage became suddenly tense. At first I didn't know why. Then, faintly, I heard the sound of a motor out in the courtyard.

No one on the stage spoke. Although the motives for fear might have been different in each case, they were bound together by it like soldiers in some lost battalion.

Harold was the first to come out of the trance. "The door ..." he began.

But he got no further. Someone had appeared in the archway to the hall—someone carrying a gun, someone mild and pale and yet taut with some neurasthenic emotion.

"I'll kill the first one of you who moves," Myra Pless said in a calm voice.

SEVENTEEN

The memory of thunder hung in the air, and then suddenly the rain ceased. I had the Luger in Nancy's ribs again. It was vitally necessary now. She was trembling like a race horse at the starting line. I didn't want any false breaks.

"Nancy sent me," Myra Pless said in the same voice of unearthly calm. "Nancy made me come here. They always tell me what to do. Nancy sent me for the envelope."

"The envelope?" Harold stammered.

"Yes, Mr. Jones. I saw you. It was like watching a play. I saw you fighting with Ballentine Black. It was at the intermission in the Opera House, up in the corridor behind the boxes. Mr. Black was demanding money from you in exchange for what was in that envelope. Instead, you knocked him down and took away the envelope and left. Now I want the envelope. You know why. You know what's in it."

The color rose to Harold's face. "Well—there are some letters belonging to Alva Creighton. I knew Black was trying to blackmail Alva. As a friend of hers, I felt it was my duty to ..."

Myra Pless laughed gently. "I don't care about the letters. I care about what you really care about. It's strange my holding this gun—

it belonged to poor Charles. He had it in the commode beside his bed. It's absurd my pointing a gun at anyone. Everyone knows I'm a harmless—" She hesitated and then spat out the words—"Utterly useless person!"

"Mrs. Pless—"

"But I can use a gun. My father always had a gun. My father—" She turned a mild light-blue gaze on Mr. Grant, who was standing close to Amy. "Father. This is your father, Miss Grant. I always knew that. I don't like you, Miss Grant, because you have humiliated me like the others. But I can sympathize with you for having a father. My father was a monster."

Nancy made the beginning of a movement forward, but a sharp jab of the automatic brought her back. Watching Myra Pless, so calm and detached and utterly unreal, I realized finally that the woman was completely mad.

Now she was saying, "I want the will!"

Amy found her voice. "Mrs. Pless, I knew that Charles made a new will two days ago—he told me about it. Believe me, I didn't want him to do it."

"All of you lie to me—Charles, Nancy, everyone. Imagine cutting me down to one third and leaving you the rest. Imagine! My money. It was my money—mine in the beginning, and mine now. After all, it's all I have left—money. I must destroy that will. You will admit it's only fair. I will destroy the will; and then the one he made earlier in New York leaves everything to me—everything!"

Harold began fighting for time. "Mrs. Pless, if that will was in your husband's safe before Black got hold of it, why didn't you destroy it yourself earlier this evening?"

"That's very simple, Mr. Jones. I didn't dare destroy it until I was absolutely certain Charles was dead. After all, it wouldn't have been easy to explain what had happened to him if by some chance he hadn't taken his—adrenalin tablet. I wasn't certain that Charles was really dead until Mr. Muldoon came to my house. Then it was too late."

"Certain?" Amy repeated in childish horror. "You mean you thought that Charles might die this evening?"

"Naturally. I was the one who put the cyanide tablet in his coat pocket this morning before he left the house."

The night, bereft of the sound of rain, was ominously still. There was only the lethargic drip of water from the eaves and the whisper of a long, drawn-out sigh from Nancy beside me. She fell back against me, all the tension apparently gone.

"I shouldn't have said that," Myra said calmly in the shocked silence. "I believe that might be considered incriminating! But you can't prove it. And after all, if no one ever knew, no one would know how really clever I am. I'm not what Charles and Nancy say. I'm not a fool!"

"You planned to kill your husband all along?" Amy whispered.

"No. Not really. Nancy imported your father with some idea of breaking up Charles's liaison with you. Then she decided to hold back for what she called strategic reasons. Nancy is always using phrases like that. But Mr. Grant got out of hand. He is a pharmacist, and he began talking wildly about poison, and he put ideas in my head. I saw at last how to get rid of my persecutors!"

"Persecutors!"

"Nancy and Charles. They used me. Destroyed me. I'm destroyed, but so is Nancy—at last. Off with terrible people like that May Bracken. If it wasn't May Bracken, it was someone else. She didn't love me, not at all. She cheated and warped and twisted and destroyed and now—now—" Her voice began to rise hysterically. "I'm surprised she isn't here herself to get that will. She still thinks I'll share the money with her. She doesn't know that she'll die on the gallows, or whatever they use in this country. She doesn't know she'll be hanged as a murderess! I've fixed both of them!"

"My God!" Harold said.

"They thought they were so clever! Laughing at me, taking my money, flattering me, locking me away from life! I won't have it. I simply won't have it! That's what I said. I bought the cyanide in Nice, and I signed Nancy's name on the register. I put it in Mr. Grant's room, and when I realized he wouldn't do what I hoped he would, I went to his room and got the cyanide tablet myself, and this morning I put it in Charles's pocket. I knew he was coming here to see you, Miss Grant, this afternoon, and I hoped it would happen then. And the knife—" She gave a soft laugh.

"The knife?" Amy said softly.

"The one I used to kill Ballentine Black. I led him into the sitting room of the box at the Opera House after Mr. Jones had left. I pretended I heard a noise, and he turned. It's amazing how easily the knife slipped into his back. He suspected too much."

"But the knife?"

"It was Nancy's. Her face went white when she saw it sticking in his back. It was a Damascus knife that Charles had given her as a letter opener last Christmas. I thought of everything! Nancy persuaded Mr. Grant to come here—everyone will think they did it between them. Nancy's knife in Black's back ... Really, it's almost funny ..."

She broke off. "Even Mr. Muldoon—I fooled him. I put a real adrenalin tablet in Charles's cabaña to put people off. And I walked along the beach in the dark when I happened to see him go down to the Bellevue Beach. I walked down from the public beach and I saw him with that girl in the cabaña. Disgusting! And I waited. The beach rake had sharp prongs, but I missed. But he isn't dangerous now, because everyone will think Nancy did it. I'll laugh … Oh, how I will laugh!"

Harold and Amy exchanged frightened glances.

Mrs. Pless said, "The envelope, if you please."

Harold moved stiffly to the commode and took up the envelope and turned back to her.

"Bring it here. I'm rather tired. It's strange how tired I get. I must go home and get some sleep. The police will probably question me, and I must think up clever answers!"

Harold walked toward her with outstretched hand. He was halfway to her when Nancy suddenly broke away. Before I could stop her she rushed into the room.

"Myra, you crazy bitch!"

If she had used other words the result might have been different. As it was, they were Nancy's last words on this earth.

She stood there for a fraction of a second, her mouth open. The little round hole in the center of her forehead looked like a caste mark. Then she toppled forward on the rug, falling like a waxen figure.

I shouted, but Mr. Grant paid no attention. He crouched for a moment in front of his daughter, then, straightening up, began to inch toward Mrs. Pless. Out of the corner of her eye she saw the movement and wheeled around.

"All of you!" she shouted, and fired again.

The little man crumpled up, just as I grabbed Myra Pless from behind and forced the gun from her hand.

It took three of us to subdue the woman. I knew even as she started screaming that her screaming would go on and on through the white empty corridors of madness.

We got her to the sofa and Harold held her down. Amy was on the floor beside her father. The bullet had ripped a hole in the little man's chest, and he had died almost instantly. Amy wasn't crying. She simply hadn't realized what had happened.

Before I went to the phone to call the police, I picked up the manila envelope from the table and extracted Alva's letters from it. I thought I might as well earn the three thousand.

EIGHTEEN

"My dear," Alva Creighton said, "It must have been like the last scene of Hamlet—the carnage, I mean."

"Four victims in one day isn't too bad."

We sat in wicker chairs on the stern deck bar of the ship as it glided out of the harbor. It was three weeks after the bloody evening at Amy Grant's villa.

"I find," Alva said, "that I can take the Riviera only in small doses. I'll be glad to be back in New York."

"It's been a dull season."

"Frightfully. Except, of course, for all that dreary business of the murders. Tell me—is it true that Mrs. Pless has been committed to a mental institution?"

"Quite true. No messy trial. No more bad publicity—at least not too much more. *Toujours gai!*"

"It's absolutely impossible to think of that Pless woman as a psychopathic murderess. Such a mousy little thing. Well, I suppose Pless and that Trippe woman deserved what they got. And I am eternally grateful to you for getting back my letters. So clever of you to have slipped them into your pocket before the police arrived."

"I wasn't any too soon. Even before we had a chance to telephone them, after Mrs. Pless had fired her last shot of the day, they were bursting through the doors. Pless's body had been discovered in his car, and the police, knowing more of Pless's love life than we had suspected, made a beeline for Amy Grant's villa."

The ship was swinging out into the open sea. Far back of us I could make out the shadow of the villa Pless had taken out on Cap d'Antibes. Suddenly I had a vivid picture in my mind of Myra Pless as she must have been during those early summer days, sitting alone in the vast, chilly villa, storing up her hatred and revenge, pallid, silently compliant, as she brought death a little closer.

"And that Grant girl!" Alva said. "Disgraceful. Waiter, bring me another champagne cocktail."

"Disgraceful?"

"Marrying that ridiculous lifeguard only two days after they buried her father!"

"I suppose she was free at last."

"Whatever that means! But really, can you imagine? She comes into two-thirds of Pless's estate. He must have been mad making that will, when he knew she was carrying on with Harold. Over a million, I'm told."

"Enough to set them up in housekeeping."

"They say Harold is already sporting a Mercedes."

"It was Pless's. They got it from the estate. They're going to live very quietly in a twenty-two-room villa over in San Tropez."

"I guess I'm just old-fashioned. What anyone could ever see in that muscle-bound Harold Jones! Impossible!"

At that precise moment a dark young man in a too-tight linen suit came up to our table.

"Oh, Mr. Muldoon," Alva gushed: "You must meet Pepe Gorgo—a very talented young actor. He has already played a small part in *Ben Hur*, made in Rome. I'm going to see that he meets the right people in Hollywood. I believe talent should always be encouraged. Pepe comes of one of the very oldest and most distinguished Venetian families."

I figured that the old and distinguished family had been poling gondolas for several generations. I got up. "I'll leave you two to discuss art."

I left the café and walked down the promenade deck. I looked back for one last look at the Riviera. The candy-box resorts, tucked in their beautiful bays, were as unreal as faded postcards. Was this all I would have of my years in Europe—a tinseled memory fading off into the sunlight? I'd been a self-imposed exile for too long, I thought. Now I wanted a cabin on the Maine coast, a dog, books, a fire roaring in a fireplace, and no one around for miles and miles.

Still caught in this pleasant dream, I went down to my cabin. The door was partly open. I pushed it in. The blonde Hungarian with whom I had discussed certain international matters in her cabaña at the Bellevue beach was lying on my bed clad in nylon stockings.

"I thought you'd never be coming," she said.

"How the hell—"

"I found your name on the list. I give to the steward the tip. *C'est bien!*"

"What are you doing on this ship?"

"I am having the honeymoon!"

"What!"

"The one Marius arranged for. The American came to Cannes to get me. He likes what he get. I ..." She shrugged. "Ah, well, it is taking me to America, anyway. And look—nylon stockings from New York! It is incredible!"

"And your husband?"

"In the bar drinking beer! We will not be discussing unpleasant things, I hope."

"You're so right!"

I shut the door behind me.

"I never forget a friend," she said.

"I'm very grateful," I answered politely.

The Riviera moved one way, Maine moved another, both away and out of time. The present was quite sufficient.

THE END

Death's Lovely Mask
By John Flagg

ONE

Hirem came into my bedroom at Bertoltotti's Palace Hotel, noon as announced in his cable, slight, sallow, mild and—on the face of it—as unprepossessing and beat-up as Arthur Miller's salesman waiting for death. He found me with a bump on my head and a disposition that could have been used to kill rats.

"Hung up again, Muldoon?" he said.

"The hell I am! Was it one of your goons who left me with a head last night?"

"Certainly not!" He gave a bilious look at the morning sun streaming over the bay of Naples. "Too much scenery," he said wearily. He sighed and sat with his back to one of the world's more spectacular views.

"Well?"

"First your rotten cable. I picked it up at the hotel desk about six last evening. It had been opened. The clerk said it had been given 'by mistake' to another American … a Mr. Wright. No Wright registered here."

Hirem permitted himself a thin smile. "Good."

"So it was bait! You hoped my room would be frisked and that I'd be conked on the head!"

"I dislike violence." But Hirem seemed damned pleased with himself.

It is not easy to explain Hirem and my relations with him, without getting into the classified field. He and his little group are so "Top Secret" that they have been almost erased from the memory of man. It's been said that should an investigation-happy Senate committee decide to get on its tail, it would have to open up Hirem's head and spread it out across one of those long wide tables and even then the membranes exposed would be in code. Exaggerated, perhaps, but not much. During the years since the end of World War Two, Hirem had called me in occasionally for some particularly dirty job he seemed to feel I could handle. We'd been together in OSS during that long-ago war and maybe his memory had added glamor to my tarnished name. Needless to say, his name is not actually Hirem or anything like it.

"You're wasting a lot of valuable time with me, Hirem," I said uneasily.

"In what way?"

"I'm not open for any jobs. Matter of fact I'm sailing tomorrow night on the *Cristoforo Colombo* for the States."

"Really?"

"Really! I'm fed up with Europe to here! I've got my eye on a cabin on the Maine coast and the smell of pine instead of Chanel Number

Five."

"Too bad."

"Listen here, Hirem—"

"Better cancel your passage."

"I have no intention of doing that."

"I believe," he said, eyes bland and innocent, "I believe that you have been able to stash about five thousand away in the Chemical National Bank of New York. What is called, with the usual vulgarity of your class, a nest egg!"

"So?"

"Certain friends of mine in the Treasury Department are taking a morbid interest in your taxes for the years '55 and '56. It would be a shame if these sordid tendencies developed into outright sadism. Why, you might never get your fanny on that nest egg to hatch it!"

"You sonofabitch!"

"That," he said calmly, "is one of those accusations very difficult to prove. Besides, save your adrenalin. You may need every drop of it. As for my T-Men pals, they are willing to listen to reason *after* you finish what I have in mind for you."

"Sweet blackmail!"

"And more to the point, you will be able to add about eight grand to that touching nest egg."

That brought me up a little. "Eight thousand? For what?"

"Two weeks pleasant living. A few questions, a few answers—nothing strenuous."

"I've heard that before. The last time I did two weeks of 'pleasant living' for you boys I was shot at four times, involved in two killings, an embarrassing pregnancy, adultery on a mass basis and several unmentionable crimes against nature. 'Pleasant living' indeed."

"Sit down, Hart."

Hirem leaned back and closed his eyes. I defied him, feeling uncomfortably like a stubborn school boy, refusing to sit but maintaining my position by the window. I stood there letting my morning indignation boil and seethe for a minute or so. The bump on my head didn't help. I began to develop an incipient case of self-pity. Here, just twenty-eight hours from sailing time Hirem was in my life again, dragging me back to what I hoped I had escaped for good. But watching him sitting there like a half-empty bag of potatoes, seeming to be a tired Joe with an advanced case of anemia, I knew I was beaten before even the tentative steps of running. Hirem could play rough when you tried to monkey-wrench his little plots and plans. No idealist, he was nevertheless dedicated, and like most of his kind, ruthless in the pursuit of his objective. Abstract denunciation of the "ends justifying the means" was something for political speeches and the voters as far as Hirem was concerned. The fact that he didn't dislike me was not going to help me out of this one.

I turned my back on him. Below, Naples fell away into the semicircle of the great bay; the morning was cloudless. Floating away in the distance like a shimmering mirage was the island of Capri and off to the south I could see the parchment-like cone of Vesuvius. It was a scene to delight the heart of any tourist, but not mine. Since the end of World War Two I'd stayed on in Europe watching—with what I told myself was cynical indifference—the world falling apart. I'd been wrapped up in dirty deals for dirty squares and shaky governments, out for hire to anything this side of the Iron Curtain and to anyone who could come up with a reasonable price. Now, I'd had too many years of Cops-and-Robbers for a fast buck that usually ended up on a roulette table anyway or in the beaded bag of some deluxe easy-laying hen. Causes advertised as noble, with ignoble ends, back-alley alliances from Paris to Cairo and back again, all hopped, skipped and jumped into a crazy pattern of my past ten years and I wanted out, preferably in some rockbound part of Maine with the sting of a November sea in my kisser.

But the moment of rueful nostalgia was brief. Hirem was not merely exercising his choppers for an expense account two-day vacation in Naples-by-the-Sea. He was quite capable of following through on that Treasury Department deal. He had me where it hurt. As a realist my course was clear; concentrate on whatever pretty little job he had on his Machiavellian mind and, of course, on an additional eight thousand to my nest egg.

During this short period of meditation, Hirem remained as calm as a black widow centered in the web, waiting for the short dash out to the entangled fly.

I turned, sat, and lit a cigarette. "All right, Hirem. Two weeks. No more."

"Good."

"Two thousand in advance. The rest, two weeks from today, deposited to my account at the New York Chemical Bank."

"Possible."

"Well then … to begin … why me?"

"Among other things … a matter of *entrée*."

"*Entrée?*"

He looked mildly at the ceiling, "*Entrée* has certain vulgar but unavoidable connotations. Charming young woman, name of Linda Pawling. Room 301 on the floor above."

I sat up straight. It was too late by some years and much experience for me to blush but I came damn close.

"Linda! What's she got to do with this deal?"

"That's one of the things we want you to find out. Maybe nothing. What do you know about her?"

I got interested in the lighted end of my cigarette. "Very little. I met Mrs. Pawling in the hotel bar two weeks ago. It seems she is a refugee from a house party on Capri. She found herself unable to meet certain unorthodox demands of her hostess. She awaits a husband. I've seen a little something of her …"

"Ah yes. We won't discuss what constitutes 'a little something' except perhaps to say that the management might be justified in an extra charge for wear and tear on the mattress."

"It's just one of those things. Husband arrives tomorrow; 'Parting is such sweet sorrow …' That's the end of it."

"No. That's only the beginning."

I groaned, "Not Linda."

"It seems," Hirem went on calmly, "that the Pawlings leave tomorrow night for Venice. By a curious coincidence it seems also that you have a sudden piercing desire to see the Grand Canal once again before you die."

"All right, Hirem," I said apprehensively, "give it to me."

He began to show stirrings of some sort of sluggish enjoyment.

"I've got about two pounds of documents for you to peruse tonight, after your more prosaic duties, of course. But in skeleton form, and simply to confuse you, here are some questions: You've heard of young Prince Sir-el-Donrd of Donrd-Arabia?"

"Now and again. He's the boy the New York tabloids call *Ali.*"

"Right. Twenty. Handsome. In his last year of graduate work at Yale."

"Didn't I read some crap about his love for rock and roll?"

"Yes. Among other manifestations of his admiration for all things democratic."

"That must please the State Department."

"On the face of it, you might think so. Ali is the favorite son of the old king Donrd … the old king is very ill … a secret well kept … and it looks as though Ali may be sitting on the throne sooner than anyone could have suspected."

"Fine."

Hirem sighed, "If only life were that simple."

"Meaning?"

"We wanted the young prince on our side, of course, but I'm afraid it has not been convenient to have him embrace all things democratic in one youthful swallow."

"Why not?"

"Donrd-Arabia is, as you know, a country existing in a feudal state. If the young prince returns and upsets the applecart too quickly, we are afraid all hell will break loose in that section of the world again."

"You mean democracy is all right … in its place."

"Something like that. The old Arab chieftains are beginning to grumble at the rumors emanating from New York … the oil interests are beginning to get skittish."

"Oil interests," I said, perking up. "That would be—"

"The German-American Oil Company. Jointly controlled by American and German capital. More German than American. They have had complete control over the vast oil reserves in the Donrd-Arabia desert for the past ten years. Too much democracy might vote them out … before it was quite convenient to our government."

"I begin to see the irony in the situation."

"There's worse to follow. Love has entered the picture in a most embarrassing and dangerous manner."

"*Toujours* et cetera. How could the kid's love life affect our foreign policy?"

"The girl in question is a student at Barnard College in New York."

"Our government prefers Wellesley?"

"Her name is Judith Garnter."

"So?"

"So … Judith's father is a senator in the Knesset … the Israeli Senate!"

"Wowie!"

"Exactly. I think you can see the implications."

"Not until I know how serious this love affair is."

"As serious as it can get! Both kids are about to defy parental wrath, nationalistic prejudices and international horrified screams of terror from the embassies of several countries."

"What about the old king?"

"He doesn't know yet and is too sick to be told. He's already indicated Ali as his heir and nothing apparently will change it. Many interested parties have tried to warn Ali of the inherent danger if he persists in his plan to marry Judith. The kid just says, 'It's a free world, isn't it?'"

"What am I supposed to do about it?"

"Well, Hart, as you can imagine, our government finds itself in a helluva spot. We can't go on record as opposing the course of young love or Ali's idealistic dreams of a democracy overnight in his country. On the other hand, if he goes through with it, the whole Arab world will boil over—everything will happen too quickly for Washington's position—it upsets a lot of carefully laid plans."

"Mice and men and the State Department. But where does Venice fit into the picture?"

"Ali is on vacation from Yale. He's visiting an American woman in

Venice by the name of Baring. Mrs. Baring, according to rumor, is only too willing to act as Cupid. We suspect Judith is about to turn up in Venice."

"You didn't call me in to talk reason to a lovesick kid."

"No. It's this way, Hart. The Russians don't like Ali and his feelings for the U.S. The Arab League doesn't like him. German-American Oil doesn't want any part of him. It's not only a question of preventing this marriage—a helluva lot of people are too goddamned interested in getting Ali out of the way. In a few words, the kid is a sitting duck."

"So? What do you want from me?"

"There are several questionable characters converging on Venice at this moment. We want you to find out what they are really up to."

"Where does Linda Pawling fit into all this?"

"We don't know for certain. We can't seem to get much on her past. But her husband is a troubleshooter for German-American Oil and they are both headed for Venice."

I got up, crushed out my cigarette and walked to the window.

"Begin with Mrs. Pawling," Hirem said behind me.

"Pretty."

"It's a little late, Muldoon, to bring up aesthetic values. Pretty or not—it's real!"

I stood there with my back to him, looking out across the great bay. Far on the horizon a ship was making a long white thread on the blue sea, heading in toward Naples. Was it the ship I would not be taking?

Finally I said, "I guess Ali isn't the only sitting duck."

"I don't know what you mean."

I turned.

"You know goddamn well what I mean, Hirem. You sent that cablegram and announced your arrival with bugles. I was lucky to get out of the first encounter with only a bump on the head. You're figuring that when they begin to take potshots at me you'll have your man ... or men ... or woman ... or women! You're dangling me in their faces like bait!"

"Something like that," he said calmly. "We'd hate to lose you."

"You're a considerate bastard!"

"You've taken bigger risks for eight thousand dollars. You've only run out of eight of your nine lives. We're betting on that ninth!"

I walked to the bureau, took hold of the brandy bottle, and helped myself to a stiff one. Oddly enough my anger had evaporated and I began to feel the old insidious excitement that creeps up on me before a big job. But I had my guilt feelings about Linda Pawling to drown. In a moment I would have to sit down with Hirem and get to the heart of the matter. I lifted my glass to him.

"For love of country, kiss and tell! Here's to the stink of it, Hirem, and the poor goddamn deluded sitting ducks!"

TWO

We had played house for two and a half weeks—a good-natured mamma and a nervous papa—but now, for her, unaware that Hirem was pulling the strings, the game was over.

"Kiss-off time, sweetie," she said. "He arrives by air early in the A.M. We leave for Venice on the afternoon express."

"How romantic."

"He writes about a second honeymoon. The first was ghastly enough. It's like compounding a disaster!"

"I was beginning to hope you had invented him."

"I wish …" She shrugged, adjusted her brassiere before the mirror, sighed. "He's big; he's nasty; he's jealous!"

Linda was under thirty, walking into some kind of personal despair, but still only on the edge of it with most of her youth intact, a quip on her lips, and a good deal of animal energy which, under certain circumstances had proved highly satisfactory. She carried her natural assets in a manner that suggested past experience in the theater or in professional modeling. Until now she had never mentioned her past, her legal entanglements, her emotional problems or her financial state. Nor had I. Our particular form of therapy had not included total recall. She dressed well and spoke well without thinking of the words ahead of time, and she had been around—maybe for the third or fourth time.

Outside the French windows, on the fancy ironwork of the balcony, a fat pigeon perched, staring in at us with lethargic indifference. Beyond the pigeon was a vast empty orange space where the last light of day hung over the turbulent city and the majestic bay. I knew that if I propped myself up on one elbow, I would see the twin domes of a cathedral directly below the hotel and that they would be copper-green in the dying sunlight. In the past two and a half weeks this hotel room had become for me something more than the setting for a classical wrestling match, something more, but of course, not enough. Hirem had managed, almost, to spoil whatever good there had been in it for me. However urgent or even noble the cause, I would have to go into this one like a heel.

Linda fished a cigarette from a pack on the bureau top and lit up. She didn't turn. She faced the mirror with an almost comic, angry appraisal which included both of our reflections.

"His ego. I've always protected it. I never sleep with any of his friends. Sometimes it's made the process of selection difficult."

"You mean he chooses not to know what he doesn't actually see?"

"Not exactly. It's more unsavory. He enjoys knowing it's happened somewhere with someone and he enjoys his own peculiar jealousy. Among other things which I don't care to mention."

"Sounds sweet."

"Oh it is! He's a helluva guy with the guys. Talks up a hearty storm on the subjects of sail-fishing, boxing, preventative war, bed jokes. Basso profundo and bourbon. Still … Still, there are reasons."

"Money?"

She regarded her own eyes disapprovingly.

"I'm not allergic to money. But as for him, not entirely. And there is something …" She hesitated. "He grew up the wrong way."

"The wrong way?"

"He learned to scratch for his own early. It's all a 'deal', you know. He likes being on the 'hep' side in a world where you're either 'hep' or 'square.' He was plenty 'hep' when he was a supply officer in the Army of Occupation in Germany. He managed to supply himself very well." She caught herself up and said in a different voice, "I'm essentially immoral, I guess. I care some, but not enough. My father was a teacher. Irrelevant."

"Maybe not irrelevant."

She didn't laugh, "Don't try to begin to substitute. I don't need another father." There was something oddly, unexpectedly intense in her manner.

"I'd like to know you better," I said and meant it, but in meaning it, was acutely aware of duplicity.

Her eyes lit up in a manner I'd found curiously exciting even in the bantering moments of our first meeting. "Look, Hart," she said, "I ask for bad things and I'm seldom disappointed. I've learned to lie, steal and cheat and darling, I'm really a case for a head doctor. Better you don't know me better." She turned and looked me in the eye.

"Come clean, Hart. It's been good for you only because there was an insurance policy with it. Your steamship ticket back to the States and the arrival of a husband. No weeping female farewells … No regrets."

"News for you. I threw away my insurance policy. I've turned the steamship ticket in!"

The vast orange space was turning into purple. Through the sudden tension in the room, the slow-gathering evening sounds of the city floated up to us, a caressing murmur that would rise with the dark hours into a crescendo of raucous sensual sound. Linda was standing very still in the twilight.

"Hart, you're joking."

"No."

"You don't want anything else any more than I do."

"You're wrong. I'm stubborn."

"But no fool." She began to talk swiftly, now, running away from the implications. "What I know about you is practically nil but I do know you're no fool. I know that you're consoling and that you're damned attractive, especially lying there in a brass bed, shameless in white shorts. I know you have an absurd name, Hart Muldoon. And I know I've become very fond of that name, Hart Muldoon. But ..."

"But?"

"You didn't cancel your passage back because ... I mean ... if I could believe—oh, damn it, I mean ... you must know we've reached the end of the line."

"At the end of the line you can still go on by foot. The going may be rough, but it can also be damned exciting."

"Jungle life has no appeal for me."

I said something more or less appropriate to the situation but she didn't laugh. I added, "I'm coming to Venice."

She stood there in front of the bureau, suddenly tense and serious in a way I had never seen.

"You're asking for something you haven't bargained for."

"For example?"

"It's different with you. And it's dangerous because it's different. I might forget to laugh."

"So might I."

That brought her to the bed, taut, nervous and urgent. She sat beside me and grasped my hand. "If you're lying, Hart ... There's something I'm in I can't get out of yet. I can't talk about it now. Maybe later in Venice."

"Why talk at all?"

I brought her down close to me.

"No!"

"Linda."

"Say it first!"

"Now, baby, don't fight."

"Say it, goddamn it."

"I love you," I said.

She stopped fighting then. Full of fresh desire and self-hatred I drew her close. After a bit the image of Iago-like Hirem drifted from my mind. My fingers touched her face. Even in the infinite lostness of the moment I felt a stab of regret and pity; there were tears on her cheek.

THREE

Now, in September, Venice had purged herself of summer's tourists; stolid Bavarians, Ohioans, Dutch, and Norwegians had returned to their homelands with photographs of San Marco for their albums, and it was possible once again to fight one's way into the offices of Cook's and the American Express. The plush International Set (meaning anything from a Hollywood producer to tattered royalty) had taken over the glittering village on the Grand Canal. I managed to snatch a room high up under the roof of the Danelli and then waited around the hotel's elegant little bar for Freddie Gorden to show. I knew I would not have to wait long; it was inevitable that, in September, Freddie would appear in the Danelli sooner or later. I was lucky. It was sooner.

I ordered him a drink. As usual he made you feel he was doing you a favor by accepting—and in a way he was. Freddie was unique. The fourth son of a British Earl, he slipped his "honorable" on and off to suit the movie stars, multi-millionaires and dubious social climbers in whose entourage he moved from one European resort to another with the seasons. He was a master of scandalous libel, an expert in such serious subjects as women's fashions (with a percentage hookup to the top couturieres) music hot and long-hair, the theater of Paris and London, modern art, sexual habits, the home life of wandering dispossessed royalties, restaurants, the juiciest items from various legations and the latest gaffes of his pet climber. A satirist without the energy to write it out on paper, he took perverse pride in his position as one of the continent's best advertised and most successful parasites. He was slim, fortyish and baleful, apparently floating somehow sober in a constant aura of Scotch, wearing an inexpensive linen suit, a mournful black necktie, and an expression of perpetual innocent surprise.

"I've run into you in some peculiar places, Muldoon," he said airily, "and I know you're not here because Venice is chic in September. Still," and then with a wave of the hand, "it is my considered belief that the gondola deserves serious study by the anthropologists. Venice regains its popularity in the fashionable world according to the rise and fall of certain sexual tastes."

"There are easier explanations. The excellent beach at the Lido for example."

"Nonsense. The beach was always there. It's simply that the direct assault which usually follows a war has given way to more subtle action."

"Where are you staying, Freddie?"

"If you mean who is paying my bills, dear boy, it is and I say 'it' advisedly, Countess Feretti."

"The name is vaguely familiar."

"My job is to make it more familiar." He turned childish eyes on a plump cherub cavorting on the wall behind the bar. "Widow of an American manufacturer of detergents. I believe the slogan was 'Your hands will adore Flor!' Apparently there was thirty million dollars' worth of adoration when he died in Ohio or Iowa, don't ask me which. Curious name of Gurgelt. Mrs. Gurgelt buried the tycoon with full honors, then waddled off to Italy with the loot, picked up Count Feretti at a sidewalk café in Rome, married him without protest, and took the Borochelli Palace on the Grand Canal for her first season in Venice. Her first season anywhere. It's an uphill battle but the food is excellent and the service acceptable. I'm even rather fond of the old bag. Last night I managed to get her invited to the shindig Barbara and the Baron threw."

I ordered another Scotch, indulged in dirty gossip, and began edging up on the point. Freddie gave me a quizzical look and said, "I'm peculiarly allergic to what your American fiction calls private eyes. I've had some rather unfortunate experiences. However, as you well know, Muldoon, there are, for various reasons, exceptions."

"So?"

"So, I'm fully aware that you didn't ask me for a purely social drink. I gather that, for a very minor reimbursement, I am to be of assistance to you. If this assistance has no particularly destructive effect on my friends who are, despite rumor, few, I believe we should, as the serious-minded say, 'get to the heart of the matter.'"

"A minor reimbursement, in my books, is a matter of installments. There are several things I want. This afternoon's work is, to be crude, worth a hundred bucks."

"Not bad for the middle of the day. Shoot."

"First: about a Mrs. Baring. Amy Baring."

His glass froze in midair halfway to his lips.

"Amy Baring! Now don't tell me they're going to turn out to be phonies. I couldn't bear it."

"They?"

"They are three. Amy. Her fabulous mother. Her brother. They have the old Czareda Palace up beyond the Rialto bridge. I like them."

"Give a little, Freddie."

"Reluctantly. They can't be mixed up in anything odd. If so, my last straw of faith is gone. Amy is fiftyish, completely charming and combines great taste with a great heart. A rare combination, I can assure you. Amy had a husband some years back who died. New

England Textiles, I believe. That sort of detail bores me."

"The brother?"

Freddie smiled.

"Miles Winthrop? Late forties. Cherubic. Well-scrubbed, exudes an aura of goodwill, philanthropy, humor and kindness. His personal tastes are, shall I say, somewhat unorthodox, but it would be difficult to recognize the Baron Charlus in any of his mannerisms."

"Ah? The mother?"

"Old Mrs. Winthrop. Fascinating. Must be eighty-five. Thin and stiff as a ramrod. Right out of seventeenth century New England! Lives in the center of Venice as though surrounded by the enemy. Sharp-tongued, disapproving and thoroughly beloved by almost everyone. They are a very close and unique family."

"House guests?"

"Well, the Czareda Palace is one of the biggest in town. Belonged to one of the Russian grand dukes. Mrs. Baring likes to have people around. Especially people she can help—artists, writers, musicians. There are usually no less than seven or eight house guests. I believe this week there has been a turnover and I'm not up on the newcomers except, of course, for Prince Sir-el-Donrd." He stopped, looked at me with raised eyebrows. "Of course! So! I should have known."

"It's not what you should have known but what you do know that interests me. For example. Why should the young Prince be visiting Mrs. Baring?"

"If you're looking for some sinister motive, you're on the wrong track. Prince Sir-el shares rooms with Mrs. Baring's young nephew at Yale. It's a case of nothing more or less than good manners. And Mrs. Baring's manners are the best!"

"When can I meet her?"

He hesitated, fighting some sort of a silent inner battle which I could not believe was ethical. Realism apparently won out without much difficulty.

"They swim at the Lido every afternoon between four and six. Cabaña three, front row, center. It's one o'clock now. Why don't we lunch and then we can take the Danelli's launch over to the Lido?"

"No. I have some things to do. I'll meet you in the Excelsior lobby at four."

"Too bad." It was apparent now that Freddie didn't want me out of his sight. Why? Surely he wasn't mixed up in this business. Had I been a dope; had I given myself away at the mention of Prince Sir-el's name?

I ordered another drink for him, paid up. First to the bartender and then a lick of a promise to Freddie, and left him floating pleasantly on one elbow. I walked out through the high, dimly lit medieval lobby of the hotel into the September sunlight. Gondolas and motor launches were drawn at the quayside. The smart launch that ferried guests of Danelli out to the Lido, was cutting in across the lagoon, past the cluster of white yachts arid steamers. I turned right, guilty with the bright romantic feeling of the day, and in a few moments was strolling across the vast mosaic sea that is San Marco square. The tables at Florian's were thinly populated, the pigeons swarmed in search of tourists, a Venetian woman with a black shawl over her head was coming down the steps of the glittering Cathedral like a character out of *Cavalleria Rusticana*. The warm September sun seemed to invade and become part of ancient faded stone. At the far end of the square, opposite the Cathedral, I entered the gloom of a narrow alley and in a short time came out into a tiny square dominated by the Café Martini. I was no sooner seated at a secluded table when the maître bent over me.

"Signor Muldoon?"

"Yes."

He handed me an envelope bearing the crest of the Hotel Grand. I tore it open and read: "Impossible, darling. He suspects. It should have been goodbye at Naples. Venice is full of beauties who will make it easy for you to forget, if you ever remembered at all." It was signed, of course, by Linda.

I sat there for a moment with the note in my hand staring at nothing. At a nearby table a woman was talking on and on in high scratchy French; the sound of glass and china and silver tinkled away into an impossibly blue sky. I crumpled the note, threw some lira on the table and left the café. I walked into the labyrinth of allies surrounding San Marco, out across small humped bridges spanning silent canals, through sunless paths curving between old façades, past the tiny shops of silversmiths and artisans of glass, out around the blue bulge of a hoary old opera house, losing as I walked, the sense of time and place. Were the activities in which I had been engaged for the past ten years part of the enlightened twentieth century? They seemed more appropriate to a time inhabited by Doges, masked murderers, poisoned wine and stilettos raised in the light of flaming torches. Linda Pawling lost her reality in this fantasy and became part of the intrigue surrounding some visiting Machiavelli.

I came out onto a small deserted bridge and stood at the parapet staring down into black waters that reflected the pink granite of a garden wall. It was very quiet and deserted. The water lost its liquid quality and seemed transformed into black glass. I thought about Linda's note. I was relieved that I might not have to lie to her again, lead her on unwittingly to her own destruction. But another reaction was more compelling and completely surprising. I was experiencing an unexpected and poignant sense of loss. No woman had been able to induce any such emotion in me for a long, long time.

Below me, the black glass became agitated; heavy oil-like ripples moved down a sunless corridor. And then, suddenly a gondola moved silently around a corner of the canal and came towards the bridge like a sinister swan. It was manned by a ferocious old gondolier with wild white mustaches. One passenger sat among the red and gold pillows; sat, and in no way reclined. It was a tiny little old lady in severe black who was as straight as a ramrod and whose entire demeanor radiated disapproval of the lush, romantic atmosphere through which she was being propelled. I was on the highest point of the little humped bridge and as the gondola moved silently towards me, the old woman looked up, caught my eye sternly, as though, in some way, I was responsible for the rococo architecture, the warmth of the day, the dramatic contrast of dark coolness below and blazing sunlit façades above.

There was something so comic, yet oddly touching, in the scene that I was held by it, completely unaware of someone approaching until it was too late. The gaze of the woman in the gondola, contracted suddenly, shifted to my left; then she raised one thin arm holding an enormous black pocketbook and shouted,

"Beware!"

My reflexes reacted without thought or direction. Out of one eye I was aware of the gondola passing from my sight below the bridge as I threw myself down along the stone rail and whirled about. There were three of them, ugly-looking thugs who obviously meant business. Two of them were placed so as to block any attempt to get off the bridge. The one closest to me was half crouched over my former position holding a mean-looking knife. It didn't take any flash of insight to see that I was nicely hemmed in a tight little *cul-de-sac* and that the nature of their bold attack permitted me only a few seconds to act. The guy nearest me came out of his off-balance crouch and, catlike, leaped toward me. I didn't wait for his calling card. I simply threw myself over the stone rail and fell with an undignified splash into the canal. I went under and tasted something unpleasant, then came up to the sound of my own splashing. Almost immediately I heard another and more reassuring sound; shouts and footsteps running on stone. Before I drifted under the bridge I saw the faces of three dirty-faced kids peering down at me derisively. Then something snatched the back of my coat collar and hauled me upwards. In a moment I was sprawled in the front of a gondola facing the stern-faced old lady I had seen a few moments before. I made a movement but she held up her arm:

"Don't move! You'll only ruin these pillows. They cost good money.

Do you speak English?"

"No. I'm an American."

"I might have known. Well, you were lucky indeed that I happened along before those foreigners snatched your wallet. We Americans should never leave our soil."

"You did."

"Duty. I have children who should know better." She turned to the sad-faced gondolier. "Take us home, Antonio."

"Just drop me anywhere," I said.

"Nonsense. As a compatriot it's my duty to see that you don't catch pneumonia, young man. Not to mention typhoid or the plague!"

Over her shoulder I saw the bridge from which I had jumped. The rail was lined with laughing youngsters. I began to feel exceedingly foolish. The bridge began to recede. The gondola rounded a curve and came out into the broad sunlight of the Grand Canal. In the hot sun my damp clothes seemed to steam. I managed to get out of my coat, opened my shirt to the waist, and began to wonder what I'd fallen into.

"My name is Muldoon," I said, "Hart Muldoon."

"You can't be held responsible for that," she said, acidly. "I'm Mrs. Winthrop. Mrs. Jonathan Winthrop. Of Quincy."

Of course! Mrs. Baring's mother. I should have recognized her immediately from Freddie's description. It couldn't have been more convenient had I planned it.

"I appreciate the lift, ma'am," I said. "I don't suppose you have a dry cigarette."

"I most certainly do not, wet or dry! Don't slouch so! Show a little backbone. We don't want these foreigners to think we're going soft!"

From among the pillows she fished a plain black umbrella, snapped it open, and raised it over her head, obviously to ward off the foreign sun.

"We have only a short way to go," she said. "However, even in that short time you might catch a dangerous chill. Inasmuch as you are already half undressed, I would suggest that, for reasons of health, you remove your trousers!"

FOUR

The Czareda Palace turned a rather tattered seventeenth century façade on the Grand Canal, but once past the main entrance, the present faded into an ornate and spacious past. Vast rooms with vaulted ceilings aflame with colors of the renaissance marble floors and grand staircases, Titians and Rubens against gilt and brocade, a tiled courtyard in the center of the building where a cool fountain tinkled, the accumulated art and furniture of several centuries, placed in space to create an almost eerie quiet, and lost, apparently, in time. Mrs. Winthrop gave some sharp and ringing orders and in no time flat I found myself in a large bedroom overlooking the canal, divested of my wet clothes, attended by a handsome young male servant who insisted on drawing me a bath in the biggest bathtub I had ever seen. When I came out of the bathroom he was waiting with fresh underwear, slacks, a sports shirt, socks and sandals.

"You're not a Venetian," I said.

"No, *Signor*. I am of Taormina."

"How is it that you find yourself in Venice in this household?"

"The *signor*. Meester Winthrop. I meet him in Taormina last winter. He give to me this great opportunity."

"Opportunity? To be a servant?"

He smiled tolerantly. "I see you are a stranger to this house. Otherwise you would understand."

"Understand?"

"My speaking of English. This is one example. Last winter I had not one word of English. Now, behold, I am a master of the language. Three nights of the week I attend the classes and in a year I will be able to rise far above my place in Taormina."

"Classes?"

"There are ten young men employed in the Palace. Mr. Winthrop has arranged for us to become more educated. Three evenings a week for three hours we must attend classes. Already Mr. Winthrop has arranged that several young men go on to university in Rome and Paris and England, even the United States. I will do otherwise. I am taking a course in automotive engineering and at the end of a year I will be equipped to work in a garage in any city in Italy. It is a miracle!"

"An odd one," I said. "And what does Mr. Winthrop get in return?"

He smiled boyishly.

"Nothing, *Signor,* that it is too difficult for an Italian to give. Is there anything else the *signor* wishes?"

"No thank you."

"*Signora* Winthrop wishes you to come to her in the loggia."

"Good. Lead on!"

Mrs. Winthrop, her tiny body encased from head to foot in heavy lavender silk, was sitting bolt upright on an iron chair in the shade opposite the fountain. Beside her on an iron table was a tray and some glasses. Before I fully realized what I was being offered, she thrust a glass of warm milk at me.

"I can't touch the stuff!"

"Nonsense. Drink it down." She lowered her voice guiltily, "I permitted them to put in a tablespoon of whisky, for medicinal purposes."

I made myself unconscious long enough to swallow the stuff.

"Good! Now tell me about yourself."

"Why?"

"I'm interested in people. My daughter and my son have gone out to that scandalous beach at the Lido. Inasmuch as I saved you from certain death by drowning, you can certainly sacrifice a few minutes of your time—which I'm certain cannot be very valuable—to a gossipy old lady. Your clothes will be ready in about twenty minutes."

"I'm not good at talking about myself."

"An excellent start! Try."

Once started I found it easier than expected and, what was more surprising, freer of fiction than I had planned. When I had finished she said, "There must have been a Puritan somewhere in the background."

"There was. Two or three generations back my mother's family went to Idaho from New England."

"Where in New England?"

"Connecticut."

"That hardly counts. Still, it's better than nothing. Well, what can you expect. Your parents both died before you were eighteen. The war. All that New England idealism gone sour."

"Could be."

"Of course it could be. You don't imagine you're the first disillusioned young man I've met! The woods are full of them these days. Give up too easy if you ask me. Too sorry for themselves! Never married. Too selfish."

"Well ..."

"Unhealthy," she said shortly. "Your New England forebearers married young, and don't you believe all those modern-day psychiatrists with their talk about inhibitions! Humph! My grandfather had sixteen children. Doesn't sound inhibited to me. Those featherbeds were comfortable and well used. Well, I suppose there's still hope for you if you get back on the right track."

"Afraid not."

"All this nonsense about being a private investigator, whatever that may be. Suppose it has to do with all this keyhole peeking going on everywhere. Sounds messy. We used to do it much better in the Bay Colony. Wasted no time. Just burned them! My son and daughter wouldn't agree. I'm fond of them. Both lost souls, of course, like yourself. Still, I try to make up for them. Charm is the curse of our times. More action, less charm would help a great deal, let me tell you. Say what you mean and stand up for it." She stopped. Her whole demeanor changed. She looked beyond me and smiled for the first time.

"Judith, my child. Come here."

I rose and turned to find before me a young woman of about nineteen or twenty; large dark eyes set in an incredibly lovely face which was almost devoid of makeup; serious beyond her years; wearing a simple blue linen dress.

"I don't want to interrupt, Mrs. Winthrop."

"You're not interrupting anything of importance. Another lost soul. Disappointed and probably thoroughly corrupt. Name of Muldoon. Hart, this child is Judith Garnter."

I managed some sort of show of innocence. Here, just twenty-four hours after I had talked to Hirem, I was face to face with the cause of all his troubles. I felt an uncharacteristic stab of pity. This child didn't deserve the trouble she was heading for. Was she aware of it? Or was it possible that the stories of her love for the Prince were exaggerated?

Judith smiled. "Don't take Mrs. Winthrop seriously. She always insults the men she likes."

Mrs. Winthrop snorted, "Don't apologize. Never apologize. I picked this young man up out of a canal. I hope it wasn't an entirely wasted gesture. He's some sort of spy."

The smile faded from Judith's face.

"Spy?"

"Oh not that kind of spy. At least I don't think so. He's a private detective of some sort. In and out of people's bedrooms, I presume. Pretends to be terribly hardboiled. Soft as a feather."

"I don't know whether to say thank you for that or not," I said lightly.

But Judith Garnter refused to be amused. She was watching me intently.

Mrs. Winthrop said, "Judith is from Israel. Her father is a Senator in the Knesset. I met Judith in New York when I was working on the Aid-to-Israel committee. I'm very much interested in Israel. It has all the vitality and idealism we used to have in America. Before we got fat and rich and smug. Israel is very like New England in the days of my great-grandfather. Why, Judith had a rifle in her hand when she was only sixteen."

"I never got to use it," Judith said. "Instead I was sent to college in New York."

"Never mind, dear. You will use it. But how thoughtless of me! Your mind is not on the brave defense of your democracy. Has that person arrived yet?"

"His train is due in now. I expect he will be here at any moment." She stopped, gave me a startled look and added quickly, "We'll talk about Ali later."

"Now, dear, don't go getting ideas about Mr. Muldoon. I'm sure he couldn't be mixed up in that business."

I was thankful that blushing had given me up years before. Judith obviously was not convinced. But she decided on a lighter attack.

"You know, Mrs. Winthrop, what happened with the last strange young man. The one you picked up in San Marco Square."

"Oh him. Well, dear, the brooch wasn't nearly as valuable as he imagined. Poor soul. Do come here and sit down. It's a shame to have to whisk Ali off to the Lido as soon as he gets here, but Amy insisted."

Reluctantly, Judith joined us. It was obvious that her mind was elsewhere. She kept looking from her watch to the door, to the main hall.

Mrs. Winthrop said, "Don't fuss and worry so, dear. No one would dare ..." She stopped, arrested by the frown on Judith's face. But after a moment she chose to disregard it. "Judith! My child. I have an inspiration."

"Yes?" Judith said, apprehensively.

"Mr. Muldoon. A private investigator. Right here on the spot. Why don't we employ him to trace down that filthy note you got this morning."

"Filthy note?" I asked, perhaps too quickly.

"Mrs. Winthrop!" Judith's voice was sharp with warning. "Please. I must discuss it with Ali first."

"As you think best."

There was an uncomfortable silence.

"I'm afraid I must be going. I'm late for a date at the Lido. Perhaps I'll have the pleasure of seeing you there."

"Perhaps."

"If you insist on going out to that modern-day Gomorrah," Mrs. Winthrop said, "you might as well go in my daughter's launch. Miss Garnter and her friend Will not be using it for an hour."

"Well ..."

"Of course you'll take it. They're picking up someone else at one of the hotels. Some stray guest of Amy's. Now, you must promise to return for tea tomorrow. I want to hear all about your sordid adventures. It makes me all the more aware of the enormity of the job some of us have to do."

I took Miss Garnter's hand. It was unresponsive. I did not like the wisp of guilt that drifted across my mind. The guy from Taormina appeared from nowhere and I followed him back to the bedroom where my clothes were waiting, miraculously dry, cleaned and pressed.

When I came down, Mrs. Winthrop was sitting alone in the loggia reading a book. She placed it on her lap as I approached, and pursed her lips before she spoke.

"You've upset poor Judith. I won't have anyone upsetting that girl. She's the finest young woman I've met in years."

"I'm sorry. I didn't mean to."

"No. I won't have anyone upsetting her. Anyone. Even the President. I wrote him a letter and gave him a piece of my mind. If it comes to that, I'll see to it that they come to life down there in Washington and do something. Even if they have to call out the Navy for Judith."

"Why would that be necessary?"

"Never you mind. I promised her I wouldn't confide in you. She doesn't trust you. I think she believes you fell into the canal purposely so that I would pick you up. An odd way to gate-crash. Still, she might be right. She's in love. Idiotic but inescapable, and people in love have funny ideas. Awful nonsense!"

"I'm inclined to agree."

"I didn't ask for your opinion. Now, young man—if Judith should be right about you—if you are up to some nasty monkey business, I'll see to it personally that you get the hiding of your life, to begin with!"

"I bet you would!" I said. "Well, I'll come to see you tomorrow if you'll permit and give you that chance."

"Good. I don't like people who just sneak out of one's life. In the meantime, as long as you're going out to that dreadful Lido place, you might as well look up my son and daughter. You'll find them in cabaña—what a horrible word—twenty!"

"I'll do that."

"See that my son doesn't get into too much mischief. His heart is good. Too good perhaps. He's already sending sixteen young men through various colleges."

I thought I caught a faint glimmer of a smile far back in those Puritan eyes, but couldn't be certain. As I started to turn away she said in a low voice:

"One more thing."

I turned back.

"Yes?"

"You've cost me a good deal of time and money, Mr. Muldoon. I don't want to see it wasted."

"I don't understand."

"It cost me several thousand lira to hire those three men to scare you into the canal just as I passed. I've been tracking you down ever since you left the Danelli."

"You're joking."

"No. I'm not joking at all. I shouldn't like to see the hydrogen bomb employed just to get Judith happily married. I may not look as dangerous as three thugs on a bridge, but I am actually much more deadly. Now go, but be back here at four P.M. tomorrow. I'll have some matters to discuss with you!"

In a daze I wandered out through the vast entrance hall to a sunlit landing platform. A smart mahogany launch with the colors of the Czareda Palace, manned by two men in white and gold uniforms, was waiting. I got into it mechanically and sank down among the crimson and gold cushions. I thought I must be dreaming.

The launch moved out away from the platform into the middle of the Grand Canal. I looked back. I wondered if the stern little old lady was sitting there over her book laughing. Had she invented the story of tracking me down? If not, what was she up to? As I looked back a girl came out on the stone quay in front of the palace. It was Judith. She didn't even glance in my direction. She turned and looked back along the Grand Canal in the direction of the railway station. Her figure receded as we sped down the canal towards the lagoon and the Adriatic. She looked terribly small and lonely and lost.

FIVE

When the launch drew up to the landing in front of the Hotel Grand, the first person I saw was Linda. She was standing near the edge of the platform staring out across the canal with cool indifference. Next to her was a big red-faced blond guy, hurrying toward forty, dressed in an expensive silk suit. As the attendants leaped out with busy deference Linda and her escort stepped down into the launch and, turning, she saw me for the first time. Her moment of hesitation was not noticeable to anyone but me. Her expression didn't change; she might have been posing for the cover of a fashion magazine. She came back into the rear of the launch and settled among the cushions, giving me the polite and pleasant smile of a lady-to-a-stranger. Her husband—for I knew immediately it was he—followed with a great show of heavy importance. He was over six feet, barrel-chested, turning beefy, yet carrying with him at least the memory of good looks, a little like the good looks on a war recruiting poster faded now and weather-beaten, forgotten for a new type of hero in a new type of war. But even the memory of good looks was somewhat marred by a too-small mouth over a too-large rounded chin.

He was overdressed for an afternoon on the Lido; Sulka shirt and tie, custom straw hat, cuff links; the works. He flashed a self-conscious smile at me, darted a look at his wife, settled down and offered a cigarette.

"George Pawling," he said, resolutely. "That's my wife."

I refused the cigarette. "Not my brand. My name is Muldoon. Hart Muldoon."

He frowned politely. "Familiar. Should I know you?"

"Not particularly."

"You must be a friend of Mrs. Baring."

"No. I know her mother, Mrs. Winthrop."

"Oh, yes. I haven't met her yet, but I hear she's a great old girl. Not only money but background. Plenty of both."

"I suppose so."

"They're tops in Boston, you know."

"I didn't."

Linda looked at me gravely, then away.

Undaunted, Pawling went on, "Matter of fact, I've never met Mrs. Baring or her brother either. I … we … my wife and I have mutual friends. These friends wrote Mrs. Baring that we would be in Venice and she was kind enough to invite us out to the Lido for a swim and a drink."

"That was nice for you."

He looked puzzled. Linda seemed fascinated by an island in the lagoon. The launch was cutting through the water now like a shark in flight.

"You in textiles, Muldoon?"

"Not at the moment."

"I see. Just sort of vacationing, eh? Gentleman of leisure."

"You could call it that."

"Wife along in Venice with you?"

"No." I didn't add that I didn't have a wife.

He laughed heartily, "Giving the *signorinas* a rough time, eh?"

I looked at Linda. "I hope not."

Linda said, apparently to the empty air, "It's extraordinary how women can be taken in by a convincing male."

George said, "That's a woman for you! My God, Linda, some of these babes operate like deadly professionals. A guy doesn't have a chance. Eh, Muldoon?"

I muttered something, not listening to him now, aware only of the ice that had crept into Linda's voice. Pawling managed to keep still for about a minute but finally said compulsively:

"I'm in oil, myself."

"That's better than hot water, I suppose."

"Eh? Oh, yeah." He laughed. "Yep. Run into all kinds of strange birds in this business. Crackpots and do-gooders always trying to mess up the works. But my wife and I know some mighty fine people. The best. People in Mrs. Baring's class, you understand. Like the

Bradley Carstairs in New York for instance. Eh, Linda?"

"We met them once!" Linda said distinctly. Then she got up. "I'm going up to the prow for fresh air."

She walked up front and stood there with her back to us like Diana heading for the Hunt. Pawling lowered his voice to a between-us-guys pitch.

"Don't mind Linda. She's always that way with strangers." And then he added with a curious touch of bitterness, "at first!"

"She's probably shy," I said with a straight face.

"Shy? Maybe. Maybe a helluva lot!" He caught himself up, embarrassed at the vehemence that had crept into his words. He flicked his cigarette into the blue Adriatic and watched the long flat island of the Lido with its luxury hotels and villas racing toward us.

Linda came back from the prow, settled once more in the cushions, regarding her husband with a long cool stare and never once looked at me. But after a moment she said:

"How long have you known Mrs. Winthrop, Mr. Muldoon?"

"Not long."

"A year? A week? A day? A few hours?"

"Why Linda, honey, that's not very …" but Pawling caught himself up short, as though come upon some delayed and unexpected radar warning. Linda was waiting for an answer.

After a moment I said, "I've known her for years. I came to Venice for another reason, to see another person. I had time on my hands. I dropped in on Mrs. Winthrop and decided to take her up on the offer to ship me out to the Barings' cabaña at the Lido."

"What business did you say you were in?" Pawling's voice was wary now, and he had, for a moment, dropped his social-climbing manners.

"I didn't."

Linda turned and looked me in the eyes for the first time. "I understand Prince Sir-el-Donrd is staying at the Baring's. Did you meet him?"

"No."

She held my gaze and her eyes were full of anger and reproach. For an instant I was afraid her cool discretion would evaporate into furious denunciation. I said quickly:

"I've never met the Prince."

"No?" Pawling's voice was hard. "Well, I have. You can have him. His father's the man for me. Great old guy!"

"Yes. I understand he's been a good front for the oil companies."

Pawling scowled. "That kind of remark comes out of someone's left wing, brother. It's a damned good thing for the U.S. that we have the old guy with us!"

Linda's face was cold and hostile. I looked at her, and for a moment, saw her naked and passionate in her bedroom at Naples. I was surprised at the intensity of my feeling. Her hold was tighter than I had suspected. Uneasily, and out of habit, I began to think. The hell with it. Give it another twenty-four hours and it will have been just one of those things. But the habit of thought didn't work as well as it should have worked.

Pawling was launched into a dreary dissertation about oil, Donrd-Arabia, and the evils of the State of Israel. I didn't hear much. I knew the words and tune too goddamned well and I knew that Linda was not listening. What did the words and tune mean to her? What had she meant in Naples when she had said, "There's something I'm in. Something I've got to get out of." Was Pawling merely a rather shady public relations guy for the oil companies, come to use Madison Avenue persuasion on the young Prince? Or were he and his wife both in over their heads in some stinking intrigue? Certainly Hirem hadn't flown all the way from the States to hunt me down in Naples in order to counter cocktail propaganda. Yet it seemed impossible that Linda would lend herself consciously to the sort of thing Hirem feared. Her eyes locked with mine again for just a second and I saw the hostility vanish to be replaced by a despairing question. I resisted a mad impulse to grab her hand, to draw her close, to explain what could be explained only without words. The second passed and she turned away and her husband's strident voice came back again, tuned in on a more realistic wave length.

The launch had sped across the lagoon that separates Venice from the Lido in record time and now we entered the canal that leads from the lagoon side to the rear of the great Excelsior Palace Hotel on the beach.

We stepped out of the launch in strained silence and climbed the stone stairs to the main lobby. Through the enormous arched windows I could see the famous beach, wide and sloping gently into the Adriatic, and the triple rows of cabañas down below the terraces of the hotel. Linda and her husband stared toward the beach entrance as I stopped to pick up cigarettes at the tobacco counter. I pocketed the pack and turned. The Pawlings were just outside the main entrance now engaged in what appeared to be serious conversation with a guy in a bikini and pale-yellow silk jacket. They seemed unaware of my approach.

"Hello, Freddie," I said, "I didn't know you knew the Pawlings."

Freddie Gorden didn't exactly jump. A raised eyebrow was for him, a manifestation of extreme agitation. The eyebrow went way up. He turned guiltily and for once seemed at a loss for words. It was Linda who spoke first, "Freddie is the mutual friend we spoke of—the one who got us the invitation to meet the Barings."

"You've had a busy day, Freddie," I said amiably.

Freddie had recovered.

"I'm beginning to feel like Elsa Maxwell."

"You look rather like her, Freddie," I said easily. "Should we go down to the kill?"

Linda said icily, "It seems, Mr. Muldoon, we have many mutual friends."

"So it seems."

Freddie's laugh was devoid of innocence.

"Hart has more mutual friends and mutual enemies than almost anyone you can think of. The price of being," he hesitated dramatically, "a private eye!"

"Private eye!"

No one said anything for a moment. Then Linda laughed. I didn't like the sound of it. "Well," she said bitingly, "think of all the places Mr. Muldoon gets into before people realize who he really is! Come on, Freddie. I want a swim badly. And a drink!"

She moved ahead with Freddie who gave me a nervous last look over his shoulder. They moved down the broad steps toward the beach. I started to follow. George Pawling grabbed my arm.

"Hold it a moment, Muldoon."

I expected either a punch in the nose or a knife in the back. What actually happened took me off guard. I turned to find Pawling flushed and excited. He lowered his voice. "Is Freddie Gorden kidding about your being a private eye?"

"No. In certain circles it's fairly well known. I'm not in Venice professionally though."

"Good! I can't go into the whole thing now. I don't want Linda to suspect. But the first chance we get, I want to have a talk with you. Business. You're just the guy I'm looking for."

"Business?"

"It's my wife," he whispered urgently. "She's been two-timing me with some bastard down in Naples!"

I managed to keep calm.

"What do you want from me?"

"I want you to find out who the guy is. He may be in Venice."

"Why?"

"Why?" The muscles of his face were drawn into a tight knot. The grasp he had on my arm was that of a drowning man on a lone plank in the middle of the Atlantic.

"My people are from Tennessee, Muldoon. We have a way of dealing with these things. When I find out who he is, I intend to kill the lousy sonofabitch!"

SIX

The cabaña of Miles Winthrop and his sister Amy Baring made me think of a cageful of tropical birds who somehow had got Spanish fly mixed up in the birdseed. Chirping and whistling, preening and strutting while sex merged into sex in indiscriminate confusion, they were wetting their beaks with champagne cocktails and the best Scotch. Except for Mrs. Baring, male and female wore the Lido uniform of the bikini, an endless supply of which hung in the dressing rooms. Music from a rhumba band on the hotel terrace drifted down across the triple row of cabañas and the wide beach and the playful bathers; its suggestive rhythms faded out across the incredibly blue Adriatic.

George Pawling and I changed into bikinis in the same dressing room. He was still on that kick about his wife. I couldn't steer him away from it nor could I decide whether he was really leveling. I suppose there was something comic about the husband and the lover stripped to Adam's defenselessness, discussing the chastity of a woman who was dressing in the next cubicle. It was hard to steer Pawling away from his obsession. I told him the job of taking spurs off a husband was not in my line. He assured me he could make it well worth my while. "Look, Muldoon, we haven't got time to discuss it now. Meet me in the bar of the Hotel Grand about seven-thirty. Linda will be dressing for dinner and we can talk. In the meantime, be friendly with her."

I shrugged. "No harm in the drink. My answer will still be no."

"I think I can change your mind."

I left him and went out to the cabaña's terrace among the excited birds.

Mrs. Baring was a cool blonde taking to middle age without protest. She affected a certain archaic "chic" but didn't ask you to take it too seriously. Her pajamas, cut by a well-known Parisian couturiere, seemed dated by thirty or more years. She made me think of a well-disposed, placid child playing a game of being sophisticated and grown-up. She seemed oblivious to the outrageous character and behavior of some of her guests, and I suppose, the most disapproving epithet in her vocabulary was "naughty." She moved through the thin air of excessive tolerance and it was difficult to associate her with her mother, the unbending New England Puritan. She was full of fashionable empty chatter about the ballet, theater, avant-garde books and poetry and international sex. The effect was unintentionally ironic. Everyone was "sweet," "so amusing," "so talented," or "so attractive." If there were villains in her world, curiously enough, they must have been Philistines resembling her mother! A birdbrain among birdbrains she chirped romantically, yet was saved from utter silliness by what appeared to be a homely, persistent and genuine kindness.

Her brother, Miles Winthrop, looked like a plump, well-scrubbed, happily extroverted stockbroker, which, of course, he was not! There was nothing in the least furtive or sinister about him; one could almost believe that his interest in all things male, especially the younger male, was purely paternal. Like his sister, there was something childlike in his obvious enjoyment of life, something naive about his curious, uncomplicated directness. He had none of his mother's granite but on the other end of the spectrum and despite his unorthodox tastes, he seemed to have little in common with the raffish crew surrounding him.

And what a crew! First, and far the most interesting from my point of view, was a dark and sultry young Italian movie actress introduced as Nina Apperatti. She was generous not only in the proportions of her breasts but in the amount exposed to public view which, save for the flimsiest string of a brassiere, was almost one hundred per cent. They rose and fell with her breathy conversation like exotic flowers seeking the nourishment of sunlight. Her English was picturesque and amusing. She affected a "young tigress" manner, popular that season with the movie set; narrowed eyes smoldering in challenge, restless hands apparently unhappy without something meaningful to grasp, and a way of moving about the cabaña from drink to drink and male to male as though approaching a state of sexual crisis.

As soon as I emerged from the dressing room she began to make a direct and none too subtle play for me. It was flattering but puzzling and more disturbing than I would have suspected. Linda's not showing at lunch, and her coolness since we had met in the launch, had left a vacuum that ached to be filled. Her manifest scorn had tensed my nerves to a blow-off point. The Italian girl's blatant approach, the sun and drinks and the aphrodisiac atmosphere soon had me seething like a bull in the merry month of May. With Linda icing me out, I began to figure on a quick where and when.

People drifted in and out of the cabaña for drinks and gossip, obviously drawn there by the whispered news that Prince Sir-el-Donrd-Arabia was expected during the afternoon. Among the more or less permanent guests drinking Mrs. Baring's liquor was a muscular male version of Nina. He was introduced without much conviction as Nina's cousin, Pietro Apperatti. He seemed to have the family difficulty of keeping vital parts of his anatomy decently concealed despite an occasional but half-hearted hitch at his postage-stamp bathing trunks. He permitted himself to bask in the intense attentions of a minor British poet much to the annoyance of the poet's friend who, it seemed, was a completely unknown painter of the abstract school.

Freddie Gorden wandered in and out while George Pawling devoted his energies to charming Mrs. Baring. Linda, carefully avoiding my gaze, seemed on the way to getting drunk and, in the process, determined to deprive the English poet of Pietro's favors.

A telephone in the cabaña kept ringing with messages for various guests of the Barings. Most of the calls were concerned with what was the main topic of conversation; a Masked Ball to be given that night in honor of Prince Ali by Countess Feretti. From what I could gather Freddie Gorden had masterminded the party for his patroness and Mrs. Baring was working all-out to make the party a success. It was obvious that she had undertaken the role of promoter out of friendship for Freddie rather than the as-yet-unseen American Countess.

The British poet, who had recently forsaken proletariat verse and a proletariat background for aristocratic sonnets and good living, underlined the social nuances of the Masked Ball:

"My dear," he said to Mrs. Baring during one of his rare lapses from the orbit of Pietro's smile. "No one, but no one would dream of appearing at the monster's Ball if you had not worked like a trojan to persuade everyone to go. Your heart is warmer than the Italian sun!"

No one seemed particularly embarrassed. Freddie joined in the chorus, avoiding my ironic gaze. "It's true! The dear Countess is about to burst through her varicose veins in excitement. And it's all Amy's doing. Marvelous! Especially when it is quite well known that Prince Ali loathes large parties."

"You exaggerate," Mr. Baring said mildly. "The Countess seems very nice. She must be nice to appreciate our dear Freddie."

"Isn't it exciting," Nina growled in my ear. "It is more fun in masks, no?"

"Perhaps."

"But of course it is. There is no one then that knows who he is and what one does and from this can result so much of the mix-ups!"

Freddie, who had managed to overhear, said ungallantly, "With you there, my dear Nina, 'much of the mix-ups' are assured anyway!"

"I'm trying," the poet said, "to persuade Pietro to go as Apollo. Wouldn't he make a divine Apollo?"

"I have a better idea," his painter friend said sweetly. "Why doesn't he go as a Persian whore? He'd be so convincing!"

Freddie stepped in quickly to prevent mild bloodshed. It wasn't necessary. Pietro merely smiled charmingly, "Both ideas are excellent. I shall consider them carefully." His big dark eyes swam appealingly towards the ruffled painter. "It is always difficult to make a choice in this world with so many pleasant possibilities." He seemed to be looking for an auctioneer.

Mrs. Baring was oblivious to the conflict. She persuaded a suddenly reluctant Freddie to invite me to the Ball. Freddie was looking damned guilty about something. I wondered how long it would take to pump up out of him his relations with the Pawlings. Linda had given up trying to wean Pietro away from the poet and was indulging in platonic drinking with the painter; a kind of tears-in-beer relationship. I could see that beneath her gay social manner she was taut and nervous. Several times I caught her glancing at her watch. Did the expected arrival of the Prince make her jittery? If so, why?

Nina panted in my ear like an impatient animal. I could almost hear Hirem's whispered warning. I knew that this modern Italian piece was not wasting her time on a no-money-guy-from-nowhere for nothing. Occasionally I caught a radar-like signal between her and her "cousin" Pietro. I was certain she was acting on instructions. But why? Did she and Linda fit into the same unpleasant picture puzzle? At the moment it didn't matter much. I went along with it as helpless and as willing as a country boob in the hands of a carnival stripper.

She had turned it on full force now. Her body seemed constantly in movement even when she was in a sitting position. Her breasts pressed against my arm as she leaned across me for a drink she had placed purposely on my other side and seemed given to a constant and highly disturbing series of unrelated undulations and curious Italian spasms as her eyes explored me. Linda, after one level appraisal of the activities in my corner of the cabaña, turned her back and began to laugh too loudly with the painter. George Pawling alternated between toothy fawning smiles for Mrs. Baring and dark threatening scowls for his wife. In between, I caught him eying me in a coldly speculative manner that made me wonder whether he was mentally measuring me for a cement coffin or something equally attractive.

All around me, despite the vacuous conversation and easy laughter, I felt a subtle growing tension. It spread to me. Prince Ali was expected any moment. Would he arrive with Miss Garnter? Linda was looking at her watch again. When a call came through on the cabaña telephone for George Pawling, I saw Linda's chin come up sharply and her glance fix questioningly on her husband as he spoke into the phone. I watched him cupping the mouthpiece close to his lips. He was apparently confining his end of the conversation to yes and no. After he hung up he stood there in the corner of the cabaña staring thoughtfully at the dead instrument for a moment, then he turned and went up to Mrs. Baring. I heard him say: "… sudden business matter. Must get back to Venice immediately."

He turned quickly to Linda. "Mr. Van Lapan," he said quickly, "only has an hour between trains. En route from Vienna to Genoa."

"Oh," Linda said bleakly. "Van Lapan. Yes."

"Stay here and enjoy yourself, darling. I'm sure Mr. Muldoon will see you safely back to the Grand Hotel."

"George," she said sharply, "I'm quite capable of getting back alone. Since when do I need an escort?"

George flushed angrily. "I'd feel safer."

"Safer?" Miles Winthrop was puzzled. "What in the world is unsafe about a boat trip across the lagoon to Venice."

"You see," Linda said with a cold ironic laugh, "my husband never did trust me with gondoliers." A reckless, slightly drunken note had crept into her voice.

George's round dimpled chin was out like a battering ram. "Linda dear, I'd like to speak with you a moment. Come with me while I dress."

She shrugged, put down her glass and followed him into one of the dressing rooms. Everyone began speaking at once. Nina redoubled her efforts as though to divert me from whatever the hell was going on in the dressing room. A few moments later Linda came out, gave me a level defiant look, resumed her former place, glass in hand and used unsparingly. She looked pale and shaken.

George Pawling didn't take long to dress. He seemed pretty God-damned anxious as he left the cabaña. Miles Winthrop said, "Thank God I'm not in business. Trouble with business is that it wastes so much valuable time. Oh look, Amy dear, the young lifeguard near the main entrance. He's the one I told you about. So gifted. I may be able to arrange a scholarship for him at NYU."

"That's nice, dear, but do remember what happened to the last one you tried to put through NYU."

"Nonsense! I never for an instant believed that he raped that dreary freshman. Or would one call it a freshwoman?"

"Whatever one calls it, it was most ungrateful of him."

The endless flow of liquor, the sound of music drifting down from the hotel terrace, the easy gossip and artificial laughter, produced a hypnotic, lotus-eating mood that pushed Hirem and his assignment off into limbo. Or almost. Linda, cool and scornful, frustrated any truce offers on my part and soon, without pain, I was rebounding toward Nina.

"Do you make pictures in Rome?" I asked her.

"One I made in the fourth month past. It is not the big part. But just the same I have already been a star in a picture only not this time in Roma."

I tried to straighten that one out. "Hollywood?"

"No." She opened her eyes, or at least half opened them, to regard me with the lazy ferocious amusement of a panther about to dine on good missionary steak. "No. This picture of which I am the star I have just quick finish last week. I make it in Egypt."

"Egypt!" I sat up a little straighter, trying to take my mind off the straining bra.

"Yes, Egypt. Cairo being the city. The picture not so good really but the money she is very good."

"Did you make it for an Italian company?"

"Oh no. An Egyptian company. For this I had to learn to roll the belly."

"That couldn't have been too difficult."

"No. I am not yet sixteen yet already I am the star of a picture in which I roll the belly for hungry Arabs. Pretty good as you Americans say. Pretty good Jack, eh?"

"Not sixteen!"

"You did not believe it. No one does. It is the truth." A veil seemed to drop over her eyes. "It is Pietro's doing. Two years ago he see the possibilities and persuaded my mamma to let me go to Rome. Pietro changed my life."

"I see. And Pietro arranged the Egyptian contract?"

She shrugged. "Friends of his. Pietro knows so many people." She laughed. "So very many people."

"I bet. You must have met some very interesting people in Cairo."

"Oh yes."

"Like officials in the Arab League?"

She looked away. "I know nothing of such things. This is not my interest."

She turned back and regarded my bikini thoughtfully. "I cannot make a decision as to the disguise I will tonight appear in."

"How about going as a well-paid foreign agent."

She smiled roguishly. "Like Mata Hari?"

"She did a pretty good belly dance too, you know, before the firing squad got to her."

She shuddered, allowing the shudder to involve most of her anatomy. "Don't be horrid. Let us talk of the party and what you will wear and what I will wear so that one will recognize the other. I love Balls!"

"So I gathered. Who knows? I may even go as a Gullible American." And then almost in the same voice I added, "Why did Pietro want you to make a play for me?"

Her smile didn't falter but she said in a low even voice, "I tell you later. In the meantime, does it matter?"

"No."

I didn't like the tense little flickering in the too-bright eyes. But of course there were other things about her I liked only too well. Especially at that particular moment. Liquor was helping the other things to a major triumph.

Someone was saying, "What in the world is keeping Prince Ali?"

I didn't give a damn about Prince Ali. I said to Nina, "Well?"

She leaned close. "You know the Duc d'Alveri?"

"No. Should I?"

"A great friend of Pietro's. Very naughty. Every day he gives something new for Rome to gossip about. Come. You will meet him."

"Why?"

"Even if he is not in, his cabaña is very fantastic. It might give you amusement."

"It might at that."

I followed her to the narrow boardwalk that ran along the front row of cabañas. I looked back at Linda. She and Pietro had stopped talking to one another and were staring at me. Her face was a mask. They paid no attention to the poet who was gushing away on the other side of Pietro. I said, "Let's go, sweetie." We left the cabaña. The sun was beginning to cast long shadows down the wide beach. Some damn fool woman out in the surf was laughing hysterically. It was a late-at-night bedroom kind of laugh, somehow shocking in the fading brightness of the afternoon. I looked down at Nina at my side. She was doing the Sophia Loren strut. For the first time I thought there was something oddly comic and touching in her brazen exhibitionism. I said, "Now tell me why Pietro set you on me."

She looked up at me. Her eyes were mocking. "You are wishing to talk yourself out of something."

I grinned. "I should know better than to examine the mouth of a gift horse."

"I have been called many things but not yet a horse."

We found the Duc d'Alveri in front of a cabaña far down the beach at the end of the front row. He was an unhealthy-looking young man with a petulant face, a white bikini decorated with a blue butterfly, and heavy-lidded dead eyes. Instinctively I looked at his arm, half expecting to find telltale puncture marks. There were none, of course, but I felt there should have been.

Without preliminaries he said to Nina, in excellent English, "Pietro. He promised to come. I've waited here. I am very annoyed."

"Pietro will be here," Nina said. "Be patient. This is *Signor* Muldoon. The American. He has expressed an interest in seeing your cabaña."

"Ah?" He gave me a cold unfriendly look. "So. Very well." He rose languidly. "I trust he will be amused. In the meantime I will swim."

These two were reacting to some wave length unknown to me. But at the moment I was only interested in getting over that threshold as quickly as possible. D'Alveri gave me a haughty and contemptuous look then went off down the beach like a sleepwalker.

"Now come," Nina said. There was a sudden urgency in her voice. "We can talk."

"Talk!" I laughed and followed her into the Duc's cabaña. She evaded me and moved to the far side of the dimly lit interior. She spoke with all the ardor of a bored conductor of a guided tour. "The cabaña of the Duc is famous in certain circles. It has shocked even the most sophisticated Romans."

I looked around, puzzled by the bitterness in her voice and by her statement. What I saw was hardly shocking. A wide couch, built for business, thick carpets, and on the walls some innocuous murals that appeared to be a scenic representation of the ruined arches and doorways of Pompey.

"The Romans shock easy," I said. I moved in her direction but again she eluded me. She laughed a rather frightening cold little laugh that had the momentary effect of checking my fast boil.

"Watch!" She reached out to a wall switch and snapped it on.

Perhaps because I was not prepared for it I felt suddenly as though roots had sprung from my feet. By some trick of lighting the murals had become transparent. Beneath the ruined arches and in the tottering doorways life-sized photographs had appeared. To say that they were pornographic is putting it mildly. Naked males and females in every conceivable sexual combination ran riot on the walls. They made the baths of ancient Pompey look like Main Street on Saturday night. But what really took my breath away was a panel directly above the couch. Here against a Roman column a man and a girl were engaged in some particularly intricate and obscene activities. The man in the photograph was Pietro Apperatti. The girl was Nina.

The sounds of the bathers on the beach were faraway sounds in a distant dream. The delicate little Duc was probably at the water's edge now greeting friends in his bored aristocratic manner. Even in the voluptuous sexual atmosphere of this room, I felt a wave of revulsion sweep over me. I'd thought I'd seen everything until this moment. Out of the dream-shock I heard Nina's voice, devoid of shame but cold with some deep anger.

"I was fifteen when that was taken. Not more than a year ago. The Duc has a family interest in Pietro and me. He is sentimental. He likes family photographs. So chic!"

I managed to get my voice and sound casual. "It pays to advertise," I said.

I turned. The brassiere was already on the carpet at her feet. She said, "Yes. Well. Come on. Let us get it over with."

SEVEN

She was expert but in the manner of an overworked schoolgirl determined to bring home an A. She deserved the A but somehow I felt like a heel. My cigarette sent hazy mist drifting across the incredible murals. She had snapped on the brassiere again and was sitting quietly beside me on the couch. I wanted to get out quick but some sense of guilt and a stronger sense of curiosity held me.

Finally I said, "Pietro told you to bring me here."

She didn't answer. The fact she didn't deny it surprised me. I turned to look at her. Her eyes were closed. She was leaning back among the pillows.

"Pietro is not really your cousin."

"Yes," she said indifferently. "He is. We were children together in Anteno. A small village. Oh *Maria mio*, such a small and poor village. It is not far from Taormina in Sicily. Pietro is four years older than am I. When he was sixteen he went to work for an American. A man who rented a villa in Taormina for the Spring. When this man went back to Rome he took Pietro with him."

"I see."

"Yes." She went on in the same quiet monotone. "The name of the American was Winthrop."

"Miles Winthrop!" I was startled.

She smiled coldly. "Yes. He did much for Pietro. He had tutors for him. He introduced him to important people. But Pietro had ideas of his own." Her voice was edged with contempt. "One day he left the establishment of Mr. Winthrop. He had met the Duc d'Alveri and a new world opened up." She laughed. "Mr. Winthrop was charming about it. He remained a friend to Pietro. What a fool!"

"And you?"

"Pietro came back to Anteno after his father died. I was fifteen then. Our fathers had been killed in the same accident. I was impressed with Pietro. He seemed sympathetic. There were ten children in my family. My mother had no time for me. Pietro told me he could do much for me. He paid my mother ten thousand lira." She laughed. "I wasn't worth it! Anyway, he took me back to Rome and I met the Duc. I was taught what the world is about. I learned fast. I wanted the things Pietro had got. I got them." She laughed again. "I thought everyone who got to the top did what I learned to do."

I was beginning to feel uncomfortable. I wanted to get the hell out of here. What had brought in this unsolicited autobiography? Why was she making me a father confessor? Certainly neither Pietro nor the Duc would approve.

She seemed to guess my thoughts.

"You are thinking: why does she tell me this? A stranger. A girl with whom I have nothing that is common except a few moments of a bed. I will tell you. You are an American. That is first. But more! You are an American," she lowered her voice, "who has come to try to stop them from doing harm to Prince Ali or Miss Judith Garnter."

There was no need to act cagey on my part. She didn't want to hear my words. She was urgently concerned with her own.

"Listen, I am supposed to take you here. I am supposed to keep you interested while you are in Venice. To throw smoke in your eyes."

"Maybe you're doing it," I said warily.

"No! We have but a moment. They said the same thing about Judith Garnter."

"You know her?"

"They arranged that I meet her. Two days ago. I was to pretend to be sympathetic with her, get her confidence."

"And?"

"The truth is I am sympathetic with her! I think it is beautiful, the love of that girl for the Prince." Her voice was suddenly almost violent. "I will not have them destroy them. You understand?"

"No."

"You must. We have not much time. The Duc ..." She broke off. "What was that?"

"I didn't hear anything." Was it my imagination that a shadow was moving behind the illuminated naked figures.

She grabbed my arm and spoke in an urgent whisper.

"The mind of the Duc is a cesspool. He has money but never enough for his tastes. You understand. He and Pietro will do anything for more money. And, well, the thrill. You understand?" When I said nothing she shook my arm impatiently. "You must understand! This love of the Prince and Miss Garnter is lovely, like a beautiful story in a magazine. The way life *should* be. The way it might have been for me if Pietro had been a different person." She gestured expressively toward the indecent photograph over the bed. "Instead, he is like that."

"Look, Nina ..." I said coolly, "I haven't the faintest idea of what you're talking about."

She dug her nails into my arm impatiently. "You think I'm tricking you. You are a fool. You must not be a fool. They are without mercy. I know. Mother of God, I know."

Still on guard I said, "What do you expect me to do?"

"Tell Pietro and the Duc that you are taking me to the Ball tonight."

"You mean you really want me to?"

"No. No. But I want them to believe you are taking me. Do you understand? It will please them. They will think I can keep you out of the way. Please, I beg of you."

"Why is it so important? What are you up to?"

"Never mind! Don't ask so many questions." She threw her head back and a bitter smile lighted up her face. "Consider it payment for what I just did with you. After all, you may be the American but you cannot get such things for nothing. Not from Nina Apperatti!"

"I'll think about it," I said uncomfortably. Then turning while she was still off guard I shot at her: "Pietro and the Duc, they're doing a job for Nasser?"

She seemed to be considering something. Then she jumped to her feet. "Come, we must get back."

"Nina." I started to get up. Behind her the door to the cabaña opened. Linda stepped over the threshold. In one split second she took in the lighted murals, Nina standing in the center of the room, me on the couch.

"Linda!" Something in the tone of my voice startled Nina; not Linda's appearance but the way I spoke her name. She looked quickly from me to Linda. In that split second of multiple reactions I was aware, among other things, of something like terror flash for an instant across Nina's face.

"I don't wish to crudely interrupt," Linda said in an icy voice. "Mrs. Baring sent me to find you, Mr. Muldoon. It seems there has been an urgent call from Venice for you."

"Venice," I said stupidly.

Nina walked quickly to the wall switch and snapped it off. The pornographic murals faded from the frame of ruined arches.

"Mrs. Winthrop wants you to come to the Palazzo Czareda immediately. Apparently there has been some sort of accident."

"Accident," Nina gasped. "Not the Prince! Not Miss Garnter!"

Linda turned and gazed at her as though the girl were some lower form of life. "I don't think so," she said coldly. She turned back to me. "I found it interesting that Mrs. Winthrop wishes to see you. Apparently you are in her employ."

"Linda ... I ..."

"The Barings have already left," she interrupted quite calmly. "So has everyone else." She glanced contemptuously at Nina once again. "Your cousin wants you to go to your room immediately."

Linda turned as if to go, then over her shoulder said: "Forgive me for having interrupted what appears to have been a charming little art appreciation class."

She disappeared. I started across the room after her. Nina intercepted me, grabbing my arm. "Let her go," she whispered. "Stay away from her!"

"What the hell do you mean?"

"Please believe me. Stay away from her."

I shook Nina's hand from my arm and went out to the cabaña terrace. Linda was already far down the narrow boardwalk. The Duc was sitting on the terrace smoking placidly. He didn't turn from a jaundiced scrutiny of the sea. He said, "In Venice, *Signor* Muldoon, there is a little-known statute of the law. It is very strict on the seducers of minors. Can I offer you a cigarette, Nina?"

"No. *Grazie.*"

"As I was saying, Mr. Muldoon ..."

I looked after the retreating figure of Linda. I said, "Yes. I heard what you were saying, Duc. It doesn't make much of an impression."

The Duc shrugged. In a weary voice he said, "It is not my concern, of course. But the girl's cousin is hot tempered."

I laughed.

Nina said, "Where is Pietro?"

"Getting laid, I daresay," the Duc said petulantly. "It's a family vocation."

"I hear there has been an accident in Venice," I said. "Do you know about it?"

Instead of answering he continued in his own vein. "Laid is such a wonderfully vulgar expression. I learned it in New York last winter from a member of the crew of the SS *Forrestal.* It might be wise, under the circumstances for you to leave Venice, *Signor.* Look how upset the poor child is."

In a perfectly healthy voice Nina said, "He can't leave before tonight. He's taking me to the Countess Feretti's Ball."

He turned and regarded Nina. The way he swung around made me think of a hooded cobra. "How nice."

Nina averted her gaze. "I must dress," she mumbled.

"Pietro wants to talk to you." He gestured towards the hotel. "In his room."

"*Sì.*" Nina gave me a furtive, pleading look. Then she turned and marched off down the boardwalk. I started to follow but the Duc spoke up. "One moment, Mr. Muldoon."

"Well?"

"The Sicilians are very hot-headed, *Signor.* Especially in matters of family honor. Pietro will bitterly resent the seduction of his innocent young cousin."

"Get off it, Duc! I'm not a bug-eyed provincial. How heavy-handed can you get?"

He turned his face up to me. The eyes seemed to hang dead and expressionless in the midst of faded parchment. "You would be very surprised!" he said, emphatically.

"Is that a threat?"

He shrugged. "I would suggest that you do not involve yourself in the domestic mess of the *Signora* Winthrop household. She is an old and eccentric woman. She is, you Americans so aptly put it, deficient in some of the marbles."

"I must go."

"Before you do. One further thought to take with you. You are too smart to play on the losing horse. It doesn't pay off. When you think it over you may want to have a talk with me."

"It's possible," I lied.

I hurried towards Mrs. Baring's cabaña caught in growing apprehension. The sun was low now, sending the dark shadow of the great hotel across the wide beach and the few bathers who still clung to the edge of the surf. I had to talk to Linda with no holds barred. It was imperative. Inside the woman's dressing room, I could hear the voices of Linda and Nina engaged in low-voiced altercation. Once, Linda raised her voice and said very distinctly, "If you insist on playing the fool, I can't be responsible for the results!" Then the words became unintelligible again.

Hurriedly I threw on my clothes. When I stepped out onto the terrace the two women were just about to leave. "I'll see you back to Venice," I said to Linda.

"I've made other arrangements," she said coldly. I noticed that Nina was avoiding my eyes. She looked pale and nervous. Linda had one hand on the girl's elbow. She said, "Come along, Nina."

"Linda!"

But she didn't turn back. I went back to the dressing room and combed my hair. Everything was suddenly desolate like a city after a bombing. I tried to shake off the feeling of depression. It was obvious that I was out in a no man's land of no return with Linda. What was worse there was no longer any question in my mind that she was up to her pretty neck in this dirty business.

I picked up the cabaña phone and asked the operator to put me through to the Czareda Palazzo in Venice. After a few crackling moments a voice said, "*Pronto.*"

"Mrs. Winthrop, please."

"The *signora* is not at home."

"Has either Mrs. Baring or Mr. Winthrop returned from the Lido?"

"No, *Signor*. Not yet."

"Where can I reach Mrs. Winthrop?"

There was a moment's hesitation then the voice said: "The *signora* has gone with Prince Ali and *Signor* Garnter to the Bureau."

"Bureau?"

"The *Carabineria, Signor.* Who is calling please."

"A friend," I said and hung up.

I stood there on the terrace for a moment trying to fight off the odd feeling of fear. Then I noticed that someone had left the dregs of a Martini in a shaker. I finished it off. It was warm and medicinal and didn't help at all. I looked at my watch. Five-twenty. Why the hell was I so reluctant to move? The long shadows of afternoon seemed to be reaching into my mind and heart. What had happened back there in Venice? What kind of an accident? I started off toward the broad steps leading up to the lobby of the hotel. I thought; she's just another dollar-happy whore! To hell with her. I reached the foot of the steps. Up above me an orchestra was playing a tango. The tea-dancers of the broad terrace looked like silly marionettes giving a wooden imitation of gaiety. Suddenly I remembered her words in that Naples hotel room: "There's some trouble I'm in, Hart."

Trouble was a mild word for it.

The sky, behind the bulking shadow of the hotel, had turned a fiery red.

EIGHT

Miles Winthrop had lost some of his accustomed good humor. He received me in the patio. The Sicilian servant I had talked to earlier in the afternoon hovered in the shadows of the pillared arcade.

"I'm afraid I don't understand."

"Your mother sent for me."

"I can't imagine why. We're a little upset at the moment. Mother is out with the Prince and Miss Garnter."

"They're still at the Police?"

He was startled. "How did you know?" He gave a quick worried glance towards the Sicilian and then said to me in a loud social voice, "Would you like a drink?"

I said whisky and he ordered two from the Sicilian, his voice warm with paternalism. When the servant had gone he said quickly, "At all costs we must not have a scandal, Mr. Muldoon. I can't imagine how you discovered about the police or what Mamma wants to see you about. So far the authorities have been most discreet and understanding. But if the story spreads and becomes exaggerated...."

"Suppose you tell me the story. Without exaggeration."

"I can't imagine why I should," he said coolly. Then he added with a charming smile, intended, I was certain, to disarm me, "Mamma is a remarkable woman, Mr. Muldoon. There is no one quite like her. I suppose I'd be lost without her. But she sometimes goes too far."

"In what way?"

"She has a way of taking things over," he said with wry good humor. "My friends. My servants. She likes to run the show. Take Alberto for example."

"Alberto?"

"The young Sicilian who has just gone to fetch drinks. Alberto is a sort of protégé of mine. At least he was until Mamma appeared on the scene." He shrugged expressively.

"I see. And it is the same with Prince Ali and Miss Garnter? Mamma has taken over from you and your sister Mrs. Baring?"

He laughed. "Well, I think she'd like to. It looks that way if she has sent for a private investigator like you."

"How did you know I was a private investigator, Mr. Winthrop?"

The color flooded his face. He was really flustered. "Why, as a matter of fact, someone mentioned it this afternoon out at the Lido. One of the Pawlings or Freddie Gorden. I can't remember for the life of me. Does it matter?"

"It might." I weighed the choices, decided to take a direct plunge. "Did they tell you I was also doing a job for the U. S. Government?"

At that moment Alberto appeared with the drinks. Miles Winthrop seemed grateful for the interruption. He launched into small talk about the Ball until the servant had disappeared. Then he said, "You were saying something about the government, Mr. Muldoon."

"Washington is worried about Prince Ali and Miss Garnter. I mean, of course, their personal safety."

Miles Winthrop took refuge in his drink. When his face came up from the glass I was aware of a stubbornness, an echo of his mother's granite I had not noticed before. "How ... er ... kind of Washington," he said ironically. Then he added: "I can't for the life of me see why Prince Ali's private life should concern any government. It seems to me to be a matter of personal choice."

"I wish it were that simple. Do any of us have complete personal choice, Mr. Winthrop?"

He smiled. "Many more of us than you would imagine, my dear sir."

I took a deep swig of whisky, marveling at the delusions under which we live. Miles Winthrop apparently was convinced that he moved through a world of personal choice. Didn't he realize that in the end he was no more than a deluxe prisoner to his tastes; a hostage to the small army of young men who smiled their way through his days.

I changed tactics and came in for a frontal assault.

"Suppose you tell me why your mother and the Prince have gone to the Police."

He sighed. "I suppose it's all right. Mamma will probably only tell you anyway. They went to tell what they know about the accident."

"What accident?"

"Mind you I am telling you only what I have been able to gather from Alberto and the rest of the servants. I have not as yet seen Mamma or the Prince."

"I understand."

"Well, it seems a young man slipped or fell from a bedroom window into the Grand Canal. Before anyone could reach him he had drowned."

Dusk had settled into the loggia. Miles Winthrop's face was almost obliterated by the ironwork design on the Venetian lantern above his head.

"Drowned?" I repeated. "Who? One of the servants?"

"Not exactly. He was a servant in a way. Not one of ours. And not really a servant."

"You'd better explain."

"I'll try. But mind you this is all secondhand. I mean about the actual event."

"Who was the young man?"

"An Arab. He turned up here yesterday afternoon. He had been sent from Donrd-Arabia by the King, the Prince's father, as a sort of bodyguard."

"Did he have credentials?"

Winthrop looked uneasy. "Oh yes. We were all of us a little upset by his arrival. We didn't know how the Prince might take to it. But we didn't have much choice."

"How did the Prince take to it?"

He looked down into his drink. "I have no way of knowing. As you know, my sister and I were out at the Lido this afternoon when the Prince arrived."

"Didn't you question Alberto?"

"Not specifically about that. Alberto did say that the Prince sent immediately for the young Arab and they were locked in the Prince's bedroom for ten or fifteen minutes. Naturally I don't know the details of the interview."

"And the accident, what time did it happen?"

"Apparently a little after four P.M."

Four. About the time I was rolling in the hay with Nina Apperatti!

He went on quickly as though afraid of some question and for a moment I wondered why. "This young Arab was an exceedingly uncouth sort of young man. I don't believe he had ever been out of Donrd-Arabia in his life. Naturally he had never seen a large body of water nor learned to swim. Alberto says he had been drinking. It's against his religion of course to drink at all and I suppose the liquor hit him hard. Anyway, apparently he leaned too far out of the bedroom window and lost his balance. He might have hit his head on one of the stone gargoyles on the lower cornice as he fell. I don't know. Oddly enough no one on the canal actually saw him fall. Several people saw him after he hit the water but by the time they reached him he had gone down. They fished him out twenty minutes later."

"Where was the Prince when all this happened?"

"Alberto tells me he and Miss Garnter were up on the roof garden, on the opposite side of the Palace from the Grand Canal. You must remember it was the first opportunity the Prince had had to be alone with Miss Garnter since his arrival."

"And your mother?"

"She was here in the loggia. Entertaining a caller."

"A caller?"

"Why yes. Oddly enough a person who had been my guest out at the Lido only a half hour before. Mr. Pawling."

"George Pawling!" I almost rose from my chair. "Pawling was here in the Palace when the accident happened?"

"Yes. Actually I believe he went along with Mamma and the Prince to tell the Police what he knew."

"And he was here in the loggia when the Arab took his nose dive?"

"Well not exactly."

"What do you mean?"

"Alberto tells me that Mr. Pawling had gone upstairs to use the plumbing. Apparently he was in one of the bathrooms when the accident occurred."

The sense of lethargic despair that had overcome me on the Lido disappeared. All my old hound dog instincts were aroused. The telephone call Pawling had received in the cabaña. The quick excuses to get back to Venice. The business appointment. Yet he must have come straight to this palazzo. And he had been upstairs when the Prince's bodyguard had toppled out of a window. Would the police make any connection between Pawling's oil interests and the death of a young Arab? It was unlikely.

"And your mother was here in the loggia when it happened?"

"Yes."

"Is there anything else you should tell me?"

"Why no. I don't think so. That's about all. Obviously an unfortunate accident. A drunken young man who couldn't swim leans too far out to get a better view of a strange city. Nothing more melodramatic may be inferred."

"You're sure that's all?"

He hesitated guiltily. Then he finished his drink. He stood. "I'm afraid you will have to excuse me, Mr. Muldoon. There are so many details I must attend to. It's not exactly the most convenient moment to talk."

"Where is your sister Mrs. Baring?"

"My sister. Why, why she's upstairs resting. Poor Amy was very upset by the news. She weeps when a kitten dies, you know."

"I see." What was nagging at the back of my mind. Some forgotten detail. I remained seated. Winthrop gave me a questioning look.

"Your mother sent for me, Mr. Winthrop. I'll wait, if you don't mind."

Miles Winthrop hesitated. He wasn't smiling anymore. He exchanged a look with Alberto who had appeared once more in the shadows of one of the arches. He turned back to me and said somewhat shakily, I thought, "Mamma has a notion she can employ anyone for any purpose, Mr. Muldoon. My sister and I have tried to keep her out of this but ..."

He stopped, arrested by the sound of voices in the outer hall. For a moment he looked like a guilty kid caught with one hand in the cake icing. "She's a remarkable woman," he said quickly, "but ..." And let it go at that.

"Thank you, Miles. You never used to say but," the familiar tones of New England announced from the archway into the entrance hall.

Miles Winthrop sighed. "Mr. Muldoon says you sent for him, Mamma. Why?"

"I'm afraid it's going to turn out to be one of those buts, Miles. The man from Guideri's is in the hall with your costume for this idiotic Ball. You'd better go up and try it on."

"Yes, Mamma."

"Try to keep Prince Ali and Judith from coming out here. I want to speak to Mr. Muldoon alone!"

"Mamma!"

"You heard me, Miles!"

For a moment I felt almost sorry for Miles Winthrop. He shrugged as he must have shrugged many times before—a mouse faced with a steamroller. With an ironically polite bow to me, he went into the hall.

Mrs. Winthrop deposited a mauve parasol on the table and began to remove cream lace gloves, working each finger loose in a ferocious manner.

"I love my son," she said. "I'm not in any manner an unnatural mother. But I would have preferred him not to be such a fool. I suppose you heard what happened here this afternoon."

"Somewhat."

"A fine thing!" She threw her gloves beside the parasol and, hat still more or less on, sat in a rustle of heavy silk. "I'm a little old-fashioned," she said caustically. "I simply can't get used to naked men falling from my house to drown in canals."

"Naked?"

"Stark!" she said.

"Miles didn't tell me that."

"Of course not. Fortunately Miles was at the Lido when it happened. Otherwise there might have been questions."

"Questions?"

"The young Arab fell from the window of Miles' bedroom!" She turned to regard her parasol thoughtfully. "Miles' bed was in a rumpled state. Apparently it had been used. For what purpose, it is perhaps better not to contemplate. There was a half empty bottle of brandy on the bedside table."

"But why your son's room?"

She shook her head impatiently. "If I could answer that I wouldn't need your help, young man! But it wasn't the only room this impossible young Arab had entered. The personal belongings, including correspondence of the Prince, were scattered all over his bedroom. My daughter's room was in the same state. And my own!"

"Looks like the Prince's father sent you a spy. A bungling one, but a spy."

She looked at me in an odd manner. "Yes," she said slowly. "Yes. That is how it appears."

"You don't believe it was an accident," I said bluntly.

"What else am I to think? The police are accepting that theory, at least for the time being. The boy had been drinking heavily. He wasn't used to it."

"Mrs. Winthrop, at the time of the accident, you had a caller. He was upstairs when it happened."

She looked at me in surprise. "Mr. Pawling?"

When I said nothing she smiled. "Oh no! You're on the wrong track. Mr. Pawling is simply a brash climber. He came equipped with engraved calling cards and a great deal of silly talk about mutual acquaintances. He rather amused me. I must say he was quite helpful after the accident. I was very grateful for his presence here."

"Mrs. Winthrop, George Pawling is an employee of German-American Oil!"

For once she lost her aplomb. "What! Are you quite certain?" And then: "But it is impossible. Even if what you say is true, why in the world would he … Oh no! Surely you're not implying that Mr. Pawling sneaked upstairs and pushed the foolish young Arab from my son's bedroom window! It's preposterous!"

"I wish I was as certain of that as you!"

She glanced toward the archway to the hall and said in a changed tone of voice: "No, I never go near the Lido. I would as soon take a one-way trip to Hell."

A voice from the archway said, "Come now, it's not as bad as all that."

NINE

Miss Garnter was standing in the doorway with the man who had just spoken. If I had had any doubts as to his identity the rapturous expression on Judith Garnter's face would have told me the truth. Prince Ali was certainly the personification of all the prince charmings Hollywood had ever dreamed up. Tall and slim, extraordinarily handsome with dark intense eyes and what Louella Parsons would probably call a "devastating smile," the guy radiated virile charm. He wore a well-cut flannel suit and seemed as remote from the desert wastes of his homeland as Noel Coward might be to a Siberian village. Judith, who had seemed attractive when I met her earlier in the day, seemed transformed by the Prince's presence into a raving beauty. Looking at them I suddenly understood Nina Apparatti's emotional reference to opera plots and magazine romance. This pair could have been manufactured especially for the readers of romantic love fiction. For a moment, even I almost succumbed. Was it some optical illusion, a trick of light, that seemed to bathe the lovers in a glow of hazy light?

"Ali," Mrs. Winthrop said with the utmost informality, "this is Mr. Muldoon."

Ali smiled. "I know. Miles just told me he was here."

"Oh." Mrs. Winthrop was somewhat deflated.

"I understand that Mr. Muldoon is very curious about the unfortunate accident we had here two hours ago." I made a note of the fact that he made no move to come further into the loggia than the archway. "I understand also that he has some connection with the U. S. Government."

"Miles always did talk too much," Mrs. Winthrop said.

"My connection with the U. S. Government is only very slim, Prince Ali. My visit here is in no way official."

He laughed. "That's what they all say!" The inflection was the colloquial cynicism of Brooklyn rather than that of Desert Arabia. "So many unofficial Joes with so many questions about my personal welfare, or lack of it. And from so many governments. Very kind. Very considerate! I can do without it. So can Miss Garnter."

"Now Ali," Mrs. Winthrop began.

The Prince interrupted politely but firmly: "I know the young man has a job to do, Mrs. Winthrop, but I'm damned if it's going to interfere with our pleasures in Venice."

"I should think the accident would have done that already."

He gave me a raised eyebrow. "Now look here, Mr. Muldoon. I understand from Miles that you have begun imagining all sorts of melodramatic nonsense about that accident."

"Perhaps you could cool my imagination down a bit. I mean with a few calm facts."

"I don't see why."

"Ali." Judith spoke for the first time. The Prince looked down at her with sudden gentleness and I saw his fingers tighten on her hand. "I don't like to be unreasonable, darling, but surely there's no harm in telling him what you know."

He hesitated a moment then said: "Very well. Perhaps it would be better if we spoke alone."

Mrs. Winthrop put her chin in the air and sailed toward the door like a clipper before the wind. "Come along, Judith. Let the men mess things up."

She took the girl's arm and they went out into the hall. Ali came out into the loggia. He grinned boyishly. But I knew he resented me like hell.

"Fire away, Senator!"

"First, let's talk about the man who drowned."

"A stinker! Impossible. I can't imagine my father entrusting him with anything more important than the watering of camels!"

"You had a talk with him?"

"I certainly did. As soon as I arrived. I was, to be frank, quite annoyed at the whole business. My father saddling me with this goon without even a warning, imposing on the kind hospitality of the Winthrops. Anyway, my reception wasn't exactly warm. And his manner didn't make it any warmer."

"In what way?"

"He was a singularly obtuse and stupid young man. He claimed he had a royal order not to leave my side. He produced a German Luger to prove his point. His manner was insufferably rude and overbearing. I suspected he had been drinking. He admitted Alberto had inveigled him into tasting some brandy but promised it wouldn't happen again. I gave him hell and ordered him to his room in the servants' quarters. He went. That was the last time I saw him."

"Did he bear any message from your father?"

Ali busied himself with lighting a cigarette. He took a moment to answer and I knew he was thinking it over carefully. Finally he said: "That I am afraid is an entirely personal matter, Mr. Muldoon. It wasn't an order not to marry Miss Garnter, if that's what you had in mind."

He stopped pretending to smile.

I used the shock treatment. "Where were you when this Arab was drowned?"

"Where was I? Why," he sputtered, "on the roof with Judith. She was showing me the view."

"When did you first know?"

"We heard distant shouting. We were on the opposite side of the roof from the Grand Canal and it didn't mean anything to us. Then a few moments later one of the servants came to tell us Mrs. Winthrop wished to see us immediately in the loggia."

"Did you know at that time your room had been ransacked?"

He scowled. "Miles Winthrop had no right to tell you that. But as you seem to know about it, no, of course I didn't know."

"And Mr. Pawling?"

"Never laid eyes on him in my life until we came down from the roof. He was in the loggia. I'm grateful for his presence. He handled all the unpleasant details and was very helpful with the police."

"I can imagine."

He looked up quickly. "Why do you use that tone of voice?"

"Can't go into it now. But believe me, stay away from George Pawling." I leaned forward hoping to catch him off-guard. "The death of this Arab is extremely convenient to you, isn't it, Prince Ali?"

"What the hell does that mean?"

"Exactly what it says."

He drew himself up and gave me a cold stare, regal for the first time. "Yes, I suppose in some ways you could say so. I have no particular regrets if that is what you mean. The boy stank of cheap perfume, he had filthy habits, he was a liar and not to be trusted. Yes, his death is convenient. His presence here was annoying to me." He smiled thinly. "But I did not kill him, if that's what you mean, Mr. Muldoon."

He turned toward the door. "Now, if you will excuse me."

"Prince Ali!"

He turned. "Well?"

"Don't go to the Ball tonight."

His face flushed. "If that's an order, you must realize a fact that seems difficult for many Americans to realize—that we non-Americans are in no manner subject to the orders of Washington."

"Nasser's agents are out for your neck!"

"Who isn't!"

"If you won't think of your own safety, there's Miss Garnter to think of."

The anger that had been seething beneath the urban façade burst its bonds. "Now look here, Mr. Muldoon. If you have a report to make to Washington, make it this: I want no more interference in my personal affairs from any quarter. Threats or warnings have utterly no effect on me! Miss Garnter and I refuse to be stampeded by fear!"

He broke off as Alberto came softly into the loggia.

"Well?"

"A telephone call for Your Highness. A lady. She would not be put off. She was most insistent."

"Ah!" Ali forgot about me. Or at least seemed to forget. "I will take it in my room, Alberto."

"*Sì*, your highness."

Ali literally bounded to the door. In the archway, he remembered his manners and turned: "We have nothing more to discuss, Mr. Muldoon. I'm sorry to be so candid but I'm afraid, at this point, you, too, will appreciate directness!"

He left me with Alberto and a state of confusion. For an ardent lover, he was behaving out of character. The mention of a lady caller had propelled him from the room like a guided missile. Before I had time to think it over, Mrs. Winthrop came marching back. She turned to Alberto. "You can go, Alberto!" Alberto left as she continued her forward movement. "I've been forced to lurk," she announced. "I loathe lurkers. Now I'm forced to eavesdrop. I loathe eavesdroppers. Although in my youth, I was conditioned to the New England party phone. Here!"

She pointed dramatically to a telephone instrument nestled among flowers on a small wicker table.

"For me and your country!" she said with salty humor. "Get to work!"

"You mean you want me to …"

"Don't be dense. The Prince has a strange woman caller. Just like a mystery book. Never read them. It's your duty to find out. You don't expect me to do it!"

I grinned, shrugged, walked to the instrument. When I put it to my ear there was nothing for a moment but the sound of heavy breathing. The Prince probably had not yet reached his room.

"Well?" Mrs. Winthrop asked impatiently. I signaled for her to be quiet. Her voice was a broadcasting transmitter turned up too high. Exasperated she looked from me to the archway as though the delay were my fault.

After a moment there was a slight click and the Prince's voice came on. "*Pronto.*"

"Prince Ali?" The woman's voice was vaguely familiar but over the crackling wires of the Venetian telephone system it was hard to place it.

"Ah, I've been waiting for your call. I was afraid …"

"Everything she is arranged," the woman's voice said.

"Good."

"Mrs. Baring is …"

"Yes, yes, I know."

"The *pension* we spoke of. Eight."

"Splendid. I can hardly wait to see you!"

The woman laughed. "Masked Balls, they are so much fun. There are always so much of the mix-ups!"

The Prince laughed. "We'd better cut this off. *Arrivederci.*"

The phone went dead. I stood there for a moment with the instrument in my hand caught in a slight state of shock.

"Well!" Mrs. Winthrop brought me back to earth.

I hung up. "How long has the Prince known Nina Apperatti?"

"Apperatti? The name means nothing to me. What was the phone call about?"

"I don't think I'll tell you for the moment," I said.

"Mr. Muldoon, you are here because …" She broke off. I turned. Miles Winthrop was standing beneath the archway to the hall.

"It's time for your nap, Mamma."

"Drat my nap!"

"Now, Mamma."

"I must go."

I started for the archway. Mrs. Winthrop swept in behind me. "I'll see you to the door, Mr. Muldoon. Miles, we won't need you. I brought you up to be polite. You know how I loathe eavesdroppers."

"Yes, Mamma." Winthrop smiled and bowed to me ironically. "Perhaps we will meet at the Ball, Mr. Muldoon."

"Perhaps."

I went out into the hall with Mrs. Winthrop rustling along beside me. Down at the far end, a servant was waiting to open the door for me. Mrs. Winthrop plucked at my arm and I stopped. She whispered hoarsely: "Be here at eleven o'clock sharp tonight. Before you go to that Ball!"

"But …"

"No buts about it, young man! I expect by that time to have some important information!"

At the door, the servant was looking elaborately into space.

"I can't promise. Love and romance are more complicated than I suspected."

"Love and romance my foot! It's sickening."

I turned and looked at her in amazement. "I thought you had assumed the role of cupid!"

"Don't be a fool! That's what I want them to think."

"Mrs. Winthrop, you shock me," I said mockingly. "Is that why you had that young Arab pushed out the window?"

She smiled. "I never resort to murder unless it's absolutely necessary." She became serious: "I like you. You're the decent type of American I understand. You're not the sort who would be at home on the Lido. I don't countenance immorality except in my children. As for drinking, it's deplorable of course, but I am forced to admit that some of my Yankee ancestors were weaned on rum. I can forgive you that. Clean-cut is an old-fashioned word, but I think you fit it."

"Look, Mrs. Winthrop, you've got me mixed up with some Eagle Scout," I said uncomfortably.

"Don't be modest." She gave me a push. "Go now, before Miles comes snooping around again. Tonight at eleven. You'll be here. I know I can count on you!"

I left her in the middle of the great marble hall and went towards the flunky and the opening door. I turned back to see a scene out of a crudely staged nineteenth century melodrama. Mrs. Winthrop erect and tall in the middle of the great hall, Miles Winthrop behind her in the shadow of the archway to the loggia and the servant named Alberto frozen in an attitude of watching halfway down the great marble stairs.

I went out to the landing to find night fallen over the canal. An obscenely fat yellow moon was rising from the lagoon. A gondola drifting toward me looked as sinister as a floating hearse. The gaudily unformed attendant signaled and the black prow swung around in my direction. I thought of the young Arab stretched out now on a cold slab awaiting shipment in refrigeration back to his native land. I wondered what he had been thinking as he slipped beneath the turgid waters of the canal, going to an undreamed-of death in a strange city so far away from home.

A clock began to boom out the hour. It made a relentless crashing sound out across the ancient rooftops of darkened palazzos, cathedrals, opera houses and hotels. The scene was threatening, macabre and unreal. I thought I detected the faint sweet odor of death and corruption rising from the black waters.

The Prince and Nina Apperatti? Impossible. Where could they have met? What was behind that terse telephone call?

The black gondola glided slowly in to the stone landing stage. The face of the gondolier was like an impassive mask. I tried to shake off the feeling of death and decay.

"Hotel Danelli," I said.

The gondolier nodded without speaking. He poled the silent craft out into the canal. Somewhere a woman was singing. The voice was weary and without passion. It seemed to symbolize the unreal sick quality of the people I had seen and talked to that day. It was like a horrible parody of love; lip service to some neurotic masquerade involving romance between sinister puppets. The last echo of the clock booming the hour died off out in the Adriatic night.

TEN

There was a message and an engraved invitation waiting for me at the desk of the Danelli. The message was from Pietro Apperatti asking me to call him at the Hotel Excelsior on the Lido when I got in. The invitation was, of course, from Countess Feretti to her Masked Ball beginning at eleven P.M. Enclosed was a stern reminder to present the invitation at the door. Without it, apparently one would be barred from heaven and all its Pleasures including the company of the Countess from Iowa. I asked the concierge where he could get me some sort of costume for the Ball. I was not the only guest of the hotel who had presented him with the same problem. He told me not to worry, that some sort of outfit would be in my room in an hour or less. When I got to my room I called the Hotel Excelsior and asked for Pietro's room. He came on strong, the oily charm dissipated on the waters of something more urgent.

"*Signor,* where is Nina?"

"I haven't the faintest idea."

"I come to her room. She is gone. Not even a note of explanation. I suspect she is with you."

"You flatter me. I haven't seen her since I left the Lido two hours ago."

"Her costume for the Ball hangs in the closet. She is due in Venice at a dinner party of the Duc's in a little over an hour. The doorman tells me she took the Danelli launch into Venice an hour ago."

"Sorry. Can't help you."

"But she told me you are taking her to the Ball. Is this true?"

I hesitated and immediately regretted it. That hesitation said too much to a louse like Pietro. I tried to make up for it. "Yes, of course, I'm taking her."

"Ah?" His voice was dark with Sicilian suspicion. "Where then did you plan to meet?"

"None of your goddamned business!"

"But you are wrong! It is my business. Everything Nina does is my business. I am her guardian."

"I couldn't wish anything worse on the poor girl."

There was a pause, pregnant with something, and breathy. Finally he said: "Nina is impulsive and young and therefore somewhat of a fool. But she is my cousin, *Signor*. I warn you to keep out of what does not concern you. And if you see her, tell her that the Duc is very, very annoyed. We are not playing games. This you may find out to your sorrow."

I invited him to go screw the Duc and hung up. But I was feeling far from flippant. It wasn't only the Duc and Pietro but the determined gang behind them. Was Nina playing with some sort of romantic fire? What the hell did the rendezvous with the Prince mean? Perhaps Pietro was in on it and his phone call was merely a cover-up. Whatever it was stunk to high heaven. The unlikely characters involved, the carnival atmosphere of the city, the drowning of an anonymous Arab, the unseen and sinister forces at work behind this frivolous charade filled me with doubt and foreboding. It was like sticking your finger into mush. Nothing came out that made sense.

As I stood there debating on how the hell I was going to track down Nina and whether I'd get to have that heart-to-heart talk with Linda, the phone began to ring. To my hello, Hirem's voice answered, "Uncle Hi."

"Good. I was about to send out an SOS."

"Come now, Hart, I'm counting on you and you alone." His voice, with Paris in the background, was maddeningly cheerful.

"I'm serious, Hi. I'm afraid your little poker game may end up this evening minus a Knave and a Queen. The boy and girl won't behave and the other characters are for keeps."

"You'll find an out for us!"

"Listen, Hirem, an Arab has been drowned."

"So I've heard. Could be worse. Get off the broads and get down to work."

"I'm serious, goddamn it. I don't think I can handle this one. You need a lousy army."

"We'd better cut this off now. Call me at one A.M. The Ritz."

"Where else!"

I hung up and called "Come in" to the knock on the door. I'd half expected the concierge with the promised costume. Instead Freddie Gorden walked in. Or rather, rolled in. He was as lit up as that tree in Rockefeller Plaza on Xmas Eve; or at least giving a damned good imitation. That Freddie drank was no surprise, but that Freddie got drunk *was* a surprise.

"Devastated," he said with syrupy mock politeness. "Should have sent up a card or something. Frightfully bad form. These chairs are, I assume, to be sat in." He sat. "Afraid I'll have to refuse a drink."

I shut the door he had left open. "I wasn't going to offer you one, you bastard."

"Didn't drop by to have my mother insulted, old boy. All right with me, though. Stuffy old bag she is. Was. Got kicked to death by an indignant horse. Motherless child. I've been thinking about being a motherless, fatherless child and I've been thinking how sorry I am for myself and I've been thinking, Freddie old boy, before you put the razors to your wrists, go out and get really stinking fried, so stinking fried I am. And boiled or fried to you I've come laden with the wisdom of my years and experience. Are you a motherless child, Muldoon?"

"Listen here, Freddie."

"No. You listen. Didn't come to listen. Came to talk. My whole career as a male Elsa Maxwell depends on this evening. Got to find a hole to crawl in and sober up before the Ball. Got to navigate, don't we, old boy? If I disgraced myself, the Feretti bitch would cut off the feedbag. Feedbags getting scarce at my time of life. Good title for a song, that. Might sell that and give up my rating as number one parasite and the world's number two or three or four prize bloody sonsofabitch!"

"I'm not interested in doing the music. How and why did you get so chummy with the Pawlings?"

"How crude these Americans," he said with mock irony. "No time for the amenities. That's what I came to talk to you about. Knew you must be disturbed."

"All right, Freddie, talk. I've got a date at seven-thirty and I haven't dressed yet."

"Thought I owed you an explanation about the Pawlings."

"Good. After taking my money, I think you're right."

"Nothing brings out the Christian self-righteousness of you Yankees more than the sound of the words 'my money.' Ah well. Another story. Another time. About the Pawlings, it's simple. I met Mrs. Pawling three weeks ago at Maria DiFaustio's in Capri. She knew I would be in Venice visiting my Iowa Countess. She asked me if I knew Mrs. Baring and her brother. I did. She expressed a desire to meet them. I said I would arrange it. It wasn't until you approached me in the bar this afternoon that I began to suspect Mrs. Pawling's interest wasn't only in getting asked to the right parties. Never laid eyes on the husband until he came into the lobby of the Excelsior Palace at the Lido with you this afternoon. My Episcopalian God's honest truth!"

"Did the Pawlings pay you better than I?"

"I suspect payment will be forthcoming in the form of a Cartier watch or something equally pawnable. After all, dear boy, you are an exception. You know my stomach doesn't turn at the sight of currency. But there is a legend that I must be treated with a certain subtlety. Sometimes damned annoying."

"Is that what you came to tell me?"

"Partly. I don't know why it should matter to me. But I wanted you to know, I want you to know, whatever is happening, whatever might happen, it's not my doing, any part of it. And … and …" He put his hand to his head and closed his eyes. "Did I tell you that I intend to put a bullet through my head before the night is out?"

"You mentioned razors at the wrists."

"So I did. Too messy. What I am trying in my feeble way to tell you, Muldoon, is … Is that my voice? I hear the words, the sound. What is it saying? Why is it here?"

I kept as calm as possible. "You were trying to tell me something."

"Ah yes. I want you to know … goddamn it, man, I've been sucked in. The Ball, all this nonsense tonight, I thought it was merely a way of pleasing some friends."

"Said friends being?"

"The Feretti, of course. She doesn't count. But the ones who put the bee in my bonnet. The ones who suggested a Masked Ball in honor of Prince Ali."

"Who?"

"Mrs. Baring and her brother, Miles Winthrop."

The room seemed suddenly drowned in watery silence. "When did all this start, Freddie?"

"A month ago. Soon after Mrs. Baring knew the Prince and Miss Garnter would be their guests here in Venice. Mrs. Baring put it up to me. Naturally I jumped at it. It was a natural, in the idiom of North America. A natural to please the Feretti, the Iowa countess. It would also assure me of a roof over my head. It never occurred to me …"

"What?"

He looked up. His eyes were brighter than a drunk's, should have been. Why the lush act? Because it made whatever he was telling me easier?

"Hear me, my friend. What I am saying is difficult. I am fond of Amy Baring and her brother. I have always felt that they were, well, gentle people. Nice people, to use the language of Chicago. It seemed incredible that they might be mixed up in some unspeakable plot against the Prince and that girl."

"Plot? What are you talking about?"

"That's why I'm here, Muldoon. A victim of illusion until an hour ago. It's this way. It's no great secret that Pietro Apperatti, his sexy little cousin and the Duc d'Alveri have been throwing money around since they visited Cairo two months ago. It won't come as any great shock to you that they are, for the moment at least, owned lock, stock and body and soul by Nasser."

"No, it's no shock."

"Well, my boy, what may come as a shock to you is the following.

You have just come from Mrs. Baring's palazzo, right?"

"About twenty minutes ago."

"But you didn't see Mrs. Baring there?"

"No. Now that you mention it. I assumed she was resting."

"You assumed wrong. About forty minutes ago Mrs. Baring could be found at a corner table far back of the shrubbery at a small café near the Malibran Opera House. And she was in deep and very serious conversation with a friend of yours."

"Friend of mine?"

"Miss Nina Apperatti!"

I stared at him incredulously, trying to drag the lie up out of his eyes. But what I saw was very disturbing. I was convinced that Freddie was not conning me. He was leveling.

"What does it mean, Freddie?"

"That's your job, Mr. Bloodhound. I'm only reporting. I do know that anything to do with Apperatti and cousin has the stink of ancient garbage. I do know Apperatti is on Nasser's salary list. You figure it out."

"But not Mrs. Baring. It can't be!"

Freddie laughed. "In the world as I've seen it, my boy, the lowest most unbelievable acts, anything, can be. That's why I'm here. The Prince and Miss Garnter. What an ironic spectacle. The world ganging up against the only thing worth a damn. Love has become dangerous and suspect. Love must be destroyed. There isn't a government in the world willing to back it. Or, apparently, an individual. Except little old drunken me who has nothing to lose but his feedbag!"

The genuine bitterness in his voice surprised me. I should have found it comic but somehow it wasn't. There was something oddly touching about the cynical, world-weary Freddie in the role of Cupid.

Touching and yet not entirely convincing. Was his story about the rendezvous between Mrs. Baring and Nina just the same sort of cover-up as the phone call from Pietro?

There must be a joker somewhere. The idea of Freddie coming to sing to me in the interests of young love was preposterous.

"I know what your nasty thoughts are, old boy," he said almost cheerfully. "Can't blame you. Wondering why I should tell you all this and more. Maybe it's because I never quite believed in your toughness. Maybe because I feel sorry for you. You've been a good guy in the past and I don't like to see you take the rap."

"Me take the rap? What the hell do you mean by that?"

"Simple enough. Those two lovesick kids are way out over their heads. No one wants them to win. And a great many people will go to any lengths to stop it. Money, millions of dollars, are involved. Also that rich, rich flow of oil. And then, too, the Prince has ideas that embarrass everyone. He actually has the temerity to believe in democracy. We can't have that, can we? Something is going to happen, Muldoon. Something really evil and this time it won't be merely an Arab servant, poor guy. And furthermore when it does happen, everyone, but everyone, including your noble State Department, will be relieved. Oh, they'll cluck their tongues in horror and weep a few crocodile tears, but believe me, my naive American, they will be relieved."

"You're a bit too cynical, Freddie. Why do you think I'm here if that were true?"

He put his head back and laughed.

"You, who've been around! Coming from you!"

"What's the joke?"

"Can't you see? It's not like you to be blinded by ego. You're the sop, the excuse, so that the boys in Washington can say they had a man on the job and he fell down!"

"You're sick."

"True enough. But perceptive despite my sickness. Do you really think, Muldoon, that if your State Department really wanted to stop whatever the hell is going to happen here in Venice, that they would have sent one lone chap who doesn't even have the power of officialdom behind him? When it happens, whatever it is that's going to happen, they'll need a …"

"Sitting duck," I said involuntarily.

"Quite. Now you're brightening up, my boy!"

I turned away from Freddie and lighted a cigarette. My hand was beginning to shake. I hoped he hadn't noticed. Freddie had merely put into words what had been creeping out of the back of my mind ever since I had arrived in Venice.

"You're having a pipe dream, Freddie."

He stood up and sighed. "I intend to go on as before. Tonight I will be quite sober by the time of Feretti's brawl. Tonight I will be as silly and harmless as I ever was and blind again. It's not my business, I always say." He came across the room, put his hand on my shoulder and said in a low voice that was quite as sober as he had promised to be later.

"It's a pretty spectacle, Muldoon. A nice comment on the times in which we live. The individual no longer matters. One of them, the Prince or Miss Garnter, will be killed and there will be rejoicing in all the capitals of this ugly little planet. As for you, you, of course, are expendable."

"Freddie …"

He moved away and raised his palm expressively. "Done my duty for today, old boy. Swan song for decency. Better to revert back to type. As for you, get out while the going's good. Nothing you can say or do will stop it. You'd be bucking too much. The ant and the mountain. Don't think it hasn't been charming."

He moved towards the door.

"Freddie …" I repeated.

He turned. "Well?"

"Suppose I don't give a damn."

He smiled. "Trouble is, you have in the past, my dear fellow. So you will again!"

He went out and shut the door.

I stood there a moment mesmerized by the hideous pink shade on the bedside light. After a moment, I went to the phone and put through a call to the Ritz in Paris. I held on listening to the lonely ringing of the instrument in Hirem's room until I knew there would be no answer.

ELEVEN

It was getting to be deep down in somebody else's dream now; too high-pitched, too unreal; lost in a vast gray area between black and white. Too many villains and too few cops. A Prince in love, an Arab drowned in the Grand Canal, a whore spouting romantic nonsense beneath pornographic pictures in a beach cabaña, hatchet men in unlikely guise moving toward a Masked Ball and a payoff, a jerk husband trying to hire me to track myself down to his wife's bed, a salty old New England character whose motives were apparently far from what I had first suspected, and above all a girl named Linda whose cool and level gaze had sent me skittering toward the cliffs of guilt. Linda whom I saw as damned and yet who had crawled in there under my skin as no other woman had been able to do in the past few years.

And now Freddie come to put the finger on the shreds of my self-esteem.

A shower didn't help much to put me on an even keel. A porter arrived with my costume for the Ball. It was the sort of thing a fifteenth century monk might have worn. Savonarola? A gray robe tied around the middle with a scarlet rope and a hood flopping back over the shoulders. It didn't look very festive. In fact there was something oddly sinister about it.

I looked at my watch. Seven-fifteen. Still time enough to keep that appointment with George Pawling. Was it wise? Still, he had been in the Winthrop palazzo when the Arab had taken that nosedive to death. Maybe I could pump something out of him. And then, too, it would be a step nearer Linda. There were a couple of empty hours ahead before it would be time to climb into that costume.

I changed quickly into a lightweight suit, went down to the lobby and grabbed a passing gondola. In a few minutes I was at the landing stage of the Hotel Grand.

I walked into the little white and gold bar and the first person I saw was Linda. She was sitting alone at a corner table. The half-finished champagne cocktail on the table before her seemed an ironic contrast to the sadness I saw on her face in the moment before she turned in my direction. All the things I remembered about that room in Naples came flooding back and my real reason for being at the Grand was suddenly unimportant. She turned and looked at me and then, through me. I walked across the almost empty room.

"May I sit down?"

She stared at the door beyond me and shrugged indifferently. I might have been someone she had met casually and not liked at a cocktail party. I signaled the waiter, ordered a double Gibson and sat.

"We can talk now," I said.

She lifted her glass and sipped some of the wine. She didn't turn to me.

"I have a date with your husband. Will he show?"

"I doubt it. I think he's changed his mind about whatever it was he talked to you about."

"He wanted to employ me to track down the man you saw in Naples. Your lover."

"Lover," she said. "What a silly word."

"Linda, for God's sake come off the ice. We may only have a moment to talk. In Naples you said you were in some kind of trouble."

She didn't thaw. "Did I? I guess I was. I let a liar and a spy into my bedroom."

"Darling ..."

"Really, I am old enough to have known better." She smiled but she wasn't amused.

The waiter brought my drink and in the silence while he was at the table, Linda hummed a little tune. It sounded like *Why Was I Born?* but I couldn't be certain. When the waiter left I tried again. "Linda, Naples was on the level. I swear it."

"On the level. What a delightful phrase. Sounds like George." And then in the same light tone, "The moment you got into the launch this afternoon and said you'd been at Mrs. Winthrop's, I knew what a fool I had been. I don't owe George much, God knows, but I owe him the courtesy of not being a fool!"

"When I met you I'd never heard of Mrs. Winthrop."

"Why don't you tell this to Miss Apperatti. She might care."

"And that business with Nina, it didn't mean a thing."

"Perhaps not to you!" Her voice was suddenly sharp. Then with an effort to regain the casual note: "I suppose sleeping with Nina was in the line of duty, too! It makes me ill!"

"If you hadn't been so cold, so remote."

"What an excuse! You're just like all the others, really. In and out of bed and crying for understanding and weak as water. I suppose you consider yourself some sort of noble martyr. How gallant! The White Knight of Capitalism!" She caught herself up, looked quickly at me, then down into the champagne.

I felt the rising tides of despair. I managed to say, "So it's that way, Linda. I didn't know. All the catch phrases, too. My God, how could you ..."

She let my voice die out without protest. I prayed for a look of silent denial but it never came. After an eternity she said: "I don't believe in the confessional, ecclesiastical or political. And kindly take your hand off my leg. I don't permit that even to the FBI."

"Linda," I pressed closer. "It's George, isn't it? Whatever you're in, it's because of that sonofabitch. Listen, we could get out of here. I mean now. Go back. Go back to Naples."

She moved away from me down the banquette.

"What twisted kind of psychology keeps you loyal to that bastard?"

"You're excessively sentimental," she said.

"Is it sentimental to try to avoid murder!" I asked, stung.

She looked me directly in the eyes and said: "I suppose under certain circumstances, yes. Anyway, I don't go in for murder."

"And Georgie Porgie?"

"Why don't you get the hell out of here!"

"Linda, get off this express train before it's too late!"

"Is that straight from the State Department?" she asked with cold angry irony.

"If you won't take it any other way, yes!"

She seemed about to reply, checked her answer, got the casual social mask back into place and said: "Here is George." I thought I detected wisps of fear in her voice.

George came lumbering toward us. He seemed to have left a good deal of his self-confidence out on the canals. He was obviously angry and suspicious but there was something curiously supplicating in the look he gave his wife. Was he scared? Had something gone wrong?

"You're late," I said.

Before George could speak, Linda said, "Mr. Muldoon is just going."

"Mrs. Pawling is mistaken," I said graciously.

"About that date, Muldoon," George said glowering suspiciously from me to his wife: "It was a lot of malarky. I was only trying to get a rise out of you. I told Linda. She laughed like hell. Didn't you, darling?"

Her look gave him the lie. "Stop fussing, George. Sit down. You're so jittery, you're shaking the room."

He turned red, lifted his voice and ordered a bourbon in a big Rotarian voice.

"Your wife wants me to go. She thinks I'm crude."

"He's been making passes at you, Linda?"

"It's the man's idea of humor, George. Don't let him get you."

"The guy fancies himself as a Don Juan. I've been hearing stories."

"Oh?" Linda said on guard.

"I just left the Duc d'Alveri." To our surprise, his face lit up in a grin that under the circumstances could have been called pathetic. "Fooling around with sixteen-year-old wop gals might get you in trouble, boy. Duc's quite a character. Knows everyone in Rome, Linda. Full of dirt and gossip. Some boy." Then to me: "The wife and I are dining with him. He's taken over Antonio's restaurant for a dinner before the Ball."

"Be careful what you drink. The Duc makes the Borgias look like kid stuff."

"He's got the right ideas!" George said heavily.

"Speaking of the Borgias," I said, turning to George with a pleasant smile: "Tell me; how did you manage, without being seen, to push that Arab into the canal this afternoon?"

George paused in the act of lifting his glass. It appeared to become too heavy for him to handle. He lowered it to the table. This time he didn't look at his wife. He kept his eye on me like a snake charmer with a king cobra. After a moment he said: "Vaudeville is dead, sweetheart. That kind of joke died with the Keith circuit."

Linda chimed in now in that too bright, social voice that was beginning to infuriate me: "If that Arab really was pushed from the window this afternoon, one thing you can be certain of is that George had nothing to do with it!"

"How?"

"Simple enough." The biting edge was back. "George never could have made such a social blunder. He's much too aware of class differences to have mistaken a lowly Arab servant for the Prince."

Too late, George's round chin came up in warning. I turned to Linda. The smile faded. "What in the world did I say?"

"Nothing much," I said. "Except that, to my knowledge, this is the first time I've heard the theory expressed that the Arab might have died because he was mistaken for the Prince."

The Pawlings lapsed into silence. George dove into the bourbon.

Linda twisted the stem of her glass. She seemed curiously indifferent, yet I sensed a tense, silent demand on George. I waited, letting him sweat it out. After a bit he said: "Look, Muldoon. I know now who you are. Who you're working for. Linda conned you at the Lido this afternoon. Smart girl. But you're wasting your time snooping around our doghouse."

"You work for German-American Oil."

"So? Since when is it a crime to work for a world-famous industry? But get this, sonny, I'm an American. A hundred per cent. I'm the kind of American who never forgets Flag Day and don't you forget it. I have nothing to hide. You can report back to the State Department that I am here to try to persuade the Prince to forget this silly infatuation. Nothing more sinister. Aside from everything else, I consider it my patriotic duty to do so. Don't begin to talk about crime and murder and stuff with me, brother. I'm not having any. That's not my line."

He was giving a damned good imitation of sincerity. Out of the corner of my eye I watched Linda as he talked. She kept her face a mask except for one brief second when the corner of her mouth drew up. What was it she couldn't stomach?

"You've got to admit, George," I said affably, "that it's a goddamned curious coincidence. The telephone call from the Lido that sent you rushing back to Venice and the Winthrop Palazzo; your being out of mind out of sight when the Arab took his nosedive."

"Maybe it is a coincidence. Maybe it was timed to look that way. I don't know. Ask the old lady. She might surprise you."

"Mrs. Winthrop?"

"Yeah! Sweet, salty, eccentric Mrs. Winthrop. All those wop servants. Maybe you don't know. The son Miles thinks they are his private property. But I've got news for you. Most of them happen to be part of old lady Winthrop's private army!"

I laughed. It was preposterous of course. But I was remembering the scene on the bridge and the way I fell into Mrs. Winthrop's lap.

George swallowed the dregs of his drink and stood.

"You'll excuse us, Muldoon. The wife and I have to dress. We're due at the Duc's dinner party in half an hour."

I walked with them to the lobby. Linda turned. She looked into my eyes and said: "It's rather touching, your concern for the Prince. Perhaps you were weaned on Romeo and Juliet."

To my surprise the innocuous statement brought a scowl to George's face. "Come on, Linda," he said gruffly. "Whatever the hell Mr. Muldoon is up to doesn't concern us."

Linda was still looking at me. There was some urgent message in her eyes I missed. She turned and followed George into the gilt elevator cage. I stood there for a moment watching as the elevator lifted slowly through the open shaft up out of sight.

I went out to the canal. Somewhere a tenor was singing in a lovesick tremolo. I signaled to a gondolier. Something whizzed past my ear. Behind me there was a clatter on stone. The doorman bent down and picked up an object.

"Did you drop this, *Signor?*"

I turned to look at what he held in his outstretched hand. Even before I saw it, I knew what it would be. It was a stiletto. The blade gleamed innocently in the moonlight.

TWELVE

"The Montagues and the Capulets were bad enough to deal with in their time. Nowadays they've expanded into whole countries."

Mrs. Winthrop sat very stiff in a very straight-backed chair. Behind her the handsome young Sicilian servant with whom I had talked in the afternoon was busy emptying ashtrays. I was uncomfortably certain that he was listening carefully to every word.

"Romeo and Juliet!" she said shortly. "Haven't you heard of them?"

"Why should you bring them up now?"

"Ali and Judith," she said. "They are going to this fool Ball dressed as Romeo and Juliet."

I remembered Linda's strange remark about Romeo and Juliet in the lobby of the Hotel Grand. It was too much of a coincidence. She must have known that Prince Ali and Judith Garnter were going to the Ball as the Lovers of Verona. How had she discovered? And why had she been so anxious to let me know she knew?

"Where are they now?"

Mrs. Winthrop tapped her fingers together. "I wish I knew. I thought you'd be able to tell me. That's what I'm hiring you for."

I managed to keep patient. I dug in the folds of the monk's robe and brought out a cigarette. Mrs. Winthrop made a disapproving face as I lighted up. The Sicilian swooped down with an ashtray for the table at my elbow.

"You must get over the idea that I'm working for you, Mrs. Winthrop."

"On the contrary. You, my dear young man, must get over the silly idea of working for Washington. It's absolutely subversive. They never get anything done down there. And I need you more than that silly administration does. I have come to believe, with some effort, that Presbyterians should have freedom of worship but I do not believe in permitting them to become a national fetish. That's another story though." She broke off and turned to the servant: "Now look here, Albert ..."

"Alberto, *Signora* ..."

"The name is Albert, while you're in this household. We won't need you now. You've heard quite enough!"

Alberto was not offended. He smiled. The look he gave Mrs. Winthrop was adoring. When he had left she said, "The morals of a cat but in every other way, absolutely trustworthy."

"Part of your private army?"

"I don't approve of armies," she said. But she grinned. "However I believe in organization!"

"Look, Mrs. Winthrop, haven't you any idea where the Prince and Miss Garnter went this evening?"

"None at all. They left here about nine. I was counting on you to track down this Apperatti person."

"I had other things to do."

"You look absurd in that Popish outfit," she said irrelevantly. "Anyway, I want you to keep a sharp eye on them at the Ball."

"Is that what you wanted to see me about?"

"Partly." She darted a look around the great drawing room like an angry pelican. She leaned forward and lowered her voice.

"The Arab was an imposter."

"The Arab?"

"The fool who got himself drowned this afternoon."

I almost dropped my cigarette.

"An impostor! What do you mean?"

She shook her head impatiently. "Surely you know the meaning of the word? He was not a representative of the King of Donrd-Arabia. He was nothing of the sort!"

"How do you know?"

"It's quite simple," she said. "I put a telephone call through to the King in Donrd-Arabia. He had designated no such person to act as bodyguard to his son."

"Does the Prince know you talked to his father?"

"Not yet. I didn't put through the call until he went out with Miss Garnter."

"What made you suspect?"

"Something Albert, or Alberto, if you will, said. He had, in some manner I do not choose to investigate further, become rather intimate with this young Arab in the short time he was with us. It seems the habits of Sicily are not too far removed from those of the Arab world. In certain unmentionable respects."

"I think I get what you mean," I said uncomfortably. "Albert remembered that the young Arab had let drop something about Cairo.

Some friend he had there and apparently missed. Even Albert had sense enough to know that Cairo is a long way from Donrd-Arabia and that the chances of a naïve young Arab boy having made that long journey was remote. I went on from there and put through the call to the King."

"You think this guy who was drowned was one of Nasser's hatchet men?"

"Yes."

"Do you think the Prince suspected as much?"

She looked away. "It's possible. If so, he said nothing."

"Then it's also possible that it might have been the Prince who tossed the boy into the canal."

She hesitated. "It's possible. Somehow I don't like to think so."

"It certainly seems to give Pawling an out."

"What's that?"

"What else did the old King have to say?"

She looked intently at a gilt cornice in one corner of the vast room.

"He's not well. Naturally he's worried about events. But he's not well."

There was an odd note in her voice I couldn't decipher. She went on hurriedly: "Ali is the son of his old age. His favorite. He trusts him to do the honorable thing. I hope he is right!"

"You speak as though you knew the King."

"When you're my age, my boy, you don't let convention stand in the way of coming to the point. I came to the point and oddly enough so did the King." She hesitated a moment, then said with unexpected vehemence: "The selfishness of youth! The unmitigated selfishness!"

If possible, she seemed suddenly to sit even straighter in the stiff-backed chair. Her eyes swung around on me like the distant point of a lighthouse beam. "Now, young man, these impetuous young people are my responsibility while they are my guests. I want you to get to that Ball, keep an eye on them and don't let them out of your sight. If we can only get through tonight ..."

"Why tonight?"

She caught herself up. "Never mind that. I'll pay you well. Better than that silly government. After all, it's the same thing. My tax money is paying your salary right now. No harm in going right to the source, is there?"

"Mrs. Winthrop, will you explain one thing to me? Why are you involving yourself so deeply in the affairs of Prince Ali and Miss Garnter?"

She looked at me for a moment and a faint twinkle lit up her eyes. "My dear boy, it's quite simple. I'm an incorrigible old busybody!"

The Sicilian servant named Alberto came into the room. He got

Mrs. Winthrop's attention almost immediately. I thought he looked pretty tense about something.

"Well, Albert?"

"There is a man here, who insists on seeing the *signora*."

"An odd time to make a call. Who?"

"He gives the name of Apperatti."

"See him!" I said quickly.

"Apperatti? That is the name given by the woman who called Prince Ali."

"Exactly. Let's see what he's up to."

"Show him in, Albert."

Alberto shrugged and went reluctantly back into the hall. A moment later Pietro came striding in, resplendent in gold cloak. Beneath the cloak his bare calves were criss-crossed with the gold straps of gold sandals.

The oily smile of greeting faded when he spotted me. Behind him I had a quick and amusing picture of Alberto's face twisted in contempt before he went back into the hall.

"Ah *Signora*," Pietro said; "I did not know you had a visitor. I would not have interrupted."

Incredibly enough he made it sound as though my call on Mrs. Winthrop involved some indecency. I suppose that in his world even that was possible. If Mrs. Winthrop got the brazen implication she gave no sign.

"This monk is Mr. Muldoon."

"Yes, *Signora*," he said. "I have had the doubtful honor." His manner was operatic and his words a bit stumbling. I realized that he was quite drunk.

"And what," demanded Mrs. Winthrop, "may we do for you?"

Pietro didn't miss the "we." He raised a suggestive eyebrow, shook some of the gold dust out of his hair and sprawled inelegantly on a chair facing us. The cloak came open around the chair revealing his costume for the Ball. Apparently he was supposed to represent Apollo or Pan or one of the least clothed of the Greek Gods. The costume consisted of a mere piece of gold mesh drawn tight about the loins. The mesh was completely transparent.

Mrs. Winthrop stiffened in shock.

"Young man," she snapped, "I am sufficiently familiar with the anatomy of the male without the need of any reminders! Have the decency to cover your sexual organs."

"Ah *Signora*, many apologies. Forgive me. Sometimes I forget. But then we Italians do not consider the body an object of shame!"

"You can carry that philosophy to extremes."

Mockingly, Pietro drew the cloak over his lap. The amusement died in his eyes. He seemed to be making an effort to remember the reason for his visit and to shake the fuzz from his brain.

When he didn't speak Mrs. Winthrop said in exasperation, "Would you be kind enough to inform us why we are honored by your presence at eleven o'clock at night?"

Instead of answering directly, Pietro turned to me. "My cousin, Nina. She is here with you?"

"I told you on the phone that I had not seen your cousin since I left her at the Lido."

"Then she lied! And you lied. You and she said you were taking her to the Ball."

Mrs. Winthrop eyed me in a puzzled manner. I said: "Who said it wasn't true?"

"It's eleven now. The Ball is beginning. Where is Nina?"

"I'm meeting her in the lobby of Danelli's at eleven-thirty," I lied.

"I do not believe you!"

"Now look here," Mrs. Winthrop began, "I don't know what you want but ..."

"*Signora!*" Pietro interrupted in an excited manner: "What do you know of this man who sits before us with a lie on his lips!"

"I beg you to remember," Mrs. Winthrop said icily, "that this room is not the setting for an opera!"

"I do not understand. But about this man. You should know the truth. This afternoon in a cabaña on the Lido, he ..."

"Shut up, you little louse!" I said as evenly as possible.

He disregarded me. "This afternoon, this Mr. Muldoon, he took my poor little cousin Nina Apperatti to the cabaña of the Duc d'Alveri and laid her!"

"How dare you use that word!" Mrs. Winthrop cried.

Pietro seemed honestly puzzled. "But it is American, is not, for when a man does this to a woman?"

Mrs. Winthrop, her face flaming turned on me. "Is there any truth in what this odious young man is saying? Answer me, Hart."

"None whatsoever," I said blandly.

"Liar!" Pietro cried. "The seduction of a minor. A very serious offense. The Duc is outraged. And furthermore, my poor little cousin, she has completely disappeared off the face of the earth!"

"I don't follow you at all." Mrs. Winthrop said quietly. She was still watching me for any telltale sign of guilt. I looked as bland and as innocent as the month of May.

"Oh *Signora*, the poor child left the Lido at about six. She was to be at a dinner party the Duc gave at Antonio's restaurant. She never appeared. Nina has never before done such a thing. The Duc, he is a patron of my family ..."

"That's a new way of putting it," I said.

"A patron of my family, *Signora*. A man of great position. He is outraged at Nina s bad behavior and I must make explanations to him. But how and where is Nina?"

"Maybe your pals the Pawlings know something," I said. "Why didn't you ask them at the Duc's dinner?"

He looked puzzled. "The Pawlings? But they were not at the dinner of the Duc's. Why would you think they were there?" He caught himself up, seemed trying to drag himself back to sobriety with a great effort of will, turned from my gaze.

I felt something cold suddenly turn over in my stomach.

Why had Pawling made such a point of going to the Duc's dinner? Why was it so important to them that I believe it? Where had they actually gone?

Mrs. Winthrop had been watching me intently. Now she said in a coldly unfriendly voice, "Hart. Look me in the eyes. Is there any truth in what this creature has accused you of? This unmentionable act with a sixteen-year-old girl?"

I tried to meet her gaze. I felt the color rising out of the depths of the monk's cowl. I felt like a six-year-old kid caught with his finger in the cake icing. Finally I felt compelled to say, "Believe me, it is not the way he has described it."

"Ah!" The sound that came from her was a cross between a snort of disgust and a sigh of disappointment. "I see that I was mistaken about you!"

She snapped her fingers and Alberto appeared. "Albert, these gentlemen are leaving."

"Mrs. Winthrop ..." I began.

"Why didn't you mention before, Mr. Muldoon, that you were so intimate with this Miss Apperatti? When I told you of the rendezvous she made on the phone with the Prince you never mentioned that you knew her well!"

Pietro who had already started for the door wheeled about. I tried to warn Mrs. Winthrop with a look but she was having none of me.

"What is this you say?" Pietro demanded. "What is this about a rendezvous between the Prince and Nina? I demand an explanation."

"You demand!" Mrs. Winthrop cried in full battle dress. "You demand nothing in this house. Now you will get out, you beastly little pipsqueak, and take your friend with you. Albert!" Her voice was a command.

Alberto looked at me apologetically but moved in on Pietro with obvious relish. Pietro didn't wait for a second invitation to leave and I knew it was useless for me to reason with Mrs. Winthrop when her Puritan sense of morality had been so badly bruised.

"As for you, Mr. Muldoon," she said in stentorian tones, "you can consider any business talks we had at an end."

"I'll call you when you cool down," I said with a grin.

"You'll do nothing of the sort."

Alberto headed Pietro and me through the hall and toward the main door. As he swung the great door open and Pietro went out onto the stone landing Alberto leaned close and whispered. "She will change her mind about you, *signor*. I know her very well." Then he added quickly: "Be careful of this Pietro and his friends."

"Thanks."

I went out onto the stone landing to face an unexpected spectacle. Moored at the landing was a magnificent gondola decorated in gold and bearing a coat of arms. It was manned by a gigantic gondolier in silk knee breeches. Seated among the crimson cushions was what appeared to be a slim young woman dressed as some sort of Greek Goddess wearing a gold mask.

The slim and dainty figure leaned forward. It spoke. The illusion was rudely shattered. From behind the gold mask came the voice of the Duc d'Alveri spouting excited Italian at Pietro. I wasn't much surprised. At this point nothing would have surprised me, least of all the fact that the Roman Duc choose to go to the Countess Feretti's ball in a woman's costume.

I stood there listening to the two of them spattering out an Italian that was too fast and too furious for me to follow. The Duc seemed beside himself with rage. But finally to some final answer from Pietro, he said "Ah," got hold of himself and said to me in English: "I am informed that you have an engagement at Danelli's Hotel. We will take you there, pick up the lady, and then all of us will go to the Ball together."

Behind me in the darkness of the doorway Alberto hissed: "*Non!*"

I stood there, undecided. I knew it was about as safe for me to get into the gondola as it might have been were I about to enter a cageful of vipers. But suddenly, as had happened so many times in my life, an impulse, half mad, overcame reason. And before even thinking I said: "Thanks, I appreciate your kindness, Duc d'Alveri."

Pietro preceded me into the gondola, settling down among the cushions next to the Duc. I followed and sat facing them. The massive gondolier maneuvered the boat away from the landing stage out into the wide expanse of the Grand Canal.

The Duc, in the dainty chiffon gown and the heavy gold mask, was not a figure of comedy. Leaning forward toward me beside the nearly naked Pietro who lolled back among the cushions, the Duc became a symbol of sinister decadence.

"Now, Mr. Muldoon," he said in a weary petulant voice: "Pietro tells me his cousin Nina had an engagement with Prince Ali. Where can we find them?"

"I wish I knew," I said honestly enough. Over the head of the two masqueraders the face of the gondolier was implanted against the stars, impassive and as indifferent as Time.

The Duc was silent. He sighed. He turned and said something in swift Italian to Pietro. Pietro snickered. We had drifted out to the far side away from the traffic in the middle of the canal.

"Pietro tells me also that you have had a disagreement with the *signora* Winthrop."

"What can I say? He heard it."

"Perhaps," he said softly, "you need an employer who is both more reliable and more generous."

"Like Nina?" I said. "I'm certain about the generosity of her terms when you babies catch up with her?"

"Nina is a sentimental little fool!" he said petulantly. "She must be taught a lesson. If it were not for me, she would now be tending the pigs on her mother's poor little farm."

"For her sake, I wish to God she were!"

He sighed again. Pietro yawned and stretched himself among the cushions.

The Duc laughed. "You take your monk's robes too seriously." He leaned closer: "Five thousand in cash tonight."

"For what?"

"To tell us where Nina is. To cooperate. You're not stupid. Why not come over to the winning side."

"You interest me."

He thought so too. "I could put you in the way of some very interesting work, Muldoon. Fascinating work. And with real pay. After all, that's what you are after, isn't it?"

I wondered how many such propositions he had made in his messy little time. Enough apparently to convince him of the invincibility of the buck.

"I'm not immune to cash," I said. It was just the right tone. The Duc leaned forward. It was all laughably simple from then on in. I got a big bunch of chiffon and bone in both hands and lifted him like a doll from its crib. The Duc was as light as his morals. He was so taken by surprise that he hadn't the presence of mind to cry out. I heaved up and out to the right. There was a small splash and in a moment, the Duc d Alveri was a blob of chiffon floating backwards away from us in the darkness.

All this took only a fraction of a minute. Pietro came into action too late. He came up out of his reclining position, half rising from the cushions. He was at a bad disadvantage. My head caught him in the chest rocking him off his axis. He clutched out wildly for the side of the tossing gondola and as he fell backwards, I caught him in the side and pushed with the weight of my shoulders. He went into the canal with a throttled watery yell. In a moment his head came up a little behind the bow and gold dust was spattered in the moonlight.

Now I turned, crouching defensively in the direction of the big gondolier. To my surprise he was simply resting on his pole watching me without even expression. From the middle of the canal, craft of all kinds were beginning to converge, brought on by Pietro's frantic cries. But the gondolier might have been deaf. From off to the left I spotted an empty gondola coming up out of the darkness. The Duc's gondolier came to life and shouted something. At first I thought he was calling for reinforcement but the other boat headed, not toward the floundering figures in the canal but toward us.

The Duc's gondolier had turned back to me. I was wary, only too conscious of the power he might wield with the heavy pole. But to my intense surprise he suddenly threw back his head and began to laugh.

The empty gondola came bumping alongside. Both men were laughing now. The Duc's gondolier broke off his laughter to say to me in English: "Quick now, you get into this fellow's boat. He will take you away, *presto!*" I managed to make the transfer without mishap. I called back "*Grazie!*" The gondola into which I hopped quickly headed away from the scene. I looked back. A launch was already fishing the Duc from the canal. I could hear his screams of rage. My new gondolier said: "It is a tragedy that they do not drown, the two of them! Where to, *Signor?*"

"The Palace of Countess Feretti beyond the Rialto Bridge."

He spat into the water.

"Every man has his own taste!" he said darkly.

"You don't approve?"

"*Signor.* I am not of the communist party. But a thing like this Ball at a time when people starve, it is almost enough to make me join." He laughed. "Still, there will be music and the people … the people of Venice will shout insults at the guests. And I suppose everyone will have a good time."

"I hope so," I said fervently. "I hope so."

THIRTEEN

The countess from Iowa was staging a super-spectacular with sixteenth century trimmings. Flickering torchlight lit the façade of the ancient palazzo as it came swimming up to me out of the night.

The wide steps from the landing stage to the famous bronze doors were lined with footmen in silk tights and the livery of some forgotten noble family. Hundreds of craft filled with rubbernecking tourists and part of the noisily derisive Venetian population clustered about the landing. It looked like a Hollywood opening on water.

The Ball had become front-page news, causing diplomatic headaches and general disapproval on two continents. The whole affair had taken on a sort of international "let-em-eat-cake" atmosphere. It was said the Countess had perpetrated an affront to the underprivileged of the world. The Countess had been quoted in the press as an upholder of aristocratic tradition. No one approved except, of course, the guests who, from what I had heard at the Lido, were determined to have themselves a Ball.

The Venetians in the crowd surrounding the landing stage in no way resembled the mobs in front of the Tuileries. They were bawdy and insulting but good-natured rather than violent. My gondola crept up the line of resplendent craft which were disgorging masked and costumed guests at the palace. I stepped out to a chorus of earthy wisecracks from the onlookers. The monk's costume brought on some ribald advice which the rest of the crowd took up with shouts of laughter. I dug my invitation from the folds of the robe and got by the bronze doors.

Just before I went in, I looked back. So far there was no sign of Pietro or his wet Duc in the long line. An impressive Machiavelli was just assisting a sixteenth century noblewoman from a gondola. There was something familiar about his important strut. I thought it might be George Pawling but I couldn't be certain.

I walked into an enormous entrance hall and a heavily perfumed atmosphere. Up around the cornices supporting the marble pillars there were damp moldy spots on the plaster. Footmen in colored tights formed a sort of cordon to the foot of a wide marble staircase. Standing beneath a stone Venus and Apollo at the foot of the stairs was an impressive figure in gold brocade who I assumed, from the manner in which she was attempting to greet the stream of guests, was the hostess. Beside her, not too well disguised as a sixteenth century court fool was Freddie Gorden. "So nice of you," the brocaded figure murmured without conviction as I went past. I leaned over and whispered to Freddie: "A nice setting for carnage."

He gave a start of recognition and said *sotto voce*: "It's begun already, only with the hostess as victim."

It was clear what he meant. Half the guests mounting the stairs went past their hostess as though she were part of the statuary group under which she stood so hopefully. Those who did pause behaved with a kind of ironic insolence. There was an ominous, loose sort of gaiety about the crowd that boded ill for the social position of the Countess from Iowa. The attitude seemed to be that a somewhat disreputable public entertainment was taking place in a shady nightclub. Everyone had come but not in the manner the American Countess expected. Halfway up the stairs I looked back. The strutting Machiavelli was bending solicitously over the hostess' outstretched hand. I was more than ever convinced it was George Pawling. Was the woman beside him Linda? I checked her costume for future reference. I suspected George had picked it out. She was a grand and pompous lady who might have been Isabella d'Este.

I waited until they came majestically up the stairs. I managed to press in close to her and whisper, "Linda." Her head came up but she didn't turn. She went on past me without any further sign of recognition. But I was no longer doubtful. I heard George say: "Remember, stay close to me!" He took her elbow and they went up ahead of me.

On the second floor was a high rotunda reaching to the roof of the palace. On the far side of this circular room stairs led down into a tremendous ballroom. We had come up only to descend again. It was quite a setting for a processional. Looking out over the vast throng crowding the ballroom floor and the adjoining rooms, I was struck once again by the curiously indecorous behavior and the insolently shocking costumes of some of the guests. Under a vaulted ceiling that might have been painted by Botticelli, reflected in the mirrored walls with their electrically simulated candlelight in great gold candelabrum, several hundred people were dancing or drinking to the music of a twenty-piece band. At the moment the tune was that well-known fifteenth century madrigal named "You Gotta Have Heart." The movements of the masked dancers and the groups in the adjoining bars and supper rooms were more uninhibited than one would have expected at an internationally advertised social affair. There was a kind of hectic to-hell-with-it atmosphere that would have been more appropriate at the Art Students Quartre Ball in Paris.

Some of the more daring guests had circumvented the sixteenth century motif demanded on the invitations by coming as Greek statues, Roman prostitutes, Renaissance dancing boys and figures from the more profane of the religious paintings of the period. One woman who seemed literally nude was being borne about the edge of the dance floor on a gilt litter by four gigantic Negroes in silver loin cloths. Courtiers clustered about the litter offering the woman champagne. She wore a bird-like mask with long trailing feathers that swept down flimsily to the nipples of her breasts. Her stalwart bearers seemed to be having some embarrassing trouble with a group of saucy Roman street boys. There was something sinister in the way she kept nodding her bird-like head.

A masked couple who had just arrived beside me at the head of the stairs disagreed about the spectacle. The woman said scathingly: "What can that Feretti woman be thinking of! This is like going to a bordello. At this rate, it may end up with the police."

A somewhat male voice answered: "Darling, how divine. I've never danced with a policeman."

"It's no joke! There's still forty minutes to go until the unmasking. The way things look now …"

They drifted away from me. I looked at a gilt clock near the entrance from the rotunda. It was eleven-fifty. Vaguely I remembered something that had come with the invitation mentioning a twelve-thirty unmasking to be followed by a processional and prizes for the best costumes. I searched the crowd for a Romeo and Juliet. They were nowhere to be seen. The room seemed stifling in some heavy perfume. The music was corny and too loud. The laughter was too shrill. My sense of apprehension increased.

Down across the ballroom I saw the couple I was sure were George and Linda Pawling go through an archway into a smaller room that had been set up as a bar. I started down the steps. There was a sudden shout of laughter from a group to my right. I turned to find a lusty Satyr had climbed up onto the litter to be received with mock ecstasy by the nearly nude Bird-Woman.

Quickly I skirted the dance floor and went into the bar. There was a mob scene there and at first I couldn't find the Isabella d'Este I thought was Linda. I fought my way to the bar and got my hands around a Scotch and soda. A brawny guy dressed as a Swiss Guard sidled in and ordered the same thing. A disheveled Nymph on my other side was arguing shrilly with reeling Columbus. "I saw what you were doing."

"Listen, honey," Columbus mumbled, "gotta see things different. This is Europe. This is fun time."

"I'll fun you, you dirty louse." The accents were pure Brooklyn.

"Try to be a lady for a change. You make trouble, sweetie, and I ship you back to New York on the first plane!"

Glass in hand I moved away from them, searching the crowd for Linda. When I didn't find her I went to the archway leading into the ballroom where I got a clear view of the main entrance stairs from the rotunda. In the shadow of the pillar beside me a Greek Statue was exploring the possibilities of a Roman Street Girl. The strategically placed rosebuds that constituted most of her costume were being scattered on the parquet. Suddenly she broke away giggling and headed for one of the balconies overlooking the canal with the statue in hot pursuit.

I downed most of my drink in one gulp. The heat and the heavy sensual atmosphere of the room, the monotonous beat of the dance band were having an odd effect. Time seemed to be slipping away. I thought: these are the Dancers of the Plague. Soon the last guest will arrive and it will be Death. Then with a start I remembered the costume I wore. Had the thoughts of Savonarola come with the monk's robes?

The Bird Woman and the Satyr were performing a satire on love and passion to the amusement of the crowd. Out of the corner of my eye I noticed that the Swiss Guard had taken a position not far from me at the pillar on the opposite side of the archway. I began to be certain that he was watching me. Whose hood was he?

I went back to the bar and picked up another Scotch. Linda and George had apparently left the room and I couldn't spot them in the mob out on the ballroom floor. I went back to my position at the pillar. I thought, maybe it's all right; maybe they have sense enough not to come here after all. But just as I lifted the glass to my lips they arrived.

It was an entrance as dramatic and effective as though it had been staged by Cecil B. DeMille. The late-comers had dwindled to a mere trickle and the winding entrance stairs were almost deserted. They came out of the topmost step and stood there, side by side, while the room below them seemed to melt away. Romeo and his Juliet were both in white; he in silk tights and a high jacket decorated with gold leaf; she in simple flowing gown cut high to conceal her breasts and a veil attached to her little Juliet hat that resembled a wedding veil. In the midst of the turbulent colors affected by the other guests the effect was stunning. They seemed isolated in their own special light.

The dancers were oblivious to their presence. Below them the muscular Satyr brushed the feathers from the Bird Woman's breasts.

None of the dancers were aware of the special radiance that stood above them at the head of the stairs. There was no pause in the laughter, the furtive giggles, the goat-like movements of the Satyr, the whirling dancers. Green, purple, yellow and scarlet, pink flesh and chartreuse headdress clashed in violent eruption across this roomful of civilized people who seemed caught in the grip of some mass hysteria, while the lovers stood above them, hand in hand, impervious to the Dancers of the Plague.

The Dancers of the Plague! The fancy still held me. Outside the world was being decimated by disease and soon the final bell would toll. In the meantime, the Lovers of Verona, doomed by a family feud, unnoticed in the hectic orgy, spoke a message whose silent truth had been long forgotten. There is something I, too, have forgotten, I thought. Something, somewhere, before everything began to happen to me. And I thought, they know, and I, God help me, have forgotten.

The orchestra was playing, of all things, "The Saint Louis Blues" with a kind of nasal insistence, devoid of feeling and life. It faded from my senses like calliope music on a summer night. It took with it, for just a moment, my well-developed armor of cynicism. I watched the lovers as though mesmerized. There was a curious sense of repose about them. They were certain about something, or at least so it seemed to me. Their world moved with them and contained nothing more. Hand in hand they watched the dancers below them for a moment and then slowly began to descend toward the floor.

I thought, no! Don't go there; not with them!

And as though my thoughts had been overheard a voice whispered in my ear: "Don't turn, we're being watched." I managed to keep facing the ballroom. The Swiss Guard was looking intently in my direction. Linda's voice went on: "The unmasking. You must warn them. But watch out, the Swiss Guard ..."

For just a moment her hand brushed mine and then I sensed her moving away from me. I couldn't resist turning. She was hurrying past the crowded bar toward the door to the supper room. The sense of doom and disaster was lightened for a moment. She must have risked a lot for that. It filled me with a curious feeling of elation. When I turned back the Swiss Guard hadn't moved. Out in the midst of the dancers I saw a Machiavelli that might have been George. And then I saw something else that made my blood run cold.

Pietro Apperatti was standing at the top of the stairs. He still wore the wet gold mesh loin cloth but he had got hold of a dry cloak, purple and gleaming, that hung over his shoulders. He stood there, legs apart, the gold mask giving his face a stiff and curiously malevolent appearance. Beside him was a curious figure. It also wore a purple cloak but pinned tight around the front, silk stockings and satin shoes that were still soaking wet. Around its head it had tied a silk scarf. At any other time it would have been a comic sight; the Duc descending from a Greek Goddess to a bedraggled street girl; but at this moment the appearance of the pair was downright sinister. I thought, the last guest has finally arrived. Time has run out.

The Duc leaned over on tiptoe to whisper something to Piero. I saw him point to Romeo and Juliet who were strolling along the edge of the dance floor on the far side of the ballroom.

In that instant—a minute, hours too late—something clicked in my mind.

Near me there was the crash of shattering glass. For a moment I didn't realize it was my own glass, fallen unheeded on the parquet floor. I was aware of encompassing many things in the flash of a second. Around me the scene was like a speeded up movie sequence: the Swiss Guard coming out of his indolent watchfulness to some sort of preparatory tension; the Duc and Pietro separating at the head of the stairs and moving out at an angle from their past position down into the ballroom, the Machiavelli guiding his partner to the far side of the dance floor, Romeo and Juliet, come to a halt and standing rather uncertainly now on the rim of the seething dancers, the sensation of the room beginning to whirl to an inevitable vortex.

Why hadn't I realized before?

Was it too late?

I took a step forward into the whirling dancers. I knew the Swiss Guard was coming toward me. But at the moment my thoughts and actions were blind to everything else but to reach the Romeo and his Juliet in time.

Suddenly the music ceased. The voices of the crowd rose in excited expectation. I got a few yards out onto the floor amid the stationary couples when suddenly there was a fanfare from the orchestra and every light in the ballroom was doused.

Vaguely I realized it was some fancy idea of the Countess from Iowa. Or Freddie's? The moment of darkness to precede the unmasking. Helpless rage and panic drove me forward now, pushing the couples aside as though they had been wooden marionettes. Aware of the Swiss Guard I deviated from my straight line across the ballroom, moving a few feet up toward the main stairs. But I hadn't reached the middle of the floor before some sense of danger made me whirl around and swing out. My fist crunched up against a face; something metallic fell against my shoulder and clattered to the floor. I crouched, jumped to one side, swung about and dug my way further across the floor among the close-packed bodies. Someone shoved me violently to one side and for a second I was squeezed against naked flesh on which a hand was moving with nervous insistence. I twisted away from them and stumbled over something on the floor falling across two entwined bodies. I realized I had fallen across the litter of the bird woman. I could hear a rhythmical kind of gasping. I scrambled to my feet. With a supreme effort I wrenched away from someone's hands and reeled on, only hoping now that in the darkness I was heading for the right spot. I was for the moment out of my senses. I heard a voice shouting "No!" and realized that it was my own. It seemed lonely and far away, lost in the laughter of the crowd.

Suddenly the lights came on. I was within three yards of my goal.

The unmasked dancers all around me were emitting shrill cries of amusement and disbelief and hypocritical protestations of non-recognition. In the vortex of senseless sound the orchestra struck up martial music. Ahead of me someone said in mild curiosity, "She must have fainted."

The blood began to leave my head. "Out of the way, you bastards!" I shouted at a simpering couple who blocked my path. Frightened by my violence they parted to let me pass.

She was lying on the floor up against the mirrored wall. The white gown was folded around her like the petals of a flower. One hand was moving slightly as though for help and even that fugitive action gave me a moment of false hope. Two men, still holding glasses of champagne were bending over her, politely but drunkenly puzzled. One of the men said: "The heat, probably, or too much champagne."

I reached over, grabbed one of them by the scruff of the neck and sent him reeling away to the right. Quickly I bent down. The little Juliet cap had fallen slightly to one side but the gold mask was still in place. When I saw her mouth moving slightly as though in prayer, I knew my dark hunch had been right. I picked her up in my arms as though she had been a child.

"Everything will be all right," I whispered.

"No," she whispered faintly.

And I knew she was right. Over her head I saw, kicked into a corner behind one of the marble pillars, the bloody stiletto. No one else had noticed it yet. It looked like an innocent trinket dropped from one of the masqueraders' costumes.

The people in the immediate vicinity had begun to quiet down and exchange glances of puzzled apprehension. Even in that moment of despair I was aware of Pietro and the Duc hurrying up the marble stairs towards the entrance in the wake of a stately Isabella d'Este and a quick moving Machiavelli. It wasn't until I began to move with her in my arms toward the stairs, hardly aware of what I was doing, that the first trickle of blood began to stain the front of the white gown. She wasn't unconscious; one hand against the back of my neck had a faint, heartbreaking pressure. I moved quickly now, through an ever-enlarging circle of silence. Behind me the orchestra was beginning the pompous music for the Grand March. I hurried up the stairs toward the rotunda. At the top, white-faced footmen parted to let me pass. Back in the ballroom I heard someone scream: "Blood!" A guy who must have been a major-domo came rushing forward and pointed toward a door at the far end of the rotunda. One of the footmen hurried ahead to open the door and I carried her through into an elegantly furnished little sitting room. Over my shoulder I hissed at the Major-Domo, "Get a doctor, quick!"

Mercifully the guy didn't ask any questions. "Shut the door behind you," I called out. He obeyed and with the shutting of the door the raucous sounds of the Ball faded to a distant merry-go-round effect.

Gently I put her down on a sofa and began to tear away the cloth at her breasts. What I saw destroyed my last lingering hope. The wound was deep and ugly; the blood gushed forth now with every faint beat of her heart. I bunched the torn part of the gown into a wad and pressed it tight against the wound.

I was on my knees beside the sofa and leaned close to her face. For a moment I thought she was already dead. I removed the little gold mask. But then suddenly the eyes opened very close to mine and very faintly, in her odd English accent, she whispered: "The Americans, they have come too late."

"Nina," I whispered.

"The Prince ... so charming ... and Miss Garnter ... so lovely ... like a dream ... and everyone else so terrible ... I once ..." She closed her eyes again.

"Nina? You changed costumes with Miss Garnter and came to the Ball in her place. Why?"

A ghost of a smile lit up her face.

"They have done the elopement ... to Spain ... someone there has agreed to the ceremony of marriage ... their faces ... so innocent ... like being in the cathedral when one is a child ..."

"Who was your Romeo?"

For a moment she didn't answer. "Poor man. A waiter from the Hotel Gruenwald ... we picked him because he was the same height and figure with the Prince ... it was fun ...we planned ... I didn't think they would dare ... but they have got away ... to Spain ..."

A spasm of pain crossed her face. Her hand tightened on mine. I knew she was suddenly overcome with the sense of time running out. With a desperate effort she whispered: "American ... listen ... no one else ... my clothes ... my beautiful gowns ... my jewels ... everything ... give them ... the Convent of the Sacred Heart in Palermo ..."

"Yes, Nina."

My hand was behind her head. I felt the sudden weight. Very close to her I whispered urgently. "Who did it, Nina?"

There was no answer.

Behind me a voice said: "What in God's name is this!"

I didn't turn. Gently I withdrew my hand. I placed her head carefully in the center of the pillow and drew her arms across her breasts. Only then did I get to my feet and turn. Countess Feretti, Freddie Gorden and the Major-Domo were standing inside the doorway.

The Countess cried hysterically: "Blood all over my beautiful sofa. Tell that silly girl to get up immediately."

"She can't," I said quietly.

I walked past them into the hall. There were a few curious guests silently waiting among the footmen. A man in street clothes carrying a small black bag came hurrying toward the room I had just left. I noticed the thin train of blood across the pink marble floor. A Strauss waltz came drifting up to me from the ballroom. I went down the main stairs through the reception room out to the boat landing. No one tried to stop me. I got into a gondola and told the gondolier to take me to the Hotel Danelli as quickly as possible. From the open windows of the ballroom the waltz sounded tinny, far away and unreal. I thought, "All right, Hirem, goddamn it. You're in for it now. I'm going to get those bastards!"

FOURTEEN

Up ahead the engine gave a childish shriek. Steam rose in uneasy clouds toward the great glass roof of the station. At the last minute there was one person running down the long sparsely lit platform. I leaned against the window in the corridor of the *wagon-lit* which was marked *Venezia-Milano-Roma*, watching the running figure as though he were someone in an anxiety dream. The car gave a lurch and the long-darkened train began to move. The running man was almost directly below me now but then I began to slide away from him. Still running he moved in close to the train, reached up and grabbed the iron rung at the car entrance. For a moment he swung crazily in space. His legs fought the movement of the train, swung back in a torturous arc and finally found the steps. As he pulled himself up one of the platform lights came slowly past and his face was suddenly very clear, like a closeup in a movie. It was Miles Winthrop.

I waited. The French *wagon-lit* attendant was in one of the compartments listening to a nasal, complaining English voice. I looked at my watch. It was two-seventeen A.M.; almost two hours since I had left the Ball at the Countess Feretti's. The train was two minutes late in leaving the station. Platform lights, smothered in steam, were sliding past quickly now. Then a dimly lit sign reading *Venezia* went rushing by and we were out on the viaduct from Venice to the mainland. After that there were no more lights; nothing but velvet darkness.

The door at the end of the corridor opened and Miles Winthrop appeared. He was pale and seemed to be near hysteria. When he saw me, he stopped dead for a second, then came hurrying toward me. I put a warning finger to my lips and indicated a door to a compartment down near the opposite end of the corridor. He paid no attention.

"Where is my mother?" he gasped.

I took his arm, swung open the door to my compartment, and guided him none too gently inside, swinging the door shut behind me. He looked blankly at the two berths made up for the night.

"Sit down. There's no hurry now. This train doesn't stop until Milan."

He sat on the edge of one of the berths. "I haven't even got a ticket. I just came as quickly as I could when I got your message."

"Good. But what's all this about your mother?"

"She's disappeared!"

Nothing about Mrs. Winthrop should have surprised me too much but this bit of news was not what I had expected. "Disappeared? When? How?"

"She was gone when Amy and I came back from the Lido airport. Wherever she went, or however she went, she apparently took Alberto with her as he too is gone."

"Any ideas?"

"Good Lord, I long ago gave up trying to give rational reasons for some of mother's actions. But I thought your urgent message to make this train had something to do with it."

"Perhaps it does. More than we think. I suppose you've heard what happened at the Ball. About Nina Apperatti?"

He leaned his head back and closed his eyes? "Yes, God help us. I've been nearly out of my mind about it ever since the waiter told us."

"Waiter?"

"The Romeo to poor Nina's Juliet. He was a waiter from the Hotel Gruenwald. We picked him because he was the same height and general build as Prince Ali. After this unbelievable event at the Ball the waiter came straight to our Palazzo ..."

"Who had the brilliant idea for this disguise in the first place ... and why?"

For a moment he didn't answer. Then he said quietly: "Look here, Muldoon, I have an apology to make to you. This afternoon I thought of you as merely a meddler. I thought it was none of your damned business ... Ali and Judith Garnter. I wish I had listened to you. Maybe that poor girl would still be alive."

"We don't have time for requiems. We never do in my business. Suppose we try to prevent further errors. You can begin now by telling me what it was your sister and you had cooked up with Prince Ali and Miss Garnter."

I gave him a cigarette and he began to talk. "Ali was determined to marry Judith Garnter over any opposition. Amy and I were in complete sympathy. So was mother, for that matter ... at least she seemed to be. But we thought it better not to let mother in on our plan. We needed cooperation ... not a General! We had to devise some way for Ali and Miss Garnter to get to Spain without the entire

International Press and the secret service agents of several countries on their tails …"

"Why Spain?"

"Ali had set up a rendezvous with a friend who has a yacht. The yacht was to put in at a small fishing village below Barcelona called Dessa-di-Mar on the afternoon of the twenty-first."

"That would be tomorrow, today really. Late this afternoon."

"That's right."

"The friend would then take them across the Mediterranean to Tangiers. There they plan to be married by a rabbi and then in the Moslem manner and present the old King with a *fait accompli*…"

I groaned. "I thought the prince had more sense than that!"

"Sensible or not, we were all for it. Amy met Nina Apperatti … the two women liked each other. Nina was very romantic about the love of Ali and Judith…. It was she who first came up with the idea of letting it leak out that the Prince and Judith would go to the Ball as Romeo and Juliet, while in reality she and the waiter would go in that disguise and give Ali and Judith time to slip out of Venice before anyone suspected. It seemed like a good idea … and lots of fun!"

"Some fun."

"Amy and I went with Ali and Judith to the airport. The Barcelona plane left at ten-thirty. Then Amy and I started for home, planning to change into costumes for the Ball. But on the way back … in the Grand Canal we came upon an extraordinary scene. We found Pietro Apperatti and the Duc d'Alveri floundering around in the water surrounded by boats. We managed to get them into our gondola. They insisted on going to the Ball, wet as they were, and the Duc borrowed a cloak from our gondolier. We delivered them at the Ball before we went home to change."

"Did you tell Pietro or the Duc where you had been and why?"

He opened his eyes, then quickly looked away. "I'm afraid I did tell Pietro."

"For Christ's sake, why?"

"Well, after all, Ali and Judith were safely out of Venice. Pietro would hardly have any reason for caring … I've known him fairly well, you know. He was my secretary for a time. I thought it would amuse them."

"That," I said with ominous import, "was unfortunate."

Miles straightened up. "Not Pietro! Surely not Pietro! He was Nina's cousin! He can be a naughty boy but, but … murder! Murder! Impossible!"

I sighed. "Go on. What did you and your sister do then?"

"We went back to our palazzo. It was almost midnight by this time. We were planning to change into costumes for the Ball. But we found the palazzo in a state of confusion. Mother had left with luggage for God knows where taking Alberto with her. I went out in a frantic search for her. The railway station … calling the airport … going to the leading hotels. I had no success. When I got back Amy told me you had called and that it was important for me to catch the Orient Express leaving Venice at two-fifteen A.M. As you see, I just managed it."

"Now let me get this straight. The Prince and Judith Garnter flew to Barcelona, that much I knew, but about this guy with a yacht—are you certain about that?"

"Positive. The owner is Pharnasis, the Greek shipping tycoon. He and Ali have been in cahoots about this plan for some time. It was difficult to arrange a marriage in the Moslem tradition or to find a rabbi willing to perform the ceremony. Pharnasis made the arrangements in Tangiers."

"If they ever get there!"

"Now it's your turn, Mr. Muldoon. What are you—what are we—doing on this train?"

"Well, first I tried to get a plane out of Venice for Barcelona but there was none until noon tomorrow. However there is a TWA plane out of Milan for Barcelona at seven A.M. This train is due in Milan about five-thirty."

"But what do you hope to gain? You can't persuade Prince Ali to change his mind even if you are able to intercept them before they board the yacht at Dessa-di-Mar."

I sighed in exasperation and decided not to explain what might lie in store for the Prince and his fiancée. "There is a couple on this train I want to keep an eye on. They don't know I'm on their trail. Couple by the name of Pawling."

"The Pawlings? But why in the world would you be trailing them?"

"They may know something about Nina's death."

"Surely not the Pawlings!"

"Now look, Winthrop, I want your help. But first, have you anything else to tell me?"

"Nothing that I can think of…. Oh yes."

"Well?"

"After the waiter came back to us with the horrible news about Nina, I put through a call to the Excelsior Palace Hotel thinking Pietro might have returned and could give me some further details. To my surprise the desk clerk said that he and the Duc had checked out ten minutes before. He had no idea where they had gone."

I groaned, "I might have known."

"Where do you think …?"

"My guess is Barcelona."

Winthrop leaned forward. "Mr. Muldoon, all this is very nightmarish and unreal to me. I thought when I got your message that you might have news of mother. Now I find myself on a train for Milan with no ticket and no change of clothing."

"Take it easy. You can get a plane back to Venice from Milan in the morning. In the meantime I've engaged this whole compartment. Damned expensive because it had to be booked all the way through to Rome. Be the guest of the U.S. Government. But now I want your help."

"Anything!" he said fervently.

"It's not much I want but it may help. George Pawling is in the restaurant car now trying to calm down his nerves with coffee and brandy. I want you to go in there, sit down with him and hold him as long as possible."

He didn't hesitate. He was as eager now as any aspiring Boy Scout. And mercifully he didn't ask any more questions.

"Tell him that your mother has gone to Rome on some mysterious errand. Get him worried and curious and asking questions. Only don't give him any answers. I mean correct ones."

"That won't be very difficult," he said not without irony. He stood and smiled charmingly. "Leave it to me, Mr. Holmes. You may not believe this, but on occasion I have been known to be quite persuasive."

"So I understand." Then before he could reach the door I added: "Tell me, Miles, about that Arab boy … the one who was drowned…."

"Yes."

"I want your expert advice."

He turned. "Expert?"

"Do you know whether this Arab, well, in the short time he had been in the palazzo … Do you know whether he became friendly, shall we say, in the sense that the Baron Charlus practiced friendship … with the servant Alberto."

His eyes didn't waver. With great candor he said: "Your guess is as good as mine. But I should say yes."

"Thanks."

He hesitated. Then he said: "Muldoon, about my mother."

"Yes?"

"She is an eccentric and sometimes maddening woman given to odd behavior. But she has always been able to take care of herself. You don't think that this time …" He broke off.

"I'm not worried about her in the least," I said with a heartiness I didn't feel.

"Good!" His relief and obvious trust in me were naïve and rather touching. "You know," he added like a small boy, "I guess without Mamma, I couldn't very well manage to navigate."

He went out into the corridor carefully closing the door behind him. For some reason I felt an odd, irrational sense of guilt at his going. Rain began to spatter the windows. Above the clickity-click to the wheels there was a dim rumble of distant thunder. I lit a cigarette, waited a few minutes, then got up and peered into the corridor. It seemed deserted. I stepped out and walked quickly down to the end of the car and compartment two.

When I was almost there the attendant suddenly appeared at the end of the car. I grinned. "Monsieur is in the restaurant car," I said with heavy inference pointing to the door of the compartment. "Madame is an old friend and she is quite alone."

He rallied as would any other patriotic Frenchman. He smiled. "I am taken with a sudden blindness," he said and walked past me down to the other end of the car.

I waited a moment, then slid the door quickly open and stepped inside. The compartment was in darkness. I closed the door behind me. There was a violent roll of thunder, quite close now.

"George ...." she muttered sleepily.

I grunted.

"Good," she said in that odd emotionless, faraway voice. "I couldn't fall asleep until I told you once again what an obscene, paranoiac, heartless sonofabitch you are."

I pitched my voice down in my throat. "Move over."

"You're drunk. Don't start that sort of thing with me. You lost your entrance ticket long ago. Now ..." She broke off. Then her voice rose sharply: "George?"

"Hello, sweetie."

The little light above her berth was suddenly turned on. She was half out of the bedclothes, drawn back now onto the corner of the berth, hand still on the light switch.

The tableaux lasted only a fraction of a second. Shock passed swiftly from her eyes. "What do you think this is? A French stage set?"

She yanked the lace nightgown down to her knees.

I said: "Poor George. He must have cold feet these nights. No wonder the poor bastard suspected everyone from the bellhops to the cabaña boys."

"How did you know we were on this train?"

"Simple. I went to the Hotel Grand. You had just checked out. I bribed the concierge. He told me you had gone to the railway station and gave me your compartment number on the Wagon-Lits for Rome. I decided to come along for the ride."

For a moment she said nothing. She looked me in the eyes, her expression cool and unnerving. "You might as well have come along for a ride on an express to hell," she finally said. "But don't forget I have prior reservations."

"I'm beginning to suspect that. But I'm curious. At the Ball you saw fit to warn me to get the Juliet out. Why?"

She looked beyond me to the door. In a low voice she said: "I beg you to get out of here before he comes back."

"Linda," I said, "you left very suddenly. Was it because of what happened at the Ball? Was it because of the murder of Nina Apperatti?"

She didn't answer. Her expression didn't change. But the hand clutching the neckline of the nightgown slowly relaxed and when she did speak the life seemed drained from her voice. "Go away."

"You didn't know?"

"Go away."

"Linda, come through the ice pack! Get out while there is still time!"

"Time?" She looked at me blankly. "All the time ran out long ago."

I sat on the berth and leaned toward her. She looked indifferently down at my hands on her shoulders. "Linda ... darling," I said. "Stop playing along with them. Your husband is nuts and you know it. Full of paranoiac dreams...."

She shook her head listlessly. "If you ever cared anything about me you will get out before he comes back."

I shook her. She was like a rag doll in my hands. I began to feel helpless and enraged.

"You're getting off at Milan. You're flying to Barcelona. George is desperate to prevent this marriage. He's like d'Alveri and the rest. He's lost all sense of perspective. You won't get away with it. They'll catch up with you."

"They! So many theys."

"I'm not getting through to you. Linda, you think that because of the work I'm doing—you think that's why Naples happened. But it isn't true. So help me God, I wasn't on any job when I met you there."

She sighed and closed her eyes. "It doesn't matter now. There are things that you can't dream of. Nightmares."

"In Naples you said you were in some kind of trouble. Can't you trust me enough to—"

"Trust you?" I felt her shoulders stiffen. Life came back to her voice and with it a sharp bite. "I heard that too, once in a dream! Not anymore. You have to do whatever you have to do and it's not my business ... my life. Cajoling, making love to me, promising me the Capitol Building in Washington ... none of these things will change what I have to do. I have no need of rescue. Go back and join the Mounties!"

"Goddamn it!" I shook her violently by the shoulder and then suddenly released her and stood up. "All right, sweetie, you're writing the ticket. Don't ever forget that! Whatever happens."

"I've known that for some time."

Just before I reached the door she added in the same dead voice: "Sometimes you're committed before you're born. I think I was. Goodbye, Hart."

I went out into the corridor and shut the door firmly behind me. It was like shutting a door on some important aspect of my life. The corridor was deserted. Rain was slashing against the windows. A sudden jagged fork of lightning rent the darkness outside. The train was traveling swiftly through the storm and as I started down the lurching corridor for my own compartment I had to resort to the handrail for support. Halfway down the length of the car I stopped. For a moment I almost gave in to the savage impulse to return quickly to Linda's compartment and to fulfill violently the function legally assigned to George. The picture of her cold remote eyes stuck in my mind like an after-image on television. But I got hold of myself and resisted the half-insane compulsion. I finally reached the door of my own compartment and threw it open. Still caught in impotent fury I went in, closed the door behind me and switched on the light.

Miles Winthrop was sprawled across one of the berths. His eyes were staring fixedly at the ceiling in a childlike gaze. There was a hole on the left side of his forehead. There were marks around it that might have been rust.

I started to turn back to the door but of course I never made it. The world came crashing down on the back of my head and I went hurtling off somewhere into the heart of the thunderstorm. A hundred heads of Miles Winthrop went spinning around in the splintering darkness and they were all whispering "Mamma" and then there were no more heads and no more whispering and I fell softly into the depth of nothing at all.

FIFTEEN

I was half awake with a train running through my head. Only the clickity-click of the wheels had become an intolerable pounding. I thought, how do you get a train to leave your head; who do you ask? Then I thought, if I can only speak to Linda about it. For a moment the pounding receded, then it came back stronger than ever, rose to a climax and faded finally to a dull clickity-click. I opened my eyes.

Miles Winthrop was under the blanket of his berth. He looked as though he were sleeping peacefully. Had I dreamed all the rest? His face was turned toward the wall. I too was lying under the blanket of my berth but I was fully dressed. The clickity-click of the wheels resolved into a persistent throbbing on the back of my head. When I tried to raise myself the throbbing turned into a sharp pain. I put my hand back there and found blood clotted over an unpleasantly large bump.

At that moment I realized the train was traveling through broad daylight.

I staggered to my feet and lurched over to the other berth. One quick look was enough. I hadn't dreamed it. Miles Winthrop was dead.

Somehow I managed to get into the tiny lavatory. I removed my coat and shirt and set to work, leaning against the basin for support when blackness threatened to settle down around me again. Warm water and soap, then cold water and finally I had rid myself of the clotted blood. The bump wasn't as monstrous as I had supposed after all, but I had vague worries about concussion. Whoever had hit me meant it to take for good and all. About ten minutes later I came out of the lavatory feeling as though sometime in the dim future, it might be possible once again to rejoin the human race. I stepped out into the corridor and shut the door tight behind me. The *wagon-lit* attendant was leaning against the handrail at the end of the corridor looking out at the sunlit fields.

"My watch has stopped," I said. "Are we due in Milan?"

He grinned. "Monsieur sleeps well. We left Milan twenty minutes ago."

I felt a sickening lurch in the back of my head. I leaned up against the rail.

"Where do we stop next?"

"Genoa. In a little less than an hour."

"I see," I said dully. Then I indicated the door of my compartment. "My friend has had a bad night. Do not disturb him until at least eleven."

"I understand." He frowned. "Monsieur has a bump on the back of his head."

"Alas," I said. "It is a malignant growth. I am bound for Rome to see a specialist."

"Oh, monsieur, forgive me. I am so sorry."

"Forget it. I think I will have some breakfast. Tell me, my friends in compartment one ... they left the train at Milan?"

"Yes. Madame looked very chic and beautiful!"

"She always does."

I went to the restaurant car fighting off the pain in my head and the feeling of complete frustration. By this time the Pawlings would probably be air-bound for Barcelona. If I got off the train at Genoa the best I could hope for was to make connections somehow with an afternoon plane for Spain. By that time it would probably be too late to prevent whatever the hell Pawling-Apperatti-Alveri and company had in mind. I went on to the restaurant car and ordered breakfast. Coffee and food calmed down the throbbing in my head. I got hold of a railway time table and looked up trains northbound from Genoa to Milan. My train, the Rome section of the Orient Express, was due at Genoa at seven-forty. There was a northbound express at eight-five that would get me into Milan about quarter of nine. It was a lucky break. I began to feel better. Maybe it was an omen.

When I left the train at Genoa I again warned the conductor not to disturb my compartment mate until at least eleven. I took him into my confidence—a note from madame. A rendezvous in Milan for the late afternoon. Thus my reason for leaving the train at Genoa. He was full of admiration. The reason was, for him, more than sufficient.

On the Genoa platform I watched the snake-like departure of the Orient Express south for Rome. With luck the body of Miles Winthrop might not be discovered until eleven A.M. and I might be out of Italy by that time. My close proximity to two murders in the space of twelve hours might be difficult to explain to the authorities. At the very least it would tie my hands and prevent me from getting to Spain.

In the time I had between trains, I made a call to Paris. Hirem's room at the Ritz didn't answer. It was obvious that Papa wasn't backing this one. I was on my own.

The northbound express was not only on time, it got me to Milan five minutes ahead of schedule. At nine-fifteen I was at the Milan airport. There I had another stroke of luck. A big trans-Atlantic plane was due to let down at Milan from Athens at ten-thirty and would stop again at Barcelona on its way to New York. Someone had cancelled and I grabbed his place. Two minutes before two P.M. the big DC-6 came to rest on the airport at Barcelona. At two-fifteen I was in the offices of The American Express just off the Rambla. Dessa-di-Mar. The young American was determined I had made a mistake. Surely I meant Tessa-di-Mar, north on the Costa Brava. No; I was firm. He doubted I would like Dessa; a dreary little fishing village. No one ever went there. However he finally produced a map. No train or bus. The only manner of reaching it was south on Nationale route ten, then a turn to the left on a dirt road, four miles of doubtful driving. When he saw I was not to be dissuaded he became cooperative. Within fifteen minutes a hired car was at the door. I set off through the streaming traffic of the Rambla, turned south into the ultramodern architecture of the University section, found Route Ten without difficulty and in twenty minutes was streaking down the narrow ribbon of road among the hills overlooking the vast bay;

streaking, that is, as fast as my little English Ford could streak.

As the road veered away from the sea, the fringes of urban Barcelona fell behind and soon I was out in the wild, thinly populated country to the south. Here and there a tile-roofed farmhouse slid past behind crumbling walls and once as I rounded a sharp curve, a fifteenth century castle, dark, foreboding and utterly unreal, rose from a mountain top against the darkening sky. About twenty miles south of Barcelona I came on a dilapidated sign reading Dessa-di-Mar pointing to the left and a dirt road that twisted away down the mountainside toward the sea. The road, after traveling a few yards, became incredible; a mere track through a rocky moonlike landscape. The little car bounced around like a monkey on a hot plate. It seemed endless and got worse as it approached the sea. I was forced at times to a mere crawl.

The afternoon light was being drained from the sky when I finally came upon the tiny village. It consisted of a few stone cottages, a church, some larger dilapidated houses and an evil-looking hotel-café strewn around a square, the far side of which opened on the beach. Fishing *caques* were drawn up on the beach and a few men were busy mending nets nearby. The village was at the head of a small bay. On either arm of the bay great black rocks, like some Mediterranean Stonehenge, stood bleak and ominous against the dying sun. I inched the car into the dusty little square. Rusted iron balconies hung from houses that once might have belonged to a prosperous bourgeois but were now falling into a state of incredible decay. Broken window panes, meagre wash hanging from the balconies, cracked walls told a story of abject poverty.

At the end of the square where it opened on the beach was the hotel-café whose faded sign read with grandiose irony *Hostel de La Regina Isabella*. Its windows were fly-specked and there were a couple of desolate iron tables set out under an arch that faced the beach. In front of the hotel was an ancient battered Hispano and a sleek little yellow Jaguar sports car. The Jaguar was as out of place as a duchess at the firemen's ball.

A woman in black came out on one of the iron balconies and stared at me with tired blank eyes. The men at work among the *caques* on the beach looked up, as though on signal, and then without expression returned to their work. When I turned off the motor the square was drenched in an intense, oppressive silence. If it had not been for the slap of the sea on the beach I might have imagined myself suddenly deaf.

Uneasily I got out of the car. There was no sign of a yacht in the small harbor. My feet made an unseemly clatter on the cobblestones as I crossed the square to the entrance of the hotel. As I passed the yellow Jaguar I noticed a gay little bouquet resting on the seat beside the wheel. A bridal bouquet.

I went under the arch into a room that obviously served both as hotel lobby and café. It was small and dark, containing two iron tables and a bar. Behind the bar stood a husky sullen-looking Catalonian. He didn't seem very friendly. The only other occupant of the room was a tall stork-like young woman in a battered straw hat, a sort of blue smock and black, tight-fitting slacks. She was sitting at one of the tables on which was a discarded copy of the *London Times*. The index fingers of each hand were resting lightly on the side of a wine glass. She stared at me with frank curiosity. I disregarded her and addressed the bartender:

"Good afternoon," I said in English. "I am in search of friends who planned to be here in Dessa on this day. I think perhaps they belong to the Jaguar outside."

The guy shrugged and shook his head.

Behind me the woman spoke up in an English that was tinged with the aggressive accents of Bloomsbury: "He doesn't speak English. At least he pretends not to. Besides, he wouldn't tell you anything. Perhaps you'd better talk to me."

I turned. She was leaning back, head tilted in a frighteningly provocative manner, glass raised as though in preparation for a toast. "I'm Angela Brooks-Carnovan and I'm damned curious!"

"Curious?" I said uneasily.

"I paint. I've been here for several weeks. Some sadist told me it was quaint and I don't have the energy to move on. No one comes. No one goes. Until today. I'm very disappointed in you, coming in a simple little Ford. The others came in style. A yacht. A Jaguar. A Rolls. A Maserati. We even had a Cadillac. Just like the cinema if you care for that sort of thing. I do. I love mysteries. Sit down and I'll give you a brandy. Don't look so frightened. I'm about as sane as anyone else."

Weakly I obeyed. She managed a few words to the bartender in halting Spanish, and scowling he came to the table with a dirty glass of some evil-looking liquid.

"I'm Will Jenkins," I lied. "American."

"Really. I'm so glad you told me. I would have taken you for an Outer Mongolian!"

"I had a sort of date to meet my friends here."

She laughed. "That's what they all said!"

"All."

"Well, I guess I'd better begin with the yacht. It came about eleven this morning. Very impressive. Filled the harbor like the *Queen Mary*. Big things make me fidgety. And this was revoltingly big. It anchored offshore and another big thing, a man, very suntanned and impressive like his damned yacht, came ashore in a small boat. He came into the bar and asked if a young couple had arrived. I was here and told him no. He seemed somewhat disturbed and exceedingly unsociable. He went outside to wait. After a bit he came back in and ordered a brandy at the bar while his minions stood around on the beach waiting for orders. Then, in about fifteen minutes the Rolls arrived."

"Rolls."

"Shiny and expensive, of course, and driven by this mad Italian. Very handsome but he wore an ill-fitting suit that somehow did not go with the Rolls. A face out of Botticelli and the manners of a waiter. My tastes don't run to Botticelli types. The fishermen here have heavenly bodies but of course that is another story...."

"An Italian in an ill-fitting suit. How do you know he was Italian?"

"I know the language and he spoke it like a native ... touch of Sicily ..."

I straightened up. "Go on."

"He came in and approached the yachtsman and said in Italian—I heard distinctly—'There has been a last-minute change of plans, *Signor*. The young couple have found it best to proceed to Valencia.'"

"Ah." I was trying to figure the identity of the Italian. The ill-fitting suit didn't fit the description of either the Duc d'Alveri or Pietro Apperatti.

"The yachtsman was very angry. He muttered something about it not being at all convenient. But after a bit he went back to the beach and was whisked off to his revolting yacht and then went steaming out of the harbor in what appeared to be high dudgeon."

"What did the Italian do?"

"Ordered coffee and sat at the table where he would get a good view of the square. He didn't have to wait long. The yellow Jaguar came charging down into town and screeched to a halt and another handsome young man stepped out, leaving a very attractive girl to wait in the car. This one wore his clothes divinely. But when he bounded into the café and saw the Italian he stopped as though thunderstruck and said, 'Alberto! How did you get here!'"

"Alberto!"

"You know him?"

"I knew him once in Venice. He was a friend of a very wicked old lady."

"I'm not surprised in the least. He was very oily. He informed the handsome young man that the yacht had been forced to leave. And then he went up and whispered something in the young man's ear. I would have given several hours of my life to have been able to overhear but, of course, I didn't. But the effect of the words was astounding. The young man seemed to wilt before my very eyes. Only a moment before he had been full of life and a sort of nervous electricity."

"Like a prospective groom."

"Exactly. But after the Italian whispered to him he literally seemed to collapse. After a bit he said in a tired voice. 'I might have known.'"

"And then …?"

"He threw the keys of his car to Manuel, the bartender, and shouted in Spanish that he would send someone for it. Then he went out with the Italian and they spoke to the girl. She looked as though all the joy had suddenly been driven from her life. The Italian took their bags and transferred them to the Rolls and then they all went off in the Rolls leaving me nearly dead of curiosity."

"Did you overhear nothing more that was said?"

"Nothing. Oh, I almost forgot. When he told Manuel that he would have someone come to collect the Jaguar, he said, 'From the castle of the Duc Garalda …'"

"Does that mean anything to you?"

"Mean anything to me! Why the castle is one of the show places of Spain."

"Where is it?"

"About forty miles down the coast. On the road to Valencia. Fabulous. A Moorish castle out of the Arabian Nights."

"You mentioned a Maserati and a Cadillac, I believe."

"Yes. Getting to sound like an international automobile show. Well, first the Maserati. It came about a half hour after the Rolls left. That would have been about three o'clock."

"You were here all the time?"

"I'm always here. Breakfast, lunch, dinner and in between. Anyway, out of this Maserati—a very flashy red sports car—came another incredibly handsome young man. Also an Italian. He was with another Italian who was not at all handsome—a weary looking dried-up young man with a fish mouth."

"Pietro and the Duc!"

"Another Duc! How incredibly romantic. You know them?"

"By reputation."

"Yes. Quite. I gathered as much having lived much of my life in Bloomsbury. Anyway, this marvelous young man questioned me and naturally I told him of the yacht and the Jaguar and the Rolls and what had gone on between these variations on transportation. I told him the couple who had gone off in the Rolls with the other Italian appeared to be headed for the castle of the Duc de Garalda. And I told him about the gun."

"The gun!"

"How stupid. I forgot to tell you. The Italian, the one addressed as Alberto, had a gun. He kept it close to his side while he spoke to the handsome young man. Manuel didn't see it. I did. I believe that is what persuaded the young couple to get into the Rolls."

"Didn't you report this?"

"Not then. It didn't seem to be any of my business. However about ten minutes ago I put a call through to Barcelona. The authorities are sending someone out to investigate. Knowing Spain, that might be tomorrow."

"Anything else about the two men in the Maserati?"

"Well, yes. After I finished talking the young man ordered two straight brandies in succession. He seemed already quite drunk. And very, very agitated."

"I can imagine."

"He seemed reluctant to rejoin his ugly little friend who was sitting impatiently in the car. He only went out when that gentleman began to blow the klaxon. I could see them quarreling about something. Then the young man got in and they disappeared up the dirt road in a cloud of dust. After that things quieted down for a while. An hour I would say. Until the arrival of the Cadillac."

"Ah, now we come to the Cadillac. Let me hazard a guess. It contained an American couple."

"Well, the woman—very attractive—didn't leave the car. The man who came in was American all right. Very self-important. Gave the impression of owning General Motor-Cars or whatever you call it."

"George Pawling!"

"You seem to have a host of friends!"

"I suppose you retold the story."

"Precisely. He seemed just as upset as the young man who had preceded him. He asked directions to the Castle Garalda and then rushed out to the green Cadillac and they too were off for the races. Well, you must admit it's a bit fantastic."

"You've been very helpful."

"Apparently. And to many and diverse people. Actually your arrival was rather annoying to me. I had—probably as a result of the day's excitement—almost persuaded Manuel to take off his clothes...."

"What?"

"I've been after him for days. Don't let anyone tell you about hot Spanish blood. They are as reticent as Puritans. Oh, the nude, you know. I specialize in the nude."

I gulped down the warm liquid and stood. "You say the castle of the Duc Garalda is forty miles to the south?"

"Yes. When you get to the fork where Route Ten branches off toward Madrid you go left and follow the coastal road toward Valencia. It is about an hour and a half to the village of San Pedro di Mar. That's where the castle is. You can't miss it."

"The Americans in the Cadillac. How long ago were they here?"

"Not more than an hour. Probably less."

"Thanks for the drink and everything else. Good luck with Manuel."

I started for the door. Behind me she said, "You know it's perfectly all right not to tell me anything. I don't mind really. I love mysteries and the solution always bores me. So much better to keep it a mystery. But I should like to ask you one question."

I turned. "Yes?"

"Yachts, Rolls Royces, Jaguars, Cadillacs, Italians with guns and beautiful women! I'm absolutely certain that all this has something to do with smuggling drugs in from Tangiers, and that you are an American gangster. I won't … what is it you say … squeal, if you'll talk."

"You're very clever," I said, deadpan.

"How exciting. If you ever need a … what do you call it … a moll, I'm available. As a matter of dreadful fact you've never met anyone quite so available in all your life. Goddamn Manuel anyway!"

I laughed. "I'll keep you in mind."

"Anyway," she said ruefully, "it's been quite a day!"

I waved goodbye to Angela Brooks-Carnovan who was perched like some gaudy, awkward bird in the midst of the gloomy room and ran to my car across the square. The woman in black was still standing on the balcony watching me with blank, dead eyes. I wondered if she were Manuel's wife.

I swung the car around and bumped crazily up the dirt road toward route ten, trying to shake off the sense of unreality left by Miss Brooks-Carnovan's recital of her unlikely day. The English woman had made everything sound like a Mack Sennett comedy, only in this case I was the lone Keystone Cop. What in hell did the appearance of Alberto in this village mean? What was he doing with a Rolls belonging to a celebrated Spanish Duc? What would I find at the Castle Garalda?

The purple shadows of night came creeping down the mountain to envelop me. The rocky landscape looked more sinister than ever when bits and chunks of it were isolated by my headlights. The comedy of the village café faded into the blackness of the vast night. I knew that somewhere down the road violence awaited me.

SIXTEEN

The Grand Routes of Spain, begun during the last unhappy days of the motoring King Alfonso and improved later by Franco as military arteries, are among the loneliest roads in the world. One can drive for hours without passing another vehicle in a country where families not only don't have two cars in every garage—they don't even have a garage! Now, with night fallen over the Iberian Peninsula, the little Ford might have been a firefly chasing other fireflies across limitless space.

About fifteen miles below Dessa-di-Mar I came to the fork in the road predicted by Angela Brooks-Carnovan. I went off to the left where the signs read Valencia and Malaga. A few miles to the south I stopped in the midst of a tiny village for gas and had a bit of luck. The attendant spoke broken English. Yes, an American couple in a green Cadillac had stopped two hours before for repairs, a matter of trouble with the distributor. It had taken a half hour to diagnose and make the repairs. The woman had been for the most part silent and preoccupied. The man had been short-tempered and nervous but then of course, this may have been only the American manner. They had gone to the café across the street for food and drink while the repairs had been made.

When they returned the man became abusive, accusing the garageman of stalling on the repairs. The woman had apologized for him. There was something about this woman that was sad and disturbing. Perhaps she had lost a loved one or was going to the bedside of a dying friend. Anyway when they had paid the bill and were prepared to depart the woman had said: "You don't imagine that you will be permitted past the gates of the Duce of Garalda. … It's madness!" The garageman had remembered the exact wording. He was a student of English and curious about the odd behavior of Americans who came through his village. Was it true that all Americans took pills to keep them from going crazy? He had heard this once from a Portuguese.

I said to the last: "Yes, it is somewhat true and not always effective." I tipped him generously adding to the crazy legend and kept my eyes resolutely off the café across the street. My stomach was making loud demands for a drink. But I had the feeling that time was running out now, if indeed it had not already run out for Prince Ali and Judith Garnter. I couldn't afford the chunk of time the drink would take from my life. It was seven-thirty. By now all of Europe must have been informed of the fact that the body of Miles Winthrop had been discovered on the Orient Express. My description had probably been flashed to every capital of Europe. Surely by this time they would have traced me to Barcelona and even beyond.

I left the garageman mulling the American dilemma under the naked arc light. The narrow tar road curved like a snake into more mountainous territory. A cold wind swept down from the jagged peaks dissipating the heat of the day. Occasionally a northbound lorry rumbled past bouncing headlights intent on Barcelona. The chill increased. Now and again the little car was buffeted by a sudden gust and floundered like a small plane in a downdraft. I had the eerie sensation of having left the twentieth century far behind and that I was heading out into a Medieval darkness.

The fork in the road came up to meet me in the darkness like a decisive decision in my life: to the right, Madrid; to the left, Valencia. I veered off to the left and pressed the accelerator to the floor. Now the road was narrow and, at times, downright dangerous. It twisted through deep gorges across sudden valleys, along the edge of cliffs overhanging a pounding sea, snaking back and forth from the silence of the mountains to the distant sound of breakers on a lonely coast. The villages were small and far between although now and again I got a glimpse of the lights of larger settlements nestled in rocky bays far down below. Once, far to the left, I saw a steamer blazing with light heading in the direction of Majorca. About eight o'clock a fat moon pushed its way up out of the sea into massive cloud banks, sending occasional spasmodic light over massive rock, twisted cypress, and olive trees, making grotesque shadows across the ancient landscape.

About fifteen miles below the fork in the road, I rounded a curve to find the glint of green metal and chrome in the trees off to the left. I jammed on the brakes and spun the car over to the side of the road. I turned off the ignition and doused the lights. The sudden silence was broken only by the moaning wind and the sharp screech of some night bird.

I dug the automatic out of my coat pocket, unlocked the safety catch and got cautiously out of the car. Standing there by the side of the darkened road with the night wind groaning down the mountainside and the distant rumble of the angry sea, I was suddenly afraid of what I would find in the car that was parked in a clearing between the trees. I had no doubt that it was the Pawlings'.

It was standing there as though for a casual night picnic. But there were no lights nor any sign of life. I inched forward around to the driver's side trying to steady my trembling hand. I managed to get my finger firm on the trigger, put my foot in the partly open door and kicked it wide open.

Nothing happened.

I crouched, aware of some slight movement from within the car, and moved forward. As though on cue the moon came from behind scudding clouds. A figure was bent over the wheel as though asleep. But the face was twisted about—what was left of it. One cheek had been blown completely off. It was like a monstrous waxworks face that had melted away. In death George Pawling was not a pretty sight. So this was the end of all the pushing and the climbing and the dirty deals. Had he ever figured this was the way the book was written?

There was another slight movement beyond him. I saw her then. She was sitting beside the corpse of her husband half-turned, looking directly, but unseeing, into my eyes.

"Hello," she said in a deathly calm voice. "So nice of you to drop in."

"Linda...." I managed to whisper.

"I've been waiting for someone. I didn't want to leave the car. I'm afraid of snakes, you see."

This was the calm of hysteria. I moved slowly, walking around the car as though I were stalking a deer. When I got to the other side she hadn't moved. I opened the door and touched her gently on the arm. "Come," I said.

She got out like an obedient child. She looked down at the Luger in her hand as though she didn't know what it was. She didn't resist when I took it from her and slipped it into my pocket.

She looked up at me. She said with quiet, heartbreaking regret: "This is not real, of course. The only real thing ever in my life was the room in Naples and the moment in which I believed you loved me."

I put my arm around her shoulders. She came along with me to my car, walking primly, carefully like a child on show before the dancing class.

"They tell me Spain is a very romantic country," she said in a conversational voice that sent pinpricks up my spine. She got in and I shut the door and went quickly around to the driver's seat. With shaking hands I managed to thrust a cigarette at her. She shook her head. "Yes," she said, "about Spain. It was in Spain that I killed my husband. He left the car to relieve his kidneys. I believe that is the phrase employed by all the best guide books on travel in Spain. The Luger was in the glove compartment. He adored it. He used it to kill a man called Miles Winthrop. But that's another travel story about another country. I took the Luger from the compartment and when he got back in I said, 'George,' and he turned and the Luger exploded in his face. Remind me to tell you about my trip to romantic Spain sometime."

Suddenly above us a storm broke. There was a deafening clap of thunder and rain ripped down out of the night. I took her in my arms. She began to tremble.

"Hart," she sobbed, "who am I … who am I...."

My lips tasted tears and then her answering lips and in the violence of the storm, time stood still.

SEVENTEEN

The storm came and went, quickly, violently, rushing off to the east, leaving a sovereign moon in the midst of a vast calm. Once I turned on the dashboard light to look at my watch. It was eleven-twenty. By my calculation we should be only a few miles north of the castle. Since we had left the clearing she hadn't spoken. We crept down the fringes of Spain as though the rest of the world had died in its sleep.

She was leaning back against the seat, eyes closed, the red end of her cigarette rising occasionally in a slow, precise arc.

After a while she said, "On the plane from Milan to Barcelona I went into the dressing room. There was a woman there. A Czech. She knew who I was. She remembered me as a child. She gave me some news."

"News."

"My father is dead."

I didn't say anything. After a moment she went on. "When I heard that I knew I would kill George."

"Begin further back."

She sighed and blew smoke out into the night. "I wasn't born an American. I'm a naturalized citizen."

"What?"

"I was brought up with English … with American rather. My mother was an American. But my father was Michael Harley. He was a professor at the University of Prague. During the war he went into the government. He was a member of the last Benes cabinet. After the fall of the government he was sent to a prison camp."

"You and your mother ...?"

"My mother died a week before Masaryk's suicide. I was fourteen then. I was sent to my mother's cousins in West Germany. Friends of my father's arranged for me to go. I adored my father. There has never been a man like him."

"And George. Where did he come into the picture?"

"He came to the house of my mother's cousins in Frankfort. Although I spoke English like an American, because of mother, I didn't really know Americans. I was overly romantic about them. I thought every American must be good. I thought of them as White Knights who would ride one day into Prague and liberate my father. George knew this about me. He played on it. In a clumsy sort of way he managed to seduce me and after that we were married. It was all unreal and dreamlike. He was still in the Army of Occupation ... a G.I. Sammy with a long way to run. But on the side he was working on some deal with the newly formed German-American Oil Company. We went to America for a while and I became a citizen and then when he was out of the Army we went back to West Germany ... to Berlin this time. One day ..." She stopped as though unable to go on.

Gently I prompted her: "One day?"

"*They* came to me."

"They?"

"Agents of the GPU—Stalin's little playboys."

"And?"

"They told me unless I worked for them my father would ... have a very sudden accidental death."

"Did you believe it?"

"Of course I did. I was frantic with fear. But I was still fool enough to believe, that despite disillusionment with him about many things, George would know what to do. I went to him. It was a horrible mistake. He saw the chance of a lifetime. We would, as he put it, 'save Papa' by working for them while he continued his work with German-American Oil at the same time. He said we might as well clean up. Can you understand?"

"Only too well!"

"I was trapped then. I had no choice. After a time I stopped believing in anything, except that my father was still alive."

Down below us I saw a cluster of the lights of a village. I slowed down.

"What did George expect to do with Prince Ali and Miss Garnter?"

"Stop the marriage at all costs. It meant thirty thousand dollars to him."

"Did he kill Nina Apperatti?"

"No. But I knew something would happen. I tried to warn you. It was the Duc d'Alveri who did it. George was only a few feet away when it happened."

"Where do Pietro and d'Alveri fit into things?"

"It's an ironic three-cornered hat. Moscow-Cairo, and German-American Oil. D'Alveri is working for Cairo and wants the credit for preventing the marriage. It means money in the bank to him. George and he are ... were ... competitors for the first prize. Pretty, isn't it?"

"Lovely. Did George kill the Arab boy?"

"No. It frightened George. He was afraid someone was trying to plant the murder on him. Actually the Arab boy was an agent operating out of Cairo. We have no idea who did it or why."

"And Prince Ali and his girlfriend?"

She pointed to the lights up ahead. "By all our information they should be there, or nearby at the castle of the Duc of Garalda. They were taken there by someone in a Rolls. D'Alveri is … was … trying to beat George to the prize money. I have no idea what we will find … who was in the Rolls or why."

"It's unbelievable."

"Most of my life is unbelievable. You will turn me over to the police, of course."

"No. And keep your mouth shut. Let me do the talking."

"Hart, there's no use. It doesn't matter now."

"You'll do as I say!" I shouted hoarsely.

We came down into the little village. Right in the center was a lighted inn. The first thing I saw was the flashy Maserati sports car parked in the courtyard.

"D'Alveri's car!" I swung the English Ford into the courtyard and came to a stop.

"What are you going to do?" Her voice was tight with anxiety.

"Maybe we can get a drink," I said in a matter-of-fact voice.

She didn't ask any more questions. Instead she followed me meekly across the courtyard, under an arbor groaning with fat grapes, and into a small room decorated with turkey-red walls and Victorian furniture. A sleepy manager or night clerk got up from behind the desk as we came in.

"Do you speak English …?"

He shrugged. "Of English I have had some little."

"Good. We are on our way to Valencia. Madame is tired and in need of refreshment. I have seen the motor car of friends in your courtyard. While you get Madame a brandy I should like to surprise my friends if you will be good enough to direct me to their room."

A polite mask didn't quite hide a certain craftiness but he was obviously bewildered. Apparently though he was unwilling to admit his lack of command of English. He said: "Brandy. For the good lady woman I am understanding. You wish also brandy for the men of the beautiful motor car?"

"Not immediately. Just tell me how to get to their room."

He frowned. I could see that he had not formed a very favorable impression of the men of "the beautiful motor car." But after a moment he shrugged again.

Linda said: "Whatever happens now will catch me sitting." She sank with a sigh into one of the overstuffed chairs. Native gallantry brought the Spaniard to action. "The brandy she will be in the lady's small hand quick."

He started for a door at the back of the counter. "The room of my friends," I barked out.

He turned and pointed to the hall at the opposite end of the lobby. "The stairs will follow you to the door belonging to them."

After he left Linda whispered, "I don't like the way he looked at you. Be careful, Hart, please. I've had enough violence for one lifetime if you don't mind."

I went into a gloomy hall where the only light came from a dim bulb at the head of the stairs. Quickly I climbed the stairs and found myself in a small square hall with a door on either side of me. Light came from under the door to my right. And something else. The sound, the unlikely sound of a man sobbing. I crept closer, got my hand on the knob and turned it very slowly. After a moment I put pressure against the door. It gave inward. Inch by inch I pushed it open, afraid any moment of some loud and peculiarly Spanish squeak. But the sobbing continued uninterrupted by any other sound. When I got the door open wide enough to get a view of the other side I found I was looking into a darkened sitting room. To one side was a lighted doorway which I assumed was the bedroom. It was from this room that the sobbing originated. Softly I stepped over the threshold and quietly shut the door behind me. Beyond the sobbing was the sound of running water which suddenly ceased. Then another voice spoke into the sobbing.

"Must you make that disgusting noise?" The voice was that of the Duc d'Alveri. The sobber went right on being disgusting. The Duc went on petulantly: "Really, Pietro, you have given me too much trouble as it is. We should never have stopped but continued right to the gates of the castle. Whoever these people are in the Rolls ..."

Pietro sputtered something in Italian. The Duc said in a warning voice. "English, if you please, the servants, the manager here, he may well understand Italian."

"But what I feel is Italian."

"Sicilian, dear boy, Sicilian. Now do stop that awful blubbering and we may get an hour or so sleep."

"Sometimes I cannot believe that you are an Italian. You are as heartless as an Englishman. You care nothing for my sensitivity ... my feelings."

"Champagne. It is always this way when you have had too much champagne. Drinking all the way over on the plane ... carrying the bottles with you in the car. It's as though you feared it was the end of champagne for you ... that there would be no more champagne in the world."

"I am as nothing," Pietro sobbed. "Less than nothing."

"Move over."

"Ah, that is the tragic story of my life—move over."

"And lucky for you it is! If this request had never been made you would probably still be fishing in that loathsome little Sicilian village."

"You forget it was Miles Winthrop who took me out of it, not you. No pity. No understanding of the heart. Poor little Nina. You swear in a holy oath you had nothing to do with it."

"My dear boy, I'm prepared to swear to anything that stops this unpleasant sniveling."

"Nina was like me. She wanted nice things … love … the admiration of the world. I wanted it for her."

"You talk as though, as though you have been interested in her … in love with her."

Pietro didn't answer. Instead he filled the silence with great baritone sobs.

The Duc said sharply: "What nonsense you speak. You know as well as I that you took her out of that village because she had a good body and would be useful."

"Ah no. I saw poor Nina doomed to a life of poverty in that village. I wanted her to have nice things … to be happy."

"Rubbish!"

"If only I had never listened to you. If only I had stayed with Miles Winthrop."

"Had you stayed with Winthrop you would never have been more than a secretary with, of course, nocturnal obligations."

"I curse my body!"

"I suggest that we curse it together! Champagne has a vile effect on you. It makes you so dishonest. You love your body as you love nothing else on this earth. The mirror is for you a device for romantic experience. I myself find such tendencies amusing. Now...."

"No!"

"Don't be dull!"

Suddenly Pietro's sobbing stopped and his voice became violent. "You have involved me in murder! I must know the truth! Was it you who killed poor Nina?"

"You'll wake the whole inn!"

"I don't care! I must know. Just before the lights went out in the ballroom you told me to cross the floor slowly toward Nina. But you were ahead of me. Then after, you said quickly we must get out! You must have known."

"My dear boy—"

"Stay away from me! I am not joking!"

"Must you be such an insufferable hypocrite. We could not … we cannot … let four million lira slip through our hands. We must have it. I am in debt. So are you. Cairo will not pay off unless …"

"You haven't answered me!"

There was a moment's utter silence. Then the Duc spoke very calmly, very softly: "You expect me to salve your provincial little conscience. You expect to find yourself suddenly as clean and as innocent as you might have been at the age of ten! Well you are wrong. You are tied to me, dear boy, in guilt...." He paused and then added in a voice that was almost a sigh: "Yes, I killed her. Now then, let us get some sleep."

I moved in on them, appearing suddenly in the doorway to the bedroom, automatic in hand. The sight that met my eyes was more than slightly ludicrous. The Duc and Pietro were in the midst of a great old-fashioned brass bed. The Duc was propped up against the pillows in silk pajamas. His face was covered with cold cream and he wore a tight silk skull cap on his head. Pietro, a picture of road company theatrical menace, was sitting up in bed, twisted around out of the sheet over the Duc. He was, as you might expect, naked. It took them a moment to unfreeze from this tableau into another one. They turned, open-mouthed and dazed, and still unable to move, stared at me.

It was not surprising that it was the Duc who recovered first. "Pawling always was a bungler!"

"Not anymore. Get up. Both of you. Get dressed, fast."

"Couldn't we have a little business talk first."

"We couldn't."

Pietro said, "I knew the day would end in disaster." His voice was curiously calm. "Where do you want us to go?"

"Out of bed ... both of you."

They scrambled out of the bed. The Duc started for the bathroom. "Never mind that. Just throw on some clothes."

"But my facial cream—I cannot ..."

"It might protect you from the ill effects of night wind."

After that they dressed quickly and in silence. Oddly enough it was now Pietro who was the calmer of the two. The seconds seemed to be robbing the Duc of his cocky self-assurance. I noticed his small white hands trembling as he buttoned his coat.

"Now. Down to the lobby."

They went ahead of me into the hall and down the narrow stairs. I put my automatic into the Duc's back and while he jumped nervously, slipped George Pawling's Luger into his coat pocket. A professional pickpocket might have admired the gesture. The Duc didn't notice.

When we reached the lobby Linda jumped to her feet and the Spaniard came hurrying around from behind the desk. The Duc, ludicrous as he was in his facial cream, bowed ironically to Linda: "Mrs. Pawling. An unexpected pleasure. I am afraid we are at the mercy of a madman!"

The Spaniard said, "Where is the meaning of this?"

"Easy," I said. "These two men are dangerous desperados wanted in two countries for murder!"

"Murder!"

The Duc laughed. "An American joke."

"Please stand over there by Madame," I said to the Spaniard.

He backed away toward Linda, his eyes fixed on the gun in my hand.

"Now then," I said to d'Alveri: "In front of Mrs. Pawling and this man I want you to say yes or no … were you not on the Express train that left Venice for Milan at two-fifteen yesterday morning?"

The Duc arched his eyebrows as though humoring an idiot. "Yes. What difference does it make?"

"A great deal of difference. A man by the name of Miles Winthrop was found murdered in a compartment of that train. He was shot by a German Luger...."

"I'm sorry to hear it. But it has nothing to do with me."

"Two hours ago Mrs. Pawling and her husband were driving south on the Barcelona-Valencia road. A car forced them to pull up to the side. The car was a Maserati. You stepped out of this car and shot George Pawling through the head."

I saw Linda's hand come halfway to her face then fall again to her side.

"You're mad!" the Duc said.

"George Pawling was shot also by a German Luger. I'm sure the police inquiry will bear me out."

The Duc turned toward Pietro. "Tell him he is crazy, Pietro."

Pietro looked at him, opened his mouth as though to speak, shut it again and turned away.

"Pietro!"

He said nothing. His eyes had an oddly fanatical malevolence, calm and determined. I tossed him the bunch of keys that I had found on the bureau top of their bedroom.

"Are those your car keys?"

He nodded.

"Good. I'm giving you a break. By driving all night you might make Malaga and a boat outbound for Tangiers. It's your only chance. The Italian police have already alerted the Spanish authorities. As a matter of fact it may be the end of running for you both. Do you understand?"

"Yes," Pietro said.

"This is ridiculous," the Duc sputtered. "The Duc Garalda knows who I am. We will go to his castle immediately. I am not afraid of the police."

"Come," Pietro said calmly. "And stop making a spectacle of yourself. There is, I suppose, a time for dignity. Even for people like us."

Linda gave me a quick, questioning look. I knew she too had been caught by the strange, almost laconic, finality in Pietro's voice.

I saw them out to the courtyard and the flashy Maserati. The Duc in his tweed overcoat and his face cream was still protesting angrily. But he climbed in. Pietro swung the sports car in a wide arc. At the last minute he leaned out and smiled. "Nina always liked to drive fast," he shouted. "Maybe she too knew there wasn't much time for her."

The low car whined out into the highway, hesitated a moment like a race horse at the barrier, then sped off toward the south.

I went back to the lobby.

Linda said, "I don't understand."

"Pietro was brought up on opera plots," I said. "I'm counting on his romantic certainty that all ends unhappily."

"I still don't …"

"Where's the manager?"

"Telephoning the police, I guess."

"We'd better get going."

"Where?"

"The castle of the Duc Garalda. Where else?"

As we went out into the courtyard she said: "The story you told … it won't help much. In the end they'll find out the truth."

"It will give you time."

Behind us the manager came running, shouting in Spanish. By the time he was in the middle of the courtyard I had the little Ford headed out into the road. High above the village I could see the lights of the great castle. I wondered what we would find there.

EIGHTEEN

Now near the end of dreaming—for the events of the past few days had become for me unreal and macabre, a sad, funny, repugnant and disturbing prelude to waking up—we came upon the most outrageous scene in the opéra bouffe. In retrospect what happened after we left the courtyard of the Inn has become a part of my memory that, even knowing it happened, strains my own sense of credibility. Yet it did occur.

The castle of the Duc of Garalda came down on us out of the night like a setting from Scheherazade. Delicate and dreamlike it floated on its mountain top, a palace of the most exquisite Moorish design, a privately owned Alhambra seemingly set in a pool of privately owned moonlight. The twisting mountain road brought us finally through open gates into a courtyard that contained several cars including a Rolls Royce limousine.

No one barred our way at the gates; in fact, the welcome mat seemed to be out. Two servants came running to open the doors of the Ford. Without words we followed them into the cool fantastic depths of the Palace. Our footsteps echoed eerily on beautifully wrought mosaic, down dimly lit corridors that bordered gardens framed in Moorish arches, gardens where orange and lemon trees hung above still pools and fountains played among the bougainvillea. The air was heavy with the scent of night-blooming jasmine. Each step brought us further away from the twentieth century. I had the disturbing sensation of walking back, back, back along the silent corridors of time.

The servant led us on in silence.

We came at last into an enormous room dominated on the far side by Moorish arches framing a long balcony overhanging an improbable view of the valley and the faraway sea. In the midst of this great room a woman was sitting at a little gilt table with a deck of cards broken before her. Apparently she had been playing solitaire. It was Mrs. Winthrop.

"I've been expecting you," she said coolly. "The village innkeeper called. He had to be placated. I didn't feel it was worth waking the Duc. The Duc is a victim of the gout. Allow me to apologize for him. He retired an hour ago."

She gestured to a sofa near her. "Sit down and rest. You must have had a very trying journey. Most of us have. Can I order you supper? It can be managed, I assure you. Or perhaps a drink of liquor, for medicinal purposes, of course. I feel it would be no more immoral than a St. Bernard offering his flask to the snowbound."

"Brandy would be fine," I said faintly.

Out of the shadows behind us appeared Alberto, the Sicilian servant from Mrs. Winthrop's palazzo in Venice.

Mrs. Winthrop gave him some instructions in a low voice and he left the room. She turned back. "I've been forced to revise some of my opinions of Sicilians," she said with a sigh. "Alberto is the soul of loyalty. Without him nothing would have been accomplished."

"Like what?" I murmured.

"Neither of us have had any sleep, or very little. I managed a few winks last night on the chartered plane."

"Chartered plane?"

"It was the only way I could leave Venice quickly. It was absolutely necessary after I heard Prince Ali and Judith had flown the coop.

The Duc of Garalda is an old friend of my family. I've known him since I was a girl. I put through a phone call and explained the delicate situation. He was, of course, charming. He has practically turned over this lovely—if somewhat heathen—palace to me and to …" She stopped.

"To whom?"

Instead of answering she looked at a card in her hand. "It is lucky I am not in the least superstitious." She jerked her wrist around to show us the ace of spades. "Gypsies and childish nonsense," she said sharply. But to my surprise I caught a note of uneasiness behind the flat tones.

"Was it Alberto who intercepted Prince Ali and Miss Garnter at Dessa-di-Mar?"

"Yes," she said dryly. "He had a pressing invitation for them and then, too, there was that odious Greek millionaire to get rid of with his vulgar yacht."

Linda and I watched her as though mesmerized. "I can't believe, Mrs. Winthrop," I said, "that I am actually asking the question that follows, but under the circumstances it seems almost routine."

"Fire away."

"Are you and the Duc of Garalda holding Prince Ali and Judith Garnter prisoners in this palace?"

The corners of her mouth twitched up in what I imagine was a smile. "How wildly romantic you are, Mr. Muldoon. But, on second thought, perhaps not romantic enough. Despite the claims of journalists, fiction is usually stranger than life. But I must admit my case has been the exception."

"I don't doubt it!"

She leaned forward and squinted an eagle-gaze at Linda. "You're pale, my girl. Where is that social-climbing husband of yours?"

"Not social climbing anymore," Linda said with tired flippancy.

"He's dead," I said.

"Oh, that's too bad, isn't it?" Mrs. Winthrop said mildly. Then to my utter amazement added to Linda in a conversational tone of voice: "A little brandy will make you feel better. I know when Mr. Winthrop died a good cup of hot cocoa fixed me up in no time. I gather he died suddenly. Asiatic flu."

"The Duc d'Alveri," I said quickly. "He was murdered by the Duc d'Alveri."

The eagle eye turned on me. For a moment she was silent then said quite calmly: "I do hope you are able to establish this interesting bit of news."

"I will!"

Linda started to say something but Mrs. Winthrop spoke up quickly,

"Don't talk, my dear. It's better to let Mr. Muldoon do the talking for you. At least for a while."

"I don't ..."

"No, of course you don't. But Mr. Pawling can't be a great loss to you or anyone else for that matter and I do not approve of hypocrisy in these matters."

"She's very tired," I said, "and somewhat hysterical."

"Tired, yes. Hysterical, no. I can see this young woman has a head on her shoulders. I can always tell immediately!"

She turned back to me. "As for you, Mr. Muldoon. I have an apology to make. I should never have jumped off the handle so quickly yesterday evening. It was that dreadful Pietro whatever his name is who unnerved me sitting there like brass in my own house with his private parts exposed. I should never have believed the story he told about you and Nina Apperatti. I mean that disgusting lie about what happened in the cabaña on the Lido. I should have known you were incapable of such a vile act!"

Linda gave me a weary side glance. I felt something suspiciously like a blush beginning on my neck. "Thank you," I managed to mutter.

"That poor girl getting herself stabbed. But I suppose that's what comes of going to Masked Balls. The news was all rather unnerving, especially after a very trying afternoon."

"Trying?"

"Yes. For me. And for Alberto. We had such a difficult time with that odious young Arab from Cairo."

"You!" I gasped. "Surely it wasn't you who ..."

"Alberto and I together. I can assure you it took both of us. The creature absolutely refused to go through that window. All rather upsetting."

"You and Alberto pushed him into the canal?"

"Well, I suppose 'assisted' would be a nicer word than 'pushed.' He was a horrid little spy and assassin. He had instructions to do away with Prince Ali by means of some vile drug. I must say Alberto is a treasure in these matters."

I managed to say: "Yes, I suppose he is." Then after a moment I got my voice and added, "Mrs. Winthrop, I have no doubt whatsoever that I am dreaming all of this. But even a dream has some sort of logic. Will you please tell me why in God's name you have mixed yourself up in this business?"

"I've been mixed up in it for a long time," she said enigmatically. "To be precise—since I was eighteen." Alberto came back with a tray containing brandy and a plate of sandwiches. He put them on the small table in front of the sofa. Automatically, Linda and I reached for the brandy.

"You have been against this proposed marriage from the beginning?"

"My heart was with them but my mind took heed. You see they met in my New York apartment. Judith was sort of a protégée of mine. Prince Ali had come to tea. When I saw the way things developed after that I tried to use reason. That failed. I wanted them where I could keep an eye on them. That's why I invited them both to Venice. But I had not counted on my son and daughter who became idiotically romantic about the whole sorry business. They plotted this elopement behind my back. I had to take action. I had another loyalty."

"Another loyalty?"

"Let us say, a loyalty to my own youth."

She obviously didn't intend to enlighten us further. At least not for the moment.

"Certain arrangements had to be made very quickly. An exalted personage, I believe the press uses that idiotic phrase—in this case it might be justified, was flown secretly from Donrd-Arabia to the Valencia airport. He arrived there not three hours ago."

I put down my glass. "Mrs. Winthrop. You don't mean to tell me that the King of Donrd-Arabia is in this house!"

Behind us, in perfect English, a deep voice spoke up softly. "The twentieth century has, I suppose, seen stranger flights on the part of rulers!"

Both Linda and I got to our feet and turned. Standing in the doorway from the hall was an extraordinary, even awe-inspiring figure. The first impression was that one of the biblical prophets had suddenly appeared in our midst. Bearded, clad in gleaming white robes and a burnoose, well over six feet tall, he filled the room with majesty.

It was only when he smiled and started to walk toward us that the picture altered into one of common humanity. For despite the initial impression of strength, this man was old and tired and obviously ill. His steps faltered as he approached. Mrs. Winthrop went forward to meet him as though to help but he gestured her away with a proud smile. He came and sat facing us and indicated that we seat ourselves again.

"You are the American agent Amy has been telling me about." He said it simply. Then he turned and gave Linda a questioning look.

Mrs. Winthrop spoke up. "Fares … this is Mrs. Pawling. Her husband was murdered this evening by some of your enemies."

The old man sighed. "Murder—hatred and murder. Will it never end?" He put his hand to his brow and closed his eyes. "The excitement of the plane trip … the joy in seeing my beloved son … the sorrowful task I had to perform … it has been almost too much."

"Fares! You must rest!" The sudden gentleness, the unexpected intimacy in Mrs. Winthrop's voice startled me.

The King opened his eyes and smiled at her. "No, Amy, I am quite all right. Rest is for the young and healthy, not for the old with so little time."

"Have they? …" Mrs. Winthrop left the question unfinished.

The old King made a gesture toward the great Moorish windows and the balcony beyond. "Behold! Perhaps one's last efforts are, after all, the best. They are saying their farewells!"

Outside on the balcony two figures had appeared silhouetted against the moonlight, like performers in some dream play. The Prince and Judith Garnter stood close together, hand in hand, their backs to us, their faces to the limitless sea.

In the silence Linda spoke up: "Your highness, you say Prince Ali and Miss Garnter are saying their farewells. Surely you don't mean that they are parting for good!"

The King turned back and said in a voice filled with an odd sort of compassionate sadness. "For good? Who knows. For the present, yes!"

"But why?"

The King didn't answer immediately. Instead he got to his feet, moved painfully toward the windows, stopped halfway and turned back to us. "Behold! This room, this palace…. It was built when my people were great and powerful. It was created out of a lust for power! It is a thing of beauty, yes, but it represents what must not happen again! There are men in the Arab world who dream again of such power, instead of peace and progress and happiness of their own people. They must not be encouraged!"

He stopped and closed his eyes as though fighting off an attack of overwhelming pain. After a moment he went on. "My son has been trained as a man of peace. He must reach the throne. If he should marry Judith Garnter my enemies will win. Ali would never reach the throne. Those who scheme with Nasser and other powers would take over. It is a time again for sacrifice."

"But your highness," Linda's boldness amazed me, "how can you be certain it wouldn't work out?"

"My child, all my life I have worked to try and drag my poor country into the twentieth century. I have had to fight every inch of the way and the progress has been slow and discouraging. My country is, in great part, still in a feudal state, composed of tribes and sheiks with no concept of modernity. But things are beginning to change rapidly now. Communications have brought the outside world into Donrd-Arabia. My son, if he mounted the throne, may be able to breach the illness of the past, the childish dreams of glory. He may yet bring my people into an understanding of peace and progress. He may make them see that the people of Israel are their brothers. But I tell you, and I know, if he marries Miss Garnter now, he will never mount the throne. The time is short. I am ill. The doctors give me two months at the most. Tonight I explained many things to these young people, and at last they understand."

"But it doesn't seem fair!" Linda burst out. "How can you know what such a sacrifice means to them!"

"How can I know?" The old man smiled sadly and looked at Mrs. Winthrop. "Tell them, Amy."

Mrs. Winthrop was sitting at the little gilt table. Her hand rested lightly on the cards strewn before her. She turned and looked at the King, then down at the deck of cards. When she spoke all the New England dryness seemed to have evaporated leaving her voice curiously soft and young.

"I do not approve of public confession. But perhaps you should know." She sighed. "It was so long ago, over fifty years ago, yet it seems just like yesterday. I was eighteen. I was visiting my aunt Amelia Littleton in Boston. Aunt Amelia was a bluestocking, went in for artists and politics and writers. Anyway, at tea one afternoon someone brought Prince Fares of Donrd-Arabia. He was a student at Yale. It was a cold raw March afternoon. I'll never forget it. We went walking that March in the late afternoons along the river and when spring came we used to ride in the swan boats out in Fenway Park ... and in that spring we fell in love."

"Oh." Linda said in soft surprise.

"Yes, I suppose it's hard to believe that an old woman such as I could ever have known love. But we were different than young people today. We didn't have to be told that from the beginning it was an impossible situation. His people would never have accepted me. We both understood. But ... but I fell in love and never fell out of it again."

"But why ...?"

"Why?" Mrs. Winthrop's voice was suddenly harsh. "Why? Duty, my girl. A word you young people sneer at. He had a job to do. My job was to try and forget. I failed at my job. Even during the years I was married to Mr. Winthrop. The man I loved became a King."

"Now I've heard everything," I said.

"Not quite everything," she said calmly. "I believe that Fares felt the same way. We never lost touch with one another, although I hadn't seen him until he walked into this palace tonight, not since that Spring of 1903."

"But things were different then!" Linda cried. "Surely the world has changed enough ..."

"Changed," the King spoke up in a weary voice. "Not for the Romeos and Juliets of this world, my dear child. The Capulets and the Montagues still are feuding and Romeo and Juliet are still lost somewhere between."

"It was an odd twist of fate," Mrs. Winthrop said. "Ali met Judith in my house … just as I had met Fares so many years before … and it happened to them as it happened to us. I only hope they will grow to understand." She looked up. "You see, love cannot be destroyed by parting."

She turned toward the King and for a moment they were locked by some deep and secret understanding. It was something I didn't understand or wish to understand. It made me uneasy. I looked at Linda. She was on her feet now. And I saw in her face a reflection of my own uneasiness.

Out on the balcony the lovers moved slowly out of sight. Soon they would be lost again in the brassy clash-by-night of the world of the Capulets and Montagues.

A door at the end of the room opened and Alberto appeared. Mrs. Winthrop said in a tired voice, "Yes, Albert?"

"The authorities have just called, *Signora.*"

"The authorities?"

"They wanted to know if we had knowledge of the two dead men."

"Dead men?"

"Five miles down the coast on the road to Valencia. An expensive sports car was driven over the edge of the cliff. It fell on the rocks far below. The men were killed instantly. One of the men had his face smeared with some sort of cream."

Mrs. Winthrop gave me a questioning look.

"Pietro and the Duc," I said. "Pietro saw too many operas in his childhood. He must have died with Verdi ringing in his ears."

In a quiet voice Linda said, "Hart, take me out of here."

Mrs. Winthrop got up and started with us for the door.

Behind us the old King said, "Come back, Amy."

"Yes, yes, of course."

At the last minute I turned back and saw the King standing straight and proud as though pain and death could be obliterated through sheer willpower. Behind him the Moorish arches built hundreds of years before by his ancestors looked like an unreal stage set. It was difficult to imagine this monarch from another culture as a lovesick youth in a swan boat in Fenway Park.

Alberto shut the door. In the hall Mrs. Winthrop said quietly, "I must go back to him."

"And then?" I asked.

She sighed. "I have my children. My foolish children. They need me. I will return to Venice."

For the first time, the sickening realization came over me that Mrs. Winthrop had not yet heard of her son's violent death on the Paris-

Rome Express. I wanted to be out of this place before she heard the news.

Mrs. Winthrop said: "Well, Mr. Muldoon, you can make a favorable report to your government. The capitals of the West can breathe easier, for a time at least."

"I suppose so. I will take Mrs. Pawling on to Valencia."

"Good." She gave Linda an odd, almost secretive look. "There is a good airport there, my dear."

Linda said, "Yes. I understand."

Now at the final moment of parting Mrs. Winthrop turned and looked me in the eyes. And for the first time I saw something unexpected there, something uncertain. "You think we're right, don't you, Mr. Muldoon?"

"I don't know," I said honestly.

"Yes. I see. Well," she drew herself up, "the King will be waiting for me. You must excuse me now. I have never doubted that I was right. Goodbye, children, and the best of luck."

She turned from us and moved back toward the great hall. She walked firmly, erect and certain. But I wondered.

Linda and I followed a servant down the long-arched corridor bordering on the gardens with their illuminated fountains. A strange and lonely silence seemed to have settled over the beautiful old palace. I thought, we must hurry or the past will trap us here. The odor of night-blooming jasmine was almost overpowering.

We got into the little English car and left the ancient courtyard. I felt that we were moving away out of some impossible dream. Linda said nothing until we were far down the mountain road. Then she said in a quiet voice, "You see, Hart, how impossible it is. The room in Naples, we were lucky to have had it."

The car swung around a bend in the narrow road and suddenly the Moorish castle on the heights was gone.

"I didn't deserve it," I said. And, at least for that moment, I was sincere.

NINETEEN

I awakened in a strange hotel room to a sense of irrevocable loss. The sun was dying along the white plaster walls. I looked at my watch. It was six-ten P.M. She was gone.

Still fighting off the remnants of a dream I struggled from the bed and saw the sheet of hotel notepaper propped up against the empty wine bottle on the bureau. I snatched it up and read Linda's handwriting:

"It can't be Naples again. I loved you. I love you. I will love you. Remember it sometimes when you are in the arms of some hungry blonde. Parting is such sweet sorrow."

I threw my clothes on, dragging the present around my scattered thoughts. This was Valencia. We had checked in at five A.M. that morning. How long had she been gone?

I soon found out. The hotel clerk was polite and disinterested. Madame had left the hotel not twenty minutes before in the airport bus. She had engaged a seat on a plane that would be flying to Athens, Istanbul, Bagdad and New Delhi. With maddening deliberation he looked up the plane schedule. The plane was due to take off at six-forty P.M., less than ten minutes from now. Yes, it was barely possible that the *signor* might reach the airport in time.

I grabbed a cab and pushed a handful of bills into the driver's hands. It helped but not enough. It was six-forty-two when the cab came to a screaming halt before the terminal building. I dashed through the waiting room to the open area bordering the gates. A big French plane was just gliding in to a landing. I grabbed a startled attendant and asked about the plane for Athens and New Delhi. He pointed to the field. Far out on the takeoff runway a big DC-6 was just swinging into position. I tried to rush the gates but it was too late. Hands reached out, pulled me back and held firm. Passengers began trickling in from the big French plane that had just landed. From far out on the field, there was a rising sound of roaring motors and the DC-6 began to charge down the runway for the takeoff. From this distance it was impossible to make out any of the faces at the portholes. Did I imagine the fluttering white speck of handkerchief? I stood there, drained of life, watching the plane as it gained momentum, left the ground, tucked its wheels up into its belly and rose like a fat duck away from the setting sun.

Someone tapped me on the shoulder. I turned, still dazed. It was Uncle Hirem, neat in gray flannel, Homburg and carrying the goddamned inevitable briefcase.

"I just got in from Paris," he said.

"So?"

"Hear things are straightening out."

I shrugged.

"But I understand the authorities may make it hot for your friend Mrs. Pawling."

I shrugged again.

"If they can catch up with her," he added softly.

"Yes," I said. "I see."

"Seeing a friend off?"

"Someone I loved."

He coughed politely. His eyes were not so polite.

"This country does peculiar things even to sane people. Time you got moving."

"Maybe you're right. Maybe it's time I got back home to the States."

"That isn't exactly what I had in mind."

I didn't give a damn. I let him talk.

"There's a blonde babe at the Hotel Continental in Paris. She's giving us trouble. I'm sending you up to see if you can handle her. Want the job?"

"No," I said. I was watching the plane hurtling out of my life into the darkening night. It was a mere speck now, its red and green wing lights winking a final farewell.

"Sure?"

"I don't want any job from you, Hirem. Ever again."

Hirem laughed.

"You will, my dear fellow," he said. "You will."

THE END

www.ingramcontent.com/pod-product-compliance
Lightning Source LLC
Chambersburg PA
CBHW050328160726
48002CB00001B/226